Looking for Leo

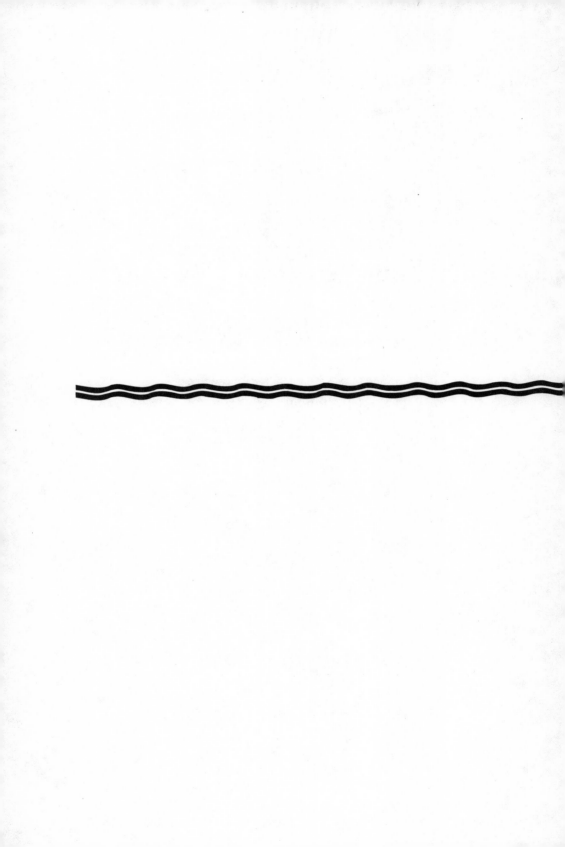

LOOKING for LEO

A Novel

Gloria Nagy

Delacorte Press

Published by
Delacorte Press
Bantam Doubleday Dell Publishing Group, Inc.
666 Fifth Avenue
New York, New York 10103

Library of Congress Cataloging in Publication Data

Nagy, Gloria.
    Looking for Leo / Gloria Nagy.
      p.   cm.
    ISBN 0-385-30655-5
    I. Title.
    PS3564.A36L66 1992
    813'54—dc20   91-43637
                                                                        CIP

Book design by Diane Stevenson · Snap-Haus Graphics

Manufactured in the United States of America

Published simultaneously in Canada

July 1992

10   9   8   7   6   5   4   3   2   1

RRH

To my father, Hal Gershman, with all my heart

Acknowledgments

I wish to acknowledge my publisher, Carole Baron, my editor, Jacqueline Cantor, my agent, Ed Victor, my cheerleader, Sandi Mendelson, my muse, Patricia Soliman and my husband, Richard Saul Wurman.

SHIT HAPPENS:

- A phrase on a T-shirt seen in Tortola, B.V.I.
- A line from *Terminator 2*
- A clever saying making the rounds
- A fact

Prologue

A CHORUS LINE OF BRIGHT, WHITE YOUNG-LADY GHOSTS pirouetted across the sky, swathed in moonlight. Delicate in their nakedness, they turned on white satin toes. Hair flying, long Rapunzel strands swirling, they moved faster stirring the skies, covering the moon. He reached up to stop them, but they twirled on.

Three of the dancers broke away, turning upside down, streaking across the clouds like small slender gulls.

The Wilis, he thought, *Giselle*'s Wilis. He tried to stand up, but the force of the wind held him.

They were over him, harridans now, frustrated maidens deserted by their betrothed. Damsels doomed to dance, to arabesque the earth from midnight to dawn, searching for the lover who left them, reeking with the rage of their humiliation, their virgin's quest endless.

Find the faithless man and dance him to death. They reached out long, spidery arms clawing the air above him, blood trickling down the sides of their ruby-red lips, shrieking at him into the storm.

"Leo! Leo! We're back. We've come for you!" Evil, ringing laughter filled his head. The mouths dilated as they lunged toward his genitals. *"Ahhhhhhhhhhhhhhhhhhhh."*

Leo sat up fast, hitting his head on the side of the upper bunk. Sweat covered him. His heart was beating so hard he couldn't breathe. He struggled to his feet, flinging open the door to his cabin and staggering across the main salon, groping his way up onto the deck. "Jesus. Jesus." He held on to the side rail, gasping for air. The moon covered his sweat-soaked nakedness, a Hollywood klieg light shining over his tall, muscled body. Breathe, man, breathe!

"It's just a dream. Relax, pal." The sound of his own voice comforted him. The sweet night breeze cooled him . . . his heart kicked back. Just a fucking bad dream.

I haven't even seen a ballet since Willa? Willa? Wilis? He climbed back down into the cabin, plucked a beer from the cooler, and wet a towel, running it over his face, his strong, sun-stained shoulders and chest. He stopped. He saw something. The faces of the ghosts. He threw the towel against the sink and took a long, deep pull on his beer. "My fucking ex-wives."

The past. The dark, fetid conch that he had so carefully buried, deep in a pirate's grave covered by the barnacles of denial, had risen up into the summer sky and found him.

He had absolutely no idea what the dream meant or why— when for the first time in his ragged, jagged, hard-luck life things seemed to be going well—it had come now. Premonition? Guilt?

One thing he knew. What every man who spent time at sea knew. When you feel the tap, you turn around. Leo finished the beer, put on his pants, and set his course for port.

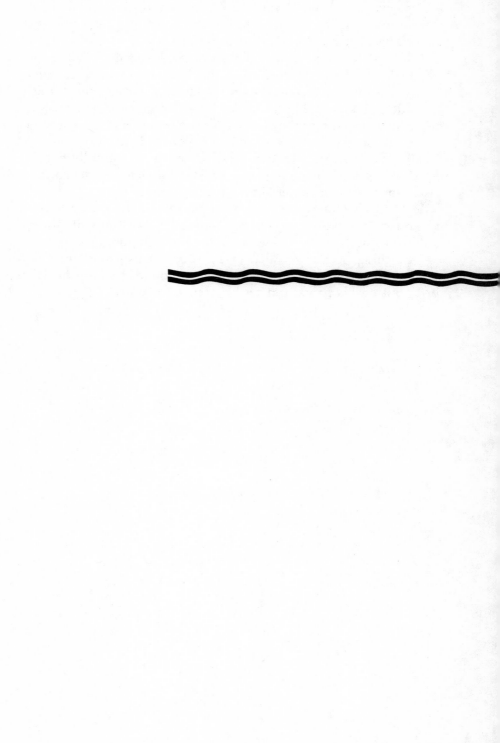

Part I

The Wives

CHAPTER 1

What's a Nice Girl Like You...

A COCKROACH WOKE HER UP. THIS WAS A CHANGE. Usually it was the janitor, banging his filthy mop against the metal pail, the breakfast carts rattling down the hall, the morning shift taking over from the night shift. Annoying, but still somehow appropriate. A cockroach, however, crawling up her leg as she tried to sleep in a "parent's sleeper chair" on the floor of the pediatric intensive-care unit of Beth Sinai Hospital, in New York City, was not at all reassuring. However, it did provide the perfect outlet for all her frustration, rage, and terror.

Never one to look any kind of gift, equine or otherwise, in the mouth, Lindy Lampi swallowed her revulsion, scooped the foul, noxious beastie up in a disposable rubber glove, and marched down the hall in her shocking-pink satin Victoria's Secret pajama suit, into the elevator, up to the top floor, and right through the Private, No Admittance door to the office of the chief administrator.

"This! This vile, disease-ridden symbol of filth and sloppiness crawled up my leg, *right* next to my child's bed! This is not, I repeat, *not* acceptable! Do you hear me? I want an army of cleaning people in Pediatrics this morning! I want Lysol. Pine Sol. Ajax. Windex. Fantastik. 409. Clorox. I want clean! Do you understand? Sparkling, sterilized, clean! Or I am taking this little sucker to *The New York Times*, whose managing editor is one of my closest friends! Children are clinging to life up there! They throw a dirty mop at the floor about once a week! This is supposed to be the best hospital in the country. What a joke! You, you . . ." She could feel her resolve giving way, the tears moving up her throat. She would not let this jerkazoid see her cry. "You . . . *administrator!*"

Actually, she thought, as she stormed out, it wasn't such a bad choice of epithets at that. It *was* one of the worst things she could think of calling anyone. Administrators—enforcers of corporate canons who never paused to consider whether the rules made any sense, rather than simply perpetuating the endless repetition of slothful bureaucratic stupidity that had gotten all of us chickens into the hopeless, oozing mess that we were calling the end of the twentieth century.

She stopped before the tall green doors and wiped the tears from her face. "Don't let her be up yet, let her sleep." It was only when Tess was asleep that she was not in pain these days. Lindy inhaled deeply, reaching out for the swinging doors that separated her from child hell. The doors held. She pushed. Nothing. Fear washed over her. They locked the doors only when there was a crisis. She waited, trying to breathe normally.

A young, skinny black girl called Dureen, hardly more than a child herself, her huge puzzled eyes overwhelming her small pinched face, tapped her on the shoulder. "Locked?"

Lindy nodded.

"Hope it's not my Wesley. He had a bad night."

Wesley was a five-month preemie about the size of a banana. His teeny body was so covered with tubes and monitors that he could hardly be seen. She put her arm around the girl's rigid, bony shoulders. "It'll be okay."

The lock clicked, and before either of them could move, a doctor and nurse with grim, tired faces appeared and reached toward the girl, taking her arms on either side and walking her off down the hall. Lindy turned away, knowing by now that the next sight would be the corpse of tiny Wesley hardly making a bump beneath the hospital sheet. Lindy leaned against the wall, hoping that Tess had slept through it (Wesley was one of her favorites). A bit of bone called by such a big name. A bit of life that never had a chance, hovered over by teams of doctors and nurses. A war zone of wounded children, each one being fought for with total commitment—a group, Lindy couldn't help thinking, that Himmler would have snuffed without a moment's hesitation.

She heard the gurney and shut her eyes, waiting for the sounds to grow fainter. "There's got to be something I can do." A flash of light. A shock wave, as if a Novocain-filled needle had hit the nerve inside a rotting molar, sending an electric spark through her brain. Leo. She blinked. He was back in her head again. Only this time she knew he was permanent. She felt the despair give way, the bloated helplessness lift from her heart. That's what she would do. She would find Leo Lampi and save her daughter's life.

The curtain was pulled around Tess's bed. She was up. Lindy sighed, bracing herself, and stuck her head in. Colleen, the young, button-nosed Irish Catholic nurse who was Tess's favorite, was giving her a sponge bath.

"Hi."

Tess smiled at her. "Hi. We heard you'd gone after the cleaning crew with a mutant cockroach."

Lindy laughed. "Good news travels fast."

Tess looked at her critically, a twelve-year-old girl beginning, sick or not sick, to see her mother as less than perfect. "You went storming around the halls like that?"

Colleen winked at Lindy. "Now, now. Don't start acting like one of those sitcom kids. She looks grand. Besides, it's barely seven A.M., and the only people here look a lot worse than your ma."

Lindy came through the curtains and handed Colleen a towel. "Damn right. You'd better watch it, or I'll turn on my Rosanne act and really give you something to be mortified about; eat Jell-O with my hands; fart in elevators; blow my nose with my fingers and wipe it on Dr. Davis's sleeve."

"Mom! Disgusting!" Tess giggled. Colleen patted her dry as if she were made of glass.

Lindy watched her. She was not used to Tess's new shape yet. That point of departure when the little girl begins to withdraw and the woman comes forward, both still sharing the same body, a pubescent metamorphosis. Remnants of the child; bony knees, baby-fat cheeks, no belly, just a button where the middle of a woman's body will appear. Then rising out of the child's chest, little round breasts; curly black hairs sprouting out of the wench's

pubis, clouding her innocence, leaving the inhabitant of this eroti-
cized chrysalis confused, forlorn, and off center.

"Excuse me, please," says Lady Estrogen politely, "I have a
little building up to finish in the mammary area. Mind if I hop
aboard for a bit?" "Screw you," replies Prepuberty, lying down
on the scaffold. "I'm not movin'. I don't want all those creepolas
ogling my boobs. I like being a little girl. Buzz off!"

Lindy had tried hard, too hard probably, to overcome her narcissism and obsession with her own body so that she would not
pass this neurotic concern on to her daughter. For years she had
watched Tess warily, wanting more than anything for her daughter
to be as different from her as possible. She wanted her to look like
Leo. She was not proud of her anxiety that Tess would come out
looking like she had looked before.

Before. It always made her feel sick to her stomach. There was
really only one person on earth still alive who had known her
before she was beautiful, and she had not seen her in ten years. She
had destroyed nearly all the evidence. She had re-created herself
and tossed off her childhood and adolescence as if she had been so
much garbage.

What if? she had thought in the middle of too many pregnant
sleepless nights. What if I have a daughter and she looks like me
before? A reminder that she was a murderer. A killer of herself.
That is what she really believed. She was not proud of any of it. It
made everything on the surface of her life (and the surface is
where she lived most of the time) a big fat lie. It dishonored Tess
too.

Tess had only seen her beautiful, glamorous, thin. A role model
without process of struggle or doubt. Her daughter, her fan.
"Momma!" she would exclaim, pointing at a catalog photo from
the day she was old enough to understand that the woman in the
picture was the woman who rocked her to sleep and took her to
the park, and covered her with zillions of rapturous kisses.
"Momma pretty!" she would announce, pressing her fat, moist
finger against her mother's smooth olive cheek. Sure. Lindy knew
the truth. She was a fraud.

She looked at her daughter's sweet, slender body overrun by
hormones and grinning, greedy Goonie cells. That's how she saw
them. Goonies. Little, lecherous microscopic monsters, dining out

on her baby's loveliness. Party Hardy on Tess's hospitality. Minute Madmen fighting for control. Like that Woody Allen movie, she couldn't remember the name. The one about sex. When Woody plays a sperm and does a whole monologue about waiting to be shot up into the birth canal. This was the nightmare version. She could see it in her head. A true war of good and evil. The Amazon progesterone, the good fairies of womanhood, in a desperate battle against the sadistic Goonie cells. Why did the Goonies seem male and the good cells female? Too bad she could no longer afford analysis, this would be interesting.

Tess did look like Leo. Leonine. Perfect name for the son of a bitch. Large bronze-blond head. Searing blue eyes, the color of aquamarine. Wide slavic cheekbones. Tess had his face, his wide-set eyes, his full brooding lower lip, and his short straight nose (thank God for the nose!). But she had her mother's black kinky hair (the Semites always win in the end). And Lindy claimed her as her own. They bonded over the impossible hair. Something physical that they struggled with together.

Tess was secretly glad about the hair, though she ranted and raved with the best of them and tried every known straightening substance, conditioner, and antikink remedy available. It made her closer to Lindy. A mother not like anybody else's mother. Her mother had modeled and gone out with movie stars and even met the President (she wasn't sure which one). Her mother had beautiful clothes and always looked perfect, even when she was just staying home. Who had a mother like that?

Not to even mention how smart and funny she was. The funniest. Her friend Penelope thought that Lindy was too sarcastic. Tess went so far as to look up the exact definition of *sarcastic* in the dictionary (*biting, cutting, bitter, derisive, mordant, ironic, sardonic.* See *cynical*). She had to agree with some of it, though the cutting part didn't fit. Her mother never said mean things. Most of her humor was on herself.

Anyway, Tess loved her sarcasm and tried to copy it, which got her in trouble with her teachers and lost her some friends, but she was learning. She had gained a little control and was keeping her mouth shut in class more. That was something else she shared with her mother. They both had big mouths. This made her happy. She liked to think of herself as "her mother's daughter."

She remembered Grandmother Segal saying that to her mother and shaking her head. It was about all she remembered of her grandmother. Her grandfather had died before she was even born and her father's family, well, actually she didn't even know if he *had* a family. I mean, she didn't even remember *him,* let alone relatives. It was just her and her mother. And they both liked it like that just fine. That was why she had to get well. She absolutely couldn't leave her mother alone. No way. Forget about it! (as Rochele, her night nurse from Brooklyn, said). She would get rid of this stupid leukemia and they would go home and back to their cozy little world.

The pain was coming back. She looked over at her mother's face and saw her watching. She was a witch that way. She always knew in a second when the pain was back. She stuck out her tongue and crossed her eyes.

"Colleen, she needs her shot." Lindy handed Tess her nightgown. Now she would do what she did every morning. Hold the spitting bowl while Tess did her teeth, brush her stubborn curls, and stand guard until the shot appeared. Then she would take her Vuitton overnight bag down the hall to the parents' lounge to take a shower, stepping over the exhausted bodies of other bone-weary parents, who had journeyed from all over the planet, flocking to this place, this monolith of miracles—using their life's savings, their pensions, their wiles, to try to find a cure for a child lying in a bed, like her child. A child with a tumor in the brain or palsy in the limbs or cancer in the bones or . . .

Only, this morning was different, she thought as she waited for Colleen to return and relieve her baby of the pain that sometimes seemed more unbearable for her than for Tess. It was the thing that she could not take away, could not protect her from or control or stop. But this morning she had found some hope. She knew what to do next. She was going to track that fucker down and bring him back.

When the phone rang, Willa Snow was just reaching to unplug it. She looked at her watch. Seven P.M. She tried to turn the damn thing off before seven. For a while, in her methodical way, in order perhaps to justify to herself her increasingly antisocial behavior, she had actually kept a log of phone calls that she received after seven P.M. and they were clearly all calls that she resented, regretted, or certainly did not need to waste her time with, when the evening hours were so short and precious.

Today was an especially good example. A day so emotionally tiring that she felt she had earned the right to disconnect the damn thing at six. But she had forgotten. The only person besides her mother (*Ha!* including her mother) that she would really want to talk to, she had put on a plane for Alaska early that morning. In one day she had sent her only child off for a summer of "becoming a man" on an Alaska fishing boat, and had watched her two favorite students graduate. Then she had spent eight endless, tedious hours in her office, closing out the year.

Usually she would be overjoyed. Months of freedom stretched ahead, time to start work on her book idea, to take a vacation with Maxwell. She swallowed. Alaska was the beginning of the end of all of that. The first summer vacation they had not traveled somewhere together. College in the fall. It was almost over. The empty nest. All the books and articles and women's group sessions from all the years of her adulthood had droned on and on about it. She should be prepared but she could hardly say the words; they stuck in her throat. Gnarled twists of twig and leaf, choking her with loss. So tonight she had planned her evening of "coming to terms with it all." She had called her mother at lunch (nine A.M., California time). Now she would run a long, hot bubble bath—"Gentile chicken soup," she called her long, hot baths. She was convinced that they cured everything. When the bath didn't help, she was really unhinged.

After her bath she would pop her Weight Watchers frozen pizza into the microwave and pour her allotted glass of white wine, to which she would add a hefty slug of crème de cassis, turning it into a luscious soda pop for tired, lonely, abandoned, middle-aged sociology professors. Then she'd pop up a large bowl of hot-air corn and settle down with one of her swelling library of classic video movies and wait for the tears.

They would find her eventually, she had no doubt of that. They had been pushing against the cracks in her cool, calm public persona all day. Eager little opportunists they were, her tears, always racing toward a promising exit sign. They knew how to find one in any language. Italian. French. Even Japanese. If she forgot to lock them all up in the morning, left even an old neglected pore unpowdered, they would find it; springing forth, clouding her view, disorienting her. Lately she had to be on guard all the time. They had been building up all week. They were hot and cranky and not at all interested in her need to maintain control of herself in public.

Sometimes she talked to them, calming them down. "Listen, I know you need the release. I really feel for you. Believe me, I could use it too. You think I don't know how long it's been since you've been out? I sympathize. The thing is, though, I've been a little overcontrolled for a while and I'm not sure, if I let you go, that I'll be able to stop when it's appropriate. Do you read me? Supposing I let you run wild and then I can't turn you off? What would Maxie think? I know you love Maxie. Would it be fair if his mother broke down, let us say in a staff meeting or in class, and started sobbing to beat the band and no one could turn her off? Not good for any of us, right? I'm all alone here, fellas. If I stop, it all stops. See? So. I know you're restless. I know you're just about ready to explode, and believe me, I'm not forgetting about you. We've got this week to get through. Let's get Maxie on the plane and get the students out, and I'm all yours."

It had worked. Now she thought maybe it had worked too well. They had taken her at her word and gone off to watch *Twin Peaks* reruns or something, and she was stuck with this throat full of weeds and these dry, twitching eyes and not a teardrop in sight. It was okay though. She had time. She was free for a while.

Willa stopped still, standing in the middle of her bathroom, unaware that she had even entered it, letting the thought penetrate. Free. She had no memory of ever being free. It seemed as if she had always been mothering someone or something. And always Max. She could no longer remember before Max. Now she was going to be alone. Alone and not old. Not young, but far from old. It was sad, but there was another feeling creeping beneath, one that she knew she would get to, way down on the list after all the despair and self-pity. A kind of excitement. A claiming of her life. A life that she had never claimed, being, as her friend Eric the Jungian said, "So other-directed you could land planes without radar."

Free. It had a nice ring to it. That was what she was thinking, she remembered later, when the phone rang, releasing the always irrepressible god of Irony into her receiver.

"Is this Katharine Willa Snow, otherwise known as Snow White? This is the Wicked Witch."

There are few people in anyone's life who can telephone after an absence of ten years and without a moment's pause, without even the sizzle of a new weld being formed, resume the connection. The giant rubber band of relationship, stretched by time, betrayal, envy, change, snaps back into place as if it had only been expanded for a second. Snap. She's back. Lucinda Evelyn Segal, alias Lindy Lampi, and Katharine Willa Snow, sprung from the cuckoo clock of random absurdity back into their five-year-old seats. Her first friend. Also her last, come to think of it. Probably neither of them had risked another such relationship.

Ten years fell away like ten minutes.

"Lucinda?"

"*Puh-leese* don't start calling me that! You know what it does to me!"

"Sorry. I had a little lapse. I just regressed thirty-eight years."

"Math was never your subject, Wills, but it's only been ten."

"No. I went all the way back to when we met."

"Too early in the call for that. We have to have a long, boozy dinner, full of recriminations and nostalgia, to get all that far down."

Willa laughed. "Right. I was just going to unplug the phone. If my memory wasn't going, you would never have gotten me. Are you okay?"

"No. The truth is no. My baby . . ."

"Tess?"

"She's sick, Wills. She's really sick. I need your help. I've got to find Leo."

"Leo!" Willa laughed in spite of herself. "Leo Lampi! Are you high, or what?"

"It's not like the nice, sensitive, WASPie little princess I knew to laugh when her best friend and fellow mother tells her that her kid's sick."

Willa gasped. "Oh, God. I didn't mean to laugh! You just caught me so off balance! Leo! I haven't seen him or heard from him since I sent him out to L.A. Since before you two got married. *You* haven't seen him for ten years. Why?"

"I'd rather not go into all the gory details on the phone. Do you think . . . could you come down to the city? You're up near Albany or some wretched rural spot, aren't you?"

"Cooperstown. Well. Sure. When?"

"Tomorrow. Please come tomorrow. I talked to Tess's doctor today. She had a real bad afternoon. She's going back on chemo, her remission didn't hold."

"Oh, God, Lindy! She's got cancer?"

"Leukemia. The Lewd Comedian, we call it. She needs a bone-marrow transplant. I don't match and you know my family tree. No one healthy left. The scourge of the only child. We've been soliciting strangers on TV, even. Nothing. And this kind of marrow doesn't come in brisket bones. I was hoping we'd find a donor and it wouldn't come to this, but this morning I had this glint of insight. I know it's Leo. He's the match. I need you, Wills. I don't have anyone else to ask for help. You're her godmother, after all, even if you haven't seen her since she was two. Besides, we shared the bastard."

"Just tell me where. I'll drive down tomorrow morning."

"Beth Sinai. Pediatric Intensive Care. Though they may move us into a regular room tomorrow, before the chemo . . . Shit, Wills."

"Oh, baby, I'm so sorry." Willa no longer had to worry about the tears. The minute she put down the phone they rushed toward the open crevice behind her heart. Out they sprang. Some of them, she thought, as she reached for the phone jack to unplug it, seemed to have been in there for more than a week. Some of them seemed to come from all the way back at the beginning.

Lindy Lampi's voice refused to leave her head. Round and round and all the way back she went. Little girls in Beverly Hills, California. Not the Beverly Hills of now, where snotty punks in Armani suits were shotgunning their parents for The Inheritance and legions of ageless women, all of the juice and vitality surgically sucked out of them, goose-stepped around banquet rooms, vaporized zombies in Galanos gowns and Cartier jewels, waltzing toward death like gossamer holograms at the Disneyland Haunted House.

No, Beverly Hills way back then had the slightly bumpkinish innocence of all newly formed places. People were doing very well out there in the postwar paradise. Better than any of them had ever expected, better than they had done back East, or wherever else they had come from, but it was still a place of fruit trees and family life. Of money so new, the owners were grateful. Grateful and respectful of the stuff. Fearful that it could vanish, pulling them back into the Depression of their youth. It had value. It was taken very seriously, this green gold, as the way out of ghettos and shame and the oppression of no options. That was glamour enough. Children were taught to respect it. They were taught that earning it was hard work and keeping it even harder, that nothing comes cheap and flaunting was not nice. The parents all worked hard, the streets were safe, the skin color was mainly white, the religion mainly Jewish, the maids mainly black, the gardeners mainly Japanese, and the family structure mainly intact.

Willa blew her nose and turned on the tub. Why was it so painful for her to look back there? Every time she went out to visit her mother was agony. She never left her mother's cottage; she hid there as she had as a child, new to the neighborhood, not one of the rich kids, not even Jewish. An outsider. A fatherless misfit living on the kindness of strangers. Shame on shame. Her mother was still in the same house, for chrissake! No wonder it was hard.

She knew something else too. She was still hiding. Hiding away in a stifling academic wasteland, as much a loner and a misfit as she had ever been. Still scared of the stray dogs and rude comments of potential torturers. It was why she had never written a novel. To do that she would have to go back, open up the root cellar to the light, and climb out head first.

Now that her son was grown she was standing again at the forked dragon's tongue of choice. She could lock herself up and wither away, turning into one of those women she saw around her. Bitter, brittle, living with too many cats and too much bile bilge from the past, poisoning their hope.

"People become depressed when they have lost the courage to live." Who said that? Kierkegaard? Go, Kierkegaard! That was her. That was why she had loped around on the outside of her life for so long.

Maxie had been enough to keep her presentable to herself and others. See! I am not a burnt-out divorced woman hiding in the sticks! I'm a mother, full of warm, cuddly sentiments and love and responsibility. See! In a way it had been true. Maxie lit her up. He was her reason for being; the oil for her lamp of China, just like in that old Pat O'Brien movie she had on tape. She turned off the water and slipped out of her robe. Or should I say *Lampi* of China? She laughed in spite of herself. Keeping Maxie safe, taking him away from Leo and raising him right, had been enough to keep her depression and longing at bay. She had done it herself and she had done pretty well, but that reason for being was in Alaska now and would soon be in Boston and she had better start working on Act Two or the play would go on without her.

She sank down into the lemony bubbles and moaned with pleasure. Heaven. Better than sex. Or maybe it had been so long since she'd had any great sex that she'd forgotten. Leo. She smiled. She certainly had great sex with Leo.

She remembered the last time she had seen Lindy. Leo had walked out on her, leaving her alone with two-year-old Tess and a totally shattered ego. Their friendship had survived sharing Leo, because Willa had already left *him* before he met Lindy. In fact, it had been Willa, feeling sorry for him out in L.A. alone, who had told him to look Lindy up. (One of Leo's great gifts was making women he had hurt still want to help him.)

What was Lindy's name then? Barnes. Yes. She was still married to the dentist. Willa blew bubbles into the water. Oh, God! The dentist with the permanent smile. The guy looked like the Joker in *Batman*. So repulsive. So nice and steady and rich. Poor Gerrold. Lindy had taken one look at Leo, and her marriage collapsed like one of Gerrold's plaster tooth molds. It didn't bother Willa, she had cured herself of Leo cold turkey.

Her only concern by then was for Lindy. "You don't know what you're getting into. This is the guy to have the passionate affair with and not pass Go. Keep moving on to Park Place. Not for marriage and forever, honey."

"Of course you'd think that way. You are not a passionate person—you've always been someone who walks around the corners of life, sniffing and nibbling. You never just tear right into the center of things, with brio. I'm not like you and neither is Leo."

"Lindy. The one passionate risk I have taken was Leo, and it was a serious mistake. So forgive me if I continue on my peripheral path."

"If there hadn't been Leo, you wouldn't have Maxie."

"Got me there. You're right. Listen. If you love him that much, go for it. I just don't want you to get hurt."

"Why should I get hurt? Because he's still in love with you? Is that what you think?"

"No. It's just that Leo is from the other side of the galaxy, Lindy. We're still the product of our value structure. He's from a whole different planet."

"That's what's so exciting! He's the last man on earth my mother would approve of! Gerrold was her dream man! You know when I danced with Gerrold, if I closed my eyes, I couldn't feel him. Just a kind of clammy emptiness, like dancing with a dead person."

"That's disgusting. It just gave me a chill!"

"A chill would have been an improvement! Nothing. We're talking absence of energy. Did you know that in some religions they describe the devil as the absence of energy. Not fire and ice picks."

"Pitchforks."

"Whatever. Well, that's Gerrold. Like the devil. No energy."

"So the devil is a nice Jewish dentist from Beverly Hills? I like this."

"He sent out holiday cards saying, 'Have a flossy New Year.' "

"You're kidding?"

"You didn't get any because I always took yours out and tore it up. I couldn't take having you see it. He was on the cover giving the okay sign, with his smile, a giant toothbrush in his pocket, and a set of uppers and lowers on his desk."

"Say no more. Marry Leo."

"Wills. Really? It's okay?"

"Listen, we've shared worse. But . . . never mind. I'll keep my mouth shut."

Leo did not want to marry Lindy, however; and as time went on she began to blame Willa, blame her for something that, in a way, she had always blamed her for. Something intangible, fizzy and slightly unsavory, a slightly bad smell drifting by that cannot

quite be placed. It had started long before Leo, but Leo had ce-
mented it. Lindy wanted him more than she had ever wanted anything and Lindy was used to getting what she wanted and had
been getting it for a very long time. Paying the world back, in a
way, for all the lonely, hapless years of her childhood. So Willa
had discarded him and he still wanted Willa and Lindy wanted
him. Thus it was Willa's fault. Willa was the winner all over again.
The blond, slender, pale intellectual, the prima in all those dreaded
ballet classes, everything that Lindy would never be.

No one had ever left Leo before Willa, and Lindy knew this was
part of it. She also knew that he was using her to heal his pride,
trying to make Willa jealous. He was also trying to impress both
of them by being on his best behavior. He was working for a
record promoter who thought he was brilliant and had "a real
future in the biz." He paid his child support and was exceedingly
polite to Lindy's mother. (Who never spoke a single word to him
or remembered his name.)

Lindy finally convinced Leo to marry her the way women have
been getting men to marry them since Babylon was the In urban
center. When she got pregnant, he gave up the hope that Willa
would reconsider and take him back, and he married Lindy. But it
ate at her. And when he left, she blamed Willa. It was not rational
or reasonable, but they both accepted it as real. They turned from
the center of the ring, sweaty satin robes thrown over their stubborn shoulders, not waiting for the bell that ended the round and
went back to their corners, to huddle in the darkness of their
thirties, alone.

When Leo left Lindy, he left. Vanished. Dissolved, eclipsed,
faded out of sight. One morning he was just gone. Neither of
them ever saw or heard from him again. He had come into their
sheltered good-girl lives like a Colossus, a giant of a guy, bigger
than life. A Real Man. An outlaw. Billy the Kid and Pancho Villa.
Hannibal and Ivanhoe. Clint Eastwood and John Gotti. Rough. A
slum kid hiding out in an Italian suit.

The kind of guy, Lindy liked to say, "who fucks first and asks
questions later." Cool. A man who worked with his hands. A
powerful presence. A man's man. A guy who never had to snow-
plow.

If the gods did not have such a wicked sense of humor, Leo

would have been born in the Wild West, a Zane Grey hero wandering the plains saving mortal men from Injuns and their frustrated wives from apathy. Slipping into the wife once or twice and riding off into the sunset. The wife unplugged and glowing with gratitude; the husband innocently waving good-bye to the greatest guy who ever mounted a mare.

But it was the 1970's, and men of decency did not walk out on women and children and trot off into the darkness. Both Tess and Maxie looked just like him. "We were just the fucking ovens," Lindy once said.

Willa put on her robe, twisted her long, fine blond hair up on her head and walked downstairs to her tiny studio. She knew just what she wanted to find. The book. The story of Lucinda and herself. A novel in progress that she had begun when she left Leo, clinging to the work through all the agonizing first months of separation, as if each page were a Coast Guard life preserver holding her up, keeping her afloat in the panic of the present.

She could no longer remember why she had stopped, but the courage to keep going, to risk writing it, had just deserted her. She had put the manuscript in a drawer and not looked at it again for all these long years. "It's time, kiddo," she said softly, and patted her own hand for encouragement. Willa sat down and opened the folder.

The Butterfly from Beverly Hills

This is the story of Lucinda Evelyn Segal (later known as Lindy Barnes), who was born in Beverly Hills, California, on November 5, 1944 (Scorpio). I was at her fifth birthday party and her wedding. She was not the smartest girl in the world or the nicest and certainly (for many years, anyway) not the prettiest, but she was my best friend for a long, long time and the loneliest person I have ever known . . .

—The Narrator,
Katharine Willa Snow

El Royal Apartments
1944

Lucinda was a mistake. The result of random x's and y's crashing together like the Liberator bombers and the Luftwaffe, a flash of light in the dimly lit bedroom of Vilma Linowitz Segal and Byron Louis Segal in a rare martini-hazed moment of passion. It was a romantic time, after all. The war had "turned" (everyone in the know said so) and American business persons such as Byron and Vilma were riding the wave of wartime booty like a catamaran. The wind behind and danger yet unseen.

They had by this time been married for almost sixteen years and had struggled together to build Lord Byron Inc. from a storefront business with two machines cranking out silk blouses for local retailers, to a thriving ladies' sportswear operation that would become (by Lucinda's fifth year) the most successful women's-wear operation on the West Coast.

They owed a lot to the war. First, because Byron was too old and small to serve (standing a mere five feet three inches made him sartorially impossible for military attire) and, second, because Vilma (who was known even then by the showroom models, secretaries, and everyone else at Lord Byron as Lady Macbeth) had a brilliant way of turning disaster into daffodils.

The disaster came in the form of a government decree (Regulation L-85) setting in no uncertain terms the war rules for the entire schmatta *business.*

"No more than two inches of hem may be used on any garment." The head designer swooned and was carried to the day bed in the ladies' lounge. "One patch pocket per blouse." The blouse cutter gasped. "No skirt more than seventy-two inches around. No collars or cuffs on coats. No belt more than two inches wide." The showroom girls were weeping quietly. Byron was coughing nervously. Only

Lady Macbeth was undaunted. Rising to her full five feet seven inches (tall for the war years), she whipped out a sketch pad and pencil and began to turn sows' ears into silk shirts. And voilà. Sportswear soared. Playsuits were born. Wraparound skirts were the answer to frozen zipper production; halters, the summer solution to fabric rationing. They put sequins on Eisenhower jackets and golden eagles and wings on narrow-hemmed evening dresses. "Fuck France!" cried Vilma as sales hit the roof. "If the war lasts till 1950, we'll be billionaires!"

On this February night in the third year of the war, Vilma and Byron had gone out on the town with several important buyers from the Midwest. It was becoming increasingly important to wine and dine these visiting firemen of the rag business. Meeting the sometimes unsavory and all-times free-loading appetites of these vital cogs in the fashion wheel, would lead the Segals to ulcers and migraines and attacks of hysteria during Lucinda's formative years. Now it was still exciting. They had taken the group for cocktails at the Hollywood Roosevelt Hotel bar and then on to the Segals' favorite celebrity-studded restaurant, Chasen's, where Lady Macbeth could make her entrance in her sleek black shoulder-padded suit, her stone martens hanging in shiny-pawed apathy around her pearl-clustered neck, to the bows and scrapes of the waiters and captains who knew the big tippers when they saw them.

They were quite a couple. Byron, immaculately dressed in gray gabardine suit and brown suede handmade loafers, his tiny frame with its already popped belly, running behind his statuesque wife. He was a nice man with a prematurely bald, white-fringed head, beaked nose, and friendly blue eyes, always ready with a little story, adoring his Vilma whom he called by a seemingly endless string of pet names, none of which seemed remotely apt ("Try the pâté, Cuddle Bunny. More wine, Sapphire-eyes?"). In the end, rather self-obsessed and weak, but always affable. A cute person, if such is a possible description of a forty-five-year-old gentleman.

Vilma, on the other hand, was not a cute person. She was a woman out of her time. A career woman in an era when women with careers—unless they were Betty Grable or the clubwomen, Red Cross Gray Ladies or Rosie the Riveters of the war effort—were heard of but not seen. She was a big person. Big of bosom and hips, with a face that seemed to have been thrown over her skull like a sculptor's first slapping of clay. It sat there, waiting to be refined, honed, smoothed out. It seemed to have no bones. The eyes were close-set and flabby-lidded, the cheeks sunken, the nose spoon-shaped and without character. Her hair, which was at this point hidden by a variety of British Air Corps–inspired chapeaus, but would spend the postwar years uncovered, was mousey brown, dyed black. It was neck-length with a fringe of bangs, of the Prince Valiant school and included a shiny bald spot at the crown, which Vilma wore, like the emperor's new clothes, with a kind of arrogant obliviousness that somehow made it acceptable. "Mrs. Segal, I could perm your hair and put it up in a chignon that would cover your bald place perfectly," said Agnes, her hairdresser.

"What bald place?" demanded Vilma, thus ending the discussion. She had beautiful legs that she showed to the hilt in black-market silk stockings and ankle-strapped shoes and three-inch fingernails painted in endless layers of silver-white enamel. Somehow, despite the fact that Hedy Lamarr was in no real danger, she had style and an attitude that made her attractive to men and worshiped by little Byron, on whose nose ring she patiently attached a silken cord.

The evening had gone perfectly, from the dry, icy-cold Gibsons to the ration-defying meal and the sighting of several celebrities, which thrilled the out-of-towners no end. When Douglas Fairbanks came in, the buyers ordered the

*entire summer playsuit line; over French champagne and
Ann Sheridan, they went for the fall jacket and dress collection; and by the arrival of cherries jubilee and Myrna Loy,
the Segals closed the single biggest order of Lord Byron's
history.*

*Thus on the high of this success and the mood of war
mania that passed in and out of everyone's nervous system,
the Segals had returned home to their prestigious midtown
apartment, whistling "Lili Marlene" in their hometown
Hoboken–accented glee; and feeling totally protected by
sixteen barren years and middle age, the Segals entwined.
It was one of those moments when life throws a curve.
Zeus blinked. Mother Nature dozed off, and Lady Macbeth was ambushed.*

North Beverly Drive
November 5, 1949

*Five years and nine months after the Segals' night of
passion, everything had changed. Lady Macbeth had survived the almost suicidal hysteria of her pregnancy (a reality that she did not face until well into her fifth month, past
the point of knitting needles and Tijuana clinics) and the
forty hours of resistance to Lucinda's relentless struggle to
get the hell out of that dark, unfriendly hole.*

*She had survived the end of the war. So long, war chic;
hello, haute couture; and endured the pressure of con-
verting both the mentality of her employees and the old
cash flow to include, once again, frantic curtseying to the
French, who sprang Monsieur Dior like a secret missile,
sending explosions of taffeta, chiffon, and ruffles across the
Atlantic. Good-bye, patriotism, victory gardens, and swollen profits; hello, postwar economy, competition, and motherhood.*

But she had survived. Byron found a quaint MGM ver-

sion of an English country house on North Beverly Drive directly across from the already famed Beverly Hills Hotel. The house had a vast tree-lined yard; a huge family room, complete with wood-paneled bar, linoleum floors, and brick fireplace; and a large bedroom suite for Vilma, with space for her two hundred suits, drawers of jewelry, and countless bottles of French perfume. Across the small hall was a slope-ceilinged room, rather an afterthought sort of space that they covered in wild-flowered wallpaper and furnished with the One from Column A–approach to baby arrival that included every conceivable gadget and luxury any newborn person could possibly require. From Column B they chose a large black nanny named Anabelle, who loved little Lucinda with more commitment because ("This here is the homeliest baby I have ever put my eyes upon").

And life went on. They were a family. The Segals' parents were all dead, and being only children themselves, the house was devoid of adoring relatives. This suited Lady Macbeth just fine. She was a second-generation Jew—not part of the immigrant riffraff, but even so, her family had been far beneath her idea of the "right sort"; thus no photo or memento was displayed and no relative was ever discussed; so Lucinda was born without a history, which may have been the genesis of her making everything up.

As she grew so did their feeling for her. She was a sweet, pleasant child, with big brown eyes that had not yet been obscured by her nose, and black ringlets that curled around her fat, shiny cheeks. They didn't know what to do with her; they didn't know how to handle her; they were scared to death to be left alone with her, but they loved her, in their way.

Lucinda was not, then, a demanding sort. It was almost as if she sensed that she had very little power and not much rope and so made do with what she had. She followed her nanny Anabelle everywhere and called her Mama and was content to sit on her fat, warm lap, listening to Stella Dallas *and Anabelle's philosophy of the world and eating what-ever was available. "Jewis people is jest Nigroes with white skin, chile. We's from the same jungle—jest a different tribe. One turned thisaway and one thataway—and if we'd stayed in de middle, we'd all be monkeys."*

Vilma and Byron were gone when Lucinda woke up in the morning and usually did not return until after she was asleep at night. Often in her sleep her tiny hands would reach up, casting shadows on the moonlit walls. She stretched her small arms up, up, tensing in her sleep—tears falling from her two-year-old eyes, and three-year-old eyes and four-year-old eyes, arms reaching, growing longer, reaching and then tensing as if trying to grasp something real, other arms that would sweep her up, hold her tight, and tell her who she was.

She was very well dressed and very clean and had every game and stuffed toy on the market. When she was three she went to New York City (Anabelle dragging behind Vilma with Lucinda and her dowry of fuzzy bears and pinafores). "In de jungle yous be nekked—so much non-sense for one baby." When she was four she went to Paris and sat on Anabelle's lap at all the couturier fashion shows, watching beautiful women whirl before her. ("Nevah saw nothin so ugly on this earth—painted skeletons—not a morsel of flesh on 'em.")

Lucinda, however, was impressed. Sitting in her nanny's lap on a skinny golden chair, she discovered make believe and the power of imagination—cracking into the heart of her loneliness, replacing the present with daydreams of beautiful French ladies and clapping hands and silk and candlelight and herself the center of all the attention. She went home with new information and took to hiding in Vilma's closet, slipping her fat little feet into high-heeled shoes and painting her face with lipstick. She sniffed in the exotic smells of her mother's power and was close to her in a way that had never before been possible.

*And so we arrive at her fifth birthday party (the first one
that was publicly celebrated). Lucinda was civilized now—
a speaking, toilet-trained person who could eat with a fork
and say* please *and* thank you *and put herself to bed. She
was ready for her debut into the perilous and foreign world
of Other Children.*

*Anabelle was sent around the neighborhood to hunt up
likely prospects. She took to the task with true jungle cun-
ning, lurking behind trees, listening for the sound of childish war cries, peeking in windows, following gum-wrapper
trails and lost puppies. It took some time, but when she
moved in for the kill, she never missed her prey.*

*Six victims were taken. In they came, followed by smil-
ing, well-groomed mothers of suitable age, whose eyes
froze at the sight of the nervous, aging, overdressed Segals,
in distaste bordering on fear. Two of the children were the
offspring of movie people and they were brought by chauffeurs. (Children of famous people were never brought by
The People, a rule that Lucinda would learn like her times
tables as years passed.)*

*The yard was decorated with balloons and pink-flowered
tablecloths. An organ-grinder and monkey entertained under the oak tree and a real live clown did pratfalls by the
bird fountain. Anabelle roasted hot dogs on the outdoor
barbecue, and a cake shaped like a giant heart proclaiming
LUCINDA EVELYN SEGAL IS FIVE! was covered with candles and
waiting in the kitchen. The fact that none of the children
talked to one another and stood in six sullen, cross-armed
states of hostility had no effect on the Segals or Lucinda
(none of whom had any basis for comparison).*

*Of the six attending children two were to be important
in the present and future life of Lucinda. The first was a
freckled, redheaded little boy named Mark Springer, who
was called Wheezie because of his asthma, and because he
was frail enough and lonely enough to allow it.*

At first it had been the teasing name given him by his

nasty older sister and her friends, after seeing Snow White and the Seven Dwarfs. *At some point, however, his father, who was a famous film producer, picked it up and soon he was "Wheezie." (The idea for the name came from a movie and they were a true movie family. Somewhere in that train of thought it became okay.) To Lucinda, however, it was the same as someone calling her Fatty and it attracted her to him immediately—comrades-in-arms in the insensitive family wars. The feeling was mutual. He followed her around from that day on.*

I was the other child of importance. I was also lonely and had just moved into this lush and bizarre neighborhood, a world as alien to my experience of studio apartments and all-day nursery schools as the moons of Saturn. My mother, Lily Miller Snow, was a widow. My father, William, had died in a plane crash on the threshold of a promising law career, leaving nothing behind but one-year-old me and a thirty-year mortgage that we could not manage. My first memory of my mother is that she was pretty in the Joan Crawford–school of beauty way and was always tired and rubbing her feet. She had taken a job as a saleswoman in the better-dress department of Saks Fifth Avenue, a job that required immaculate grooming, elastic smile muscles, and the legs of a defensive tackle. They never let her sit down and she developed hemorrhoids and varicose veins, and finally, by my fifth year, was forced to surrender her attempt at independence.

Her surrender worked out fairly well. She was hired by Mortimer and Mitzi Mitchell as a sort of feminine Our Man Godfrey. *The Mitchells were a semiretired but still famous song-writing team, who had written the scores for many hit Broadway and Hollywood musicals.*

The job came with living quarters of our own. Down an oleander-shaded path, on a separate lot in back of the tennis court, was a cozy, spacious two-bedroom guest cottage that became our first, last, and only real home. We had a lawn in front and a private patio in back. There was a small but perfect country kitchen completely stocked with Wedgwood china, fiddleback silver, and English crystal; two sunny four-poster bedrooms with a blue-and-white tiled bath between; and a large knotty pine–paneled living room furnished with chintz-covered sofas and expensive reproductions of English antiques. On the south wall, between the sofas, was a flagstone fireplace that reminded my mother of Gary Cooper movies, and on the wall above it was a real Turner seascape that could have hung in the Metropolitan Museum (and did too, later on). We had our own phone, radio, and small TV. I thought it was paradise. My mother knew better.

On the day Anabelle found me chasing Mitzi Mitchell's toy poodle, Garbo, round and round the circular driveway, I had been living up the street from the Segals for one month. I was a moderately pretty blond girl with almond-shaped green eyes and a slender, flexible body that led me to a frantic, and at times neurotic, devotion to ballet class. I was smart, a little sassy, and tied to my mother like Hagar's bastard, believing passionately that we were all alone and bonded together in the world. At the time it was perfectly true.

I did not share Lucinda's problems of overweight and lack of attention, but she did not share my poverty and half orphanhood. Everything considered, we were about equal. The truth of this must have been beamed out on some level of consciousness, because by the end of the highly unsuccessful afternoon, we were friends. (The film siren's ratty son proclaimed on departing, "All in all, your party stunk.")

Because both our mothers worked all day Anabelle took charge, gathering Lucinda and me from kindergarten and taking us home to play.

"What's yo' full name, chil'?" she asked me on my first postbirthday excursion. "Katharine Willa Snow. Willa for

*my daddy William who crashed from the sky and burned
all up."*

*"Well, now, Katharine Willa Snow, you listen here.
Don't never tell Lucinda's Momma and Poppa that yous
not Jewis and yous not rich, and everythin' be jes fine."
And I never did either.*

*"Katharine Snow?" Lady Macbeth swooped down on
Anabelle, her bald spot glowing under the overhead fluorescent light of the kitchen. "That's certainly an unusual
name for a Jewish girl."*

*"Um-un. Mis Segal. The Katharine is after that Hep-
burn movie star. And the Snow part is changed. Her
Momma changed it from Schmeck—I think yous can un-
nerstan' why. What Momma wants her baby risin up as
Mis Schmeck?"*

*Even Lady Macbeth could follow that reasoning, and so
I was accepted in the Segal household with as much gra-
ciousness as was available.*

The Beverly Hills Hotel
April 1954

*She is sitting on a bar stool near the glass doors, down-
stairs at the soda fountain. She considers it her stool, for she
spends most every afternoon there doing her homework
and breaking her diet. No one bothers her and she can
think. She is almost always the only kid around, except
occasionally when some visiting VIP or movie star's brat
comes in to run up the tab as a way of paying Mommy back
for ignoring them. They never talk to her and she doesn't
really care. Today it is quiet. Only she and Myrtle, the
waitress, who has worked at the hotel for a thousand years
and gives her extra scoops of ice cream and free cookies and
never minds writing "cottage cheese" instead of "French
fries" on the charge account, so that Lady Macbeth won't*

know she is violating Dr. Tibor's Baby Fat Elimination Plan, Phase I.

Two men in shiny dark suits, whom she figures must be agents, enter and sit as far away from her as possible, smoking cigarettes and drinking coffee. Everyone else seems to be in their room or at home glued to the television screen, watching that weirdo McCarthy foam at the mouth. The week before Lucinda had said that she thought G. David Schine was groovy and Lady Macbeth had slapped her face and sent her to her room. So much for the First Amendment.

The soda fountain is a small room containing only a long counter rounded at one end and a dozen tall wrought iron-backed stools. The walls are green flowered paper and the carpet is worn and it smells of freshly grilled cheese sandwiches and lacquer and nail enamel from the beauty shop next door. Lucinda knows every nook, crook, and cranny of this hotel. She lives right across the street, and since Lady Macbeth never learned to drive, it is where she took Lucinda on rare mother-and-daughter outings, to sun by the pool, eat lunch in the Polo Lounge, get her hair cut, buy French perfume and handbags, and wait for Lord Byron to take them to dinner after his Saturday golf game.

As soon as Lucinda was old enough to cross the street alone, it became her corner store, her haven, her escape from the series of dour housekeepers in whose constant care she found herself. Everyone there knew her. "Hey, Lucinda, how'd the spelling test go?" The midget in the red uniform, whose face adorned the Philip Morris ads, would shout to her as he raced across the lobby with a page message in his tiny white-gloved hand. People spoke her name. Cocktail waitresses kissed her forehead and she could sit in a corner of the lobby and read her horror comics until her eyes fell out.

She saw Marilyn Monroe one day and Rosemary Clooney and Frank Sinatra (for whom she would gladly die) and even Adlai Stevenson, who patted her on the head though her parents never believed it.

At Christmas the big white tree went up and she helped the maintenance men hang the decorations. And there were parties every day and so many beautiful and fancy people around that she would stand in the corner, movie magazine in hand, and look them up, putting stars by everyone she guessed right. And carolers dressed like angels sang in the ballrooms and gave her all the free Christmas candy she could eat. In the summer she helped the gardeners on the lush green lawns, cutting back the bougainvillaea that cascaded down the pink walls of the hotel, suffocating the buildings with their brilliant purple beauty.

The manicurist buffed her nails and let her use the pale pink polish and old Mr. Levine in the smoke shop gave her free bubble gum. "Go on, sweetie—all those teeth will fall out sooner or later anyway. Enjoy!" Often she told people that she lived there, that her mother was an Arabian princess in exile. She made up endless stories about herself when she was little, and she never stopped when she grew up.

Now she is nine years old. She is fifteen pounds overweight "for a girl of her size and background," says Dr. Tibor, the Hungarian sadist child-hater. She has thick black hair that frizzes from her scalp in a violent Semitic act of freedom, causing horror in her mother's soul and remorse in her father's pale blue eyes. She has a large hooked nose, whose bridge starts so high that her beautiful brown eyes are lost behind it, and a wide space between her crooked front teeth. Her ears stick out, denying her the joy of ponytails and braids, which are in vogue, and her feet are too big and almost completely flat, which gives her a ducklike walk and causes her ballet teacher to rush from the room in occasional bouts of hysterics. Her skin is clear daughter-of-Judaea olive, and she has plain but rather nice hands with double-jointed thumbs, which she uses to upset her new Austrian housekeeper.

No one pays any attention to her. At school, the teachers don't know her name, and she has no real friends except Wheezie, who is a misfit like herself and so doesn't really count and The Narrator, who has become popular and less malleable and so doesn't really count either.

And so this rainy late April day she sits, overeating and pretending to do her homework while eavesdropping on the conversation of two shiny-suited businessmen. She was wearing her horsehair slips under her pink cotton skirt and her fuzzy angora sweater, her saddle-shoed flat feet dangling beneath.

Her stomach hurts. Two double-thick chocolate malts, one triple order of French fries, and a cheeseburger threaten to return to Lucinda's empty plate. She looks at her fourteen-karat gold Bulova watch. It is past five and she is late for her piano lesson. Tears fill her eyes and she wipes at them with her greasy napkin, leaving ketchup stains on her nose. She hates going home to that horrible Austrian witch and that lonely, empty house. Her parents are away on a selling trip. They have been gone for more than a week. Wheezie has bronchitis, and I have taken up with a more fashionable playmate, who has her own horse and a groovy twelve-year-old brother.

She is all alone. If Lady Macbeth would only let her have a puppy or a kitten, it wouldn't be so bad; but the mere mention of the subject causes her mother's chest to heave as if it would spring from her body, and her father doesn't dare take her side (though she secretly suspects he'd like one too).

She signs the bill, leaving a big tip for Myrtle and slides awkwardly off the stool. The men glance at her and smile to each other. She wants to kill them. She wants to kill Leroy, her piano teacher, too. She hates the piano. She hates ballet and gymnastics and tennis and art class and modern dance. Mainly she hates them because she has no talent for any of it and so is continually embarrassed and filled with a sense of failure.

This sense of failure follows her everywhere. She sees it in the mirror and radiating from the disappointment in her parents' eyes and in the eyes of other children's parents and all her various teachers. Everywhere she goes failure follows, breathing down her neck with its putrid nasty breath.

She uses her own key to open the front door and tiptoes into the living room, hoping to escape the Austrian Nazi's wrath. The smell of pork chops and onion frying in a pan fills her nose, sickening her again. Leroy sits at the baby-grand piano bought, supposedly, as her ninth-birthday present (just what she'd always wanted) but really on the advice of the Segals' decorator, who could no longer cope with the gaping hole in the northeast corner of the living room. Patti Page is softly singing "The Tennessee Waltz" on the kitchen radio. The Austrian has forgotten to open the windows, and the room is stuffy. She resists the temptation to sneak up behind Leroy and smother him beneath her bouffant skirt.

He turns. "You are late, Miss See-gal. Mozart was never late."

"I'm very sorry, Mr. Leroy. I was attacked by a huge dog as I was crossing the street. He chased me for two blocks, and I climbed a tree and couldn't get down until he stopped barking and ran away. It was horrible."

Their eyes lock. He wavers. She meets his gaze, unblinking, brown eyes widening in steady sincerity. "The first rule of lying," Lucinda taught Wheezie and me, "is eye contact. Grown-ups never believe you can look them straight in the eye and lie. And they give themselves *away*. They always say, 'Look me in the eye and say that.'"

Lucinda had discovered lying in a flash of guileless wisdom. "See, once you don't care if it's the truth, I mean you aren't afraid God will punish you or your parents will torture you, then it's easy. You just do it and after the first

*time it's easier and easier and then you can be so much
happier. Everything is really much simpler."*

*We would listen in open-mouthed adoration and try. But
neither Wheezie nor I could ever get past the look-me-in-
the-eye phase and we gave it up, except for life-or-death
situations. Lucinda just smiled her secret smile, as if she
knew things that we were much too young to understand,
and went on lying.*

*Mr. Leroy burped. His stomach let out one of its infa-
mous high-pitched wails as if some living thing were
trapped inside his skinny, cheated body and wanted to get
out.*

*"I wouldn't have thought there were wild animals in
such a fine neighborhood. Sit down and begin. My time is
much too valuable for this nonsense."*

*She began. Large, clumsy fingers pounding up and down
the keyboard, struggling over notes she was too bored to
try and read. "Can't I learn 'Sha-boom' or 'Heartbreak
Hotel'?"*

*"You can't even seem to learn 'Row, Row, Row Your
Boat,' Miss See-gal. Just look at your fingers. The piano is
not a chopping board, you do not smash at it. Your hands
must arch and move quickly, gracefully, and above all with
strength. Now, watch me."*

*The keys danced. Leroy was showing off, using Lu-
cinda's lesson as his excuse to play a fine piano before any
audience, no matter how small and sullen. His pianissimo
made her head swim. The pork chops' greasy fumes and
Leroy's body odor made her dizzy with nausea, and his
contempt filled her eyes with tears. His stomach gurgled in
her ears, his bony fingers rose, the cold, empty room swam
before her, and as Leroy reached his smug and lyrical fi-
nale, she vomited. One violent and thorough spasm all
over his hairy hands.*

*It was not how she had hoped to end her short, unhappy
piano career, but it* was *most effective. Leroy and the Aus-*

trian Nazi shrieked and carried on. *Both accused her of doing it on purpose and she was sent to bed without a backward glance or an offer of tea and toast, and no one even asked if she was all right.*

When she woke up, the Nazi was gone, walked out bag and baggage, leaving her alone with a note stuck under the salt shaker. "I called your Momma. I hat enuf. Goot-bye."

She was famished and dressed quickly, running across the street to Myrtle, to order two grilled cheese sandwiches with bacon before calling a cab to take her to school. When she came home that night, Lady Macbeth and a sour-faced Scots woman were waiting.

We were, above everything else, children of the Fifties. War babies without a war; nine-year-old girls caught in the middle of the twentieth century. We carried the guilt of our innocence, "Of course, you're too young to know what it was like during the . . . war," and which *war depended on whether we were being admonished by parents or grandparents.*

It was a time when parents and children were not supposed to communicate. We were wrong and they were right. Traditional values still counted. But traditional values for Beverly Hills, California, were not those of Ozzie and Harriet, or anything that the newly rich parents and their guilt-ridden children had ever heard anything about.

We had not stood in bread lines or fought for our country or gone to jail for our beliefs. We were nine-year-old girls with at least six crinolines each and our own bedrooms, bopping along with American Bandstand *and curling our hair.*

No one ever told us anything. We hung there, spoiled and meaningless, mamboing our way into puberty as if nothing had ever happened; *caught in the middle of the century like painted puppets on tangled strings, trying to work our way free. Try to move a leg, and an arm popped*

*you in the eye. And that would be the story for most of our
lives.*

*At night in her room Lucinda used to pray, "I am inno-
cent—I am separate, it's not my fault." She told me this
much later and when I asked her what it meant and where
it had come from, she said that she hadn't the slightest idea.*

Life in General
Christmas Vacation, 1957

*In the alley with the cats she is special. They gather
around her, licking, purring, leaping, rubbing. Here she
reigns. Sitting on a cement step just outside the old inciner-
ator, her pocket filled with kitty treats and dog bones. She
is waiting for Wheezie and me. She has been waiting for
almost an hour. We had planned to walk over to the hotel
and have lunch—Segal's treat.*

*She is hungry and cold and her rear end still stings from
last night's punishment. She pulls the Mitchells' tom onto
her lap, feeling the heat of his fat, furry body. She is thirteen years old. She has large breasts, which fascinate us,
and braces on her teeth. Big clumps of her hair have fallen
out, the result of her experimentation with a home-applied
Negro hair-straightening preparation.*

*She has crushes on at least five boys, none of whom is
aware of her existence. She wants to kill all of them.*

*Upstairs on her bed are stacks of brand-new clothes from
Lord Byron. Wool skirts, cashmere sweaters, silk shirts,
slacks—a complete fall wardrobe. She refuses to wear any
of them, slipping on what Lady Macbeth refers to, in horror, as her Filthy Beatnik outfit. It had all come to a head
last night. She had been requisitioned from the new English maid's nutrition program to join her parents and two
buyers from New York for dinner at Chasen's. The Segals
had been on edge lately. They were still on top, but the*

perch was precarious and the competition more brutal each season. The entertaining and placating of the ever-increasing hordes of out-of-town buyers was beginning to sap their energy and self-respect.

They were at this time both over fifty, and the pace was finally getting to Vilma. Her nerves were shot. A Christmas trip to Hawaii was hastily planned. Lucinda refused to go unless I could go with her. I was invited. I was ecstatic.

Lucinda sulked, never having been on a vacation, knowing only big-city trips, business trips, lonely room-service nights in hotel suites. Hawaii was just one big factory, as far as she knew. Besides, she couldn't swim a stroke. It was the one thing she would have loved to learn that was never considered. Lady Macbeth did not know about swimming. She knew about sportswear and East Coast things like ballet and piano, it had never even occurred to her to add a pool to their endless yard.

It had also never dawned on her that, for a child living on the verge of the Pacific Ocean, in a town where the number of swimming pools actually affected the level of humidity, not *swimming was a severe social handicap. So what would she do in Hawaii? The same thing she did at the rare swimming parties to which she was asked—plead chlorine allergy and sit under an umbrella reading* Seventeen *magazine and feeling miserable.*

We were set to leave the day after Christmas and stay through New Year's. But after last night Lucinda was not so sure.

Her parents had come home at six, to change for their dinner engagement. Lady Macbeth had gone upstairs immediately, thrown open the door to her mammoth walk-in closet, switched on the light, and screamed. For the first time since she was four years old, Lucinda had been caught. She was sitting in the corner, wearing her mother's most expensive black silk pumps, her face covered with a black mink jacket, playing with herself.

"What are you doing in here? Are you trying to kill me! Do you want to see me have a nervous breakdown?"

Lucinda bolted up in her mother's shoes. She tripped and fell forward at Vilma's shapely feet.

"Lucinda, get up immediately and tell me what on earth were you doing sitting in my closet in the dark? I want the truth!"

Lucinda focused her black-lashed eyes with steely innocence.

"I'm so afraid you won't believe me."

"Of course I'll believe you, if it's the truth."

"I was looking for the trap door."

"The what?"

"The trap door. My homework assignment was to read this story about a haunted castle in England that looked a lot like our house and it had a trap door in the lady's boudoir that led to a hidden treasure chest and so I was trying to do what it said in the story. I bet it sounds silly."

Lady Macbeth put down her dagger and smiled. "How sweet, dear. It's so nice to see you using your imagination and reading something literate, not just those awful comic books. But you gave me an awful scare. Mother's very nervous lately, you know. Now, I don't ever want you in my things again. You have so many of your own lovely things, any girl would be envious. My things are my *things. Now, go get dressed for dinner. Wear that lovely new pink shirt-dress, and let Hortense do, uh, something with your hair."*

Lucinda smiled, kissed Vilma's cheek, and went into her room. She took a long, hot shower and put on her Filthy Beatnik outfit. This ensemble consisted of one black turtle-neck sweater (no young ladies under sixteen wore black anything), a moth-eaten, skintight, black wool skirt salvaged from the Mitchells' garbage can, black tights and ballet slippers. She put black eye pencil around her eyes and white pimple stick on her lips and haughtily made her way downstairs.

"Here's your martini, Sweet Potato—nice and icy, just the way you like it," Lord Byron purred.

"This has been the worst day of my life," her mother moaned.

"Now, now, Lamb Chop, nothing's so terrible. We'll be off to Hawaii soon and you'll be fine."

"I'm getting old, Byron. I'm slowing down."

"No, no, never, never, Petunia Petal."

"Yes, yes."

"Never."

Lucinda appeared in the doorway, interrupting this poignant scene and causing Lady Macbeth to drop her martini into her pure silk-covered lap.

"Look at her!" she shrieked, losing the last thread of control. "She's trying to kill me! How could she do this to me! All those beautiful clothes! Look at her! A filthy beatnik!"

Lord Byron ran to his hysterical wife's aid. Somehow he managed to remove her, soggy and sobbing from her leather swivel and half carried, half pushed her upstairs to bed.

She had waited out the scene sitting in her mother's chair, finishing off the remains of her father's drink. She waited passively, most likely not really understanding why she had chosen to act out her hostility in such a self-defeating and desultory way any more than anyone else ever did. Or maybe, simply, what happened next was exactly what she wanted.

Her tiny, pot-bellied father stood in the doorway, his face stern, giving him an eaglelike appearance. "Get up to your room and lie down on your stomach on your bed." Lucinda rose immediately and followed him up, the sounds of her mother's sobbing echoing under the door. Byron Segal, for the first time in his or his daughter's life, was angry.

"Take down your pants!"

"Why?"

"Do what I say!"

She did. Off came his gold-buckled alligator belt. Slap. Slap. Slap. Her buttocks turned red. Her eyes stung with the pain, but she did not cry. In fact, she rather enjoyed it and was in no real hurry for it to end. Slap, slap. Byron continued, his mouth tight, his small hand, white on the buckle, tears in his eyes. It was her first spanking. It was also the first time in her entire life that she had been alone in a room with her father or had his full attention.

When it was over, he left without a word. She got up and opened her bulging closet, studying her bottom in the full-length mirror. Fiery red stripes lined her backside and the tops of her thighs. She stripped off her Filthy Beatnik outfit, put it in a plastic bag, and threw it in the trash. This particular game was over.

Lindy's Inauguration
Rodeo Drive, January 1964

She is standing in front of the Luau, smoking a cigarette. She is waiting for me to pick her up. She is looking at herself in the side mirror of a Corvette parked in front of her. She smiles. She frowns. It is not what she had wanted. She had wanted Jackie Kennedy. That is what she had asked for. That is what she had planned. When the bandages first came off and she saw her new face—new nose, dermabrasioned acne scars, pinned-back ears—she had screamed so loudly that two prospective young patients fled the stunned doctor's waiting room.

So she wasn't Jackie Kennedy. She was beautiful. She could tell by the naked shock in all the pretty blue eyes and most especially my green ones. There she was, big as life, Lucinda Segal, twenty pounds lighter, hair ironed into a thick, wavy pageboy, huge brown eyes mascaraed and braces off, lips sticked.

Since she had emerged from her three-week Christmas exile, her secret transformation, her revenge on all of us, she had floated like a fetus in a gauzy sac of unreality. Isolated, upside down, dreamlike. For every two waking hours she spent one staring in disbelief at this new creature in the mirror.

This was not Lucinda Evelyn Segal, foil for the pretty girls, last to be chosen, first to be taken home. She would wake at night—her arms stretching toward the ceiling as she had done as a child, terrified, recoiling from nightmares of her new face being smashed, melting, changing back. She would sit up, her heart pounding, her nightgown drenched with sweat and crawl across the floor to the bathroom, crouching in terror, afraid to look. Slowly she would pull herself up, eyes closed, praying. Snap. Lights on. A beautiful princess smiled back. Someone who had absolutely nothing to do with her. Lindy would be her name. She rehearsed it inside her mind, shared it with the princess in the mirror. Lindy Kennedy, second wife of the President. Lindy Sinatra, new bride of Frank. Hans Christian Andersen was right, after all.

Her parents beamed. For the first time in her entire nineteen-year life, eyes did not look at her with disappointment. She wore this new visage like a private joke, a Superman suit, Mr. Hyde's hat. Part of her mourned good ol' reliable Lucinda with a piercing sadness that doubled her over with stomach cramps and made her head ache. The other part of her was in ecstasy.

She takes out her compact and pats her hair, dropping her purse onto the hood of the car. A face appears behind her in the mirror. A man's face. She turns.

"Hi, beautiful," he says.

It is the first time this has ever been said to her.

"Hi," she replies.

"What's your name, baby?"

"Lu-Lindy."

"Nice. Mine's Damon. Want to go for a ride?" He nods to the Corvette. She is too nervous to speak. He is handsome. Tan. Blond. Probably an actor. He is also old. At least thirty.

"I can't. I'm waiting for someone."

"I'm only in town for a few days. Got a suite at the Beverly Hills Hotel. Come on. You're too good to pass up, beautiful."

That word again. He is talking to her. *She has not been found out. He likes her new name. He is not turning away. She is not melting. It is real.*

"Okay."

It is getting dark. The room smells of Scotch and stale cigarettes. She has never been in a room here before. He is lying on his back, naked. His belly is a little soft, and he seems even older than he did before. He is breathing loudly. His hand is in her hair, spoiling the wave. Her throat is dry.

"Put it in your mouth, baby."

She does as she is told. It is not the first time, God knows. But it feels like it. It is the first time as her. *It is Lindy's first time. It is the first time anyone wanted her. The first time she has not done it to pay someone back or on a dare or because she was only asked out when she did it.*

"Faster, baby."

She obeys, head whirling backward. Myrtle's malts. Cats in the alley. Grilled cheese sandwiches.

"Sit on it, dolly."

She climbs onto his hot, foreign body. She has never done that before. She has never been all naked in a room with a man before. She does as she is told. Riding him as if her life depended on it.

"Yeah, bitch. Do it to me, pretty bitch!"

Pony rides. Puppy dogs. Anabelle's lap. Lord Byron's after-shave. Christmas carols, ballet class, chocolate Cokes.

"Now, baby. Now. Ride it. Now!" He cries out and

grabs her buttocks. In a moment it is over and he is asleep. She doesn't know what to do, so she does nothing. She sits there, afraid to move for a long time. Her leg is asleep. She bites her lip, and as quietly as she can, she climbs off him and tiptoes into the bathroom.

Her hair is sweaty, springing back into its natural form. Panic fills her. She is melting. He will come in and find her, a she-wolf at full moon, Dracula at dawn. She takes a shower, washes her face, tiptoes out, gathers her clothes and purse, and returns to the bathroom.

She pulls her hair straight back (nice flat ears opening up at last the world of the ponytail) and carefully applies fresh makeup. Her heart slows down. Lindy will escape unscathed. She puts on her clothes, turns off the light, and tiptoes back. She waits for him to wake up. To say the magic words again. It is late. Dinner will be on. She clears her throat. She coughs. Nothing. Finally she stands, takes a pen from the desk, and writes her new name and number.

She walks slowly down the green flowered hall, with her ten-year-old ghost, then through the lobby of her girlhood and into the cool night air.

. . .

Willa closed the folder and stood up. She put it in a large mailing envelope and carried it into the kitchen, flipped on the news, needing a moment of distraction, poured herself the long-overdue glass of wine, and took her diet pizza from the freezer. *Low fat, low sodium, low calories, no sugar, no animal oils, no tropical oils . . . No taste.* Willa shoved it into the microwave.

Someone on the local news was shouting about air pollution. She punched the dial. Someone on one of the interview shows was shouting about street crime; Patti Davis (former First Daughter of the Tussaud President) was on a tabloid program, wearing a bikini and babbling about the dolphins. Willa kept flipping. Station by station, black, white, Asian, Hispanic people with puckered faces were complaining about everything.

Willa sipped her drink, letting the cool, dry liquid soothe her, a trickling, teasing caress gliding down the center of her being. A group of heavy women on motorcycles with T-shirts that proclaimed DYKES ON BIKES was roaring down Market Street in San Francisco in some Gay Rights parade. Behind them a transvestite wearing a jock strap and covered in gold chain mail was bumping his pelvis and waving a flag that said SCREW CHILD ABUSE.

Willa sighed. Sometimes she wished everybody would just shut up. Abortion Rights, Animal Rights, Pro-life, Anti-life, Pro-veal, Anti-veal, Alcohol Abuse, Drug Abuse, the Homeless, Teen Runaways, Greenpeace, Nukes, No Nukes, Mind/Body proponents, Vitamin C proponents, Smokers, Nonsmokers, Passive Smokers, Fetus Rights, Carrot Rights, Christ, Antichrist. Why don't they all just shut up. Someday soon we'll all be back living in caves, running around naked and eating berries. Every other option will have become too offensive to some group or other, too toxic, or too indulgent.

It had always been so clear to her that fanatics were the most dangerous people of all. Nothing was more dangerous than an absolute belief that there is no other side. There are no *good* causes for zealots and fanatics. It was all so depressingly pathetic. All these people filled with rapacious zeal, reeking of intolerance and hate, pumping their meager personal value up by caring about cows, or radon, or whatever. Enclaves of righteous fascists pushing everyone else around.

One day last fall as she was strolling down Madison Avenue, feeling light and happy, a unique moment when she was not on guard, a crazy-eyed, but well-groomed black man had jumped in front of her, his face contorted with hate. "Animal murderer!" he had screamed, pointing to her modest fur-collared wool coat.

For a second she was frozen, stunned by the invasion; then outrage flooded her. "You don't love animals, you hate people!" she shouted back, but he had already run off, a bully in the end.

What did he really hate anyway? What did most of them really hate? People who had more money than they did. She did not like to admit that she thought this. Not that she had any money. But compared to him, to them, she did—they all did, all the well-dressed, well-educated achievers who filled the co-ops and shopping streets of American cities.

All everyone really seemed to care about anymore was money; rich or poor. Every city was broke, every state, every charity, museum, foundation, halfway house, AIDS clinic, social service. Beggars and bag ladies banging their cups on the curb; Donald Trump banging his cup on the mahogany desk in Chase Manhattan's boardroom. Money. Money. Money. All of a sudden *no one had any money.* We couldn't keep the Persian Gulf crisis going without NATO's money! Unbelievable. America! The savior of the planet. Country of deep pockets and endless reserves, whining with the rest of them.

It was harder and harder for her to take anything seriously. Everyone seemed to be hurtling toward the millennium on their own monogrammed rocket of frenetic madness. The week before, at a perfectly civilized dinner party at the home of the college provost, she had been seated next to a writer of literary criticism. Fueled by more than a moderate amount of Napa Valley zinfandel, he had leaned close to her and whispered somberly, "We as a world are facing two profound threats."

"What?" she had asked with quasi-flirtatious interest.

"The first," he murmured conspiratorially, "is a plague caused by deer ticks, which is really being spread by rats that have come in contact with petroleum by-products. A plague. It will wipe out millions."

"And the other?" she inquired, fascinated now.

"We are being punished by God for taking uranium out of the earth," he slurred. "In the earth, you know, uranium is perfectly harmless. Only when it is removed is it deadly. That is what I am going to devote the rest of my life to. We must put all the uranium back."

"Well, that ought to keep you busy," she said, smiling sweetly, and turning to the buck-toothed chaplain on her left.

The very next day she had watched a parade on television for the Mandelas. A joyous, surging ticker-tape parade the day after The Man had said on national television that Castro, Arafat, and Khadaffi were his close friends and his allies—and great humanitarians, to boot. His wife's bodyguards were already on trial, implicating her in the savage murder of a young boy; and the streets of South Africa were running black with blood, tribe on tribe terrorizing their own people and making the Afrikaaners look

positively bovine by comparison, and America is giving him a
parade on Wall Street! Winnie and Nelson grinning and greeting
the adoring hordes—hair sprinkled with confetti—two chocolate
ice-cream cones come to conquer. Arthur Krim is hosting a party
on Park Avenue, where wicked Winnie will arrive outfitted from
head to toe by a famous Jewish fashion designer; then they will all
tango off to TriBeCa for a movie-star bash thrown by Robert
(Bobby, baby) De Niro and attended by every right-thinking celebrity from Madonna to Bart Simpson.

It all made her head hurt. She had first come East because she
had written a book of cultural essays entitled *After the Ever After*
that had garnered good reviews in the respectable literary press
and had even been praised in *The New York Times.* They were
mainly essays on contemporary marriage and the absurdity of urban young adulthood; but they had been her ticket out of San
Francisco, and then, after Leo, out of New York City.

Carter College was a small, nicely endowed liberal-arts college
founded by Lutherans. It was rated "highly selective" in the col-
lege-listings books, which meant it accepted rich kids from the
Midwest who couldn't make the Ivy League schools and whose
conservative, WASPie parents wanted the prestige (and biannual
theater and shopping trips to Manhattan) that went with a child in
an eastern college.

Willa had jumped at the offer to teach cultural sociology and be
an ad hoc writer-in-residence, hired on the hope that she would
do another book, thereby gaining brownie points for the school
and tenure for herself.

She arrived from Manhattan with eight-year-old Max, feeling
like a refugee from Remedial U.—half orphaned and mildly edu-
cated. All she had been able to afford was two years at Santa
Monica City College and two years at UCLA. She had no graduate degree or any real qualifications for the job. The book had
gotten her to New York, into magazine editing and the teaching
program at The New School extension, and she had done well
there. But when Carter called, she couldn't help feeling somehow
a giant mistake had been made.

Terror would be an understatement for her first year there. Between her drive to succeed and to make up to her son for the
desertion of his father and the peripatetic displacement of his early

childhood, years had passed before she even looked up and realized she was in the middle of a life.

But she had done well at Carter. The students loved her course and she had published several articles, which were compiled into a second book called *The Bell Doesn't Ring Without the Clapper*. It was not as successful as the first one, but it seemed to please the tenure committee. She had a snug, pleasant, reclusive life. Too snug maybe. *Stifling* was the word that came to mind.

Willa pulled her pizza from the microwave, picked up her wine, tucked the envelope under her arm, and went upstairs to her room. She settled down on her bed and switched the TV on muting the sound.

Where would she go if she left here? She was far too shy to begin anew, join a garden club, take up folk dancing, bicycle across Burgundy with a nutritionally aware singles group, follow a spiritual leader, or march for Rat Rights. She was just not the type.

She could not throw herself into the midlife, new-town whirl of "networking" and compulsive socializing that she had seen so many of her newly single or newly transplanted friends do. The whole idea for a solitary soul like herself was basically unbearable; an endless series of concert nights and small dinner parties with "interesting" new people. She would rather retire to a studio in Queens and watch game shows.

The truth was that no life that involved a "style" or was rated by the number of well-known people one knew, was of any interest to her. If she had been different, more ambitious maybe, she would have stayed in New York City, networking to beat the bloody band and building her reputation.

She would have hired a press agent like what's-her-name and started showing up at PEN events and literary soirées, wearing thrift-shop men's wear and smoking a pipe. She just hadn't had it in her.

Not that Leo would have minded. Leo loved the idea of her becoming a celebrity, however minor, and taking the heat off him. It was very clear by then that her belief in Leo's deeper side, the brilliant musician she had thought him to be, was a lover's illusion. Their unspoken marital agreement was that she would work and he would try to compose music. They gave it their best shot. She plugged away at her day job, writing press kits for real estate developers, and working on her essays at night—plus, of course, Maxie—and Leo wrote music, made demo tapes, played in gigs up and down the coast with unknown groups of hopefuls like himself. Nothing came to anything.

New York was the last hope. They would appreciate his talent in a way San Francisco couldn't. New York would save them.

Half of this hope came true. It saved Willa. They accepted her talent and put Leo in his permanent place. New York City did not cotton to any illusions, lovers' or other kinds.

Leo was like fresh buffalo mozzarella or Beaujolais nouveau. He didn't travel well. Leo was not an East Coast guy. Leo was a sunshine-and-seashore guy. A West Coast or Southwest type. She didn't even *know* where he'd really been born. (Part of his sinister appeal had been his strong, silent refusal to talk about his childhood. How mysterious! How manly!) Here was a guy who would never be caught dead at a Save the Whales rally. This was a guy who would simply dive into the water, swim out, and *lead them.*

Willa chewed the last bite of crust and turned on the sound. A surly James Dean type from some teen crime show was being interviewed by an overly eager toothy blonde. (Weren't they all?) "Johnny, what do you like?"

Johnny slumped down so far in his seat she might as well have asked him to recite the Torah. "Uhh. Well. Um. I like drinkin' coffee. Um. Uh. I like sleeping."

Willa hit the zapper. Nan Kempner, New York's most famous and emaciated partygoer, was whirling around in the kind of dress that can only be worn if you are being transported by crane a distance of no more than fifty feet and do not plan on sitting, eating, breathing, or urinating for some time.

"Why spend five or seven thousand on a dress, then go to a party and see three or four other women wearing it, when you can spend a tiny bit more and have something really special? My husband doesn't see my point. He says, 'Nan, have you *seen* what the market's doing? Be careful.' But what can I do? He married a clothes-crazy gal!"

Zap. Willa sipped her wine. She was proving her own point.

"Hi. I'm Jessica Hahn. When people hear my name they think of headlines, scandal, and controversy. But no one knows my side of the story. Now I'm willing to tell all. You'll be shocked and amazed by the real Jessica Hahn. For the first time I'm willing to share the real me, to bare my soul. Call 555-1000. Twenty-five dollars plus two dollars for each additional minute. Now hear from some of our other *Love Phone* participants. Remember, we all want to be loved."

Jessica's plastic face faded and another one appeared looking just like her, only with dark hair. She was sitting in a chair with several male and female clones in evening dress. "Hi. I'm Candy. I like guys who do all sorts of fun things. I'm a party girl who likes dancing till dawn. I love music, long walks on the beach. I'm looking for someone who's *innerested* in honesty and world peace. He should have a dynamite smile, be a nonsmoker . . ."

"And have a sixteen-inch penis." Willa zapped the Off button and turned out the light. Funny, no one in any of the personals ever says, "I hate music, the beach, and staying up late. I want a guy with no sense of humor who's into crime and war."

It was time to think about it now. She was getting herself into something tomorrow, and she did not know what it meant or where it would lead or even if she was ready to cope with it. "It" being *her*. Lindy née Lucinda. She had stopped Momming the masses. She was no longer the first person to leap forward in a crisis with arms spread and endless energy to spare on other people's problems. Of course, Lindy was different. She loved Lindy. There was no way on earth she could turn down her plea. Just the thought of something like that happening to Maxie made her entire being scream. But where were the boundaries of it? Lindy had always been lousy at boundaries. She really was the Saddam Hussein of female relationships. She just took what she needed. Of course, that was all a long time ago. We grow up. We change. Lindy sounded changed. It wasn't just the agony in her voice—she sounded more vulnerable and not so armored. She had always been scanning for the raised psychic fist, the invisible blow, so that staying close to her was an endless mine field of hidden verbal traps.

For the first time in Willa's life she was really in a position to be available. She was not teaching summer school. Maxie was gone. She had some money in the bank. She just had to be careful, to let herself see clearly. She had been badly wounded by this woman; deserted without so much as an explanation, for something (Leo's departure) that was certainly not her fault. She had a drawerful of unanswered letters marked RETURN TO SENDER and not much else to show for an almost forty-year friendship. It still hurt.

She stretched. She would take the manuscript with her. Maybe she would give it to Lindy and maybe she wouldn't. She would see. What the work had showed her was how much she had cared. It was also clear why she had stopped writing it. She was still seeing Lindy when she'd stopped. There was no way she could have gone forward after the Luau vignette without losing her.

The next several years of Lindy's life had not been very flattering. She was one wild, wanton, furious young cupcake. After graduation ("Oh, Halls of Beverly/ We love you!") Lindy had set out in as premeditated and methodical a manner as any out-of-control, recently released young butterfly could, to pay her parents back for their benign neglect and all the other girls and boys for their scorn.

In the kind of small, movie-company town that Beverly Hills, California, was in the early Sixties, there was a group of pretty young girls who wanted Gene Shacove to cut their hair, Warren Beatty to ask for their phone numbers, and the bartender at the Daisy to know their first names. They bought their sweaters at Jax, where all the saleswomen looked like Audrey Hepburn and the owner hung out with movie stars and was seen with only the youngest and most beautiful models in town; and their immediate goal was to meet a successful actor or producer with an XKE convertible, who would take them to dinner at La Scala and get them a contract at Twentieth.

These girls were called starlets, though many of them had never starred in anything, but all of them had let a fair number of older men explore their eighteen-year-old Milky Ways. These were the girls who had eschewed college, feeling that a degree from Beverly Hills or Hollywood High School and good skin were more than enough to set them off on the nervy, curvy road to fame and fortune. Few of them really believed that they would end up on the wide screen as anything more than a flashy frame, a bit player, a catalog model, or one of the chirpy, fizzy-faced mannequins that add eye interest to auto shows and beauty pageants.

The real goal was the Guy. The one with the Lincoln Continental and the house above Sunset, the Chinese houseman and the intimate dinners attended by people they had read about in *Modern Screen* and *Confidential.*

A movie producer. Even an *agent.* Directors and screenwriters didn't figure in their fantasies, these bubble-cut girls with long, long legs and short, short skirts, three sets of false eyelashes, and Capezio pumps.

In those days only people in "the biz" really knew what film directors did, and writers were too intellectual (they thought) and not powerful or interested enough (they assumed) in going out and spending a lot of money. It was the guys with the flash, the cash, and the heavy-lidded, lustful eyes that the starlets were after. Being the wife of a man like that is what they had planned for, and that is what they would achieve. Most of these girls were not from the traditional wealthy families that spawned The Little City that Could. They were the daughters of divorcées and opportunists living in prewar Spanish-motif apartment buildings on the literal wrong side of the tracks (in this case, below Santa Monica Boulevard).

Their mothers, and sometimes fathers, saw their daughters as the way up. In a town where looks talked, having a beautiful girl-child was better than having a macaw in parrotland. These girls were groomed for this future; the promise of bright lights and big bucks. Marilyn, Liz, Lana, Ava—why not their own darling dear?

The starlets got through Beverly High, being elected class princess on occasion, but often not, those crowns going to the more conventional, well-rounded, popular, and less threatening girls; the cheerleaders and drill-team strutters who joined clubs and went to football games and sat on the student council.

These girls had a plan, and while they may have felt bitter, burning envy toward their better-protected and pampered classmates, they hid it behind a facade of icy, regal remoteness, as if all the teenage nonsense was just so, so silly, as if they knew something better lay ahead and all this adolescent idiocy just had to be endured.

Even though Willa was probably pretty enough (though she never thought so), and had the other qualifications, namely, a widowed mother, no Jewish blood, and blond hair, she had never been remotely attracted to this group, preferring the company of the Drama Club and the Dance Club (of which she was president) and writing for the paper and being serious about poetry. Lucinda, however, after her transformation, went right for them; a brown-eyed fly to the sticky golden web of pretense.

The girls accepted her with the insouciant amusement of the superior class. It did not for a moment hurt that she, unlike they, was from one of the fine families and treated them to a perpetual sugar-plum flurry of movie tickets, double malteds, and Susie Q fries with tartar sauce at Delores's Drive-in.

And, of course, Lucinda (just newly Lindy) had a car. A metallic-turquoise Buick convertible, perfect for cruising Sunset on Saturday night, hair held under fourteen coats of Aqua Net, pug noses tilted high, never for a moment condescending to respond to the rude remarks of silly boys who tried to get their attention.

A creamy convoy of Beverly Hills bitch beauties who would never return a glance unless, of course, it came from someone cute and driving an XKE, Chevy Impala, or better.

Lucinda wooed them and Willa stepped back and when high school ended and real life began, Lucinda opted to follow. "I'm going to be an actress," she proclaimed, causing her mother to collapse in hysterics, pulling out what was left of her hair and leaving her petit prince to deal with The Daughter.

Every now and again, in an old movie from the time, a movie starring Sandra Dee or Annette Funicello, the face of one of these girls will appear; a line or two will flow blandly from a pouty mouth and she will vanish, a flicker fading out, replaced by another. None of them ever really came to anything from their talent. But a fair number of them achieved their goal: marrying older wealthy men, some of them hanging on to this very day. Others fell by the way, victims of drugs, drink, or a passion for the wrong kind of guy, someone who left them with battered beauty and babies to raise.

Lindy, in the end, came out pretty well. Partly because she had a family, however out of their depth they were with her new lifestyle of resumés, acting class, eight-by-ten glossies, and older men. Mostly what they didn't know didn't hurt, and they knew only what she wanted them to. (Lindy held the title Master of the Manipulated Parents Truth conversation.)

They did not know about the pot, the pills, the abortion in Mexico; the big-time agent of Lord Byron's age who forced her hand onto his cock while screeching down Sunset Boulevard after a dinner party in the Palisades and refused to let go, even after they sideswiped a car and almost crashed head-on into a giant palm tree somewhere near UCLA.

They did not know about the tennis player (later top assistant to the head of a major studio) who beat her with his racquet and the real estate superstar who got off watching her take showers. (Often very long showers.) Or the broken promises, the auditions that left her eyes stinging with humiliation, sending her psyche reeling back to the days of Mr. Leroy; reminders of her worthlessness and powerlessness in the world of accepters and rejecters.

The thing about Lindy was, she never gave up and eventually she started to work, first as a runway model for Lord Byron, then for other design houses as well. This at least was respectable, her parents thought; and to encourage her, they set her up in her own apartment and offered all the parental perks available.

She found an agent and started to model for catalogs and soon she was making real money on her own. This was an experience so foreign and so magical to her that it brought her out of her moral languor, and out of Baal, the wasteland of golden calves and golden girls that had used her needfulness as legal tender. It gave her self-respect and she began to take life more seriously.

She went to work in New York for a year, showing up on Seventh Avenue runways and in Sears catalogs, Saks Fifth Avenue holiday ads and Gimbel's summer-sales brochures. Having no rent and no responsibilities, she saved her money, bringing her bank books to her father, which made his little paunchy chest swell tight across his handmade English cotton shirts. "It's all right, Bunny Cuddle, our little girl is going to be all right." He would beam, patting Vilma Segal's silver-taloned hand and allowing himself to get old.

If her father hadn't died, she would have kept going forward, doing just fine. But he did die, on the dance floor at the Cocoanut Grove, in the middle of a mean fox trot with his billowy bride, he died. He just stopped moving, releasing her hand, dropping as neatly as everything else he did, and died.

Her mother was left to wander the phony English halls of her Hansel and Gretel house, baying at the moon of misery with Lindy beside her. Returned, regressed, Lucinda once more, back in her baby bed beneath the attic; alone and frightened, slapped by the fiery-hot hand of fate.

What was the reason for doing anything if not to aggravate or impress them? It had simply never occurred to her that it was possible for one of them to be gone. And certainly not her father. The conciliator, arbitrator, diplomat nonpareil, the benevolent buffer between her and her horrible mother. How could he go and leave them alone with only each other to turn to? It was quite simply unbearable.

Willa had finished college, taken a job in San Francisco, and met some guy named Leo, who had drop-kicked her brain into Silly Putty. And she was back home on North Beverly Drive with *her mother*!

Under the circumstances, Lindy did the only sensible thing. She married her dentist and moved to North Maple.

In Beverly Hills, California, in the late Sixties, there was a group of affluent young married couples who, though the concept would not take a definable form for another twenty years, were the forebears of the Yuppies. They were mainly the offspring of the first-generation families who had made their mark on the West Side of the City of Los Angeles, raising sheltered, traditional heirs who went off to college, then law school, med school, or business school, only to return home and settle in close by their parents, matched hybrid salt-and-pepper sets of past and present. The sons, who were not ambitious or brainy enough for higher education, settled for a cushy executive slot in the family business, cutting short the process of making their own way in the world, and often, as if in short-circuiting the years of struggling to achieve on their own, they had cross-wired their genetic timetable; they seemed to segue dramatically from youth to middle age, losing hair and adding fat to their alligator-strapped waists, taking on the look of their fathers, old before their time; acquiring automobiles and stereo systems; houses in Holmby Hills and boxes at Dodger Stadium, as if the symbols of prosperity could eradicate the need for an experienced life; a journey toward, replaced by a spin around the block in a custom-built sports coupe.

These young old men married girls from similar families, combining assets and neuroses, joining Brentwood Country Club, and having babies named Joshua and Jennifer. Everyone knew everyone else and had watched one another grow up, had followed the rise to riches and the falls from grace that were publicly few. It was a world as narrow as a knife blade and as conducive to personal growth as an incubator without an air supply. This was the world that Lindy had struggled against all her life, but it was the only one she knew and it was the one she flung herself at, lashing herself to the French provincial mast of new-money marriedhood, in a fiercely fearsome act of self-denial.

Small wonder that after seven years of interior decorating and Friday night dinner parties (escargot served in the shells on special little silver plates and standing rib roasts with doilies on the bones and homemade mint sauce in the middle); Thursday night gin games with matching married couples; mixed Sunday doubles at Brentwood and lox and bagels at Nate-n-Al's; manicures at Shacove, lunch with the "girls" at Hamburger Hamlet, and Saturday night sex with Gerrold, she was ready to run.

Gerrold the Dead, the Joker, the Dentifrice Demigod, who thought she was the most beautiful girl in the world and also the most fortunate, to have him. Gerrold, with his curly black hair and his small, perfect features and pearly white teeth and adoring parents who worshiped him, praised him, pampered him, and gave The Couple anything they wanted (and a whole lot more that they didn't).

Gerrold, who had a needlepoint sampler on his office wall that said NO TARTAR MAKES YOU SMARTER! and thought cunnilingus was a gum disease.

Small wonder that when Leo Lampi rang her solid brass bell one night—Leo, Willa's discarded man of mystery, just landed in town and all messed up—that Lindy was struck dumb with desire. She opened the door in her Friday night finery, her group of matching marrieds settled in the rumpus room, drinking martinis and talking about real estate; and the schoolmarm met the outlaw. So what if the schoolmarm had modeled lingerie and been chased around hotel rooms by panting men twice her age? She was now a nice, married, proper young Jewish lady, with several pieces of "serious" jewelry, a full-length mink coat, a marble bathroom, and a husband who had root-canaled some of the most prominent people in Hollywood and took her to Paris for Christmas and let her sleep as late as she wanted, even on weekdays.

A husband who lovingly tweezed the bristly black hairs from around her nipples and tirelessly instructed her in the proper way to floss. Gerrold, who believed in the importance of daily elimination, higher education, dermal exfoliation, mutual masturbation, and nonverbal communication. Gerrold, who exclaimed, his small, immaculately clean hands sweeping the flagstone driveway, "This is the house that bad teeth built!" Who addressed their unborn children by name (Rachel and Rodney) and thought that sustaining an erection for more than five minutes led to high blood pressure and glaucoma. (Or at least this was his justification for why he never would, or could.)

Leo was Lindy's savior. "Hop on, little lady," said the High Plains drifter, galloping her off across Wilshire Boulevard, away at last from her child-self. Away from the life she had never wanted and into the one she most feared, her own.

Lindy sat curled in her sleeper chair in the dark, watching her daughter sleep. They had moved to a semiprivate room. There were no private rooms in Pediatrics, even if she could have afforded one, which she couldn't; but so far the other bed was empty. Compared to the ward or the IC unit, this was positively luxe. The Ritz Carleton of hospital rooms. She smiled. It was astonishing how quickly you adjusted to an altered reality. It was probably a lot like what happens to hostages: One day you're the American ambassador to Lebanon or Kuwait, with your Italian chef and French cotton sheets and Indian valet, and the next day you live in a cell filled with lice, a pot to piss in, and a cup of bread and water. Within a week it's a real treat when they unlock your wrist from the radiator.

She was now so used to sleeping in a chair, waiting in line for a communal shower, and never having any privacy, that she could hardly remember what it felt like to sleep through a night or close the door to her own room.

She had not eaten with anything but plastic for weeks and had almost forgotten what sitting at a real table or cutting her food was like. Her friends thought that she was making it too hard on herself, that she should get out of there and go home at night. But she would no more leave her baby alone in *that* place with *those* people than take a nice stroll through Central Park at midnight. Dangerous choices both.

In addition to the cockroaches, the overworked staff—some of whom forgot how to speak English after ten P.M.—there was the unpredictable rotation of residents, interns, and nurses, who ran the gamut from great to gruesome, with only an objective observer (namely, a mother) to differentiate. The hospital was just a microcosm of the way the city was these days, with doctors being attacked in their labs, nurses raped in the back stairwells, and drugs stolen. There were signs posted in every patient's room: DO NOT LEAVE ANY VALUABLES ANYWHERE IN THIS ROOM. Well, the only people coming into the rooms, besides families and friends, were *the staff,* so one needn't be a rocket scientist to figure what that meant.

Visitors passed grisly tales of dying patients whose wedding rings and heirlooms had been lifted right off their moaning bodies. It was enough to make you ill, without the presence of the real problem. The main event itself. A hospital, Lindy was convinced, was no place to leave a sick person, alone.

It was almost pleasant to have this quiet night with Tess before whatever roommate would arrive in the morning, not as horrible, she hoped, as the last one; the sixteen-year-old bald beauty, in from Connecticut for the removal of her third brain tumor, with the impassive, stone-faced mother crocheting compulsively. "She just keeps growing the damn things," she said, as if she were talking about potato plants.

A truly terrible woman, Lindy had decided, a woman who went shopping for shoes the morning they took her daughter off to surgery and then that night refused to help her when she had thrown up, dizzy from the anesthetic and the terror; leaving her retching, sobbing child. "I'll get your nurse, that's what she's paid for," she announced, storming off down the hall, leaving Lindy, who could not bear it, to hold the poor girl's head and wipe the mucus from the corners of her swollen, cracked lips.

Maybe you just go through so much, you harden up, she had thought, trying to give the woman the benefit of the doubt. But the next night when she and Tess had pulled their curtain, so that she could give her a sponge bath and they could watch *Jake and the Fatman* together privately, the Harpy from Hartford (as Tess called her) had ripped back the curtain—akin in hospital etiquette to barging into someone's bathroom without knocking—and demanded that they share the TV since her daughter was watching something "silly." At that moment Lindy's heart had filled with hate, and she had turned all of her helplessness on the other mother. "Don't you ever do that again!" she yelled, snatching the curtain from the startled woman's hand and resealing it, her body shaking with outrage. Tess went red with mortification, nothing being worse for a twelve-year-old girl than a mother making a scene, but Lindy knew that she was really glad she had done it.

Tess opened her eyes and saw her mother sitting with her knees drawn up, alone in the dark, the moon shining in the window, casting dark shadows on her face. "Momma," she whispered, her throat dry. "I had a bad dream again." Tears slid down her cheeks, glowing in the night-light.

Lindy came to her, lowering the safety bar and taking her free hand. "I'm here, baby. It's okay. Want some water?" Tess shook her head. Her voice didn't seem to be there, just a big sticky lump.

"Any pain?"

The lump wouldn't move. She shook her head, sending the tears flying.

"Want to tell me about it?" Lindy dipped a swab into the pitcher of ice water and wiped Tess's silky white face. "Got the lump back?" Tess nodded.

"Want me to talk for a while? I've got some things to tell you."

Tess nodded again, reaching out for the cup Lindy had filled with ginger ale. "Okay. I talked to Willa tonight. I know you don't really remember Willa. You haven't seen her since you were a squirt, but you've heard me talk about her forever. She was my best friend, from when we were kids, little kids. And she was married to your dad. In fact, I've told you about Maxie, her son? He's your half brother, but you've only met him once. He's eighteen now, I guess. Anyway, I called her because, well, because she still is my best friend and I miss her, and also, Tess, because I need to find Leo. We need that bone marrow, baby. Right now he's our best bet. I'd hoped it wouldn't come to that but it has, so I'm going to ask Willa to help me find him. We're going to round up the bum and bring him back here and get you well."

The lump moved down. Tess could feel it in her chest, pressing against her heart. Everything inside her felt too tight.

"Momma! No! He hates me. He won't come."

"He doesn't hate you, baby! Why would you think that? It was *me* he left, not you. It had nothing to do with you. It was him. He just couldn't handle the responsibility of being a parent (or a husband or a grown-up, for that matter). He left Maxie too, and he knew him a lot longer than he knew you."

Tess's eyes, Leo's wide silver-blue eyes, stared into her, hurting her heart. "Will I have to see him?"

"No, darling, not if you don't want to."

"What if he won't come? What if he's dead or something, even?"

"Oh, no. Not a chance. He's somewhere out there. And he's coming, if he comes tied in a body bag in the back of a police car. He'll come."

Tess swallowed. The lump moved lower. She watched her mother, looking for things she had not said out loud, searching with the clear, uncluttered eyes of innocence, for the truth. "I don't want you to go away, Momma. I'm scared. I don't want to be, but I am. The dream I had. I'm this dwarf, this sort of hunchback little dwarf and I'm wearing this really disgusting wig, because of the chemo and I'm driving this great huge crane. I'm really into this crane and I keep sending it down into this huge excavation, like where archeologists go? Like Egypt or someplace. And all these people are watching me and everyone's afraid because they think that there's some terrible monster down there. I'm afraid too, but I keep going deeper and deeper. Every time I whiz around and nothing's there I'm relieved, but I just keep saying to myself, I know there's something more down here. I've got to keep digging. Isn't that the weirdest?"

Lindy put her daughter's small, silky hand to her lips and sniffed in the skin smells. "I like that dream, Tessie girl. I think that's a really gutsy dream. I'm not sure what it means, but I know a good solid unconscious when I see one. Don't be afraid of that dream. It's strong. You're strong."

"Momma. There's something else you're not telling me. Tell me the truth."

Lindy looked up at her. "Boy. You are one tough little taco. Okay." Lindy took a deep breath. "You remember my mother,

Grandmother Segal. We came to New York and sort of never saw her again?"

"We never saw her again because you said she was in a coma in Florida or someplace, like a vegetable."

"Did I say that?"

"Mother!"

"Okay. See, a lot of this stuff was from my lying days, but I thought I had already turned over my Tessa leaf by then. Okay. Well, the truth is that she is not in a coma. What she had was a little stroke. But she's fine. I mean, as far as I know. I haven't seen her in years, but we exchange letters. When I left my first husband for your father . . ."

"Lord Plaqueless?"

Lindy laughed. "Who?"

Tess raised her knees, shaking with giggles. "Don't you remember? He sent me a Chanukah card when I was little. It said 'Happy Holidays from Lord Plaqueless,' and it had a picture of him dressed in fox-hunting clothes with a mansion behind him and a hound beside him wearing a collar made of toothbrushes. I remember because I felt so bad for you that you'd been married to such a dork."

"Oh, my Lord! I forgot all about that. When we get home, we are burning that card. The very first thing we do, before we unpack even."

They smiled at each other. Believing in this mission and using it to take away every other possibility. Lindy braced herself. "Okay. Let me get this over with. It's a sad, sordid story, my lady. I wish I had a more elegant history to bestow on you but I don't, kiddo. I'm sorry."

"Don't say that, Momma." Tess looked hurt. "You're the best mother in the whole world. I love your life. It's not just dull and ordinary like other mothers'. Besides, it's ours, it's what makes us special."

Lindy's heart was breaking. This is what they mean by that, she thought. This is what heartbreak is. Huge cracks, love tears, emotions so thick and dense and ragged and tender that the poor little muscle cannot hold them all. Bottomless love and passion for this child flooded her.

"Tess. Your grandmother was so mad at me for leaving Mr.

Toothbrush that she cut me off and out of her life. She sold everything and moved to Sarasota. That's where she is. I'm going to call her up and go down there and bring her back to stay with you while I go find Leo. Between Colleen and Rochele and your grandmother, you'll be okay. Not as good as me, I know. But we have to do this, baby. Trust me. You know I'd never leave you for a Siamese second if I didn't absolutely have to."

Tess blinked back tears. She was very tired all of a sudden. She knew the next question she wanted to ask, but she wouldn't. She didn't think either of them could take it. But she knew what her mother was saying and she knew that she would have to be stronger than she had ever believed she could be. She had to make her mom think she would be okay. She had to let her go. She thought about the dwarf on the crane. She would think about that. About what her mother had said about it. She would try not to let her down.

Willa was early. She had planned to meet Lindy around eleven, knowing from her limited experience with hospitals that the mornings were loaded with doctors' rounds, bathing rituals, bed changing, and medication delivery. It was only ten. She parked her car in one of the hospital lots, bought the papers, and went into a coffee shop near the Emergency entrance to clear her head. It was crowded. Hospital personnel on breaks and coming off shifts, shoppers and business people from the neighborhood. Willa took a seat at the counter and ordered coffee and a corn muffin.

She had enjoyed the long, predawn drive down, a drive that always reminded her of the good things about California; car rides with the radio loud and only your head for company. She opened the *Post* first, working her way toward the *Times* as she did each day. Dessert before dinner, she thought, zeroing right in on the cover story.

BUTCHER OF BEAUTY PUTS
BODY IN BUCKET

The man accused of dismembering his girlfriend, a beautiful former Martha Graham dancer, led police to the

*young Swiss woman's skull and bones, which were stashed
in a sealed white plastic bucket. Police sources said the East
Village crazie, who confessed to stabbing the girl during a
lovers' quarrel, spent much of the next week dismembering
her, flushing parts of her down the toilet and boiling the
skin off her bones. The deranged drifter, who fancied himself the devil's disciple, had first met the gifted young
dancer in Tompkins Square Park, where they smoked marijuana together and she invited him back to her apartment.
The crazed Satan worshiper never left, pulling the girl into
the seamy underworld, where just two weeks before her
death she was working as a topless dancer to support her
killer's mounting drug debts. "I beat her and I boiled her,"
the madman told a neighbor who had walked in to find
him boiling the woman's head in a pot.*

Willa shuddered, slugging down a large hot gulp of coffee. She
had been clipping stories like this for a piece she was working on.
She had an entire file full of pictures of seemingly sane, attractive
women, some more fortunate than the Swiss Miss, others not, who
had fallen under the spell of highly visible psychotics. Women
who married men in jail for wife murder and child abuse; a police-
woman who married a Bronx policeman accused of beheading his
first wife, who then proceeded to "molest, assault, rape, sexually
abuse, and endanger" her twelve- and thirteen-year-old daughters.
(The woman relinquished the girls to foster care in order to stand
by her man.) There was the beautiful young psychology student
who fell in love with the Napa Valley maniac doing life for the
slaughter of his young wife, her sister, her mother, and the throat-
slitting of all three of his tiny daughters, leaving one clinging to
life and surviving to tell the tale. "I love him," the pretty woman
boasted on prime-time television. "I want to marry him and have
his child."

It blew Willa's mind. Who *were* these women? What fairy-tale
fantasy had they swallowed with their mashed Gerber dinners?
What was wrong with women? Every talk show, every radio call-
in, overflowed with stories like this. What women did for love. It
fascinated her. Not just the violent and bizarre extremes but all the
gradations she saw and heard from women around her. Feminism

seemed like a dream, a Brigadoon they had wandered into, while taking a fitness walk in the woods. Even old Ivana, a perfectly gorgeous woman, carved herself up to keep The Donald, only to receive as a reward, "Who'd want to touch those plastic tits anyway?" Willa had seen scores of intelligent single women in relationships with married men, waiting for other women to finish with them, like bums waiting for Yuppies to discard their soda bottles. Anything, even a can will do. So what if it's sandy, capless, chipped? I'll clean it off, fix it up, and redeem *him.*

Most of her married friends treated her with a kind of benevolent superciliousness. *Poor thing* silently beaming from behind their frozen married eyes. No matter how often their husbands were unfaithful or how horribly they were demeaned in their marriages, no one left anymore. "Anything is better than being out there alone" seemed to be the postfeminist motto of the Nineties. Anything? Willa smiled. For instance, a boiled head?

Maybe it was her worst hidden fear. That something like that could happen to her. She would be swept away by another Leo, but someone so much worse than Leo that she would end up emptied of herself. Was she so afraid that she could no longer risk loving anyone? She took a bite of her corn muffin. Don't tell me I'm going to turn out to be one of those women who spend their best years alone, in therapy and intellectualizing, when all they really need is a good fuck. The thought made her laugh out loud, causing the well-dressed older lady beside her to turn slightly away.

One minute it had been sexy, swinging, and admirable to be single, and the next, everyone had crawled off into whatever relationship they could resurrect, salvage, or leap on.

She and Lindy were different from the middle-aged women she knew who had never married or had children; there was something lost in those women who had lived their entire lives without a frame of commitment to anchor them to anything.

Some of them were anchored to jobs or careers, and that steadied them. The others tended to be wanderers, the kind of women who seemed more like girls, not just because they often looked younger but because they lived without any responsibility to a person, a child, or a community that cements the process of growing up.

These were glamour-job women who often turned up in exotic lands. They moved around. Looking for something or running from themselves. It was hard to tell. But they were not like her.

She and Lindy lived more like married women. The only thing missing was a man. This heretofore unexamined absence was beginning to make her uncomfortable. Empty Nest again? Probably.

She looked at her watch. Ten-thirty. Her stomach tightened. She was more nervous than she wanted to admit. She scanned the paper, too preoccupied to concentrate, and let the voices of her fellow counter-dwellers pass over her.

"So I said to the waitress, one of those trendy, snotty types, I said, 'Don't you have anything without arugula in it?' And she says, 'No. Everyone who eats here is pretentious and anal retentive and they all want arugula!' "

"My aunt is coming to stay with me for a week, and she's gone blind. I'm not up for this."

"Well, at least you don't have to worry about cleaning your apartment."

"My son took me to see Tony Randall in *M. Butterfly*. Lousy! I called it *Felix Goes to China*. Shoulda had Jack Klugman playing the Chinese fruitcake."

"Wouldn't you consider machine-gunning six Jesuit priests to death and ripping their brains out of their heads a human-rights abuse?"

"You owe me four sixty-three. Your part of the tip comes to exactly thirty-two cents."

"So she made him get circumcised. Now she wants six thousand bucks for a nose job. All the coke she did collapsed her nose. So I told him, 'Take the skin from your dick and stick it in her fuckin' nose.' "

Willa sipped her coffee, enjoying herself. She loved this theater of the absurd that was called daily life in New York City. Tucked into her cozy counter seat away from the downside of the motley streets; this is what she had come East for in the first place. It was so unlike her childhood. As different from Beverly Hills, California, as the other side of the moon. She loved the way people flung themselves into life each day. Out there, as it were, with no time for bullshit. No time to tidy up the psyche for its daily bludgeoning.

Not like her life: at Carter there was all kinds of time to dust the internal picture frames and make sure the psychic antimacassars were starched and draped just so. She finished her coffee and picked up the check. She realized that she had never been in a New York City hospital and had no idea how it might be different from the pastel, palm tree–guarded, art-filled hallways of California-style medicine, her only basis for comparison. She stood up, passing by two nurses with tired faces waiting for her seat. "People should be like supermarket turkeys—when they're ready, a plastic button shoots out and says *done.* It would save us all a lot of time and money."

Willa's stomach tightened. No, this would not be like a California "wellness" experience. She only hoped that whatever lay ahead for Lindy and Tess didn't include a plastic pop-out wand.

What was it that her grandmother had always said about having her name in the paper? When you're born, get married, and die? Willa was standing at the main elevator bank, waiting along with nurses coming from breaks with apples and carton coffee in their hands; relatives with flowers and boxes of store chocolates; doctors with little black bags and somber, blank faces; and patients in wheelchairs, trying to gather their dignity around them, a veil of primitive protection against the curiosity and pity in the eyes of people like herself, the temporarily more fortunate. The visitors rather than the visitees. Was that a word? Willa thought about her powdery Presbyterian grandmother's prim, smug little motto. The same was true of hospitals. Willa stepped into the elevator and was pushed back against the wall by a surge of impatient patients and practitioners. Definitely. The only time you should be in a hospital is when you're born, give birth, and die.

She tried to take a deep breath, but the air was dense with humidity and foreign smells. Perfume and surgical soap and wilting carnations and cigarettes, and always, the perennial sick smell, the slight underodor of urine and rot that permeates all clinics, hospitals, and nursing homes. The common smell of sickness, waste, humiliation, and torpor. Nothing ever got rid of it. No amount of cleaning, deodorizing, or scrubbing quite harnessed it. And no one who had ever smelled it could ever forget.

It remained in the head, behind all the merry, frothy, pleasant smells of life, waiting in the air shafts and hard-to-reach corners of the senses, a reminder that someday, somewhere, it would waft toward them again, taking the joy of fresh air and deep breaths with it. Fouling the invisible shields of good luck and good health that propel all us bold-faced bombardiers forth into each new day.

Willa got out on the children's floor not knowing what to expect. She followed a cocky-looking little man in a white coat with a stethoscope around his neck, who seemed to be heading somewhere central. The man had a narrow face with lots of bad teeth all pushed toward the front as if someone had stepped on the sides of his head. He looks like a cockatoo and he's mean to his wife, Willa thought, having no idea why.

The doctor stopped at a glass-walled room filled with children. Willa stopped behind him. A clown was marching around the room, honking his nose and handing treats and candy to the kids. It took Willa a moment to absorb what she was seeing, to understand how this was different from any other magic show she had seen. Laughing faces, balloons, a fat-bellied funny man in purple polka dots.

It was the children. Some were lying on gurneys; some sat in wheelchairs, tubes and monitors hanging over them; some leaned on crutches. A wispy-haired boy with one leg gone clapped his small, thin hands with gusto. A curly-haired, freckled little girl wearing a Mets cap sat in a wheelchair, her legs and back shackled with metal braces, giggling with joy.

Two Down syndrome children jumped up and down, mucus running from their noses and mixing with pink frosting on their lips, while a nurse tried to wipe them clean. Round and round went the clown, pulling pennies out of ears, a stuffed rabbit out of his bowler hat; spreading hope and a moment of majesty at the Mad Hatter's tea party. A fun-house room of phantom reflections, optical illusions, distorted lenses like a cheap prescription, a glass house of nature's tricks. Willa blinked hard trying to clear her vision, day-blind, goggle-eyed by the sight before her.

The doctor was talking to her, asking her something. "I'm sorry?" she said, her voice seeming to come from far away.

"Can I help you? Are you looking for someone at the party?"

Tears filled her eyes and she brushed them back, not wanting him to see. "I don't know. I mean, I'm not sure. I've never been

here before. I'm looking for my friend, Mrs. Lampi. Her daughter
Tess is a patient."

He nodded his head, his lips barely closing over his mouth.
There was something insidious and smug about him. Willa tried
not to judge people so harshly or so quickly, but she instantly
despised this birdman.

"Yes. Yes. She's right down the hall. Room six. I think she may
still be down in chemo though." He grinned, transforming his
cheated face into a beak. "I'm sure Tess will be happy to have such
a lovely visitor. My name is Dr. Fava, like the bean. Heh-heh. If I
can be of any help." He winked, slipping his card into her pocket.

Willa was stunned. The first man to flirt with her in so long, she
could hardly even remember and this was it. A hook-billed asshole, who would put his scaly claws on poor sick children. How
dare he tell me about the chemo; trying to ingratiate himself. He
doesn't even know who I am. Finding this human dart board to
aim her panic at helped Willa prepare herself. She had an opening
now. A meeting place with Lindy. A common enemy in this verte-
brate, this sexualized clay pigeon who had taken liberties with her,
right in front of the glass cage that held the wounded chicks.

Willa stormed past the perpetrator of her outrage, marching
purposefully down the hall and flinging herself into Room 6.

Lindy sat curled in her day chair, staring at the television, passing the tense, officious time called "waiting for your child to return" that hospital motherhood required. Only this time was different. This time she knew what she was waiting for. She knew
how sick Tess would be; the spasms of violent nausea, the chills,
the night sweats, the clumps of thick, shiny hair in the brush. This
time it lacked, or rather, *she* lacked, the passionate, restless hopefulness. This time it was more like a last-ambush attempt, knowing the enemy troops were already massing at the border.

There had only been three moments since that day six months
ago, when life as they knew it had ended for Tess and Lindy
forever, that she had felt herself giving way. From the morning
that the "flu" turned out not to be; when the drawbridge that
linked them to ordinary concerns and daily life had been lifted
behind them, and complaining about the prices at the corner Korean market and going to the movies and talking on the phone and

ordering in Chinese and bitching about her job and all the rest of
the spicy stew of their orderly one-big-person-and-one-smaller-
person universe. There had only been three flashes when Lindy
had felt she would not be able to cope with this.

The first was when the Nurse Who Should Be Shot had called
her at work and quite matter-of-factly announced to Lindy, who
was in the process of finding an Armani pantsuit in just the perfect
shade of beige for one of her very best Texas socialites; "Mrs.
Lampi, the doctor wants to see you right away. He said he'll meet
you at Beth Sinai, not the office."

"Beth Sinai? For a flu report?"

"Oh, honey, her white cells are just crazy. I'd say leukemia. But
you'll have to wait for him. Better hurry. He's got a real tight
schedule."

She had put down the phone, handed the suit to her assistant,
said something polite and acceptable to the Texan, picked up her
purse, walked down the stairs and out the front door of Bergdorf's, hailed a cab, and as the words "Beth Sinai, please" left her
mouth, a feeling of total cosmic horror had gripped her, sliding
into every blood-filled crevice of her being. I will not be able to
stand this, God. If what that witch said turns out to be true, I am
putting you on alert. I cannot take this.

That had been her nightmare. That these feelings would swamp
her and she would be useless, helpless to do what she must do for
the only person on earth that she had ever completely, uncondi-
tionally, and unselfishly loved.

The second time was the morning Dr. Davis told them the remission hadn't held. The third had been this morning when they
wheeled Tess away. The last straw waving before them like a
farmer's late harvest.

She held on by watching TV and waiting for Willa. What would
she be doing now if she hadn't called Willa? Being that vulnerable
to someone she hadn't seen in ten years, made her cringe with self-
loathing. Really pretty pathetic in terms of a support group, dear
girl. But maybe, in the end, all any of us really has is one ear that
will not go deaf. One face that really turns our way.

Lindy pondered while Kitty Dukakis plugged her autobio on
some talk show. One of the blond shows, where all the hostesses
ran together in her mind. They all had the same nose job, face lift,

hair style, and jeweler. They all seemed to be the same woman. Some sort of mythic, intruding Jewish mother prying into the seamy side of famous narcissists' lives. In fact, Lindy thought, the whole interview format was giving narcissism a bad name.

Kitty, a little overbalanced by the lithium she had just admitted taking, seemed to be believable.

"In your book, Kitty, you describe your husband Michael, the Democratic presidential candidate at the time, coming up to your room on several occasions, when you were due at some major event, and finding you passed out on your bed in a pool of vomit, an empty vodka bottle beside you. That must have been very difficult?"

"Oh, no. That's how we got off. A bed full of vomit is a great turn-on, you Barbie-brain." Lindy loved this. It was a great outlet.

Kitty droned on, mouthing current recovery propaganda as if she were reading it off cue cards.

"Was there ever a time during all of this when you or Michael felt that separating might be a solution to this painful problem?"

Kitty snapped to. "No. Oh, no. Never. Not for a second."

Lindy smiled. "Kitty! Kitty, you dog! You lying dog! How about every fifteen minutes, you thought about it? How about every ten for him?"

"Kitty, I know how difficult this is, but your courage . . ."

"Courage! How about hundreds of thousands of dollars in royalties and speaking fees? He's history. It's *your* turn to shine. Courage! You've been sober for thirteen seconds!"

"It would help others who are struggling with this sickness to know . . . in your darkest hour what substances did you ingest?"

"Here it comes." Lindy clicked up the dial. "Here she goes. This is what we've all tuned in to hear, Kittala."

Kitty sat up straight, paying the piper. "I ingested mouthwash, nail-polish remover, rubbing alcohol . . ."

Willa raced through the doorway as if being chased by wolves.

"Lindy! I just had the most horrid conversation with this Dr. Bean. I mean Fava. The one who looks like a bird? He . . . I hope he's not Tess's doctor, he—"

"Shhhh. Come here. You've got to see this. Kitty Dukakis is reciting her industrial-cocktail list. Nail-polish remover! Willa.

She drank *Cutex*! No one in their right mind would get all dressed up in pearls and red silk, have their hair done, put on eye makeup, and go on national television and admit drinking nail polish remover! There is not enough money in the world for that! God. I feel like such a . . . a strong, normal person! All of this shit and I never once, even once, even with my sordid chemical past, came anywhere near the Listermint!"

They both stopped. Two dervishes, whirling back into each other's life without missing a step. Kitty whined on about the future and they stood smack in the middle of the present, Snow White and the Wicked Witch with new parts to play.

"Jesus," Lindy said, her voice wavering. "You're starting to look like your mother."

Willa laughed. "You too."

They moved into each other's arms and held on, swaying until they were dancing together, dancing to the music coming from the TV commercial, the way they had danced through their childhood, playing the boy-part back and forth. Leading and following into adulthood. They had always danced together. It had given them a way to be close, to garner comfort and mothering, to investigate smell and sensuality and romance without risk. More than anything it had made them feel safe. So they danced, *American Bandstand* babies stepping without words around the green linoleum-covered floor of an empty hospital room.

Later they sat side by side in the corner by Tess's empty bed, trying to catch up on ten years of living, linking themselves together for what might turn out to be a journey to nowhere.

"I don't know why New York seemed like a good idea. I'd had a terrific year here when I was modeling, and I wanted to get as far away from home as possible. Also, I guess, maybe because my parents came from here. I know that sounds ridiculous—my father was dead and my mother wouldn't speak to me, but I felt like my roots were here. And my mother was in Florida, so I guess I felt more connected somehow."

Willa's eyes widened. "Your mother is in Florida? I thought she was dead!"

Lindy laughed. "Yes. Well, that was the scenario of innuendo. I didn't want her to just pop back into Tess's life after the way she behaved when I left Gerrold. She cut me off completely. Disinherited me. Wouldn't take my calls. I never actually said she was dead, did I?"

Willa frowned. "Gee. No. I guess not. Something about a stroke and a coma. Then I guess we stopped communicating, and I just assumed she must be."

"Good. I wasn't as bad as I feared. I had to tell Tess last night.

"Where was I? Oh, New York. Well, off we went. I had a little money from my father—actually I had a lot of money, but Leo went through most of it on one get-rich-quick scheme or another, so by the time I got here I had enough to buy an apartment and get Tess into private school. But I was already in my thirties and this was a little before 'mature models' were In. I was too thin for the Forgotten Woman and too fat for Saks. It was pretty grim." Lindy looked at Willa, trying to decide how much openness to risk. "If I tell you something, do you swear you will never, ever tell anyone, even under torture?"

Willa grinned. "Lindy! You know me. The Sphinx. I don't know about torture. I mean, if the Marathon Man was drilling away and he said, 'Tell me what Lucinda Segal told you or I'll drill all the way down to your ovaries,' hard to say. Otherwise your secret is safe."

"I turned tricks. I worked for a fancy call-girl service for six months."

Willa tried to keep her face impassive. "The truth?"

"Would I make that up? I've never told anyone that. I couldn't get a job and I was desperate. Don't be shocked, it wasn't so horrible. I mean this was a very Mayflower Madam kind of scene. Actually a lot of the men were more attractive and nicer than most of the ones I slept with for *free*. Don't think *that* wasn't depressing."

"I'm sorry, honey."

"Why? I just said it wasn't so bad."

"Lindy, I'm sorry that I wasn't there to help you. It must have been really lonely and scary."

"Not any worse than North Beverly Drive in the Fifties. Anyway I finally landed a job as a showroom manager. Now I'm running the personal shopping service at Bergdorf's. Now there's an ironic twist: I'm waiting on all of the women that my mother wanted me to become. Old models and divorcées never die, by the way—they're all selling designer sportswear at Bergdorf's.

"I figure if I can hang on until Tess finishes college, that's a wrap. Then I'm off to the old hookers' home." Lindy put her head down. "God, Willa. College." Sobs shook her body. Willa sat beside her, not knowing how to comfort her. Not wanting to mouth words, facile pep patter that only made everything worse. She put her hand on Lindy's back, patting softly, silently, letting Lindy lead.

She stopped crying and sat up. Her mascara was running in rivers, giving her face a warrior look. "Cripes. I need Kleenex." She jumped up and found her purse, poured water from the plastic pitcher by the still-vacant bed, and wiped her cheeks. She looked tired and older than she was. Her face was hard and soft at the same time, Willa thought, the way it had been before she was beautiful.

Lindy sat down, pulling a pad and pen from her purse. "Wills, let's talk about this now before Tess comes back. Will you go with me to Florida to get my mother?"

Willa sighed. "Wait. Just slow down a minute. First. Why don't *I* go to Florida and get your mother? I know you don't want to leave Tess until it's absolutely necessary, and it's cheaper. Let's talk about *money*. I have a little saved for the summer and for Maxie's education. It's all I have between here and the homeless shelter. What we're talking about, or not talking about yet, could cost a fortune. He could be anywhere on earth! We need expenses, plane fares, maybe a private detective. How do we do this?"

"Well, I know we're a little moldy, but maybe my old madam."

"Lindy, seriously." They both laughed.

"Sorry. It was too good to pass up. Okay. I have some ideas. First, I'm setting up with the hospital to do another TV news plea. If Leo hears it and calls me, our worries are over. I've also placed ads in *USA Today, The International Herald,* those "Please call your ex-wife" kind of messages. I don't say why. If he thinks money's involved, he might ring up. If all this fails, then there's my mother. She's loaded and we're talking about the life of her only grandchild. I'm hoping she'll have mellowed enough to help us. If not, I'll try to refinance my apartment, but that can take months. Everything else I have, or had, has gone to cover what my medical insurance doesn't."

Willa felt like crying. "I could ask the Mitchells. They've always been like second parents to me. My mother still lives there, for chrissake. They were always crazy about you and they don't have any heirs, unless you count cocker spaniels. I can't imagine that they wouldn't help. The only thing I own is my house and it isn't worth much. I don't have any collateral."

"Tess is our collateral! Let's not get too reasonable about this. We are not applying for a home improvement loan or a Dunkin' Donuts franchise. Even my *mother* wouldn't ask for collateral. At least I don't think she would. If she does, I'll go down there and pull her silver-white fingernails out of her cuticles." Lindy smiled. "We've come full circle. We're back to nail-polish removal."

"Okay, then it's settled. You call your mother and prepare her. I'll go down and escort her back here. After the chemo can Tess go home, or does she have to stay here?"

Lindy rubbed her eyes. "Home. I am not going to leave her here without me. I'm trying to get her two favorite nurses to work private shifts for us for a while. My insurance will cover it if we're at home. I'm taking her out of here before we leave. The doctor said he thought it would be fine."

"Good. That makes it easier on your mother too. I have another idea. Maxie. I can try to reach him in Alaska before they ship out and have him come back. He could be a match."

Lindy looked at her solemnly. "Wills. You are really something. Naw, let the kid have his summer. I don't think it'll get to that. But thanks."

"Lindy, it's not your style to be coy. He's her half brother. Without Leo, Maxie's the best shot. He'll be in Sitka tomorrow. I'm going to try to reach him. I think this may be more character building than fishing with Eskimos anyway."

Lindy took her hand. It was not easy for her to accept what Willa offered. It never had been. "I don't know how I'm ever going to make this up to you."

"It's not a loan, Lindy. It's friendship. Besides, I can't *make* Maxie do it. It's still his choice. He's eighteen years old! So save it. He may say no."

"If he's a match, the procedure is really painful."

"I'll tell him."

"What I remember about Maxie—he got very Sarah Bernhardt over a paper cut."

"That's Maxie. Not Mr. Stoic. But I've got to tell him the truth."

Lindy smiled. "All those lying lessons I gave you and Wheezie, what a waste!"

When they brought Tess back, she was asleep. The orderlies lifted her with the kind of prudence associated with the transporting of nuclear warheads. She sighed when they lowered her onto the bed, turning her wan white face, stripped now of all its rosy healthiness. She was smiling in her sleep.

Willa stood awestruck at the sight of this female version of her son. It was almost uncanny. The resemblance was so close that the love she felt for Maxie moved over to include this girl child, as immediate a bonding as the moment an infant enters a mother's arms. She felt love. There was no way back from this place now. Now it was not just for Lindy. Now it was for Tess, who had lived only in a mist of memory, with so many other floating shapes from the past. Now she was real. A half sister for her son, a half daughter for herself. Not since the moment when she admitted that leaving Leo was no longer an abstract possibility but a vital necessity, had Willa felt anything like the sense of direction and purpose that she felt now, standing over the fallen angel who wore her son's fine features.

They watched her, palace guards of the sleeping princess, breathing when she breathed, not daring to move, to disturb her peace.

A door opened behind them, and a bustling presence broke into their reverie. They turned to confront the intruder. A tiny hatchet-faced woman with an ill-fitting black wig plopped on her head, like a Sunday chapeau, clattered toward them, a tray of medical paraphernalia in her hands and a stethoscope around her wrinkled neck.

Lindy glared at her. "Can't you let her sleep?"

"Sorry, girls. Gotta check her. She had the five-course blue-plate special down there. Don't want to take any chances with the customer."

Willa and Lindy exchanged glances. Willa could sense Lindy's tongue fighting to stay quiet inside her mouth. "I'm her mother."

The little woman banged the side of the bed down and reached for Tess's wrist. "Hi, *her mother.* I'm her gramma Alice. That's what all the kids call me. Don't you worry about nothin, Mother. I'm gonna stay with her now till morning. Why don't you ladies go have some fun or somethin'? Nothin' you can do till tomorrow, not with me here. 'Cause I won't let you. Tess and I are buddies. I was with her through the whole meal. She's a real trouper, this kid. Brave as a Seminole. I'm quarter Injun myself, so I know whereof I speak."

Willa could almost see Lindy's tongue forking. "Well, good for you, Pocahontas, but I don't leave my child alone here. I am perfectly capable of taking care of her. Tess and I have been through this before."

Alice let go of Tess's wrist and turned to face Lindy, her black eyes sparking. She smiled, revealing a poorly fitted set of false teeth, and sized up her opponent. "Okay. Here's the deal. See this wig? That's 'cause of *my* cancer. See how skinny I am? Only got a quarter of a stomach left. But I'm still a chemo nurse. I work double shifts 'cause I don't like to leave my kids. I know what they're goin' through and they know I know. And forgive me, *Mother*, but she's gonna get a lot more of what she needs to feel safe right now from me than from you. Ma or no ma. You know I'm tellin' the truth. So you two give yourselves a break and beat it. You're not gonna get another offer like this from somebody as good as me." Alice stood her ground, her tiny feet spread. "Pocahontas. I like that."

Willa leaned over and whispered in Lindy's ear. "She's right. We could really use some time to plan everything, call your mother. This is really a blessing. I think she's okay. We can call every hour."

Lindy stiffened, struggling with her ego. The magical-thinking demons made her believe that it was her physical presence that was keeping Tess alive. What a crock, she thought. I've always felt that I was beaming protection into Tess and the Lewd Comedian just jumped up on the stage and grabbed the mike right out of my heroic little hands. She touched Tess's arm, fighting the tears. "Will you tell her I went home because you made me?"

Alice gave her a surprisingly hard slap on the back. "Believe me, she ain't gonna notice. But I'll tell her. Go. Have a nice bottle of *vino*, toss a couple for me too! Live a little. Too much hospital ruins the point of view. Well people have to be with well people. Sick with sick. The other combos lead to no good. Believe me, I speak from experience. Never know when it's gonna be your turn. So go, have a few laughs. It'll make her happy. She wants you to. She's worried 'bout you, she told me."

Lindy's shoulders relaxed. She picked up her purse, pulled out a card, and handed it to her tiny surrogate. "I'll be here if she—if you need me."

Willa took her arm and led her out of the room and into the corridor. Lindy swayed against Willa, dizzy from the act of walking away—even for a night—from everything she had on earth that mattered to her.

"Come on," Willa said, trying to lighten the mood. "I've got my car. We'll curl up like old times—talk, watch movies, and eat compulsively."

"That's what I do every night." Lindy braced herself and walked out through the revolving doors, spinning herself for the first time in weeks back into that other life.

They sat across from each other curled up in their terry-cloth robes, a bowl of potato chips and an open bottle of California chardonnay on the table between them. They were waiting for Vilma Linowitz Segal to return Lindy's call. They were exhausted but too anxious and excited by each other's presence and the reasons for it to even consider trying to sleep.

"I always thought that you had secrets. That whatever you told me, there were also lots of really shocking things going on in your life that you never shared. It used to drive me crazy." Willa sipped her wine.

Lindy laughed. "That, my dear, was the point. If it didn't drive you crazy, where was the fun?"

"I hated that! Well, did you? Or did you just act like that to manipulate me?"

"I guess. I was really fairly fucked up in the olden days." Lindy yawned. "Ten more minutes, I'm calling again. I've got to do a press conference in the morning. I've been working on the damn thing for a week. Those TV slimeballs didn't want to do it unless Tess was on camera with me, like they did with that other girl, Alison Atlas? I got a little testy about it. I am my mother's daughter, after all. Anyway I guess the missing-husband melodrama is enough, because they backed down, but I don't want to look like Mary Lincoln. I'm hoping for pale, gaunt glamour. Tell the truth, do you see my mother's jowls starting? Should I have my cheeks liposucked?"

"Which cheeks?"

"Willa Snow, what a saucy tongue. I heard some plastic surgeon interviewed on TV once, and he said the one thing women complain about more than anything else is that they're starting to look like their mothers."

"God. How sad. Wouldn't you hate to think of Tess feeling like that someday? Why is it such a horrible thought anyway?"

"Why? Dear girl, you know why. You've met *my* mother. Do you know what she said when Tess was born? She stood there, her arms crossed in that imperious way she has, watching me feed her. 'Babies are just luggage that eats,' she said, and walked out of the room."

Willa laughed in spite of herself. "Did she really? That's hilarious."

Lindy's face darkened. "Not then it wasn't. It was bloody mean. It hurt. It must have been the way she'd felt about me too."

Willa watched her, debating. "Lindy. I brought something with me. Part of a manuscript I started years and years ago about you and your family. I was always afraid to show it to you, but I thought now . . . I don't know, I thought it might be useful. There's a lot about your mother in it."

"Oh, great. I love science fiction." Lindy took a handful of chips and munched aggressively. "You really wrote a book about me?"

"Started to. I totally forgot about it until you called. I think you could use a little current reality about your mother. I mean, she was a little over her head trying to be a parent, but I do think she loved you."

"Well, one can only hope. All I know is that our last conversation was about as relaxed as a Manchester soccer match. I'm really nervous about this."

"Look at me and my mother. I didn't call her for two days once. *Two days!* The first thing she said to me afterward was, 'I was ready to drag the lake.' "

"Now, *that's* funny."

Willa smiled. "I get your point."

"Your mother was always very dependent on you. But she was jealous of you too, Wills."

"Me? Why?"

"Get real. You were fresh and clean and full of talent and hope. Who knew you would lose your mind to Mr. Macho and end up at Cow College trying to be an English spinster. I'm sure she thought you would have the life she was cheated of when your father died."

It hurt, but Willa knew she was right. "Did you ever notice how all genteel Englishwomen seem like spinsters, even the married ones? I am doing that, aren't I?"

"Sure." Lindy shrugged. "I am too, though our styles of camouflage vary remarkably. I'm more Kela the love goddess. With men present, docile and subservient; but alone, jealous and bloodthirsty, violent, and powerful. No tea and crumpets and setting off on a steamer to darkest Africa like you British dingbats, but the result is the same. Did you ever meet that little songwriter Leo was screwing when I met him?"

"Honey? Once. She wasn't so small, was she?"

"Small? Her teeth were bigger than she was."

"She did have very large teeth. I remember. He brought her with him to pick Maxie up right after we separated and I had a fit."

"I had one of those he's-my-man-now scenes with her. I was pregnant and she called and asked me to meet her at her apartment. She was living in the old Sunset Towers in Hollywood. I went up there and she started in on how Leo was just using me for my money. There was a moment when I thought, I could pick this Hee-haw up by her osteoporotic little cunt and hurl her out onto the Sands Hotel sign, which had a huge blow-up of Wayne Newton on it. I could have impaled her on the end of Wayne's twenty-foot cardboard arm. Pure Kela. I decided later that if murder was not on my list of goals, I would be better off not being in love. I really could have killed her, but then what? Leo was a pussy hound from day one. If I kept Kela-ing around, the bodies would be piled up, blocking traffic all over the city. Think of the carbon dioxide. Not environmentally responsible at all."

They were quiet, recovering. The phone rang.

Lindy jumped. "I'm cool. I'm not nervous about talking to my mother for the first time in three years!" She reached for the phone as if it were a live grenade.

Willa sat forward.

"Hello?"

"Miz Lampi? Alice. Our girl's doin' fine. She's sleepin' now. Don't worry 'bout nothin'. Doctor was in and he's real pleased."

"Wonderful. Did she ask where I was?"

"Uh-huh. I told her that I chased you off with my tom-tom. She got a kick out of that. Said if I called you to say she loves you. Okay?"

"By all means. If she wakes up, tell her I love her too."

"Listen, I'm not Dr. Ruth. Tell her yourself in the morning. 'Night."

Lindy hung up, relieved about Tess and the momentary reprieve from her moment of truth with her mother. "Alice of the Beth Sinai Alices. What a trip."

"I like her," Willa said. "I was thinking that if she could do it, she wouldn't be a bad choice to come and stay with Tess."

"The woman's got cancer, no teeth, no hair, no stomach. She and my eighty-four-year-old mother who couldn't boil water with Julia Child standing beside her and who thinks children should only be seen properly dressed and between six and seven P.M. on weeknights? Great. I'm really scared now."

"Lindy, I know it's not ideal, but I have a feeling about that nurse. I think she'd be good. Let's wait for your mother. If she's too frail, I'll call my mother."

"Your mother drinks."

"Not so much anymore."

They looked at each other, and screamed in unison. "*Ahhhhhh-hhhhhh!*" One long release of tension. "God, how pathetic!" Lindy said. "No kindly aunt. No devoted sibling. No loving mum. Where are all those relatives I always see when there's a hostage crisis? All of those devoted, sober, sane, committed fami-lies of adoring relatives who rally together, run around tying yel-

low ribbons on oak trees, writing Congress, never giving up hope!
Why can't we clone one of those guys? Where's Terry Anderson's
sister when you need her!"

Lindy stood up and poured more wine for both of them. She
picked up her glass. A slow, sly smile slipped across her face.
"Getting back to the beginning of our conversation. I *do* know
something I never told you."

Willa put down her glass. "Tell."

Lindy grinned at her. "I fucked Wheezie."

"Stop it!"

"Fucked his little Woody Woodpecker head off."

"You did not! That's like incest. Not Wheezie!"

"I did too. The night before I married Gerrold!"

"You did not!"

"Could I make that up? I'm not the *college* professor. I don't
write."

"Why didn't you tell me?"

"That was back in your morally indignant, professional tight-
twat days, and I thought it would totally horrify you. Besides, I
knew you'd never be able to look poor Wheezie in the face without falling down in hysterics. It seemed better to keep silent."

"You're right. I would not have approved." She could feel the
laughter building from down deep in her stomach. In her mind's
eye stood knobby-kneed, rabbit-eyed six-year-old Wheezie and
voluptuous, voracious, grown-up Lindy. "I'm going to have hysterics."

"No you're not."

"Yes I am. Wheezie!" Willa started giggling, then laughing, then
chortling. It was the funniest thing she had ever heard. She shook
with mirth, wave after wave releasing her.

"I'm peeing in my pants. Right now, I am peeing. Oh, God!
Wheezie!"

Lindy watched her, enjoying the show immensely. "Want a
bedpan? I always keep a spare these days . . . He was good."

"He was not! Don't tell me he was good!"

"Better than Mr. Dental Floss, *and* he was a virgin. That was a
real turn-on. Very Deborah Kerr. It was great. Then he got too
excited and went into an asthma attack, and I had to rush him over
to Cedars and get him a shot of Adrenalin."

Willa was breathing too fast, tears were running down her face, and her pajamas were wet, but she was trying to calm down. "I'm okay now, under control. He really had an asthma attack?"

Lindy wasn't through with her, not just yet. "Um-hm. I asked him to go down on me and—"

"Oh, Lord!" Willa was off again.

"There he was, down between my legs, his little red Brylcreem pompadour just nodding up and down. I think he must have gotten caught in my bush—you know what a Brillo pad I am—and he just inhaled some hair or something. Maybe it was just all too evil. Anyway one minute he's bobbing along like the old red robin, and the next minute he's gasping for air. Can you imagine if I'd killed him the day before my wedding!"

"You made *Wheezie* go down on you? You harlot!" She started all over again. Lindy sat back and sipped her drink, absolutely delighted with herself. She had not done anything so bitchy in years. Playing the Truth game. This stuff was part of the past, from before she had Tess, when she still told lies and was not a good person. Obviously part of her still wasn't.

"I lied."

Willa stopped in midscream. "What!"

Lindy grinned at her. "I never did Wheezie. Got you!" Now it was her turn. "*Haaaaaaaa!* I got you! You were totally lost! Peeing in your sensible cotton jamies, you were. What kind of whore do you think I am, Miss Scarlett! Wheezie was ma best male friend. Like a bro' to me!"

"I will now kill you. I will now break your surgically perfect nose."

The phone rang. They both froze. "So much for mood breaking." Lindy grabbed it.

"Stall. I've got to change my pajamas!" Willa ran into the bathroom.

"I am trying to reach a Lucinda Evelyn Segal. Please tell her that her mother is calling *long distance.*"

"Hello, Mother. It's me."

"You're not in jail, are you?"

"Death row. They strap me in tomorrow at dawn. This is my last call."

"You always had a smart mouth."

"Obviously hereditary. I don't talk to you for three years and that's your first question?"

"I gave that question considerable thought, actually. It was a choice between jail, which had some pith to it, or 'You must need money.' But I knew you wouldn't *dare* call me up after three years and ask for money."

Lindy's chest tightened into a tense, hard knot. The edifice of last resort lay in rubble. "Good choice, Mother. I haven't called because nothing has changed. I have no redemption rabbits in my hat. I've done everything I can to make it up to you for leaving Gerrold. It's all a long time ago. Are you well?"

"I am very well, thank you. I have just undergone a complete medical examination, and the doctors find me to be biologically at least ten years younger than my age. I was, in fact, at Tango Night with my instructor, Mr. Pedro, when you called. How may I help you?"

Willa ran into the room, wearing one of Lindy's nightgowns. Lindy gave her the thumbs-down sign. Rage and a burning sorrow filled her. They had started wrong and there seemed no way back now. Too little, too late would be their epitaph. "How could the doctors calculate? Not even Daddy ever knew how old you really were."

"They were sworn to secrecy. Doctors, I can trust."

The point was made. Daughters, she couldn't. Lindy's hand tightened around the receiver, draining the blood from her knuckles. "Mother. There is a reason for this call, not the one you think. You know I haven't asked you for anything in my entire life.

"My little girl is sick." The tears found her again, loosening the fist in her chest. "She's really sick, Mother. She has leukemia. She needs a bone-marrow transplant, and so far, it seems, the only match that looks really possible is her father. I have to go try to find him and I can't leave her alone. Willa's here. She's going with me to help. I'm calling because you're her only relative. I know it's a lot to ask, but if you're well enough, could you come up and stay with her? I'll have a nurse and everything. You won't have to do anything. Just be with her, so she's not all by herself?"

Silence. She could almost hear her mother thinking. "What if that Larue person can't be found?"

"*Leo.* I can't think about that now. I have to try."

"You know that I have never been any good with children, and I am considerably less good now than ever before. But I'll come. Of course I'll come. She's my granddaughter, though God knows what you've told her about me. She probably thinks I'm dead."

"Mother!" Lindy flushed with guilt. "Thank you. Tess is a wonderful girl. Much nicer than I was. Willa can come down there as soon as you're ready and bring you back here."

"Katharine Willa Snow? I thought she'd been exiled too."

"Mother. I know fact is not one of your fortes, but it was *you* who exiled *me.*"

"That is not the way I remember it. I am perfectly capable of bringing myself to New York. I'll also bring my maid."

Images of horrible Segal housekeepers flashed before Lindy's tired eyes. "That's great, Mother, but you know how I've been with your housekeepers. I don't want anyone mean or cold near my baby. She's too sick to be upset like that."

"The problem was not with my housekeepers, missy. But this girl is a very nice young Jamaican girl, who even you will be able to get along with. Besides, you won't be there and I will be in charge. I also resent the implication that I would be insensitive enough to inflict pain on my only grandchild."

Lindy felt like screaming. It was as bad as she had feared. They were like two punch-drunk pugilists, lashing out with deadened fists, eyes swollen shut, brains numbed by a lifetime of uppercuts and shadowboxing. The pain of her mother's coldness sliced into her. She was back on North Beverly alone in her overdecorated room, so starved for mother love she could feel it physically, a cramping need that doubled her over with hunger.

"Fine, Mother. I really appreciate it. How soon do you think you can get here?"

"Two days."

"That's good. She's having another round of chemo. She'll be in the hospital for at least that. When she comes home, she'll have to go back once a week or so for treatments, but we'll have a nurse by then, so you don't have to worry about it."

"This is very, very upsetting, Lucinda. That such a thing could happen to *my* grandchild."

Lindy fought for control. There was no point in saying anything. Those circular agonies that never opened even a millimeter into a brain like that. She could go at her with a blowtorch or a chisel—not a dent.

"Will you call and let us know when you have your reservation?"

"I'll call you in the morning. Give Katharine my regards."

Lindy lowered the receiver. Her head ached. She must somehow be a really awful person, to have earned this much contempt. She heard the thought whistling through her brain, even after all her analysis, there it was. Bottom line, top of the ninth; *whack*. It was still in there. The little black box of self-loathing. I deserve this. She shuddered.

Willa came over and sat down beside her. "Bad?"

"About as friendly as brunch with Yasser Arafat and Abu Nidal. But she's coming. Forget money though. Not a chance. I'd rob a convenience store first." She burst into racking sobs and Willa held her, feeling the power of her anguish. "God, Wills. She hates me. She really does. There's no one there. No one."

"I'm here, baby," Willa said. Comforting them both with the same truth. They rocked together, curled into the discount leather couch, falling asleep finally in each other's arms.

Six A.M.

"Wills?"

Willa tried to wake up. For a moment she had no idea where she was or who was calling her name. She opened her eyes. Lindy sat beside her, dressed to kill, makeup perfect and a suitcase packed and ready.

"Listen. I'm going to the hospital now to see Tess before the press conference. Can you be there at eight-thirty? It starts at nine, sharp. And after it's over I'm catching a plane to L.A. I thought of where I can get the money, in the middle of the night, *boom*, I got it.

"Remember all that scrumptious jewelry Gerrold gave me? Well, when I left, in one of my rare selfless moments, I gave it back. I just didn't feel right taking it. But he was really nice, I'll give him that. He said that he had bought it for me and it was mine and it always would be mine and he gave me a key to a safe-deposit box. He said if I ever needed it, it would be there.

"Well, I completely blocked that. I don't know where in the hell the key went, but I called him late last night and he said he has it, so I'm going out to see him. I mean, he's a medical person, he knows about the Lewd Comedian. I'm hoping he didn't just drape the stuff all over his second wife. Anyway I'm going to tell Tess and talk to Dr. Davis about Maxie. Will you see about Alice? I think you're right about her. At least she knows what she's doing."

"Do you have enough money?"

Lindy kissed her. "I have enough plastic. See you at the hospital."

Willa lay in the dark, morning light beginning to stream in through the decorator blinds, leaving stripes on the parquet floor of Lindy's condo box. She stretched, the black leather folds of the sofa creaking around her. Her neck hurt from sleeping curled sideways on a sofa, but she thought she had never slept more deeply in her life. She could have lain there forever, she was that tired. Her eyes closed again. One more hour. She could sleep one more hour. How was Lindy doing it? She was exhausted and they hadn't even started yet.

Today would be her first day with Tess. She would need all her energy. She had no map to follow on this road.

Heaviness pulled her down. One more hour and she would be okay. In her sleep she felt something stir inside her. Moving gently from her belly into her womb and down. She was aroused. The deadness was gone. She moaned. How improbable. Here? Now? In the middle of all of this she felt horny? It was such a welcome reunion with this long-traveling part of herself that she didn't want to think it to death. She was just so glad to have it back. It was as if from that other moment, when her phone had rung, a switch buried deep inside her had flipped back on. The pilot relit, the engine sparked, her long winter frost finally beginning to melt. She lay still, not touching herself, allowing the tender pulse of need to cover her. She relished it and was in no hurry to end it. She felt superstitious about what was happening in this quiet morning light on her best friend's couch. It was a sign that wherever she was heading, she was on the right track.

CHAPTER 2

I Love L.A.

LINDY STOOD IN FRONT OF BAGGAGE CLAIM AT LAX, WAIT-ing for Wheezie to pick her up. Willa had wanted to have her mother get her, but the thought of going back to North Beverly Drive and staying with Willa's mother in the Mitchells' guest house was just too depressing. Being back there at all was bad enough.

She squinted into the California sun blasting into her overcast East Coast orbs. How long had it been since she'd been home? Almost ten years. It hardly seemed possible. She had left soon after Leo had walked out. There had no longer been anything there for her. Her father dead, her mother removed to Sarasota swank, Willa in some remote burg. She had taken Tess and moved to New York City and never looked back. Most of the remaining friends she had were in and out of New York on business, and she saw them there. L.A. had receded into the moss of memory. She was no longer anxious to return to its warmth.

The press conference had gone well, or as well as a ghoulish media event could go. Dr. Davis had been serious and eloquent. She had been urgent but, she hoped, not whiny. Leaving Tess was the worst, but leaving her with Willa made it infinitely easier. It was quite amazing how quickly they had connected. She took a deep breath, feeling the toxic air move through her lungs. *I might as well start smoking again, if I'm going to inhale this shit.*

A large silver Mercedes pulled up to the curb. "Lindy!"

She squinted, bending over to see into the car. "Wheez?"

"The one and only. Hop in."

She picked up her suitcase and slid into the plush silver leather seat beside him. "Way to go, Wheezie!" She knew he was an agent at William Morris. But she didn't know he was *an agent* at William Morris. She felt guilty remembering last night. Having fun with Willa at Wheezie's expense. Maybe she really should have seduced him. He was the only nice man she had ever known personally. She wondered why he had never married. Maybe he was gay. Naw. Not Wheezie.

"Looking good, kid." Wheezie had an entirely new Hollywood image. She had seen others like him, nerds beyond belief in high school, now running movie studios and wheeling and power-dealing around town. She had gotten used to it. Sometimes she shot him a reminder, the Mouth having a life of its own, but most of the time she just let him enjoy himself. The new Wheezie was, of course, never called that. He didn't even let his parents or sisters call him that. He was Mark Springer to everyone on earth but her. This was even nicer, considering that she refused to let him call her Lucinda, terms that he grudgingly accepted.

"Wheez. Pretty fancy. You aren't one of those agents that runs a little drug ring on the side, now are you?"

Wheezie grinned, his white-lashed freckled face crinkling impishly on the sides. A Tom Sawyer type, who would never look like a serious grown-up. He was one of those men who become more attractive as they age, and Lindy saw this now for the first time. His physique was well developed, and his face was stronger and less vulnerable.

"I left Morris. I've got my own company now. I'm doing great. Name a hot female singer and she's mine. They love me."

"Sinéad O'Connor."

"Yep."

"No shit. I *am* impressed. Wait till I tell Tess."

Wheezie reached over and took her hand. "How's the kid?"

"Not so good. Did my news bite run out here this morning?"

"Yep. I caught it. You looked terrif. I cried. Really. If he heard it, he'll come running."

"Yeah. Got a cigarette?"

"You haven't smoked since you left town."

"Yeah, well, I'm back. So I'll smoke till I leave again. If I'm going to breathe here, I may as well get some pleasure out of it. The air's going to kill me anyway."

"No kidding. My doctor says that if I don't get out of here, I'm going to have one granddaddy asthma attack that will carry me off to the great pollen park in the sky."

"Wheez! Get serious. You can't stay here. You're talking about your life!"

"Without Hollywood I'm dead anyway. Five more years, I'll be able to retire. Then watch my smoke." The car phone rang. "Mark Springer. Yeah. Right here. Hold please."

Wheezie pushed the Hold button and turned to Lindy. "It's Gerrold's office. I left this number in case of a change in plans."

She took the phone, not knowing what to do with it. She had never actually been in a car with one before. "How does it work?"

Wheezie smiled patronizingly and flicked the switch. "Where do you live, in a cave?"

"Don't start that hip Hollywood stuff. I'm traumatized enough being here . . . Hello? Hello?" It was hard to hear.

"Mrs. Lampi? I'm Dr. Barnes's secretary. He told me to call and ask you to meet him at his house. He said if you get there ahead of him, just ring—his wife is home. Do you have the address?"

"Yes. Thank you. We're on our way." Lindy fumbled with the buttons, thrusting the phone at Wheezie. "Here. Get it away from me. I hate this. I bet people here are crashing into each other all over the place. It's not natural to talk and drive at the same time."

"Easier for some than for others."

"If you say one word about my coordination, Wheezie Springer, I'll squeeze the styling gel right out of your little red brushcut."

"Okay. Okay. I'm out of my verbal league."

Lindy pulled the address card out of her purse. "Bel Air, no less. Stone Canyon Road. Gerrold has risen. God. I can't believe I'm doing this. Do you know the wife?"

"Nope. I've seen her picture in his office. I know she was in the biz. Music end. He tried to get me to handle her one time, but then she dove into motherhood and being a rich matron and I never heard anything about it again. Thank God. He's a great dentist, I'd have hated to lose him over his wife's career potential."

"They have kids?"

"Yeah. Twins, I think. Girls. Big fat ones."

She laughed. "No kidding. Fat?"

"Yep. At least from the picture in his office. Two ten-year-old chubbos."

"What about the second Mrs. Barnes? Porcine?"

"Nope. One of those stringy little blond bottle jobs. The kind who overexercises and lives on Lean Cuisine. At least that's how she looks in her pictures."

Lindy sighed. They were heading down Sunset now, toward Bel Air. At least she wouldn't have to face the hotel yet. Later she would. Wheezie lived in West Hollywood. She'd have to drive past her old neighborhood. Why was it this painful?

Wheezie swung the car onto Stone Canyon and up the hill. She read the directions to him, keeping her head down, filled with dread.

"We're here." He pulled up into a long driveway where a phony French mansard-roofed chateau stood at the end.

She shuddered. "The house that bad teeth built."

"What?" Wheezie turned off the motor.

"Nothing. Something Gerrold said about another house once. Are you coming in?"

"I'd rather have braces again. I'll be down the street at the Bel Air Hotel. Got a meeting scheduled." He reached into his pocket and pulled out a neatly typed sheet of monogrammed stationery. "My secretary put the number of the restaurant and the car phone, just in case you like it there. If I have to leave, I'll be in the car. Just call and I'll come right back and get you."

"Thanks." She opened the heavy, silent door and picked up her bag.

Wheezie watched her. "You sure you're okay? I was only joking—if you want me to go in with you, I will."

"Naw, this is definitely a solo. I'll call you. Keep your eyes crossed."

Wheezie's face crinkled again. It was something he used to say when they were kids. He waved and turned on the ignition of his glistening machine, looking like a six-year-old carrottop with no male friends, gliding by in his father's car.

She watched him go. Then, gathering her courage and slipping into her New York "mess with me and you die" attitude, she crunched up the white gravel circular driveway and pushed the polished brass bell.

All hell broke loose. Fearsome sounds of large, dangerous dogs baying and barking, racing toward the massive golden-maple portals as if dinner, at least, waited on the other side. A detached voice was yelling at her from the top of the bell.

"Who is, please? Who there?"

"Mrs. Lampi, to see Dr. Barnes."

"He no here. *Momento.*"

The dogs were flinging themselves at the door. Even for Tess, Lindy was not sure she could cross that threshold.

"Yes. Who is it?"

"It's Lindy Lampi. I believe I'm expected." Must be Lena Cuisina herself.

"Okay. Just a minute. I've got to get the dogs away and turn off the security system."

Sounds like good thinking to me. She smiled. So it's come to that. Bicoastal barricades. Everyone living in some version of a paranoid prison. The day of the unlocked door and the neighbor dropping in now part of the nostalgic folklore of the past, buried in the family hope chest, right beneath the bustles and spats.

A hand appeared, parting the ivory silk moiré curtains that covered the leaded-glass side panels framing the door. A small, somehow familiar face peeked out.

Just checking to see that I'm not an ax murderess doing an impersonation of Gerrold's former wife, I assume. Lindy fought the strong desire to smash her palm against the glass.

The door opened, revealing a wiry blond woman wearing a fluorescent-orange body suit and running shoes, her hair fashionably messy and tied up in that egg-beater way, with strings and strands falling around her tense, angular cheeks, striving to look casually done but having taken, Lindy knew, considerable time and effort to achieve that "just got up and threw a pin into it" tousled look.

"Hi," she said, in the hollow, California-friendly way that Lindy hated. "I'm Gerrold's wife. Come on in."

Lindy entered, not saying anything. She was trying to figure something out.

The stringy orange woman bounced before her, leading the way. "Come on out to the kitchen, the girls are having a snack."

Lindy watched her. She knew her from somewhere. She was one of those overtan, overtrim, over thirty-five California girls who never seem to exist anywhere else on earth, except possibly select sections of Colorado. It was easy to mix them up, but somehow this one was familiar.

Lindy trailed along, through a hideous assortment of showroom-ornate chambers. Each one represented a different decorating style—flowing from deco den to postmodern dining as if a victim of multiple-personality disorder had been in charge of the design. Overdecorated and underexperienced, contrived to impress then left in darkness, unused and unloved. Rooms like this always made her feel sorry for them, as if they were people. They reminded her of the Segals' living room and of her own childhood. Projecting again, dear girl, she thought, her heels clicking across tile, then hard wood, then thick pile—a flooring cornucopia created by big budgets and bad taste.

The Latin girl from the intercom was spooning some whipped yellowish substance with small bits of red swirling through it into large glass bowls. Two little girls—bloated white chunks of children—sat side by side in the black-and-white marble checkerboard kitchen, looking at the glop with surly distaste.

The Gerrold's wife person turned and smiled at her. "These are our girls, Bethany and Tiffany. This is Mrs. Lampi."

What? No Brittany? No Sodomy? And where's little *Gluttony?* "How do you do" she said, keeping a civil tongue. She did know this twit.

"We're watching our diet. Corazon has been trying some new fat-free desserts for us all."

"It looks like a bird abortion," said Bethany, winning Lindy's heart forever.

She put down her purse and sat beside the twins, a former fatty who understood. "You're right and it probably tastes like one too."

The twins looked up at her as if some magical fairy godmother had just swooped down to save them from the evil queen. "Let me try. There's no diet dessert on the planet that I haven't tried."

They passed a spoon over to her, not daring to look at their mother.

Lindy took a big bite. They stared at her, entranced. "Hmmmm. Yes. Definitely a bird abortion. Probably parakeet. No, wait! Dove. Yes. But not at all a *bad* bird abortion. Needs a little NutraSweet."

The twins giggled gleefully, cupping their mouths with their pudgy pink fingers. Lindy didn't have to look—she knew that Gerrold's wife was not happy. She could feel her behind her steel hi-tech stool trying to regain position.

"The girls have a glandular disorder. We are trying to reset their basal metabolism."

She grinned at them. "Horseradish. They're fat because they've never met a food group they didn't like. Right, girls? Takes one to know one. I was fat and then when I hit my teens, I just lost it. You will too, when you're ready and also because you're very pretty and that will motivate you."

"You were fat?" They looked at her with hope. She nodded and winked at them. Corazon nodded too. Gerrold's wife bounced into the picture. Lindy was staring at the twins. Something was out of sync here. They were all so familiar.

"Bring some coffee into the library, please." The wife had not gotten the reaction she desired from showing off the house and the perfect family, so it was time now to get serious.

"Let's go somewhere private and talk. Gerrold should be home very soon."

Lindy waved at the twins. The Behemoths, she thought. That is what they were like. Two wonderful Behemoths, torturing their mother in the only way they could. She knew and they knew she knew. She felt a searing moment of rage at the fluorescent female in front of her. Watch the mouth, Lindy. If you offend her, she won't let Gerrold help you. Don't be stupid here. The Behemoths had been risky enough, but that she couldn't help.

"Let's sit here." Gerrold's wife plopped down in an oversized paisley-covered armchair. Lindy sat down in its duplicate. The blonde smiled. Corazon swayed in and set a tray before them. Gerrold's wife did not say thank-you. Corazon took her time retreating, hoping for some dialogue.

Lindy waited, using her presence to buy some time. "I know you, don't I?"

The blonde smile spread. A bit Cheshire, Lindy thought, bracing herself.

"We met once, a long, long time ago."

"This may sound like a weird question, but did you used to have bigger teeth?" She swallowed, her heart speeding up.

"Gerrold filed them."

"Honey?"

"That's right. The Sunset Towers. Twelve years ago."

Oh, God. Now she knew. The twins. Leo's eyes. She felt sick. She didn't know what to do. "How? Where did you . . ."

"Let me explain quickly before Gerrold gets here. He doesn't know any of this and if you have any eensy thought of telling him, forget it—or whatever you want, probably money, you can kiss good-bye. I know about your daughter. I saw you on the news and put two and two together."

A potential Nobel laureate, one can see. Lindy sat on her mouth.

"When Leo left you, he came back to me for old times' sake, I guess. Also, he was broke and needed a place to stay. Anyway I thought I'd try your trick and I didn't wear my diaphragm. I got pregnant and he split so fast, he left his clarinet. You know how he was about that clarinet. So I had a brainstorm. I needed a tooth filled and I decided to go see your ex. I knew all about him from Leo, and because I was pretty obsessed with you when Leo left me the first time; I wanted revenge. I still blamed you for everything. Well, these nice Jewish boys, they don't know from Texas white trash. He never had a chance. I did him right in his office, in the chair. The next day I sent him a tape of a song I had written about him: 'I met a guy, Gerrold is his name. Since we met, I've never been the same. Oh, Gerrold, Gerrold, where can you be!'"

Lindy gasped. "That's not yours, that's Paul Anka's, Donna!"

"Sure. But what did poor gullible Gerrold know. He cried, he was so moved. Three weeks later we got married." She smiled, enjoying the moment. "Twins are often early."

Lindy's mind was racing. The twins. Robust young bones. Same father. Two more shots at it. She was beginning to think like a vampire, judging victims in terms of keeping Tess fueled. Honey looked at her, reading her mind.

"No. I know what you're thinking and the answer is no. If you test the girls, Gerrold finds out. It would kill him. He adores them and he's the only father they've ever known, not to mention what it would do to my life. *No!* You can have money, medical help—anything you want. I've already told Gerrold to give you whatever you need; he thinks I'm a saint for it too. The price is, you keep your mouth shut and stay away from my girls."

"If I can't find Leo or if he doesn't match, my daughter is going to die."

"I'm sorry about that. I am. But it's your family or mine. I'm partial to mine. I have everything I ever dreamed of. Things rich girls like you take for granted. The way you took Gerrold for granted. Well, you got what you deserved—Leo! I've got your cast-off and I'm the one sitting in a mansion in Bel Air. No one is going to mess with my life. Am I clear?"

"Like Baccarat." Lindy felt dizzy. She should have thrown her out of that window, no doubt about it. There was a new pain inside her. She felt it deep in her heart. Leo had been with Honey right after he'd left her, probably even the same day. Jealousy. She was jealous. What did that mean? Oh, God, she did not want to know this. She was still in love with the son of a bitch. She stood up, feeling faint. "I promise. Your secret is safe. I need to use the bathroom." She was not going to faint in front of Lucy Lycra.

Honey pointed a matching orange fang at the wall. "Just push." She watched Lindy, enjoying her moment of triumph. "One more thing you might find of interest, before Gerrold comes. It may help you in your search—there's another wife."

Lindy whirled. "What did you say?"

"I said, there's a third wife. She's a singer. Bee Bee Day. A friend of mine ran into them about five years ago."

"Do you know where she lives?"

"Nope. Don't know if he's still with her either. Could be Vegas. Not here though. She shouldn't be that hard to trace—she still works. The guild must have a record."

Lindy made it to the wall, and into the john. She sat down on the seat, lowering her head between her legs and trying not to pass out. Okay. It was going to be okay. Honey didn't know about the jewelry, and she now had—if, God forbid, she needed it—something on her. She had to get to a phone and call Willa.

When she emerged, freshly powdered and back in control, Gerrold was waiting for her. He had lost most of the top of his curly black hair and added a layer around his waist, making him look vaguely like an eggplant. "So, you've met my girls," he said, flashing his perfect smile, as the Behemoths and the Blackmailer posed around him.

Poor Gerrold, she thought later, watching him maneuver around his study, handing her the duplicate key to the safety-deposit box, offering support, additional funds, whatever she needed. The guy hasn't got a chance. One of these days the Texas Two-step was going to deal him one from the back of the deck, or should I say, another one. She felt sorry for him and the Behemoths. Innocent victims of Honey's hunger.

"Gerrold. I want to say something." They were standing in his driveway, waiting for Wheezie. "I'm sorry. I behaved like a real jerk and I hurt you. I'm glad you're happy now."

He reached into his shirt pocket, smiling at her with such twinkly sincerity that, for a moment, she thought he was going to present her with a dental gift. A new toothbrush or a tiny plastic bottle of mouthwash.

"Thanks, Lindy. I guess everything works out for the best. Oh, I almost forgot. Here's where to go to sell the jewelry. I had it reappraised for insurance last year. I think you'll be surprised by what it's worth. One thing: Promise me you won't tell Honey about it. Money she doesn't mind my giving you, but if she ever found out there were jewels sitting around that I had withheld, I'd be in the dog house."

More like the lion's den, Lindy thought. She leaned over and kissed his cheek. "My lips are sealed." She paused, fighting the urge to march back in and drag the Behemoths home with her. "I like your kids, Gerrold. Maybe sometime they could come and visit us. I think I might be able to help them with the weight thing."

His eyes, she thought, darkened slightly. Could he suspect something?

"Well. That would be up to Honey. Let's get Tess well first.

Better get right over to the bank, the manager's staying open for you."

Wheezie's car appeared at the bottom of the driveway. "Bye, Gerrold, I'll let you know what's happening." Lindy waved and ran off down the path toward freedom. She was so full of new information, she felt like an overinflated helium balloon in desperate need of a pin. She flung open the door, threw her bag in first and herself in after it. "City Center National Bank, Camden Drive, and step on it."

Wheezie took off, excited by her urgency. "We are talking major daytime drama!" Lindy exhaled. "Can I call New York on this egg beater?"

"Yep. Give me the number." Lindy handed him the card.

"I've got to get Willa at the hospital, now! Everything you are about to hear is never to leave your food hole. Promise me on Sinéad's life."

Wheezie raised one small, freckled hand. "I promise."

She could hardly sit there while Wheezie put the call together. Her head was going too fast. What if it was that simple? He was with bride number three, somewhere nearby. She knew Leo's macho. He would be shamed into coming with her. What woman would stand for her man not running to the aid of his stricken child? Unless, of course, the woman knew nothing of any children. Her heart sank.

"She's on."

"Wills?" There was static on the line. It was like talking from a midtown street corner.

"Lindy, I got Maxie! He was just leaving the hostel to ship out. He'll be here tomorrow. I think he was relieved, actually. I didn't go into great detail, but you know how teenagers are. If they put up anything less than a tantrum, they don't really mind. He's very excited about meeting Tess. Also, Alice said okay. Apparently she's got a ton of vacation time coming, and frankly, I think paring down to one kid will be a rest for her. So we're doing fine at this end. Tess is still pretty weak, but her spirits are great."

"Well, I can keep my ball in play. Guess who Gerrold is married to? The one with the teeth that Leo knew."

"Honey?"

"Guess what else. She has twins by Leo. Two ten-year-olds that

Gerrold thinks are his. They've got Leo's face, only they're chunky. She told me if I told, she'd stop him from helping us."

"But they could be a match."

"We danced to that one. No way. But I've got the key, and we're on our way now. I'm telling you, the guy should be rounded up and castrated. There is probably a trail of little Lampis all across the land. We should have a reunion—the discarded wives and seedlings of Lurid Leo annual potluck supper."

"Twins?" Wheezie was so engrossed, he missed the light at Roxbury and Sunset and came within inches of running up onto the curb.

"Calm down, everyone! We're in a car here. Willa. I'm on the car phone, if you please, and Wheezie almost killed us with that last bit of information. There's more: Leo has a third wife. A singer called Bee Bee Day."

Wheezie hit the brake, Lindy pitched forward. "I said, calm!"

"I know Bee Bee Day! She's in Miami."

"Willa? Did you hear that? Wheezie knows her. She's in Miami! I've got to get the jewelry now. Gerrold's set it up for me to sell it in the morning. If all goes as planned, I'll take a red-eye back tomorrow night."

"Wait a minute! That name is so familiar. Let me look at the messages. Lots of calls came in after the television spot ran. Yes! Lindy, there was a message from someone named Bee Bee Day. Just says it's about Leo, and there's a phone number. I'll take care of it. Call me later."

"Roger. Over and out, or whatever they call it." She handed the phone to Wheezie, no longer interested in its magic. "Tell me about her?" She could feel the other feeling, the jealous, flaming agony of unfinished love, tracking her.

Wheezie pulled into the bank parking lot. "She's unique. Very talented. She writes a lot of her own stuff and it's not highly commercial. Sort of feminist cabaret style, the kind that, if you're lucky, gets you a semipermanent gig at the Algonquin or the Carlyle and eventually a concert on Broadway. If you're not so lucky, it gets you what Bee Bee has. A niche in a smaller town. She's very popular there. She even has her own *Music World* show. She interviews visiting entertainers. Jesus. She's married to Leo? How could I have missed that one?"

Lindy swallowed. "Does she look like me or Willa?"

"Ha! Neither. She's very, very tall. A really big girl, kind of coppery short hair. Showgirl type. And young. About thirty-two or -three."

"Well, thanks. That picked me up considerably." Lindy reached into her purse and took out the key and the piece of paper Gerrold had given her. She was trying not to feel competitive. She was a more mature and less superficial person than this. Sure she was.

Wheezie turned off the motor and looked at her the way men look at women they think they know, when they realize that there is no way to know any woman. "Did I say something wrong?"

"No. Just a little rough on the ego. The jerk left me, remember? I'd have preferred Grandma Moses."

"How 'bout no tits. She had a preteen chest. Flat as a flapjack."

"Better. Not great but better." Lindy opened the paper and read. "Oh, my God! Wheezie. The appraisal was one hundred fifteen thousand dollars! We're rich. He can run now but he can't hide. I can hire Remington Steele. Columbo. Kojak! Let's go!"

Wheezie ran around and opened her door and they were off, racing toward the Emerald City, a city of dreams and rainbows and silver linings, even if the backs were all cardboard and the dreams rarely came true.

Lindy sat hunched down in the seat beside Wheezie, her purse, now holding her precious sack of jewels, clutched against her chest. She had never had anything more than a couple of hundred dollars in cash in her purse in her entire life; the thought of six figures' worth of gems in her handbag was more than unnerving.

"Wheez, I'm feeling pretty strange about this. What if I get mugged? I can't take any chances with this. This is Tess's hope I've got in here."

Wheezie was heading toward Beverly Hills High School. "Relax, this isn't New York City. No one gets mugged here."

"Sure. They just pull up beside your car and blow a hole in your head. That wouldn't do me much good either. Maybe I should just go sit in the police station until tomorrow morning."

"They're safer with us than anywhere else."

Lindy was not reassured. She looked up and saw where they were. "What are you doing? You're heading toward the school!

You're not planning some kind of weird nostalgia trip, are you? Turn this heap around right this minute. The hotel was bad enough. Stop!"

"Lindy, I wouldn't do that to you. I'm taking you to Jimmy's with me. Just for a little while. My dad's being honored by the Limelighters, he just donated his film library to their charity. I'm an hour late and I've got to show up. Besides, my family wants to see you. I'll have Jimmy put the stuff in his safe."

Lindy sighed. "Wheez, I haven't spoken a word of small talk to anyone since Tess got sick, and this scene I couldn't handle ten years ago. I'll wait in the car."

Wheezie looked hurt. "Fifteen minutes. I don't want to leave you out there alone. I'm sorry. Everything ran so late."

Lindy softened. She could hardly remember existing before Wheezie was part of her life. They had been through childhood and puberty together. In Lindy's value structure surviving puberty together went a long, long way. He had been there when she had married Gerrold *and* Leo and the night Tess was born; and after she had turned away from Willa he had been, at times, her family as well as her only real friend. All the so-called business trips to New York that were really to spend "uncle" time with Tess and shore her up. She never went there. He always came to her.

"Okay, but don't expect much. I've never been more nervous in my life. You know what happens when I get nervous. The mouth moves faster than the mind."

Wheezie laughed. "Oh, yes. I remember a Friars' dinner for my dad when I introduced you to Rudy Vallee and you said, 'Oh, how nice to see you, I thought you were dead.' "

"Oh, God. I did, didn't I? Will he be here tonight?"

"No. Now he really is dead. That was the night you started calling my old man's shindigs the dead-movie-star parties."

They pulled in the drive. Every car parked or arriving was a Rolls-Royce or a Mercedes. She pulled her compact out and feverishly patted the shine from her face. "Actually, a dead movie star would look better than I do right now. Come on, let's get this over with."

Wheezie ran around and opened the door for her. "You look beautiful. Give me the stuff. I'll meet you inside."

Lindy shook her head, holding on to her purse as if it contained the secret of life itself. "Nope. I feel better having it within fast-exit reach. Besides, this crowd has enough of their own baubles—no pickpockets in this group. I'll just keep them."

The room was buzzing. Local celebrity reporters ran from group to group, pad and pen in hand; small, middle-aged men in cheap suits, cameras wrapped around their dandruff-speckled necks, racing behind them. Hooray for Hollywood, Lindy thought, following Wheezie across the room with the same enthusiasm she saved for mammograms and annual Pap smears.

The famous faded faces that filled the room were not part of the new Hollywood. These were not the hot stars of the Nineties, the Michelle Pfeiffers and Tom Cruises, or even the hip, older guard of Jack Nicholson and his pack. Nor were they part of the power structure, the producers and studio heads who ruled the city and made careers and projects with a single one-syllable word. Yes. No.

The group that Wheezie's parents belonged to, and the one in which both of them had grown up, was part of the past; the history of Hollywood in the days before it was hip. When glamour was in and actors, male as well as female, would no more be seen in public without a perfectly corseted and masked exterior than let an unretouched photo see print.

They were all old now, though some of them still looked wonderful, and they were mostly unwanted by the other Hollywood. They survived in a world of their peers and the columnists and sycophants from their glory days, to whom they were still the stars, part of the good times when they were all young and wanted and worked whenever they chose. They came out on nights like this, bravely elegant, tucked and lifted, jeweled and coiffed, posing for photos with one another, with the effortless glide into angle, degree of smile and profile, and the invisible tightening of abdominals, mastered by the seasoned veterans of center stage.

Cesar Romero and Anne Jeffreys, magically handsome and gleaming with the gift of born beauty and good genes. Buddy Rogers, silent-screen star and protective spouse of Mary Pickford, looking as though he could still leap over a tennis net or samba a bevy of Busby Berkeley babes across a mirrored floor. All the actors wore white suits—setting off the silver in their perfectly groomed hair.

The comedians held court at a table of their own. Morey Amsterdam, Jack Carter, Henny Youngman, Sid Caesar, eyes darting, minds clicking; a sensibility as far away from that of Andrew Dice Clay and Robin Williams as *The Wizard of Oz* is from *Blue Velvet.*

The people who laughed at their jokes were the people from their generation, whose sense of humor had aged with the humorists; the jokes and bitter ironies of one generation lost on the members of the next.

George Burns sat among them, the only one who had crossed all the boundaries, starting over in his seventies when most of them were playing to their friends at benefits or occasional nostalgia nights like this one, or appearing in commercials for arthritis preparations or denture glue. The little man with the cement-mixer voice and the fat cigar had managed to keep the whole population chuckling.

He seemed to represent—even to kids who had never heard of Gracie Allen or known anything about him before he'd played God—a link between times. His presence was reassuring. He tottered out and made fun of himself, old age, loneliness, the loss of sex and youth and love, and even teenagers responded.

He was the world's favorite geezer. He had become an icon, a link that hooked vaudeville to *Saturday Night Live.* He was a show-business god, an adorable living god of Comedy, a god of good humor and compassion. A milk-and-cookies god, who would give a wink and always understand the foibles and fears, the ragged rage and striving to be human without being venal. "It's okay, kid," god George would say, puffing on a Havana and working on his gin game. "Life's like having to follow Coco the Contortionist—you'll sing your heart out, but they'll still be clapping for Coco. Relax, kid. Look at me. Never can tell when you'll get to open the Palace." In a way, he was the best god around.

In this world where time had stopped, Virginia Mayo was still a chick and Zsa Zsa Gabor a sex pot. Parties like this at places like Jimmy's and Chasen's, where Sinatra and Jimmy Stewart were regulars and Maude Chasen still moved gracefully from table to table, greeting her guests as if it were 1950, were a viable reassurance to the aging giants of Movieland, that they were still part of the action, still stars of the bright, busy night.

Wheezie handed Lindy a glass of champagne and guided her through to his parents. "Look who I've got!" he announced, proud to bring them someone from his childhood. It seemed, as time marched on, that to all of their parents, the only people from their children's lives that they remembered or were able to sustain any interest in, were those who held the remnants of the past. The friends from the years of family life, when they all were young and full of hope. Manny and Doris Springer's faces sparkled at the sight of them together.

"Lucinda! How good to see you! How's your mother?"

Lindy snapped instantly back into the manners and form of her girlhood. "She's just fine, Mrs. Springer. She lives in Florida now."

"Good. I hear it's lovely there. Manny made a movie there once, with Loretta Young, I think. She'll be here tonight. Isn't that wonderful! She never goes to these things, but for Manny—"

"It wasn't Loretta Young, it was Jeanne Crain and she *is* here. Hi, darling girl! You're such a stranger, got to come up to the house for brunch. How long's it been since Doris made her white-fish salad for you?"

In fact, Lindy thought, it had probably been *thirty* years, but who was counting? They enfolded her as if she and Wheezie had just ridden their bikes into the driveway and raced in for a Saturday afternoon snack. It was quite unnerving.

Lindy had told Tess on numerous occasions that she wanted it known now, that when she got to the point of showing up in public with inappropriate color combinations, dressing like Baby Jane, or putting her stockings on backward, that it was Tess's duty to put her out of her misery. She would have to add "total loss of timeframe" to her list of when she had stayed too long at the fair.

Doris Springer smiled at her with such a look of longing for the good old days that Lindy, not knowing how to handle this mothering kindness at a time when she so needed it, put her arms around the small, plump mother of her friend and hugged her.

Hugging her also meant that she didn't have to look back into her eyes, which had obviously been victimized by a skin-happy plastic surgeon who had removed so much of poor Doris

Springer's eyelids that she was unable to blink. She stared out of her bright, shiny mask of a face like a death's-head with mascara.

Mr. Springer watched the touching sight and patted Lindy's hand. He was wearing a silky midnight-blue suit with a frilly open shirt, the tip of his bypass scar emerging from under his solid-gold Star of David necklace. He was so tan that the creases around his eyes had white stripes in them. He wore a dyed black toupee, which rose straight up on his head, making him look like an eighty-year-old Jewish raccoon.

"Lindy?" She retracted herself from Doris Springer's embrace and turned. A tall, ash-blond woman, her hair piled high on her head, wearing enormous, blinding sapphire-and-diamond earrings and a matching necklace, was grinning at her with the myopic, overattentive gaze of the very loaded. The woman was wearing a skintight red evening gown of the kind not seen since Rita Hayworth had made them fashionable. Her middle-aged breasts were pushed up into the strapless heavily boned bodice, making the aging flesh pucker in the middle.

Wizened cleavage, Lindy thought, how attractive. She made another mental note for her list. Women over forty who wear strapless low-cut dresses. If I ever turn up in one, cover me quick and take me to the Home.

"Lindy, it's Heather! Heather from Beverly. Heather Hickey. Well, it's Heather Stockton now. I'm married to *Stewart Stockton*. Stockton Films? Why, I haven't seen you since we were extras in that college movie. The one with Fabian? Remember? We had to do the hully gully on the beach and you kept losing your balance and falling into the lights! What a hoot!"

Lindy remembered only too well. Her feet were so flat, she couldn't balance in the soft sand. Miss Diamond Mine had amused herself and all the cute male extras at Lindy's expense. She was one of the golden girls from Beverly. One of the flashy fake friends that Lindy had kept in movie tickets and Mars bars for two desperate, frightening years. Just what she needed tonight. She looked over Heather's shoulder trying to find Wheezie. This was now beyond duty to her pal.

"Of course. Nice to see you, Heather. Are you still acting?"

Heather threw back her head in a forced theatrical way that she must have seen in some old Ava Gardner movie. "Heavens, no!

Just keeping all our households running is more than I can handle. I guess you don't watch much television. My husband *is* television. It's a wonderful, crazy life. I haven't thought of my career in ages."

Since your "career" consisted of three Beach Blanket movies where you bounced your boobies around in a crowd scene for thirteen or so celluloid seconds, I think you made the right choice, dear.

"Well, it's great to see you, Heather. Excuse me, I have to find my friend." Before she could escape the specter from her untamed youth, a small, emaciated older man appeared beside her nemesis. His eyes bugged out of his head, and three hairs, parted somewhere below his ear, were plastered across his small, pointy head. "Darling. This is Lindy, I haven't seen her since just after high school. We went to Beverly together and we were in that Fabian film. Isn't life a hoot!"

The husband, who looked like Peter Lorre with anorexia, gave Lindy a long, languorous, appraising smile. Lindy smiled back. This was getting interesting. She knew this guy. He had been a frequent customer of her former madam's. She had double-dated with him once though, thank God, she had never had to be with him herself. She had heard that he was quite fond of wearing black silk stockings and garter belts.

"Hello," she said, thinking how sweet it was to meet a tormentress from adolescence and realize that you no longer envied or cared anything about her. Living with Popeye there wouldn't be worth all the "hoots" in a hillbilly hoedown. "Haven't we met?" Lindy said, wishing she had another glass of champagne.

The TV titan's smile froze on his face. Heather shot him a fast, vicious look. "No," he replied in a high, thin voice, the kind of voice, Lindy thought, that one would expect from a gent who wore ladies' underwear after midnight.

"No. I'm sure not. I always remember a pretty face. Come, dear, we have to be at the Pecks' in ten minutes."

Heather recaptured her devil-may-care grin from her bag of party tricks.

"I told you. It's a crazy life! Bye, dear. Call me. We'll do lunch!"

When Annette Funicello plays Gertrude Stein, we'll do lunch. Lindy gave a little finger wave. Mr. Television glanced back over his shoulder at her, confirming her suspicions. She blew him a kiss, grabbed another glass of champagne from a passing tray, and went roaming through the throng of gabbing, gaudy, gilded guests, searching for Wheezie.

Conversation floated over her. She inhaled it, thinking how different West Coast party talk was from East Coast cocktail chatter.

"So I went into the bathroom, and our wedding rings were lying side by side on the sink. All of a sudden I saw them as a symbol of everything wrong with us. My ring was heavy and dense. His was thin and light. I filed the next day."

"I was lying in the ICU after the mastectomy, all of these tubes in me and my first conscious thought was, Now maybe he'll leave me alone."

"She's got to stay away from the construction guys and all those black fighters. I told her, Give up the navy-blue cock or you're going to end up in Divorcée Dead End. He's gonna dump her when she hits forty anyway. She's got to think about her future."

"I told *Vogue* I wanted to create a perfume for the *little* women. The ones who'll never drive a Mercedes, have a quality fur, or shop on Rodeo, but when they put my scent behind their ears, they'll feel a part of all this."

"I never have to show anyone more than three houses. I'm infallible that way. The sheikh from Saudi Arabia? He only wanted to spend *seven,* but you know what that buys. So I took him to the one on Mulholland for *twelve.* He flipped. Only asked one question: Had anyone died there? Part of their religion or something. He didn't want a house someone had died in. That's why he didn't want the Menendez place. Bad karma. A steal, but bad karma."

Wheezie waved at her. He was stuck between Ruta Lee and Mr. Blackwell. Lindy pointed toward the door and headed out. No way she was moving into that group, not this sober anyway. He caught up with her.

"Our friendship is now on the line."

"Okay. We're out of here." He was smiling at her. "A nice quiet dinner and then I'll put you to bed." He handed the car guy his ticket.

"Seems like old times. My mother was completely unhinged.

She wants you to come spend a week with them. She said we could stay in my old room, just like fifth grade. We could even set up that old pup tent in the yard and camp out."

"You are pushing your luck, Wheezie Springer. This was like walking into one of those time-warp flicks. Take me somewhere totally un-Hollywood. No Morton's, Chasen's, Bistro—none of that. Take me somewhere where everyone has their original jaw-line."

"We're talking about Omaha, then."

"Very funny. Be creative. Take me to Glendale or Culver City."

After dinner they went home. Wheezie was shy, eager to show off his success. He made drinks and they sat in his house in the Hills, the lights of the sprawling noncity glittering far below them. It was so quiet. They sat in the darkness reminiscing in whispers.

"I don't know, Wheez. I've really fucked it all up. Some of what Gerrold's bride said to me is true. Most women marry The Leo first, get all the negative romance out of their systems, then find Mr. Nice Guy and settle down to the comforts of someone you can depend on. I did the whole thing backward. Now I've had one of each, there's nothing left. He broke my heart, you know. I've never told anybody that, not even Willa. I've never even told my-self. He did. I was really totally overcome by that man."

Wheezie's eyes looked red. He rubbed at them, keeping his face away from her.

Lindy sighed. "Well, that was lighthearted. Hey, Wheez. What about you? Where are the starlets? Remember Lana Blenstein?"

"Blenheim."

"Yeah. Boy, did you have the red-hots for her. I heard she changed her name to Whitney White and became a porn star. So, why no wife?"

"You," he said, his voice quavering.

"Me?"

"I've always loved you. I loved you when you were Lucinda with the wonderful Roman nose and crooked teeth and fat thighs. I loved you all the way through and it's really screwed me up."

For the first time in her entire life she was speechless. No one had ever said anything like that to her before. No man who had wanted her had ever known anything but the After side of the snapshot. Even her parents had changed toward her after she was presentable. She could see it in their eyes and hear it in their voices when they introduced her to people. Pride. She heard pride in their voices for the first time. It had never even occurred to her that anyone could have loved her before. She had never thought of Wheezie like that, maybe that was why.

She found her voice. "Wheez . . ."

He looked up at her, tears streaming down his anguished face. "Mark! Call me Mark. Just once, treat me as if I were a man and not a neurasthenic little weirdo."

"*Mark.* I . . ."

He stood up and paced back and forth before her. "Do you know what my wildest dream has been? That one day you would really look at me, see me, and know that I'm the right one for you and we would get married and I would adopt Tess. I love her, Lindy. I've always felt like she was mine, even though I know how ridiculous that sounds. Good old Uncle Wheezie, the poor neutered little schmuck."

She reached out to him, but he was lost in his confession. It was too much for him to reveal. He felt ashamed. "I've had too much to drink. I'm sorry. I'll wake you in the morning." He left the room without looking at her.

Lindy sat in the dark, stunned by his truth. What could she do? He might as well have confessed that he was a man from Mars. Not once had she ever fantasized that Wheezie felt anything more for her than friendship. How blind and self-absorbed was she?

Could it be that for all those years, right in front of her narcissistic little puss, he had been the right man and she had so totally blocked the idea that she had never even seen him as male? God! Funny that she should have gone into that whole seduction number with Willa. The old reliable unconscious. Maybe she had not been so totally unaware of him as she wanted herself to believe.

She put on her shoes and picked up their glasses and ashtrays and made her way in the moonlight to the kitchen. She washed the glasses, stacked them in the drainer, poured herself a glass of Perrier, and carried it into the bathroom. She ran a tub, sinking in and letting all the surreal, anxiety-loaded events of the day seep out of her. Wheezie. She smiled. Isn't life a pisser?

She got out of the tub, wrapped herself in a large bath towel, and brushed her teeth very carefully as if trying to decide something. She rinsed her mouth, applied moisturizer, eye cream, lip cream, and hand and body lotion. She was conducting an auto-pilot equipment check, switching the panel lights on reflexively. Legs shaved. Underarms smooth. Nails polished. She looked at herself in the fog-covered mirror. How long had it been since anyone had touched her, even someone who didn't care about her? *Long.* She sighed. What the hell. She picked up her glass and swaying, barefoot and woozy from the water and the emotion, she made her way down the hall to his room.

"Mark?" He was lying in the dark on his back, tears still running down his face. She stood in front of him, waiting for a sign. "Want some seltzer?"

"Thanks," he said, reaching out his bare arm. She handed him the glass, waiting while he drank. When he set it down, she undid her towel. "Better late than never," she whispered as if they were still children, lying down beside him like a virgin bride on her wedding night.

Willa will *kill* me, was the last thought she had before he touched her.

CHAPTER 3

But Seriously, Folks

BEE BEE DAY STARED INTO THE HARD RING OF LIGHT FRAMing her mirror. She had made four attempts at a rendezvous between her new false eyelashes and her slightly swollen upper lids, and it was now too late for another attempt. The left one was still crooked. It made her look a little cockeyed, but it would have to do. Besides, it was the second show on Saturday night and everyone out there would be too cockeyed themselves to know the difference. Good.

Since she had heard that damn news conference she hadn't been able to concentrate on anything, even eyelashes. She was off. Way off. She had even lost her train of thought during her morning interview with Julio Iglesias. She had just blanked out on the last question. Luckily he never paid any attention to the questions and just kept on smiling like a Latin Garfield and plugging his concert tour; but that had never happened to her before.

"Five minutes, Bees! Got a group out there so gaudy, even your Revos wouldn't cut the glare. Half of the exiled dictators of the Spanola-speakin' world and their date-rape prospects. Lots of Dom and Napoleon floatin' around. Need anything?"

"Nope. Just tell me, how crooked do my eyes look? I couldn't get the damn lashes straight."

Trudy Dale, Bee Bee's manager, leaned into the small square of female clutter that filled her dressing room, squinting through her omnipresent metallic blue–rimmed biofocals. "Just tilt to the left and you'll be fine. You're crooked but cute. See ya after, I'm gonna go soak my dogs. Oh, by the way, you got a call from some dame in New York, name of Willa Snow. Said it's about the press conference at the hospital. Says you called her. What the fuck is that?"

Bee Bee reddened. She always told Trudy everything, but she had not been ready to talk about this. "Tell you later."

"Okay. Just remember, no benefits this month. No sickos, AIDOS, druggos, or winos. We got taxes to pay."

Trudy closed the door and Bee Bee went to work on her lips. Her hand felt shaky. This was ridiculous.

Come on, girl. Put all that stuff out of your head now. You'll have plenty of time to flagellate yourself with the Leo songbook later.

She blotted her lips and stood up, dropping her robe and stepping into her one concession to Saturday nights at Serena's, a full-length bright green sequined evening dress that she hated, not only because it made it difficult to breathe—let alone sing, and left deep red marks covering her body like Lilliputian cookie cutouts hours after she removed it—but because it totally misrepresented her act. The rest of the time she wore a black pantsuit and a white T-shirt with the word WRONG in black letters across the chest.

It is what she had worn the first time she performed here, and it is what she would be wearing when they carried her off to the old cabaret show above.

Serena, who was the most successful nightclub owner in Florida and had given Bee Bee her break and her permanent club home, had asked her to sex it up for the Saturday crowd. She owed her that. She zipped herself in, pausing to arrange her newly implanted cleavage, still unfamiliar with the joy of real breasts and as unsure as a female impersonator with how to handle them.

Both Trudy and Serena had been after her for years to do it. "You're a stunning girl, but you've got a chest like a little boy with TB. It don't play in Pottstown," Trudy had told her. Pottstown was Trudy's worst criticism. Anything—a new piece of material, new song, or new friend—that got the "don't play in Pottstown" judgment was gone before bedtime.

Breasts had never been very important to her. She remembered Errol Flynn being interviewed once when she was a kid, before she knew she would not be touched by the Bosom Fairy's wand.

"Breasts are highly overrated as erotic symbols," Errol had purred. "They only turn on men looking for their mothers. You can't do a bloody thing with them. You can't make love to a mammary gland. Legs, calves, ankles, thighs, buttocks—now *there's* where a man can get interested." Well, if it was okay for Errol (whom her mother idolized), it was good enough for her. But this was business. And all she had that mattered now was business, so she had agreed.

The day she had gone in for the operation the admitting nurse had pulled out her clipboard and started firing health questions at her before she had even taken off her coat. "Any false teeth?"

"No." She shot an I'll-get-you-for-this look at Trudy, who was hovering over her as if she were a prize pig at the county fair, which in a way, for Trudy, she was.

"Glass eye?"

"No!"

"Wig? Hair piece?"

"No."

"False fingernails?"

"Bitten to the quick."

"Any prosthesis?"

"Shoulder pads."

The nurse blinked as if considering whether a joke was being made or she had a lunatic before her.

"That was just a little hospital humor," Bee Bee said, putting the poor dear out of her misery.

Now she had breasts. Big deal. Leo hadn't cared. He was one of the Errol Flynn types. She didn't care either. So the breasts were for the roomfuls of leering, boozy, bad boys, whose names she would never know, and whose faces she could never remember.

It did, however, make her pretty damn impressive. A great big girl, now fortified in front as well. Six feet tall in her heels, she had, as they said on the circuit, presence. It kept the wolves at bay and gained the awe and respect of their women. Besides, it was a tax deduction. Which Trudy kept telling her was very important.

Go, girl. She picked up her earrings and left the dressing room to face her audience.

*   *   *

Sometimes Bee Bee thought that all of human nature could be subdivided between the Night People and the Day People. The simple choice of when to be awake and when to be asleep carried with it a chain reaction of life forms and fashions.

By definition, Day People were more conventional. They got up in the morning. They ate breakfast at breakfasttime, opened their morning papers, made their gourmet drip coffee, walked their well-trained pups, did their NordicTrack while the *Today* show crackled in their shower-fresh ears. They faced the day.

Sunshine and Filofaxes, subway trains, carpools, power breakfasts, dental appointments—every hour of their mornings was filled with the normal workaday hustle of contemporary life.

The very fact that almost everyone else was doing almost the same things at almost the same times offered enormous comfort. All those well-manicured hands, spreading all that low-cholesterol margarine on all those whole-wheat bran muffins was enormously reassuring.

The Day People were not afraid of being seen in full morning light. They lived in the presence of one another, secure in the subtlety of their makeup, the closeness of their shaves, the sweetness of their breath, and the dryness of their underarms. Hair was clean and properly combed. Shirts crisply starched and ironed, suit collars free of unsightly speckles of dandruff or dust. Shoes shined and level-heeled, teeth white, eyes clear.

No werewolves or vampires among the Day parade. No bleary-eyed rummies or victims of disfiguring diseases, bad dry-cleaning, or poor dental hygiene. The Day People, secure in the correctness of their cheery, overorganized, overachieving, unspontaneous, diligent, responsible, orderly, structured, and above all else, acceptable daily lives, had nothing to hide.

Day, by its very definition, meant sunny, healthy, happy, cheerful, and part of the A team. One wouldn't find Barbara and George hanging around afterhours clubs or working the night shift in an Atlantic City poker parlor. Right-thinking people, people with kids and dogs and civic involvements, got up early every morning. This was the American way.

Farmers, fishermen, bakers, and stockbrokers opened each day. By dawn the roadways were already crammed with commuters, truckers, Federal Express deliverers. The parks and streets pounded by joggers, bikers, fitness walkers—the whole, healthy, harmonious, workaday world buzzing along from first light.

It had even become a subject for competition. The earlier one rose, the less sleep one needed, and the more one had accomplished by the time the paper hit the doorstep, the better a person one was. The Day People ran the world, of that there was no doubt.

The Night People were another breed altogether. They filled the wide and small screens as horror-movie fiends, rapists, murderers, muggers, thieves, cat burglars, prostitutes, pimps, junkies, drunks, boozers, losers, barflies—those best kept in shadow. Those with skin not quite so clean, eyes not quite so bright, hair less shiny, clothes less tailored. These were not crisp people. The Night People.

Jazz musicians and show people. Singers, actors, dancers, comics, bartenders, security guards, office cleaners, subway conductors, nurses, cops, watchmen, waitpersons, cabbies, mobsters, and socialites. People who came out at night, like jasmine and mosquitoes, chasing off the day lilies and hummingbirds. Night People saw life differently, their perspective tinted, night-blinded by shadow and sorrow. Things that went bump, a darker view of the truth.

They lived in an artificially lit tunnel of awareness, shaped by the mental masquerade, the smoky room of midnight dementia, the hours of bleak, black truth before sunrise. These were princes and princesses of darkness, not daydreamers or doers. They walked more slowly, thought furtively, dressed flamboyantly, lurked, prowled, stalked, seeking the secrets that cannot be found in daylight. Dark secrets, Halloween tricks, treats of the masked men and maidens who ate breakfast in all-night diners and slept while the Day People conquered the world.

The two groups never bothered each other much, except at the junctures of chance—the meeting between New Jersey housewife and Harlem drug dealer, rapist and woman who missed her bus, insomniac and all-night convenience store clerk. But these encounters, whether cordial and impersonal or violent and unexpected, were all haphazard; not harmonious or in keeping with the interests of their band. Like class and race. The Night People and the Day People did not belong together. They did not share a

lingua franca. They were not in any way alike and when they
wandered into each other's world, strange, unpleasant things occurred.

Once in a while someone who should have been a Day Person
was caught in the world of the Night or vice versa, and this person
would suffer in the unique and desperate way that a soul living out
of step with its natural order suffers, but generally people found
their way, quite early, to their proper clique and everything else in
their lives, from their choice of lover to their job, flowed from this
preference.

Bee Bee had always been a night person. Even as a very little girl
she would lie awake, luxuriating in the velvet-soft darkness, wandering around the room she shared with her brothers, watching
over them, thinking her night thoughts.

Of course, growing up in Las Vegas, Nevada, didn't hurt. If
there was ever a town that thrived on the night, that was it. Her
parents both worked nights, her father as a lounge pianist ("Star-
light" was his signature piece), her mother as a showgirl, then as a
cocktail waitress, finally, until she got sick, as a blackjack dealer,
all hardly wholesome daytime professions.

It was hard on her parents, being Night People and trying to
raise three children, who by law if not by inclination were Day
People. Five-year-olds could not go to night school, not in the
state of Nevada anyway.

Bee Bee could never remember her mother not being half asleep
and staggering around. Somehow she always made it though. She
got up and got all of them fed, dressed, and on the school bus, got
the kitchen tidied, threw a load of laundry in, and made the beds
before falling back to sleep.

Sometimes her parents were still asleep when Bee Bee and her
brothers returned from school, and those were the lonely after-
noons that set the pattern for Bee Bee as the one who took care of
"the boys." It seemed that she had been taking care of "the boys"
—her brothers, her lovers, her friends from the time she was old
enough to reach the stove. It was just the way it was. She took care
of those who needed it. When she was bigger, she took care of her
parents, too.

She loved them. They were pretty people, childlike and simple,
cheated of their promise—the promise that good looks and mod-

est talent had held, wooing them forward, beckoning them into the darkness with the long, skinny finger of the trickster's lure. "Come, come, my pretty, right this way, all your dreams will come true, step right up."

They had fallen in love with each other's beauty and hope, believing that together they would rise to the top of the town. Las Vegas. They did not dream of Hollywood or Broadway, they knew their potential better than that; but in their clotted, shimmery, green neon pond, they believed they could triumph.

They married young and when Bee Bee was born, her mother took off her spangles and put them in a box with her illusions, storing both neatly at the back of her closet.

The Sixties began and Las Vegas grew hotter and hotter. There was work and her father worked; he opened for Shecky Greene at the Riviera, and Don Rickles at the Sands. But the competition was fierce and every year, as the town spread, new talent poured in. The city grew fatter and flashier, phosphorescent and blazing with the raw, crude power of money and the tinselly seduction of the saloon singer's romanticism, the intoxicating delusions of a city in the desert, created for Cimmerian pleasures and the people who want them. He was passed by. Passed over. Snuffed by the shadows.

He sang "Moon River" and "Nancy with the Laughing Face," and "Moonlight Becomes You" and "Blues in the Night." He kept his wavy black hair and lost his high notes. He worked then like any night-shift guy. He got up at five P.M. and had breakfast (western omelette and home fries, a side of bacon, and three cups of coffee) in the all-night coffee shop of whatever hotel he was playing. Unlike train conductors or power-company repairmen, he wore a burgundy tuxedo and a white carnation and did not carry a flashlight or a lunch bucket, but the job had become for him just a job. Dead dreams, too many sunless hours, three kids to feed, and a wife who was weakening.

Sometimes Bee Bee thought that the reason so many Las Vegas people ended up like her parents, was that they had gone against nature and nature was paying them back. The desert of the Bible was a place for the Day. Night was for finding water and traveling by camel. They had come into this pristine white, flat holy land and torn it asunder. They had turned it into Sodom and Gomorrah, a madman's mecca, a sinner's haven, filled with phantoms and golden gods.

Temptation lurked behind every palm tree. Concrete and glass pounded into the sand, pushing the very land away from its roots. Air-conditioning whirred in fluorescent glass boxes, where in other deserts shepherds in their tents and slave girls fanning nomads, had endured.

Now the Arabs were in *their* desert, driven in chauffeured white stretch limousines, to bet fortunes at the roulette wheel and put their harems up in royal-blue silk-walled suites, where they ordered cheeseburgers and chocolate milk shakes from room service and watched *The Days of Our Lives* while their keepers played.

In this town where nothing ever closed; where people in evening gowns did their laundry at three A.M. in neon-signed Laundromats with slot machines next to the soap dispensers; where studio apartments were rented mostly by the week; where people came and went, got lucky or folded—up and down, in and out, a blinking, blinding, nocturnal nation of passers-through—there Bee Bee grew up, believing this was the way everyone lived.

It had never occurred to her to do anything that took place during the day. School had been an aberration from the very start. It didn't matter that she was smart. "You're so smart," her teachers would say. (Teachers—part of the Day world, strangers whose skin was tan and who went to bed before her parents went to work.) What did smart have to do with school?

She had started writing little songs when she was four years old, and her father taught her how to put them to music. Writing songs and singing them was all she had ever wanted to do, but even her creativity was dimmed by the umbra of Las Vegas. Lounge lizards and show Gypsies, their feet always sore and their hair always in curlers. None of it looked very glamorous. The world of the Sinatras and Minnellis, and the other headliners who drew the crowds, was too remote for her. She had not aimed very high for a long time. Too long maybe.

Until she was eighteen and went on the road she had never seen a wood floor or a solid-colored carpet. (All of Las Vegas was covered with swirling, multi-colored carpeting that showed no wear and softened the sounds and harshness of the night light.) She did not know anything about real clothes, meaning plain and without glitter and stage appeal, or uniforms of some kind. Everyone she had known growing up worked in a hotel as a bellman or dealer or waitress or showperson. Everyone wore uniforms unless they were off, when they mostly wore nightgowns and pajamas or dancer's exercise stuff.

The road opened the world of subtlety, good taste and art, foreign food and low-heeled shoes; but Vegas was her nursery. The city of keno and crap tables, pastrami sandwiches for supper, and false eyelashes on the kitchen sink. This was her security blanket. The world of the Night.

When she was sixteen, her mother died and she gave up school and took over whatever she hadn't already taken over. Her father seemed to grow old overnight. It astonished Bee Bee. One morning he just wasn't handsome anymore. Nothing had really changed. He had not gotten too fat or too thin. His hair hadn't gone white or sparse. Her mother had gotten sick and died—and the next thing she knew her father wasn't young anymore and he didn't seem to care.

He was still kind to her, if distracted. Not unkind but rather uninterested. He still performed, though the hotels were farther down the Strip and the spots shorter and never at peak crowd times.

They went on. Zombielike. Night creatures lost in their sadness. Motherless, wifeless creatures, wandering till dawn. They never really mourned and they never really stopped.

She kept her mother's old costumes in a box at the back of her closet, and she wore her wedding band on her middle finger. She wore it there when she needed to remember something. Her father had given it to her and she had put it on her right ring finger, but it was too loose. One morning, not long after her mother's funeral —a Day Person's ritual, for sure—she had wanted to remember a lyric, a song she was writing about her mother called "Betty Ann," and to help her remember until she found a pen and paper, she had slipped the ring onto her middle finger as a reminder. She had done it ever since. If the ring was on her ring finger, there was nothing important she needed to think about.

Somehow the ring had become her mother-memory, like "Eat your spinach" or "Wear your rubbers." It made her feel guided. It made her feel safe. She always slipped it onto her middle finger before she went onstage. It was her stage voodoo, like "Break a leg" in the theater. If it was on, she would never forget a lyric. And so far she never had.

When she was eighteen and her brothers were old enough to care for themselves, she wrote an act for herself and her dad. She sat him down in the cramped, green shag-covered living room of the ranch house three miles off the Strip that had been their home since she was three, solemnly took his place at the piano, and proceeded to perform both their parts for an entire ninety-minute show.

He remained seated before her, rigid with shock, never before realizing, so lost had he been in the pitchy cloudiness of his own despair, how talented she was. He was awestruck and he was ashamed. When she finished he put his wavy Grecian-tinted head in his hands and sobbed like a child.

At first she was hurt, thinking that his tears were for her, because she was being foolish. But then he reached out to her and she went over and curled onto his lap, as hard as that was for a big girl. He pulled her down and held her. "I'm sorry, baby," he said over and over, and she understood then what his tears were about.

When he calmed down, he took her out for a drive. It was twilight, the sun setting over the sand, streaks of purple-orange light shadowing the sky—primal, real light, more powerful than all the neon shrieking across the downtown twenty-four hours a day.

"I can't," he said, and she nodded, relieved in a way, knowing it was permission to go forward, that he did not expect her to take him with her.

Six months later she had an agent and a contract for a third-string Oriental cabaret tour. The road had called her. A road that led her through spotlights and cigar smoke, dirty powder puffs and foreign towns; years of nighttimes, sometimes starlit, sometimes glittering, often lightning-struck or rain-dappled, foggy or frightening, but never without the familiar mothering radiance. It was her homeland, the land of moonbeams and solitude; wee, small hours and the truth. Bee Bee believed in it. The truth of the Night.

"Ladies and Gentlemen, *Señoras, Señoritas y Hombres,* Serena's *de* Miami is proud to present Miss Bee Bee Day."

She slipped her ring onto her middle finger and walked out onto the stage. She liked it here. After all those years on the road Miami felt like coming home. She was tired and she had come here to rest. At least that was what she thought she was doing. That was before Leo.

She looked into the crowd and smiled. Trudy was right. Miami was becoming what Las Vegas wanted to become but never did. It had the glitz and glamour, but it was also a real city, a sun-and-sin city of the future.

Everyone wanted to be in Florida. Drug dealers, old people, Yuppies, real estate developers, and bankers. People just kept pouring in from everywhere. The Cubans had livened up the palette, tapping the town with their music and flavors, smells, and colors. Of course, there was a dark side, but for better or worse many people found that attractive.

The restaurants were filled with smooth young men, cellular phones in hand, strutting back and forth across Joe's Stone Crab making deals. Wheeling and probably stealing in perfectly pleated linen slacks and sockless Italian loafers.

These guys had more juice than a Florida orange grove, and they set the pace for the city, bringing with them gorgeous girls in tiny black dresses and everything else that flashy cash needs to operate; gourmet food boutiques, French couture, wine shops; and personal trainers, who in turn brought athletic apparel emporiums, NordicTrack, and Magic Stair salesrooms, sports-medicine doctors and holistic practitioners; and employment agencies that provided butlers, chauffeurs, nannies and au pairs; real estate salesmen scouting the town from Coral Gables to Biscayne Bay; manicurists and facialists and plastic surgeons and jewelry designers and call girls and yacht brokers.

A daisy chain, a pyramid game—started by one guy in a white linen suit, strutting into Joe's Stone Crab, and slamming his portable phone down on the dinner table, setting it in between the blue stone crabs and the melted butter, as if anyone who wasn't important enough to need a phone on his dinner table at nine-thirty on a Saturday night should pack up his troubles in his old Hermès bag and move to Atlanta. "I'm here and it's happening" was the message that arrived with this guy and all the others who had followed him.

Cities get hot the same way people and trends do—they flower, bloom then if they're lucky, settle into the comfort of a warm, well-watered pot, a secure middle-age, not quite so lush, but still in the silt. Unlucky cities, ravaged by race wars, corruption, and greed can fall as far as any fallen star. Miami had been up and she had been down, and the karmic chain of events that had led to her current rebirth was giving a lot of people a great deal of pleasure, not to mention money and power.

It was a good city to be in at the lip of the century. It was a city of history, of the founding of America—of Magellan and Ponce de Leon, the fountain of youth and the creation of the new lands— and it was a city of the pure, primal present. A city that worshiped beauty and youth, money and instant gratification.

The hotel lobbies brimmed with overdressed South American millionaires who wore mink coats in May and gave lavish parties for scores of expatriates like themselves, flaunting their wealth and comfort without fear.

A city of the *sol* where Savile Row–suited businessmen and heavily made-up matrons had tea with the wives and mistresses of the rulers of third-world police states, while pianists in tails diddled out salsa tunes.

Weddings were lavish, and any excuse to dress up—Cuban Confirmation parties or wedding anniversaries; any event providing an opportunity to puff and fluff, parade and primp, pull out the Rolls, the Rolex and the gems from the safe-deposit boxes in the Bank of Miami—was embraced with innocent, atavistic glee. It was a city for showing off. A dazzling bubbling, champagne-popping place grasping the present in a ferocious attempt to stave off the future, and the running down and possible running out of the American dream, leaving only a few cities still ripe with hope.

Miami was shining at the top, the last frontier before the millennium, the beginning of the century that no one would live to see through. The time when all the doomsayers may be vindicated and the ozone may vanish and the pipelines may powder and the seas and rivers run to poison. Food will grow in laboratories, babies will grow in bottles, and there will be no more fun. No more juicy guys in white Ferraris with a blonde in the master cabin and a villa on Fisher Island. The future did not interest most of these people who had come to Miami to defy the death of such dreams. For them it was a perfect place.

It was one of the only towns where someone like Bee Bee, a Night Person, an entertainer who could do a ninety-minute act of Broadway show tunes or Cole Porter from memory, could work steadily. It was not that she was totally through with the road. In fact, she still had a gig in Hong Kong to do. It was just that she needed a home and Miami had become that to her.

When she arrived here, she was twenty-seven years old with two marriages behind and nothing much before her. She was childless and rootless and tired. She was tired of singing "Tomorrow" and never getting to perform her own work, though every club owner always promised to let her. She was phoning in something that she loved with all her heart and that was killing her joy.

The only place they had ever let her do her own stuff was Switzerland. It didn't even make any sense why there, but the Swiss loved her quirky, angry songs. But so what? Bee Bee had never even been able to describe what a Swiss was like. One night she and Trudy had stayed up till dawn drinking Swiss beer—or Swiss piss as Trudy called it—trying to figure out what a Swiss looked like.

They were a people without a definable physical presence. Bland. Punctual. Not tall or short, dark or light, young or old. Neutral and Swatched, clean and cold, like the River Reuss. The *raclette* melting, the trains arriving, everything on time, little men marching around pooper-scooping each turd from the tidy streets. Underneath all the gliding swans and ticking gold watches, there were junkies and crazies, needle parks and brutal blandness; but the top was perfectly starched.

It was a deceptive place for Bee Bee who had style, however brassy, and that may have been why they liked her. She was nothing if not definable. And it was there, that night when they drank beer and she had cried and told Trudy about her childhood and her two husbands, that she had decided to find a home.

Dexter Jones was a tall, melancholy violinist with a soft, deep voice and an effete, shy manner that made Bee Bee feel protective and needed. He recited poetry and talked of spiritual journeys to places that she had never heard of and this seemed to her, the desert kid away from home for the first time, wonderfully romantic. They met on a flight to Singapore. He sat beside her, two tall people miserable in their short-people seats. It was the first real conversation that she'd had with anyone since she'd left home. They talked about music and this brought them close in that deceptive way of lonely strangers with a common interest and Bee Bee, a virgin with no knowledge of men or herself, was captivated. Three days later they were married. She did not even know where he was from.

Dexter beguiled and betrayed her, taking her money and leaving her after only a month with a note on her hotel-room pillow. A hotel in Bangkok, where she had gotten sick from a piece of tainted fruit at the Floating Market. "I cannot do what I wanted to. I cannot be a husband. I must seek a spiritual and monastic path. I am going to India to reclaim my soul. Forgive me."

What was she to forgive him for? Leaving, robbing, searching, what? She had decided to forgive him for all of it and go on with her tour. They had married in Singapore when she was singing at the Sheraton, and she went back there to end it.

Bee Bee figured that any country that stamped in red on her entry visa "Dealing in Drugs Is Punishable by Death" (an idea that seemed to her far more potentially effective than "Just Say No") was a country where an annulment was not something to be taken lightly. She had done it, crying all the way through the court appearance and gone on to the next booking. Seduced and abandoned and not yet twenty. She had never even told her family.

"Never sleep with anyone who has more problems or less money than you do," her mother's wise friend, Esther the hairdresser, had told her just before she left Vegas. Sound if unromantic advice, she knew, but like most advice, only as valuable as the recipient's retention skills.

After Dexter left she was more careful, not letting her heart lead her. She was a great big sexy young American girl a long, long way from home, with no one to protect her or help her out of a jam and a lot of people, male and female, were only too willing to suck off her strength. She had to be careful.

Manfred Stein was a German-Jewish concert promoter thirty years Bee Bee's senior and down on his luck, with a kind, courtly manner and a warm, hearty laugh. She had never known anyone like him. He said, "Let me take care of you, you need someone to watch out for you," and the words were so welcome, the promise they held as lyrical and hummable as a Tony Bennett ballad. Yes.

He was a widower who had lost his only son, and he needed her as much as she needed him. "I'm going to make you a star, Bee Bee. Leave everything to me. I don't want you to have to worry about anything ever again. You just use your energy for your music, I'll do the rest." It was as if some sardonic fairy godmother had tapped her, and for her particular reality he was perfect.

He taught her about sex, an almost virgin with the strange particulars of a child of the Night, who had grown up watching topless women move their bodies for the enjoyment of strangers, but who still possessed the guileless innocence of a child raised by two limited and unworldly teenage sweethearts. He told her and he showed her and he opened her to the pleasures of love.

What he could not open her to was her own orgasmic self. "We have time," he would whisper to her when she lay in his arms, sweaty and frustrated by her failure to reach that hidden place, a place she was not really sure she wanted to go. "We have all the time in the world, my baby girl. My beautiful *Day.*" He spoke to her softly, with his gentle foreign accent, and she curled against him, feeling safe beside him in a way she had never felt safe before.

He taught her timing, how to breathe into a song, where the control came from. He taught her to trust herself when she wrote.

He would hold her hands and look straight into her eyes when he told her things. "When I was young, Bee Bee, I trusted everyone. Then I went into the world and I learned that people were mostly not worthy of this trust. Don't forget I came from a country of shame. I became very hard and for a long time I trusted no one, believed nothing anyone said. Now I believe about half. But I still live as if I believe only what I know myself. A belief means you've stopped seeing, and so it is very dangerous to believe anything. You must keep seeing and staying open to what comes forth inside your head. It is not easy to live like this. There are so many voices in one's head. You must listen to them all, then feel what's right and move on. Don't get stuck in theories. Not even this one."

She tried hard to understand what he told her, as if in a way she knew he was preparing her to go on alone. They were married in Vienna on her one night off, just before her twenty-third birthday.

Two years later, when his plan for her was in place and her act in wonderful shape, he had fallen over in her dressing room while she was combing her hair. She remembered later that she had just said, "You know what I'd love to try? I'd love to try My Earthquake song tonight." It was something she had been working on all year. A tough, bluesy song that no one had ever let her put in the act. He had not responded and it had hurt her feelings. She had been afraid to look at him, afraid he would see her disappointment. She felt a thud. Felt the sound like a physical sensation. He was lying facedown at her feet and he was dead.

Later she found out that he had known his heart was weak, and she could see then why he had reached out to her with such total attention, such urgent commitment. She had no basis for comparison. He had been her only real lover, teacher, friend. And there had not been enough time.

She took his body home to his town in the hills outside Munich and buried him. She stayed on there for a while, living in an old castle that now served weekenders on holiday. He had left her enough money so that she didn't have to work for a while and she stayed in her castle room, not doing anything, trying to figure something out.

She had been in so many hotel rooms in her young life; they were the only homes she had known and she treated them kindly. She thought of the rooms as people, believing that they waited for her, eager to please, cleaned and fresh and wanting to charm. She hated the way she saw other entertainers treat them. "Room rapes," she called it. They stormed in, tearing the paper tapes off toilet seats, ripping robes off hangers, throwing trash and empty brandy bottles on the floor, messing the soap, tossing wet towels on lovingly made beds, staining washcloths with lipstick, burning dressertops with cigarettes. She felt so sorry for the rooms that had waited, so full of expectation for a pleasant companion who would appreciate the effort made to please. She always felt like apologizing for them. "Sorry, guys. I know you tried your best. You're a great room, really. He's just a jerk. I've seen other rooms he's left. It's nothing personal."

She always treated her rooms well, with respect and consideration. She wiped her makeup off with Kleenex and folded her damp towels and placed them on the side of the shower or tub and put her trash in the wastebasket. After Manfred died and she afforded herself a nicer room to stay in, she treated it reverently. Someday I'll have a home of my own and I'll never take any of it for granted.

Being kind to her room, her pillows, and ashtrays helped her be nicer to herself and she stayed on, being polite and well-mannered until her money ran low and it was time to go on with her life. She had lost all sense of what that meant. She had always lived rather spur-of-the-moment, without any real goal or plan, drifting around in her life, waiting for something to happen. She did not want to admit it, but even Manfred had not felt so much like the happening as still part of the waiting.

At night, in her grieving terror, she thought, If I end up like one of those Vegas girls surviving on unemployment in a week-by-week studio, waiting for my big break, I'll slit my throat. Well, she didn't know what she wanted, but at least she knew what she didn't want. That.

She went forward. She played Tokyo discos and Caribbean cruises. She kept Manfred's voice in her head and trusted only those she had to, for the minimum amount of time and with the least amount of belief possible. One of the rudderless, waiting women. She did not know who or what she was waiting for. God knows, she never thought it would be Leo.

Looking back, Bee Bee found it interesting that a girl who had grown up in the desert and was a grown woman before she had seen the ocean, or any large body of water, should have met the two people who became the most important influences in her life, on ships.

Bee Bee met Trudy Dale on a Princess cruise to Bermuda. Every night when she went on there she was, a lanky bleached blonde with bright purple lips; a long, narrow, hard-luck face; a pair of bright blue wide-rimmed glasses; a cigarette holder stuck between her crooked yellow teeth; and a pale, portly bald-headed man always beside her, always silent and always smiling sweetly at everyone. They were in the front row for both shows each night and Bee Bee began to look for them and sing for them. The last night of the cruise there was a knock on her cabin, which was also her dressing room, and there they were.

"Kid. I'm Trudy Dale, this is my husband Mikey. Let me get right to the point: We like you, you've got great potential. I been a talent manager forty years, Mikey too. I think you need us and we can get you moving forward. Ever recorded?"

Bee Bee's trust antennae went up. She was not going to be anyone's meal ticket. "No," she said, waiting for Trudy to reveal more of what Manfred had called, "The mouse part of the cat game."

It had taken almost a year from that night for Bee Bee to agree to let the Dales manage her. What had finally won her was that Trudy understood her. Trudy was nothing if not pushy, but she had seen Bee Bee's resistance and respected it. Trudy Dale was the kind of woman that she could trust. She had been around women like Trudy since she was a baby. They were all women born out of their time: ballsy, tough, smart, crackling with thwarted energy—but part of a generation of women who were supposed to marry young, breed fast, and not give their men any aggravation.

Trudy was one of that generation's misfits. A person who desperately wanted to be someone herself, but without the looks, talent, or education required from the world *and lacking* the ability to procreate or stand quietly behind a husband (who would rather stand behind her anyway), she did the best she could with what she'd been given. She put her drive into other engines. She managed, mothered, lived through, and for, people like Bee Bee.

There were very few couples like the Dales left in New York, Vegas, or anywhere else by the Nineties. They were part of the old-time Tin Pan Alley mentality. They lived their lives in arcane sheet music and dusty eight-by-ten glossies-jumbled offices and apartments, in rundown brownstones off Times Square, living on container coffee, Camel cigarettes, and stale kaiser rolls. They handled variety artists (what was left of them), singers, comics, ventriloquists, impressionists, and tap dancers.

Theirs was the world of *Broadway Danny Rose* rather than the world of Madonna, MTV or live concerts at Madison Square Garden and the Universal amphitheater. Their acts still worked Vegas, cruises, European and Oriental cabaret tours. Sometimes they got lucky with a *Tonight* show bit or a sitcom guest shot or a small part in a Broadway show, but mostly their acts had aged with them and they lacked the panache and sensibility to the look and sound of the Now that would attract any new talent.

Bee Bee was a miracle for them, even though they had tried hard not to show it. She was young and certainly striking and talented, and her talent was rooted in a musical tradition they understood. They were rooted in a show-business tradition that Bee Bee understood and could trust.

In the end what won her over was that they needed her so much. It was probably the same seduction that had worked with Manfred. She found it touching and reassuring.

They adored her, pampered her, but always told her the truth. She was the child they never had, but she was also a lifeline. Children are not supposed to provide that service for their parents, and all of them understood this irony. If the rules of the relationship had not been clear, the point where patronage becomes manipulation, parentage exploitation, and the lifeline turns into a noose, they would not have survived Leo.

The night Bee Bee met Leo Lampi she was twenty-eight years old and had never been in love.

Dexter had been a romantic misstep, the act of an achingly isolated and naive young girl with so little knowledge of men and relationships that she had married him without even considering whether the feelings of sensual yearning and excitement were love or spring fever.

Manfred had certainly been about caring and affection, but "madly in love" would never be the way to describe that marriage. Bee Bee had led a rather cautious emotional life. The external factors in an unstable, high risk career being so risky, the only way to survive with sanity and dignity was to keep tight rein on her feelings. This personal history does not bode well for a young woman about to embark on the most treacherous, mysterious, delirious, and delusory of all human adventures.

Bee Bee and Mikey and Trudy Dale had set up shop in Miami. The Dales had sold their apartment in New York, a move that was long overdue and in keeping with the shift in club bookings from New York to Florida. They rented a spacious three-bedroom house on an unfashionable canal in Miami Beach with white wall-to-wall carpeting and a small baby-blue pool. They had a rehearsal piano in the living room; the spare bedroom was used as an office; and Bee Bee had the master, with a large, mirrored walk-in closet for her show clothes and a view of the water. Theirs was an instant family and they were all besotted with glee. A home of their own, with billowy marshmallow clouds above and bouncy blue water below and sunshine every day and phones that rang with good news.

For the Dales, who were pushing seventy and had never lived on street level or without grime and crime, it was, as Trudy said, "Better than heaven." For Bee Bee it was almost the same.

Bee Bee changed in Miami. It was as if the physical rooting helped her internal garden as well. She lost weight and started to swim and run. She cut her hair, letting it turn copper in the sun. Her voice grew stronger and her songs grew bolder, angrier, freer. She started adding more humor to her act.

Onstage she was mysterious, sharp-witted, sultry. Offstage she was shy, reserved, and self-conscious. Settling down into an orderly and protected daily life, a kind of re-creation of a childhood fantasy where she was tended, pampered, and encouraged helped the two sides, public and private, find a more comfortable living arrangement within her own, now golden, skin.

The night she met Leo was a major event in Bee Bee's Miami life. Trudy had booked her onto a fund-raising gala aboard the yacht of one of Florida's most prominent philanthropists. It was a star-studded, big-ticket evening, where anyone who was trying to be someone fought for an invitation to spend thousands of dollars on overcooked spare ribs and watered rum punch. It was a coup for Bee Bee not only because she would appear on a program with far more famous entertainers but because many influential people in the recording and nightclub business would be in the audience.

The three of them were thrilled and shaking with nerves when they arrived. Bee Bee had never been at a party like this. This was not Vegas. Silver-haired millionaires with matching wives, foxtrotted around a polished maple dance floor set onto the deck of the biggest boat owned by a single human being that Bee Bee had ever seen. Middle-aged couples with bronzed skin and black shiny clothes, diamonds gleaming on the wives' ears and necks, moving in perfect step, faces impassive, pulled artificially tight, mirroring one another, seemingly oblivious of the others but in fact checking out every single arrivee. "Did you say Hello to Tina, dear?" "No, but I'll say good-bye to her." They twirled by, perfectly coiffed, secure in their right to be here with the others of their station. Bee Bee was wide-eyed at the sights and sounds of this private, privileged world.

Trudy practically had to push her forward through the fashionable throng and down to the entertainers' makeshift dressing room. They were separated from the revelers, kept below and away, fed different food, and told not to mingle, drink, or make their presence known before show time.

The star attractions, of course, were also guests and invited to circulate, raising the pulses of the socially weary party-goers, their presence a further reassurance that this was indeed the top of the world.

Bee Bee, the band, and the others like herself, who were not being paid, but were being "given a great opportunity" were treated as such. She had clomped down the stairs to the green room, wearing her black pantsuit, more nervous than she had ever been before a performance.

Sitting on a stool, a cigarette hanging from his full, pouty mouth, his strong-boned face tan and windblown, his sand-colored hair pushed back out of his eyes in that impossibly sexy, casual way only Robert Redford, and maybe God, ever get hair to look, sat Leo Lampi.

He looked up at her over the languorous layered lids of his sea-colored eyes and smiled, and something deep inside her—not quite where she thought her heart or stomach or anything important was—gave way. A physical opening, as if a tap had been turned. The sensation was so powerful she stopped dead, causing Trudy to almost tumble on top of her as she barreled down the narrow wooden steps into the cabin.

"Hey, Lampi! Come up here and check the piano! The fucking humidity's thrown everything off! We aren't goin' to get rehearsal. Get up here!" an anonymous voice called.

Leo stood up, rising tall, his broad athletic shoulders straining his tuxedo shirt. He walked straight toward her slowly, cigarette still held between his lips. She was in his way, standing dumb-struck, as doomed as a highway squirrel with bad timing. She was stuck, the tourist's car barreling toward her, unable to time her dash.

"Hi. I'm Leo Lampi," he said, amused by her wide-eyed awk-wardness. "Got some music for me?"

"Sure," she croaked, her voice quavering up from the gurgling, rusty place turning on inside her. She fumbled with her bag, pull-ing out the sheets. He reached for them, his large, warm hand touching hers and she jerked backward, hitting her head on the hatchway.

"Hey. Easy. I'm not going to steal it." He touched her arm and grinned at her, locking her into his eyes, eyes that had been places Bee Bee had never thought of and seen things no one wanted to see.

"Leo! Get up here!"

Gently, amused in the way that men who know they affect women are amused, he moved her ever so slightly out of his way and she let him, stumbling against Trudy, a startled squirrel out of luck, dashing to safety one second too late. Street Soup, she was. *Thwack.* Impact. She was lost. All she could hope for now was that the driver would be kind enough to stop and carry her twitching, shivering self over to the side of the road.

"We are very fortunate to have with us tonight, at this most worthy event, one of Miami's bright new stars. She's just recently returned from a world tour and has graciously consented to per-form for all of you generous Friends of the Wetlands. Miss Bee Bee Day."

Leo watched her enter, giving cues to the band. She was going to start with her own song. She was in no shape to take such a risk but she was lovestruck and didn't care.

"Good evening. It's a great pleasure to be here tonight. I'd like to do one of my own songs first. I hope you like it."

Bee Bee looked at Leo, he nodded and she walked forward close to the audience. Everyone was silent. Her private intensity—the energy that the sheer presence of this stranger at the piano was releasing in her—was sending currents across the crowded salon and into the guests.

After waiting around for years,
Hiding from myself in a cozy vale of tears,
I stayed home last night,
In my room all alone.
I waited it out without touching the phone,
And I pushed past my panic of no one at home—
I moved past myself to the world.

And I saw me and the people,
People with faces,
Personal places, things that they own.
They wait at the bus stops, batting at the haze,
And stare out their windows in the earthquake
of their days,
And I drink coffee in the morning,
Tea at noon,
Bourbon in the nighttime
to fight back the gloom.

After waiting around for years,
Hiding from myself in an endless trail of fears,
I stayed clear last night
in my bed all alone.
I waited it out without touching the phone,
and I pushed past the panic of no one at home—
I moved past myself to the world . . .

They loved her. The applause turned the tap further. She strode over to Leo, braver now. "I'm going to go with my stuff, just follow me." She could smell him when she leaned over, and the sensation—inhaling his clean, lemony maleness, the sea salt and sun, soap and cigarettes—filled her with moaning, lustful longing. The faucet was wide open now. She had nothing left to lose.

There are worse things than being alone . . .
Just to name two, there is being with you,
Or a party where no one is gay.
There are worse things than breakfast for one,
Or days without sun, you'll agree.

So though scared as I am
At having no plan
But dinner in bed and TV,
There are much worse things
Than phones that don't ring
Than being alone with me . . .

On it went. She could do no wrong. For the very first time in her life she was singing her own songs full out, not one snuck in between "Rain Drops Keep Falling on My Head" and "The Way We Were." Stealing the time as if the acts of her creativity were something stealthy, dirty, and shameful. They were always doing her a favor to let her sing one. She suddenly felt the full weight of her rage at all the years she had passively allowed this. Years of creating without having been able to express it. The anger opened with the other feelings, unleashed by the blasé, completely insouciant presence of this tall blond stranger. A fire-storm of frustration. It was part of the lust, for sure, but a more positive part. It was as if she were high, snorted up with dangerous, exotic chemicals. Flying on feelings she had never known she carried.

Women are strange,
I could say deranged,
Pretending they're weak
When they're strong.
They act out a part
from their head,
Not their heart,
Pretending that the creep
with whom they sleep
is a captor to
whom they belong.
It's a tripper,
the way those head games
they play
Just get hipper
the minute some dude
Hits that zipper . . .

He's a liar and a loser,
and an all-time woozy doozer,
He's a bully and a bastard,
I work and he gets plastered—
Six kids and no *dinero,*
Think I'd hand him his sombrero.

Ties me to a chair,
Messes up my hair,
It's so sick that I care about him,
And worse, I could easily do without him.

And someday when I am ready to face the world
without a home,
I'll pack up, I know I'll do it:
I'll just split and he can screw it . . .
All alone—
Momma's not at home!

The dogs are chasing birds
In the park these days, or haven't you heard
'Bout those crazy-headed dogs
Trying to fly,
Trying to catch some birds.

Hold me, hold me, baby,
Love me through the night
'Cause the whole world's gone crazy,
And I really need your love tonight.

They wouldn't let her go. Tiers of silver-domed winners, stomping and shouting for her. "Who is she?" they whispered, enraptured by her own current, pumping across the deck, fueling them all.

It all started lying in my bed
With a piercing migraine headache,
Wishing I was dead,

So I went into analysis
To relive my misspent youth . . .
At one hundred bucks an hour,
I went searching for the truth.

The doctor said he could cure me
with his psychic-sexual power
On his brand-new leather couch . . .
And he charged me for the hour.

Too many nights and too many fights,
Burgundy wine clouds my head,
Looks like the time has come
To pack up my dreams and run . . .

But when I loved you
And you loved me,
the two of us together
for the world to see . . .

When she was finished, she was dripping wet, her WRONG
T-shirt plastered against her little-girl chest. Tears ran down her
shining cheeks and she bowed, unable to turn to the man at the
piano who'd led the band. Finally they stopped applauding and
she recovered herself. She turned to Leo and claimed her stage.
"To the band!" she said. "Leo Lampi and the band." He took his
bow and bowed to her. "You play piano like a horn player," she
said.

He looked at her quizzically but with respect. "I left my horn
in California."

She laughed. "I know a guy who left his heart in San Francisco
—maybe you should call him."

The audience roared. They adored them. A fresh experience.
Wasn't life grand? Sitting in the sea air, drinking donated Chablis,
candles flickering, and these darling show folk giving their all,
delighted beyond delight for the chance to show their stuff for
such an élite and important group. Bravo!

Bee Bee took her final bow and made her way through the main salon and down the stairs. She was soaking wet and more excited than she had ever been before in her entire life, onstage or off. She closed the door to the tiny bathroom, grateful to have outrun Trudy and have a moment alone. She looked at her dripping face in the mirror.

Something else had happened to her out there. Something so outrageous that she could not meet her own eyes in the mirror. She had had one. The place that Manfred had worked so patiently to take her. All alone on the stage, in the rapture of these new sensations, she had come for the first time. The guy had never even kissed her. Street Soup, for sure.

Three A.M. Bee Bee is sitting at an empty table at the back of the club. She has changed into jeans and a fresh T-shirt. She is eating a club sandwich, drinking a lite beer and waiting for Trudy, Mikey, and Serena to join her. The club is still packed. A stocky little Cuban man, wearing a pink silk dinner jacket and elevator shoes, leads a very young woman with waist-length white-blond curls, a skintight white satin body suit covered by an ornate rhinestone-covered coat, her shapely body thrust forward on six-inch spiked heels, her pretty face buried under layers of makeup, past Bee Bee and onto the small, crowded dance floor, looking over his narrow shoulder to see who was watching her.

Bee Bee smiles and chews her dinner. She likes this time the best. All the tension of the day is over. The hours from the moment her eyes open midmorning until her final bow were filled with the knowledge that, at some point, she would have to go out there and perform. The anxiety of this daily fact never leaves her until this moment. Her makeup off, the deed done; she can disappear into the shadows, unwind, feel the release of good hard work and let go until tomorrow.

No one pays any attention to her now, out of costume, her inner spotlight off, and she can watch them; the watched watching the watchers. She likes to watch. If you look long enough, you start to see things more clearly. You start to figure people out.

Watching people dance was a real head opener. Only the Latins were an exception.

The Latins always seemed to be dancing, even when they were sitting down. They made the transition from private sidelines citizen to undulating exhibitionists with gliding grace. The hips swayed more lavishly, the soft ecstasy in their faces grew lusher, but there was always a careful control to it all, a sense of boundary. The Latins would no more throw themselves on the floor, bucking and twitching like some of the Americans did, or lift their dresses over their head, or begin shimmying and shaking in arrhythmic and inappropriate abandon, than be seen improperly dressed or without their dark glasses.

Everyone else was up for grabs. A middle-aged southern couple danced by. The man was wearing a red bandanna around his head and several heavy gold chains. He was a large, florid-faced southerner who had been to see the show before. His wife was a small, dowdy woman, circumspect and polite until she hit the dance floor where she jerked around, thrusting and stomping, looking to Bee Bee like a person just diagnosed with a severe case of crabs. Her husband jumped up and down as if he were trying to put out a fire with his feet.

According to Serena they were enormously rich. "Where you-all from?" Serena had asked them on their first visit.

"We're from Georgia, missy." The big man had grinned, downing his third double tequila.

"What do you-all do down there?" Serena had cooed, always looking for big spenders from new watering holes.

"We live off ma daddy's money, honey lamb." He replied, grinning like a Halloween pumpkin.

"Well, then, What does your *daddy* do?" Serena countered, not about to be upstaged.

"He lives off *his* daddy's money," said the Georgian, closing the conversation.

The music pulsed on. Last call on Saturday night coming up. The weekend peaking, no one eager for it to end or for bloody Sunday, with its various kinds of hangovers and routes back to reality, to begin.

Sunday was the beginning of Bee Bee's weekend. Sundays and Mondays, and Tuesdays too, off-season. But now she had her TV shows to tape, so only Sunday was left to really rest. She needed it. Now more than she ever had. Now it was not just a day of rest, but a time to recover. Often she stayed in her room, sleeping until she could no longer keep her eyes closed, then just lying there, looking out at the boats blowing back and forth in the canal. Trying to heal her hurt.

"I know he's bad, but when I get home and squat on his face, all my troubles are over." Two pretty, young black models at the next table were talking about men in that candid, bottom-line way that made Bee Bee blush but that she also envied, associating the verbal freedom with a more fluid and direct connection between the head and the heart.

"May your tongue rot and fall outta your mouth! That man is gonna mess your mind. My granny always said, 'Women are violins and men are drummers, and a good woman needs at least a bass player.' This motherfucker is a *bongo* man. He's gonna break your heart."

"You're just jealous. You've never been in love like this. I was hard and he melted me down. He gets me so hot, the walls sweat."

"That's all you'll get from that jive ass, you can count on it. A messed-up head and a bunch of peeling paint. He went with my cousin's roommate. That girl had *beard* burns on her inner thighs. The guy is an animal! He's not even at the top of the food chain, girl. Don't come knockin' on my door when he dumps you. All you're gonna have left are several contagious diseases. This ain't love. You're just in a feedin' frenzy. This is the clit talkin', honey, not the heart. I gotta get through to you!"

Bee Bee finished her beer. Where was a friend like that when she'd needed one? She motioned to José, the waiter, for another beer. Trudy, Mikey, and Serena were moving toward her. She was not looking forward to the next ten minutes. She wiped her mouth. What she had just thought wasn't true. They had all been there warning her. It had done no more good than the girlfriend at the next table was doing. It was painful to hear the feelings coming out, however crudely, from another woman's mouth. It was too familiar.

An overweight, overdressed Brazilian widow, who spent half the year at the Grand Bay Hotel, stopped Serena before she reached Bee Bee. Trudy and Mikey slid by, making a quick escape.

"Serena, dear. You've lost weight! How I envy you. The only diet that ever works for me is travel. I go to hideous countries and order the worst thing on the menu. In Salvador I lost a pound a day. Bliss! But it doesn't work in Italy. There isn't anything horrible on the menu in Italy."

Trudy turned to Bee Bee. "The upper crust. A bunch of crumbs held together with dough. Listen to that dame. Reminds me of my aunt Millie. Remember, Mikey? She went to India or some hellhole and she got sick. Real sick. The Indians, who *know* from sick, told her, 'Go home, lady. You're losin' weight, you need American medicine!' So she finally is well enough to get out of there, gets off the plane, half dead—a walking skeleton—and her bridge group is waiting to pick her up. 'You look great, you're so thin,' they tell her. Remember, Mikey? Poor Serena, that one starts, she never shuts up."

"The French are never wrong. Absolutely never wrong about anything. I should know, darling. I was married to several of them."

"Oh, brother." Trudy motioned to Serena, trying to give her a reason to end the chatter. Serena waved back helplessly.

Mikey, who almost never said anything, patted Bee Bee's arm, sensing her distance. "Penny for your thoughts, baby?" He smiled his sweet, spongy smile at her. Mikey looked to Bee Bee like one of those old Shmoo inflatables from *Li'l Abner.* She had one when she was little and she'd loved it. It was so agreeable, friendly, and accepting. No matter how many times she and her brothers bashed it in the face or straddled it or deflated it, it always forgave, smiling its wistful smile and absorbing whatever they threw at it. That was Mikey. It was impossible not to like him. It was also impossible to really know him.

"Actually I was thinking about lemon-filled doughnuts at Velvet Creme. The one on the Tamiami Trail? I think I could possibly eat ten of them." It was the truth, if not exactly the whole truth. She had been thinking about her after-show conversation with Willa Snow in New York City, and that led to thinking about the Tamiami Trail to the Everglades and the last trip she took with Leo—the doughnuts had followed.

Now she had two entirely new people in her life: Willa Snow and Lindy Lampi. Two women with children. Children fathered by her husband! Women and children she had never heard of, whose existence was no more real to her than that of any other invisible member of the universe, until yesterday morning, waiting to tape her show, when the national news bites were being fed into her monitor and the anguished, tired face of a woman had appeared. A woman with Leo's last name, pleading for help. It was devastating, impossible to absorb. Two phantom wives and children, whose existence had slipped his mind.

It had filled her with terror. If all she really had in the end was her own judgment, what Manfred had taught her about listening for the right voice, and she had been this deaf, had chosen this badly, then how could she ever trust any decision, or any other person ever again?

Shame flooded her. Now she would have to tell Serena and the Dales. She would have to tell them because Lindy Lampi and Willa Snow were coming to see her and if there was any way that she could help them, she was going with them. A child's life was at stake. It could have been her child. She swallowed.

It was as if each of them had a piece of a puzzle that Leo had left, but no one had anything close to the whole picture. The wild thing was that *she* had known about his *first* wife. Lindy and Willa had never even heard of her! When Willa said, "You're number three," Bee Bee realized that they knew nothing about Corrine!

"Corrine?" Willa Snow had almost screamed. My God, what a ship of fools they were. But one thing she knew. They were shipmates. They were all discards, flotsam and unfastened square knots from Leo's sea chest.

She was going to help them find him. Part of it too was that she wanted to take another look, the way she watched the nightclubbers, trying to see more clearly. She needed to figure out what had happened to her so that she could find the courage to go on with her life.

CHAPTER 4

Love Is Always Having to Say You're Sorry

MGM GRAND AIR IS AN AIRLINE THAT COULD ONLY have been created by Hollywood. It served a purpose, filling a gap left by the limitations of commercial first class and private jets. First class was now filled with frequent flyers and holders of bonus-mileage coupons, engineers and accountants on company payrolls; thus the quality of service, the people-watching, and the possible deal-making had gone steadily downhill.

The trouble with private jets was that no one saw you. The chance encounter with a possible investor in your next film project was nil. It was often more stimulating to board the Magic Kingdom air palace, sliding into your leather-cushioned swivel seat, nodding to the overly solicitous steward that it was time for your large bottle of iceless Evian, setting up your laptop, signaling for the delivery of your air phone, and surrendering to the anticipation of exciting possibilities epitomized by the other illustrious passengers filling the surrounding seats.

Not that the flyers of MGM were frivolous. This was not a Surf 'n' Turf, champagne and tenderloin group. These were motion-picture and television-industry executives. They did not fly for fun. They did not do *anything* for fun. Fun was for losers, not for bicoastal movie execs, their Pierre Deux and Vuitton carryons crammed with scripts, their ostrich-covered Filofaxes engorged with important memos, phone numbers, and an endless vertical

database of power-meal appointments. What went on aboard the
L.A.-to-NYC flight was serious business.

Not one of them would be caught dead napping, eating, reading Danielle Steel or *Vanity Fair,* stirring a spicy-hot Stoly
Bloody Mary with a perfectly chilled celery stick. God forbid.
They were above the temptations of ordinary travelers, people
who thought that if you were paying big bucks for free booze
and hand-tossed salad, well, shit, man, get your money's worth!

These were California-brained and -trained entertainment
moguls, who no longer had any room for or need of just being
alive. The business of deal-making had clogged their hearts with
as much plaque as four tons of caviar eggs (which they would
never touch—at least not in public). They were the epitome of
what some wise social commentator called "the new generation of
pleasure anorectics." They would most likely make a lousy crash
or hijack group, not easily relinquishing the business at hand.

"I don't give a fuck what your cause is, Abdul, you can't just
take my *phone*! I'm waiting for Eisner to give me a Go."

"I'm dreadfully sorry, Mohammad, but I simply can't sit on a
plane with unrecirculated air. It causes a build-up of free-floating
radicals, and I don't have my deoxidizing megavitamin packs with
me. You'll have to work this out some other way."

"Listen, I know this isn't the best time, but before you kill the
next hostage, I'd like to talk miniseries with you. I have a deal
memo—standard form in my briefcase. Pal, I don't want to be
crude, but think about it. I mean, in the next few hours of terror,
think concept, okay? I can get you high fives, maybe low sixes,
depending on how much shit goes down."

This was not Lindy's group. But the ticket was Wheezie's go-
ing-home present and so there she was, waiting in the trendy,
uptight private lounge for her flight home.

"Well, I know everyone in Marin is buying llamas, but it's just
about played out and I really don't think they make very good
pets for children. They can be quite temperamental and they ruin
the foliage. We're really very high on the Vietnamese miniature
pigs. They are to die, adorable! Just the cutest little things and
smarter than dogs or cats! If you can still find one (the Europeans
are snapping them up). They cost about five thou and they use a
little box to do their business, just like kitties!"

"I'm not wearing my Rolex anymore. I put it in the safe. I'm wearing a cheap copy. I just heard the third story this month of someone getting killed or beaten for their watch. One man was wearing that forty-five-thousand-dollar gold one, the limited edition? Well, you can see why he resisted. The maniac had a chain saw and he just cut off his whole hand to get it! It isn't worth that. I'd wear a Timex first."

Oh, God, was she ready to go home! It had taken them three days to settle the sale of the jewels and get the bank draft. Tess had been released and her mother was already there. Maxie had already been tested and was not a match. Lindy had known he wouldn't be—she didn't know how, but she had. Funny, how her instincts were so strong. She had been gone for five days and it seemed like five years. The pain of leaving Tess was so engulfing that she had to physically shut herself off, or she couldn't have functioned at all. Willa had been handling things terrifically, and if Lindy weren't so exhausted and so grateful, she probably would have been jealous.

Alice, her mother, her mother's housemaid Glenny, Maxie, Willa, and Tess; an instant Brady bunch, clicking along just fine without her. How bizarre life was. An external fun house crammed with breakaway floors and distorted mirrors, always waiting to throw you off, confuse, startle, and challenge your inner resources. There was always one more mummy in the linen closet.

They called the flight and she fell into line behind a movie producer wearing a Sergeant Pepper–style, gold epaulet–braided jacket and tiny round eyeglasses, whom she recognized from some interview show. L.A. was full of women like this. Young producers with development deals at one studio or another. Their qualifications seemed to be based mainly on a combination of being thin and from the East Coast Ivy League, running five miles a day, drinking legendary quantities of still mineral water, and having a husband who ran a studio, was a leading actor in a hit series, or both. (Of course, if the lady was fortunate enough to achieve the husband first, she could forgo the other qualifications.)

A glossy middle-aged couple wearing matching Rolex watches and bright blue jogging suits came up beside her. Lindy toyed with the idea of warning them about the Rolex chain-saw maniac but thought better of it. For all she knew, that could be where they had gotten the watches (at a steal) in the first place.

God, she was cynical. Even the Wheezie Week, as she was now calling it, hadn't tempered her pessimism. She settled into her swivel, grateful that she had been able to book a single and did not have to sit in one of the highly desirable private compartments, where the deal-makers could wheel in secrecy. For an outsider it would be like spending five hours under the table at a *Bund* meeting.

She sat back and closed her eyes. Wheezie. Who would have ever thought, in a hundred million years, that the best sex she had ever had in her semisordid, promiscuous little life would be with Wheezie Springer! Better than Leo, she had told him that first night, making his friendly face flush with bashful glee.

It was true. And it could not have come at a nicer time, helping to neutralize the blow of admitting she still loved the creep. She and Wheezie had fastened their easy, sibling friendship one notch tighter and found passion. Where it went next was certainly up in the air, and she had been brutally honest with him about that, but she knew that neither of them would ever regret it. In a way, it might allow him to let go of her finally and find someone else. Someone better, she thought, tears filling her eyes. Why was that always the way she thought of herself?

For so many years of her early life Lindy had thought that this hunger—this fuzzy, restless, aching place inside her—was her fault. She must be unlovable. No one could blame her parents, housekeepers, teachers, or peers for making fun of her, ignoring her, not paying her any mind. She was unlovable. Homely, lonely, a mean, lying, nasty little girl.

Now she had a broader view. The unloving had started before she was any of those things. It had started before she was even born. Therefore—even a child could see—it could not have really been her fault. It wasn't even personal. In the midst of being so cool and objective about this thing, she realized that if it hadn't been for Anabelle, one person whose heart she had really touched, she might have ended up in much worse shape.

How she had ended up was sardonic. It was the legacy of the improperly loved. She no longer really believed in the better nature of her fellow beings, or in the possibility of one true love. So much of love depended on need, physical appeal, and convenience. She shuddered. Cynical, even for her.

But probably true nonetheless. We all railed on, beat our breasts about how we loved this one or that one, and could not imagine life without them. The pure fact was that some people lost everyone and still managed to live on, putting nonchlorine bleach in the washer and not forgetting the egg shells in the coffeepots. That was the way it was: Holocaust survivors going to the dry cleaners and paying the rent like everyone else.

Who really ever even knew anyone? We were all strangers in the end, cursed by the first person singular, the five-finger exercise that played the scales inside our famished heads. The closest Lindy had ever come to real intimacy had been with her child. And it had taken the Lewd Comedian to push them forward to that level of bonding. Much too high a tab, thank you anyway, Dr. Freud, Mr. God, or whoever was in charge of relationships up there.

Now that she had lost her illusions about other people, lovers, friends, even children, she actually felt more hopeful. Maybe now at least she had a chance of forming relationships based on the limitations that went with being a person, rather than on the neurotic, deprived child's yearning, the palpating need for mother love.

Either way at least she was better protected. The wound inside was not healed—let us not give psychotherapy more than its due. But at least now she had covered it with a proper shield; it was shrouded and not so raw, apparent, and open to infection. At least it didn't hurt all the time. The fact was that she had not found a whole lot to admire in human nature. People were not so great. Most of the time she was ashamed to be a person herself.

God knows, she did not want to feel like this. She wanted to be one of those cheerful, chirpy, New Age—positive beige sort of women, always seeing the best in everyone. One of the get-lemons make-lemonade types who were active in political causes and really believed that tying up their newspapers and J. Crew catalogs with twine and putting them out in their morally superior recycling pile, would change something. *Puh-leese!*

It was harder and harder to take any of that stuff seriously.

But what did that mean for Tess? She did not want to pass this dour, negative view of the future on to her child, who, God only knew, needed every single solitary ounce of positive vibration to face what might lie ahead. She knew that, no matter what she said, if this was how she truly felt, Tess would pick it up. The very idea horrified her. It was the most selfish kind of loving, then, wanting Tess to live, because her own life would be so empty and futile without her. She had to find the hope inside herself, if she was to give it to her baby. She just had to.

Somehow it all came back to finding Leo. He was her quest, her Grail. She would not be good old patient Penelope, she would be Odysseus; she would move out of her own frozen existential end zone and reach for something hopeful. She needed to believe in something miraculous. This journey seemed to be as close to changing wine into water as she was likely to come upon in her immediate future.

They were all waiting for her when she arrived, except Alice who was out filling some prescriptions. She dropped her bag and headed straight for Tess without even really saying hello (a slight that she knew her mother would make her pay for later). She was lying in the shaded afternoon light, sleeping. Lindy closed the door softly and stood watching her, not wanting to wake her but needing to make contact, to reassure herself that Tess was okay. Tears slid down her cheeks.

When she was with her every day, she was less aware of the changes. Now she could see the dark circles, the bony edges of her face where there had been adolescent fullness. Her hair was bound in layers of tight Ace bandaging, which somehow helped keep down the hair loss, or so they thought this week—the theories changed continuously. She was much weaker. Lindy could see that even while she slept.

She moved closer, wanting to hear her breathing. How beautiful she was. Despite her own disillusion she realized, standing over her, that it was unbearable to think that if Tess did not get well, she would never know what it was to be in love—would never experience the first moment of being a woman with a man, of being touched. She would never be made love to, see love in the eyes of a man, hear the words "I love you, Tess. You're so beautiful," words every little girl dreamed of, carrying the fairy fantasy forward until the moment it became real.

Maybe it was just silly and old-fashioned, but she had never heard any woman wish for her daughter; "I long for her to be a state senator and fly her own plane." Mothers still wished, no matter how unrealized their own girlish dreams, for their daughters to be well loved. It was not tolerable for Tess to end up with less than she had. Tess was supposed to have more. There was no other acceptable resolution.

Tess smiled in her sleep and opened her eyes. Lindy wiped her face, not wanting her to see the tears. "Momma!"

Lindy tiptoed over and lay down on the pink-sheeted brass bed beside Tess, taking her in her arms and holding her the way she hoped, someday, a man who adored her would hold her, tenderly and totally. "I missed you so much, baby, I couldn't even eat ice cream."

Tess giggled, sinking into her arms, all the struggle of pubescent child gone, embracing mother love without fear or rebellion. "Wow, that's really serious. I had ice cream every day."

Lindy kissed her cheek, sniffing in the sweet, sickly smells that were now Tess. "Yeah, for about fifteen minutes."

Tess laughed. "Yeah, right. Barf City. I'm better now. They've been trying some new drug on me, and it really helps the nausea. Gramma Alice got it for me. She is totally crazy, Momma. I love her! She told us the funniest story. She comes from this really weird Italian family. And all her cousins and aunts lived with her mother who spent, like, her entire life in the kitchen, cooking for all of them. Well, finally, last year her mother died, I mean she was ancient! Alice was really sick and everyone in the family is pretty decrepit, but they all managed to get to the funeral, and her one cousin who has, like, no life, she starts crying and screaming and carrying on. Then they lowered the casket into the ground and this woman just freaks. She dives onto the coffin and rides it down, sobbing and screaming all the way, 'No more ravioli! No more ravioli!' Isn't that a riot!"

"I think it's one of those you-had-to-be-there stories." Lindy held her tighter, not wanting Tess to see how much the macabre anecdote had upset her. "I thought she was an Indian."

"Just a little. All the rest is Italian." Tess pulled away slightly.

"You didn't laugh because it was about someone dying. I'm sorry, Momma. I made you sad."

"Tessie. No! No! I'm just tired and I'm so glad to see you." She paused, trying to change the subject. "Uncle Wheezie sent you something in a very fancy little box, from Tiffany's, no less. He's going to come see you when Willa and I go." She tried to swallow. Her throat felt like it was stuffed with mashed potatoes.

"Willa said you found another wife in Miami."

"Yep. We're thinking of starting a Girl Scout troop."

"Momma. You are so warped." They held each other, finding their way back together.

"Maxie's a little gorgeous, wouldn't you say, Tessie?"

"Totally! I mean, if you have to have a mystery brother, he's not bad. He's really sweet too. He makes me the best tuna-fish sandwiches and he brings me breakfast in bed. Some concoction he calls Maxie's famous scrambled eggs. He doesn't beat them up, he just tosses the whole thing in the pan with butter and then mushes them all around. They're great! Willa says he's been making them since he was six. One morning on Mother's Day he appeared in her room with this tray. 'Have some of Maxie's famous scrambled eggs,' he said. He could hardly reach the stove. Isn't that really darling! Momma, it's been great. I mean, too bad we had to meet like this, but better than not at all."

Lindy stroked her forehead, thinking of all the wasted years. She could no longer even remember why any of it had happened. That Leo would have loomed so large that she had sacrificed Willa and Maxie to a ghost rider—a man whose exact features she could barely remember. God, the vanity, the insanity of romance.

"Okay, one more to go. How was your grandmother Segal reunion?"

Tess turned toward her and kissed her. Lindy smiled. "That bad?"

"No. I mean, she's been very nice to me. Well, *nice* really isn't the word for it. I don't know how to describe it. I've never met anyone like her before. I mean, she acts like some kind of royalty or something. She just orders everyone around. Not Gramma Alice though. Oh, Momma, you would have loved this. One night she storms in here and says to Gramma Alice, 'Is that disgusting pot of vile-smelling substances on the stove for my granddaughter? Don't you *dare* feed her one bit of that!' Well, it was this really yummy Italian stew thing, called osso something . . ."

"Buco."

"Right. Osso buco. I loved it. I mean, you know how the chemo is—nothing tastes good. So Gramma Alice had made this stuff and she said, 'Kiddo, even throwing up, you'll love it,' and Grandmother Segal just lays it on her and I got upset. I mean, it's my grandmother, but Gramma Alice is my friend, and I got scared she would quit and Willa wasn't here! So Gramma Alice, she just puts her hands on her hips that way she does and she walks right up close to Grandmother Segal and she says, 'Listen up, toots . . .'"

Lindy gasped. "She called her *toots*?"

"Uh-huh. She says, 'Listen up, toots. This here is my responsibility. Nobody's makin' *you* eat it and Tessie loves it.' I was totally speechless!"

"What happened then?" Lindy loved listening to Tess, bubbling with her old energy, caught up in the excitement of all these new people in her life.

"Nothing! I mean, Grandmother Segal just turned around and left with her nose in the air. Gramma Alice did a great impersonation of her later. You know the way she kind of struts with one hand on her hip like Mae West or Bette Davis in those old movies? She never said another word. She's been trying. She bought me all of these really beautiful clothes. I just feel bad for you. I mean, I'm glad she wasn't *my* mother. She must have made you really unhappy. I guess I'm old enough now to see stuff like that."

Lindy hugged her tight. "You're the best, baby. I guess I'd better go out there and greet her. I was fairly abrupt on the way in. I'll be back in a little while. Can I get you anything?"

"I'm fine. Just hand me the remote. I'll watch TV."

Lindy handed it to her, fluffing her blankets and making herself leave Tess to greet her own long-lost mother. "May the osso buco be with you."

Tess laughed and hit the remote.

Maxie was waiting outside the door, carrying two glasses on a tray. "Aunt Lindy, is she awake?"

It was hard to look at him. He was so much like Leo. Smaller and not as jagged, but certainly his son. "Yes, Maxie, it's so good to have you here. How about a hug? Last time I saw you I had to bend over—now you'll have to." He juggled the tray, hugging her with one arm. "It's really good to be here. Can I go in?"

"Absolutely."

He let her go and moved past her into the quiet room, carrying two large glasses of Glenny's fresh orange juice and sat down beside Tess. She was watching one of the cable-channel religious programs. A fundamentalist preacher, with a pompadour that looked as if a silver foxtail had landed on his head and at least three rows of chalk-white teeth, was offering his flock a "miracle update":

> *Jesus said, "Come unto me" . . . I just sensed the presence of God—reaching out now. On this very broadcast He's going to bear witness. This is your day, my child, to be delivered . . . to be set free. Today God is going to break the yoke of hardship, praise the Lord!*
>
> *There's nothing more exciting than knowing that God is a person. He's your friend . . . He needs you to show that you trust Him with what belongs to you. Do you trust Him with a thousand dollars . . . five hundred dollars? Have you ever noticed how your faith increases after you have given?*
>
> *The owner of a failing yogurt shop in Alabama with a lump in her breast . . . she doubled her pledge and she was healed! I have a letter from the owner of that yogurt shop, "I just knew if we gave the five hundred dollars . . ." the owner writes. "The Holy Spirit even instructed us on what the name should be—Super Natural Yogurt." Just as I have taken those lumps out of uh, uh, uh, Jackie's breasts, you need to give a gift to God that's valuable to you. I know some of you don't have much, for some it's one hundred dollars . . . for some it's five hundred . . . one thousand. But I sayeth, the Lord has the power to make your business prosper—your yogurt business, whatever. I hear someone . . . you have trouble in*

your life. You need to make a pledge of one thousand dollars. If you do it, you will see a change! Hallelujah!

Maxie groaned. "You like that mind milk?"

Tess flushed. She didn't want him to think she was a flake. "It is funny. Though, I must admit, since I've been sick—I know it sounds dorky, but sometimes I wonder if maybe it could be true. I mean, about praying and miracles and stuff."

He felt ashamed of himself. He wanted to be able to do something for her, and he couldn't even seem to say anything right. "I'm really sorry about my test. I wanted it to be me helping you." He felt his voice closing. He didn't want her to see him cry. It would only make her feel worse.

She smiled at him. It was such a nice thing to say. "Don't feel bad, Maxie. I'm kind of relieved actually. It's supposed to be a really painful procedure."

They looked at each other. Their relationship was so new, neither of them was sure how to conduct it.

He cleared his throat, calming himself down. "Do you think about him much?"

"Who? Leo? Not much. More now. I mean, I was barely two! Do you? I mean, you really knew him. What was he like?"

Maxie shrugged. "He was like some big-screen dad. Sort of larger than life. He took me sailing. Skiing. He taught me how to play tennis and golf. We went to the park and played ball. He taught me how to shoot baskets. We went fishing. All that boy-and-his-dog kind of stuff."

"It sounds great."

"Yeah, great. Until one day he went away and I never heard a word—not one single word—from him ever again. I mean, he *knew* me. I was a real person, not a baby. He just disappeared."

"I guess some men just can't handle being fathers. That's what my mother says. He just couldn't take the responsibility." She wanted to make Max feel better, but she wasn't sure how to go about it. She really knew very little about boys, even the ones her own age. "Don't you think it's kind of weird that both of our mothers lost it for him. I mean, they are so different!"

"Boy, you're right about that. I mean, my mother is so level-headed and serious. She analyzes everything. We love to travel, right? So she's always sending away for guidebooks to exotic places that we want to go to someday. Well, when she gets one, the very first thing she turns to, even if it's somewhere like Tahiti, she always turns to the Practical Information section."

Tess giggled. "My mom would head right for Shopping, Eating, and Night Spots."

"Exactly. But Leo pressed both their buttons. Grown-ups are so twisted."

"I guess," Tess said, zapping the preacher and replacing Jesus with a *Cagney and Lacey* rerun. "But they're all we've got."

"Tea, Glenny, and bring in some of those sugar cookies you made yesterday and the brownies." Vilma Segal motioned for Lindy and Willa to sit on the sofa, taking her rightful place in Lindy's one good chair, Empress Eugenia interviewing day help.

They sat docilely, the clock ticking backward to North Beverly Drive, 1957. Two guilty kids in the fading afternoon light, side by side on the Segals' herringbone-tweed sofa, still sweaty from their daily *American Bandstand* workout, waiting for Vilma to hold her inquisition about one suspected sin or another. Willa, terrified, hoping she would be able to hold up under questioning, pass the eye-contact lie test and not sacrifice Lucinda to her mother's wrath.

"For a sick, fatherless child, your daughter is quite wonderful." Vilma crossed her still shapely, if somewhat bandier, long legs. Lindy noted that she had not surrendered her black silk stockings and spike heels.

"Thank you, Mother." She was determined not to react defensively, which was what her mother always expected. "You're looking very well. Really, you haven't changed a bit."

Vilma gave her version of a smile. "Thank you, dear. In the end, self-discipline is its own reward. Everything else lets you down. A lesson you young people had better learn."

Willa moved her hand over and pinched Lindy's thigh.

Glenny appeared. A sweet-faced, caramel-colored girl, shyly keeping her face lowered over the tray.

Willa stood up. "Here, let me help you."

Vilma shot her a look so burning, it would have sent Smokey the Bear running for his water pail. "Sit! Glenny can do it."

Glenny, so nervous now that her face was almost in the plate, lowered the tray and practically ran from the room.

Willa and Lindy slid their hands together, hanging on to their spirits and using all the accumulated years of dealing with authority figures for additional support. She could be one hundred and twelve and we could be eighty and it would still be like this, Willa thought, squeezing Lindy's fingers.

"Katharine, it's obvious that you have never had help. In fact, your poor dear mother *was* the help. I realize it's not your fault you don't know how to treat them, but you have been watching me now for several days. You cannot do *that*! It only confuses her. Now, do have some tea and let's talk."

Willa and Lindy did as they were told. The tea was hot and strong and the cookies so moist and buttery and oozing with vanilla and the brownies so chocolatey-rich and crunchy with walnuts, that for a moment, it was all okay. It was okay to be chastised as if they were children, regressed and diminished, patronized and bullied in the way of mothers of the old school.

At least here they knew what was expected of them. Someone formidable was in charge, setting the rules of the game in clear, broad letters on the invisible blackboard of their confusion. Someone in charge with absolutely no ambivalence at all about the role of responsible adult. A superparent willing to go all the way out on the spiny limb of decision-making, immune to self-doubt, angst, or a need to be fair to those smaller or in their care.

A parent who felt no need to be anything but, who never looked back, regretted any decree or action, and thus had no sliver of hesitancy toward the task of speaking out as freely as possible without fear of damaging, insulting, enraging, or horrifying the listener. If the listener was her child, she was most certainly not entitled to any of the aforementioned emotions. The parent was the parent, after all.

They munched, forgetting diets and nutrition awareness. The sweets held whatever comfort was left from their memories of North Beverly Drive. They tasted the same. The recipes were Mrs. Segal's own and she was quite fanatical about their continuation from housekeeper to housekeeper. Preparing them exactly right had always been of great importance.

Lindy held in her senses all the tastes of her mother's table.

There was a wonderful lemony salad dressing that she could summon up at will, the memory of a taste so friendly and comforting, so long lost, so mourned. A pot roast like no other, with browned potatoes that crunched on the outside, then melted in the middle, filling her mouth with joy.

Since Willa had spent so many years of meals at the Segals', they shared these memories, and they both felt the piercing loss and the seductive warmth of the cookie caresses and the brownie hugs.

Maybe this was enough. Maybe what Vilma had brought with her was all the mother memory anyone needed. Someone in charge who still got the cookies right. Someone still present to define them for themselves. It couldn't be so bad; they couldn't be so old, lost, frightened, unfocused, if a mother was present to tell them their seams were crooked, their hair was in their eyes, and they had forgotten for the one thousandth time to close the back gate when they went out.

A mother to inquire as to their plans for the afternoon, the condition of their fingernails, their homework, the thank-you note to the neighbor for the birthday present. If they were still sitting in silent, submissive unease, munching their cookies and brushing the crumbs before such a presence, then everything must still be okay—safe and linear and correctable. They could always run back and close the gate.

They sat in the ebbing light before the inquisitor, Lindy as always, doing the talking, saying what she wanted her mother to hear, then waiting for the chastisement, moving ever so subtly to the left or right of the jab, patiently continuing on the long, desolate path to completion.

She was paying for the sugary sweets, and it seemed to her, listening to herself while she told her mother about Bee Bee Day and their departure in the morning for Miami . . . told her that Gerrold and Wheezie and the Springers were fine and their plans were uncertain; that what she was giving her daughter by bringing her mother back into their lives was what she had secretly wanted for herself. A chance to go home again, to sink into the safety of any mother at all who was willing to take charge for just a little while.

Tess would not get approval or kindness or affection from her grandmother but she had that from her; what she would get was someone whose way of loving involved freshly baked treats, daily fresh linens, serious attention to hygiene, manners, rituals, and the sense of child safety that such form brought with it.

It was not her style. Tess was used to "There's a five on the dresser, baby, get a bagel on the way, I *cannot* get up yet" and endless cartons of Chinese take-out. Maybe they both needed this kind of a mother now, even though the very thought sent shivers of horror up Lindy's back. Somehow she was swallowing all of this, because her mother represented something her baby needed that she herself had not provided, even when she was there. It was an amend she was making.

She wanted to tell her mother this because it held a part of her love that Vilma could accept. It had been, Lindy realized, the only way her mother knew how to express her love. She wanted to tell her, but she did not know how and so she prattled on, relaying as delicately as possible the sordid details of their safari into the un-mapped jungles of Lampiland.

"Well." Vilma sighed dramatically. "I can't pretend to approve or understand. The very thought of your father behaving in such a way is beyond comprehension, but I do see that it is probably your only choice. We will be just fine here.

"Maxie is a fine young man, Willa, and even that perfectly dreadful old woman, who seems to have dragged herself in from some street gang, is very thorough with Tess. I loathe her, but if there is one thing I know, it's good medical help. So I'll just have to overlook her incredible coarseness, not to mention the rude-ness and the inedible slop she cooks. One thing about running a major company for thirty-odd years—you learn how to get along with all make of man."

Vilma stood up, looming over them as if waiting for them to fall to their knees and kiss her enormous emerald ring. "Better have your showers, girls, it's almost cocktail time and those cook-ies have probably spoiled your appetites. We're having pot roast" —she paused, looking into Lindy's eyes for the first time—"and butter lettuce salad with that lemon dressing you always liked."

It might have been her own exhaustion or the fact that her contacts were dried out from the flight, but for a second Lindy thought she saw tears in her mother's eyes.

"Oh, Mother, my favorites! Thanks."

Vilma stiffened as if Lindy had leapt into her arms and smothered her with kisses. "Well. I just hope you have room left after all that sugar." She turned, mannequin-style, and strutted off to dress for dinner, as she had every night of her adult life.

Willa and Lindy collapsed into each other's arms. "Some things never change," Willa said, giggling into Lindy's neck.

Lindy whispered into her ear. "Remember how we used to eat a whole tray of brownies and then stick our fingers down our throats so she wouldn't yell at us for not eating dinner?" Lindy pulled back. "I just realized something. Where did she go? Where are you sleeping? We've only got two bedrooms."

Willa pointed toward the front door. "Your mother rented the apartment across the hall. The owner's in Paris for three months. She got it for practically nothing. I think the broker was completely undone by her. It's huge—*four* bedrooms, so we've all been living in style."

Lindy laughed and picked up her suitcase. "Well, let's use my room, she'll never hear us in there. We've got a lot to talk about before tomorrow. I want to hear every single thing, no matter how trivial. You deserve a medal for valor, dear friend."

Willa followed her. "Oh, one thing, not so trivial, but I can't wait any longer to tell you. Bee Bee told me there's another *wife*. She's in Washington. Her name is Corrine Brandmore. He was married to her before any of us. That makes four so far."

Lindy stopped dead. She turned around slowly, all the color gone from her face. "God, Wills. We are talking Henry the Eighth here. I do not fucking believe this. He never said a word!"

"Not to me either."

Lindy took a long deep breath. "Well, on the positive side, since I'm now questing for healthy, plump marrow, maybe there's another offspring."

"Bee Bee said no, honey. But I think we should go see her."

"Grand. A spouse quartet."

They tiptoed down the hall into Lindy's room, shadowed by their girl-selves, sneaking off to tell secrets, have a smoke, shave their legs, curl their hair, empty their stomachs, or whatever other necessary and forbidden outlet was now required.

* * *

Many months later Willa would look back on the dinner they all had together that night, wondering what they might have done differently if they had known the future. Sometimes thinking about it was too hard, but at other times she could relive it and experience from a distance some of the magnetism of that meal. If it was a Last Supper of its kind, it was a helluva feast and they had all embraced it with full, if overburdened, hearts.

Glenny and Vilma had outdone themselves. The meal held all the frustrated energy of a woman who had stopped being useful and whose pride had prevented her from finding her way back to the only people she had left, to be useful to.

It was also, possibly, Vilma's last opportunity to show off. The combination of reasons brought out the best in the grand old dame, the Queen of California Sportswear, the Women's-wear Wartime Wonder. She had been relegated to the wings for far too long, and she knew this was a last chance to vamp down the runway.

Everything at the table of the ornately decorated rental apartment was perfect. Candles glowed, fresh-cut roses filled vases all over the living and dining rooms, Mozart sonatas played softly in the background.

In addition to Glenny, she had hired a pale, nervous young waiter. When Lindy, Willa, Maxie, and Tess crossed the hall (Tess insisting that she was strong enough, even though Maxie was really holding her up), they were greeted by a slightly frenetic man in a black tuxedo who showed them into the parlor and took their drink orders as if it were the bar of the Carlyle Hotel. Tess and Maxie were impressed enough to forgo their usual teen insouciance, sitting up too straight and speaking in carefully modulated and complete English sentences.

Willa and Lindy, who had the insiders' advantage of having dined Segal-style before, had dressed properly and looked calm and serene, the result of hot showers, several bouts of hysterics, a good long cry, a sawed-in-half Valium, and a sweet, quiet talk with Tess and Maxie.

When they were all settled in, glasses in hand, mouths full of tiny caviar-filled blinis, Vilma made her entrance.

Willa had to hand it to the old broad—she really knew how to enter a room. She was covered in ropes of pearls and yards of black lace, her wrists wrapped with diamonds, her Prince Valiant bob lacquered to her head, a red silk handkerchief dramatically held in two silver-taloned fingers. The heels on her black satin pumps were so high that Willa or Lindy would have spent two days in traction just from walking across the room, but she sauntered down the hall as comfortably as if she were wearing Nikes.

It touched Willa to see her. In many ways she had known Vilma Linowitz (Lady Macbeth) Segal better than her own mother. She had practically lived at Lucinda's house from her sixth year until her seventeenth, and the fact was that those years still held more reality for her than any of the years of her womanhood. Her character had been formed there, her doubts and demons had been born, and her values shaped by what she saw and how she felt about what she saw.

Lily Miller Snow, her own mother, was still so opaque. Whenever she thought of her, even when she was with her, Willa's impulse was always to reach out and brush away the cobwebs; focus the blurry, overexposed film that had always kept her from really seeing her mother.

It was not that her mother had been unavailable. She had no social life and she was always home, wandering around in her robe and mules, her hair pinned up, some rejuvenating cream or other on her face, slightly dreamy, sometimes groggy with the aftereffects of sleeping pills, nerve pills, or whiskey-sour pills.

Her mother had the manner of one of those women in B movie melodramas; unlucky in love, fallen below her expectations, and too disappointed to do much about it. Her mother's life had stopped with her husband's death. Everything since then had been conducted in slow motion, as if she were waiting for the handsome Prince to return from the crash and rescue her from her fate.

Willa sometimes thought that her mother had refused to finish mourning, because if she did, it would really be over; he would really be dead and she would really be responsible for herself and her daughter. She had chosen instead to wander, a wounded widow in the wind, a specter in her own life; waiting to be saved.

From Willa she needed continual reassurance and frequent phone calls and not much else. She was too preoccupied with her own desolation, vanity, and the effort to part the internal fog long enough to perform the services required by the Mitchells.

Luckily these services were never too demanding. What the Mitchells seemed to need more than anything else from Willa and her mother, was the psychic comfort of younger people in their orbit. A child's laughter, a pretty woman's smiling face at dinner, someone to walk with and play bridge with.

Willa often wondered what on earth would have happened to them if it hadn't been for the Mitchells. They provided the cushion that allowed her mother to function, but it also kept her mother from facing herself and so she was never real to her. A mother of "That's nice, dear" and "Ummmmm," not able to ever really experience Willa as a separate being.

Even now she could not think of one original thought, idea, hobby, favorite song, special activity, or ritual that identified her mother for her. Her mother never hit, rarely scolded, and had left her alone to practice her barré exercises, spend every minute with Lucinda and Wheezie, read her brains out, write her poetry, do whatever she wanted.

Of course, there was little risk in this. She had been as dependable, studious, and well-behaved a child as ever drew breath. Whether these traits developed out of an instinct for self-protection—if no one is going to see to you, guide you, or tell you, you had better figure out how to do it by yourself—or was the by-product of her mother's benign neglect, she could not be sure.

What she had gotten from her mother was freedom and permission to develop and explore herself and her passions without interference. She was not rebellious like Lucinda, because she had had nothing to rebel against. There would have been no reason for fingernail or homework inspection. One was always clean and the other was always done.

Willa once told Lindy that she must have saved all of her bad-girl stamps until Leo. After all those quiet, virginal, good-as-gold years, she had lost her mind for a man as dangerous for her as the Hillside Strangler. Even then there was no one to stop her.

Her mother had smiled dreamily, kissed her forehead, and said, "He's such a good-looking fellow, almost as handsome as your father."

Lindy thought that Willa's mother had sounded relieved because she knew that Willa was not getting a better shot at happiness than she herself had had. It hurt Willa to think that about her own mother. If it was true, it was like never having been loved at all. But whatever the reason, no one intervened.

As she watched Mrs. Segal glide across the room, she knew what she had gotten from her that her own mother had not been able to provide: a vivid female force, a role model, even one to rebel against.

Whatever Mrs. Segal's limitations, she was a presence; she was not fey, veiled, or cloudy. And so on this surreal and special night, a night that she would never forget, when they were all gathered there, pilgrims before the progress, Willa felt grateful to this complex, arrogant, and difficult woman. Out of her own narcissism, but also out of her concern, she had created this banquet and granted them an opportunity to laugh, partake, and prepare one another for a journey from which some of them might not return.

"Don't you think it's interesting that in commercial fiction the female characters are always enormously successful, but in serious fiction the women are all housewives, spinsters, working in low-paying dead-end jobs, or under the thumb of convention in some way?" Lindy was working on her third helping of pot roast.

Willa nodded. "Absolutely. No one sees rich or successful people as empathetic. Especially women. They don't even see one another that way.

"It also reflects our own prejudices and illusions. If life is not mean, simple, and thwarted, it isn't serious. These characters also become raging stereotypes, but the critics never seem to notice. Maybe the only unique, truly original character to emerge in the last decade is Owen Meany, and he is sort of a cross between Yoda and the Little Old Winemaker."

Maxie laughed. "Mom, remember that lecture you gave about how the media makes us think of famous people as all being brilliant and unique?"

Willa smiled. "Maxie, you remembered that."

"Sure. You just think I don't pay attention to you. Yeah, it was after that TV play by that playwright Wasserman . . ."

"Wasserstein." Vilma sipped her burgundy.

They all turned toward her. She raised her jet-black brows until they disappeared under her bangs. "Just because one grows old does not mean one does not keep up. Wendy Wasserstein. The play was *Uncommon Women.* It took place at Mount Holyoke. My very own alma mater, in point of fact."

Lindy looked at her mother as if seeing her for the first time. "I didn't know you went there. I always thought you went to work right after high school. How come you never told me that?"

"I was only able to stay one year. My parents could not provide the funds and I was not gifted enough for a full scholarship. So I left and went to work. I probably just found it too upsetting to relive. I did spend one glorious year there. If you remember, it was the school I had hoped you would attend."

Tess was listening so hard, her teeth were clenched. "Momma, you didn't go to college, did you?"

"No, baby. I was a very foolish girl. I wanted to be an actress and I didn't think I needed it."

"Learn from your mother's mistakes, Tess. She wouldn't listen to me, but I did go to college, so I knew what not having that education meant. I have given a considerable amount of money to Mount Holyoke, so if you should find it interesting, it would give me great pleasure to finance your education there, or wherever you may decide to attend."

Tess looked at Lindy, not sure how to respond.

Willa broke the tension. "I know what Maxie was referring to about the Mount Holyoke play. They showed it once on public television and afterward they had a round-table discussion. All the actresses were there to talk about it, and Wendy Wasserstein was the den mother.

"Anyway, it was just ludicrous. All of these mildly famous actresses sitting around in this restaurant, self-consciously offering their theories on Pro-choice, the Berlin Wall, modern culture. So I gave a lecture on what celebrity has become in the Eighties and Nineties.

"If you are famous for any reason, then somehow that makes your opinions on subjects that you know nothing about as valid as if you were an expert. Here are these *television* actresses expounding their beliefs, and millions of people are listening to them for no other reason than that they are on television.

"What next? Hedda Nussbaum and Joel Steinberg on the Miranda decision; Leona Helmsley, Sukreet Gable, and Ivana Trump on the invasion of Kuwait; Madonna and 2 Live Crew on the space program." Willa stopped, her cheeks red. "Oh, my. I gave a speech."

"You're right, Katharine," Vilma sat forward. "Why, just the other day at the hair salon I was leafing through a magazine and I came upon a full-page color ad for Jockey underwear and there was this family all in their underclothes sitting around a table, grinning like idiots. I simply could not believe my eyes! Why on earth would any couple not totally corrupted by the media celebrity cult allow themselves to be photographed with their children like that for a national magazine?"

Lindy looked at Tess. "Tessie, didn't you have a crush on some boy who posed for one of those underwear ads with his father?"

Tess flushed. "Mom! I *never* had a crush on him. I think he's mentally and physically repulsive, but we've been friends since preschool. We used to eat dirt together!" Tess shot a quick look at Maxie to see if he was laughing at her.

"I'm sorry, baby. I always thought he was cute."

"He looks like an anteater."

"I always liked that look."

Vilma rang the bell for Glenny, subtly changing the conversational tone. "We're having lemon meringue pie and petit fours. My granddaughter has never had my lemon meringue pie, and it is in her honor."

Tess smiled at her. "Thanks, Grandmother Segal. I love lemon meringue pie."

Lindy laughed. "Wills, remember when we had that horrible old Scottish housekeeper and she made two lemon meringue pies because my parents were having some buyers over for dinner and we came home from school famished and each ate an entire pie?"

"How could I forget! She chased us across Sunset Boulevard with a broom! We were so full we could hardly move. If we hadn't ducked behind Wheezie's poolhouse, we'd have been dead meat."

Tess's face closed ever so slightly.

Lindy responded as if they shared a nervous system. She leaned over, whispering in her ear. "You okay, baby?"

Tess nodded, not wanting to be taken away from this wonderful night filled with people she loved and the smells and sounds of normal life. "I'm fine."

Vilma rang again. "What in the world is keeping Glenny? She cannot remember any instruction for more than a second. Her attention span is so short, she couldn't read straight through a fortune cookie."

Lindy and Willa looked at her and burst into peals of laughter.

"Mother, you made a joke! I've never heard you do that before."

Vilma glowered at them, but it was clear that their response pleased her enormously. "There's a lot about me that you know nothing of, dear girl. Your father always said I was his woman of mystery. Remember that, Tess. Always keep a little bit of mystery, some surprises up your sleeve. No man ever left a woman who had mystery."

Willa looked at Lindy, who had stopped laughing. It hurt, whether her mother had meant it or not.

Tess felt it and took her mother's hand. "I just want to grow up to be like my mother. Whatever she has is good enough and mysterious enough for me."

Maxie raised his glass. "Hear, hear. Let's make a toast to our mothers, the most wonderful women in the world."

They all raised their glasses.

Lindy stood up. When she opened her mouth, her voice was quavery, surprising her. "I'd like to make a toast to my mother for this wonderful evening. It's been a . . . very long time since Tess and I have had a family dinner. Thank you, Mother, for everything." Her hand was shaking so that she could barely raise her glass.

They all stood and toasted her mother. And Vilma raised her glass, solemnly accepting her due, more aware than any of them, Willa thought later, of the fateful nature of the occasion.

Willa turned over and looked at the time. It was after two and she still couldn't sleep. She wanted to be rested for their flight tomorrow, knowing somehow that once they set their search in motion, there might not be any time to stop, think, or regroup for quite a while. Her head was too busy. Maybe she should just give up on sleep and write in her journal. They had to leave for the airport at seven, it was hardly worth it to keep trying.

Disparate images and thoughts flitted in and out of her head. She remembered an obituary she had read before this all started. A Park Avenue fashion star had died of breast cancer at forty-eight. In an interview, before her illness, the woman had said that she had achieved all of her dreams: an apartment on Park Avenue, a handsome husband (actually four of them), a successful career, a country estate, a closetful of Chanel. She believed it had all come about because of her spiritual commitment.

This girl had tried it all—Buddhism, macrobiotics, channeling, crystal collecting, Scientology, est, all the New Age voodoo. When she became sick, she refused all conventional medicine until the cancer had crawled, then trotted, then cantered, then galloped through her seaweed-cleansed superwoman frame, ravaging every inch, leaving her deaf, blind, bald, and finally, dead.

Willa couldn't get the image out of her mind. But what if it was true that harnessing this extra power from the universe, the rocks and minerals and mind men of the other dimension, could really work? All the New Age stuff had always seemed false to her—even if *false* meant using all the right things (brown rice and quartz deodorant, Buddhist meditation and tofu cuisine) for the wrong reasons. If movie stars and chic, Chanel-suited doyennes used it for material success, it was as phony and misguided as any hollow fanaticism. Using spiritual techniques to achieve temporal goals—chanting for a beach house or a profile in *New York* magazine—was a rather enormous missing of the point.

But her ambivalence had returned as she watched Tess struggle through the tortured and limited possibilities of traditional healing. She almost wished she could believe in some form of metaphysical magic. Cured by carrot juice, something to hold on to and share with Lindy. She rolled over onto her stomach. Sure! Lindy was even more wary about that stuff than she was herself.

She did not want to share with Lindy the details of the last five days. How that child had suffered. She had been frightened by what she saw in the eyes of the peaky old nurse. Eyes that had personally come very close to the other side of the light. Eyes that did not close when the truth burst in. Willa felt her heart skip.

"Mom? Are you asleep?" Maxie's face poked out from the dimness of the doorway.

"No. Come on in, baby." Willa flipped over.

He moved across to her on his long, narrow feet, Leo's feet, and sat down beside her on the bed. His face was swollen.

"What's wrong, honey? Have you been crying?" She sat up.

He nodded. "Yeah. Sort of. Mom, it's weird. I mean, a week ago I'd never even really heard of any of these people and now they're, like, my family. I was thinking, maybe I should go with you and Lindy. I mean, maybe you need a guy around to help. If you find Leo too. I mean, what if he won't come? I could help."

"Oh, darling, that is so lovely of you. But I think for now a man is needed here more. Tess just lights up when you're around. I think she's trying harder because of you. But if something happens and we need back-up, believe me, we'll call."

"I'm not a kid anymore. I might even be bigger than he is."

She watched him struggling with his feelings. "Why were you crying, baby?"

"It'll probably sound dumb. I started thinking about Leo. I mean about him maybe coming back. I guess I've always had this fantasy that someday he would come back and beg for my forgiveness, like in one of those 'hit men with a heart of gold' movies or something, and we would go off into the sunset together. Well, I was thinking about that in bed and all of a sudden, I realized that that was impossible. I'm all grown now. It's too late. I mean, even if you find him and he comes and he's all sad about leaving and begs for forgiveness and everything; it's still too late, because I'm too big now. It can never be like I dreamed.

"And then I started thinking about you, how you never had a dad at all, and I felt so sad for you. At least I know what it's like. I have some memories, but you never had anything. I just wanted you to know that I think I understand more about how you feel about things now."

Willa reached out and pulled him to her, his large frame settling against her with the reluctant shyness of a young man wanting one last infusion of little-boy comforting.

"Oh, Maxie, you are really something. You give me so much. You don't have to torture yourself. It's going to be okay, baby. It is."

He kept his face tight against her shoulder. "But what if you don't find him? What if she dies?" His whole body shook with anguish.

"I don't know, Maxie. But I think God's got his hand under Tess. I just believe that. He's not going to drop her. He's saving her for something special. Just try to keep thinking that. She's going to make it."

He held on to her. "I'll try."

Willa held him, infinitely grateful for the gift of this being in her life. "I know you will," she said, kissing his forehead and rocking him gently.

She could put to rest her preoccupation with the other paths—witch doctors and psychic healers. She believed in what she had told her son. She believed, ultimately, in the simplicity of the hand and will of God. She'd had no idea that this ghost of childhood bedtime still roamed behind her tense, watchful, reality-trained eyes, but there it was.

Bee Bee had just gotten out of the shower when Lindy and Willa arrived. She opened the door in her robe, a towel wrapped turban-style around her wet hair, and they stood there nervously, not quite knowing what to say. Lindy relieved them. "Well, at least the guy wasn't hooked on a specific physical type."

They laughed together, and Bee Bee led them into the sparsely furnished white living room, where a fresh pot of coffee and a plate of Danish were waiting. They all went for the morning treats like old friends at a sleep-over.

Bee Bee studied them. She envied their friendship. The idea of a friend overcoming even jealousy and man-lust to come to your aid was totally foreign to her. Her mother had been kind, but she had died before it was possible for them to bond in that female way, and she had lived in a world of men. She had never had a real girlfriend. Trudy probably came the closest, but she was more of a mother figure than peer.

Maybe that was part of her desire to help. Maybe what she wanted from them was to be one of the girls, to be part of a team, a family of women. At least they all had Leo in common. That was certainly more than she had in common with any other women she knew.

They settled in slowly, using the breakfast interlude to introduce themselves, share miniature life histories, occupational anecdotes, assembling a foundation—however hastily constructed—on which to build trust and allow the next step forward in this landfill of possible disasters.

Bee Bee poured more coffee. It was time to test the pilings. "I've got to tell you, I haven't been able to think about anything else since I saw Lindy on television. I can't sleep. I can hardly work. My manager's ready to brain me."

She stood up and walked barefoot across the synthetic white carpet and pulled a file out of a cabinet that looked as if it had been bought for a drug dealer's mansion. It was ornately carved, sprayed gold and decorated with trompe-l'oeil swirls and figures from Italian church frescoes.

"I pulled everything I have from the last months Leo was here. Also, I called Corrine Brandmore in Washington. She was very nice. She's quite a bit older than Leo and it has been a long time, but apparently he sometimes sends her birthday cards. Well, as it happens, she still had the card from her last birthday."

Lindy licked her fingers. She could feel her anger growing. "What a mensch. Funny, he couldn't manage to send one to his kids."

Willa sat forward. "Was there a postmark?"

Bee Bee smiled. "Hong Kong. Leo was mad about Hong Kong. He was always pushing Trudy to book me there. I suspected he had something going on that was not so savory, but I wasn't really willing to know about anything like that then.

"It just so happens I have one last commitment from the Leo days in Hong Kong. I called the club and asked if I could switch bookings and come now and they said yes. So if you want, I can go with you. I know the city and I know where he'd be if he's still there. It may be a wild-goose chase."

"Hong Kong! That's always been one of my fantasy places." Willa wiped her mouth with a small pink napkin. "Don't we need visas or shots or something?"

Bee Bee laughed. "No. It's still one of the places that wants us to come. At least for the next six years. I've already called the airlines and made reservations to Washington and then on from there to Hong Kong. Corrine said she'd be glad to try and help us. Listen to this; her present husband used to be just under Bush at the CIA! We're talking *inside* Covert City.

"Now he's secretary of some agency and very well connected. She said, and these were her exact words, 'I don't want to discuss this on the phone. If you come down here, I'll see what I can do.' I think what she meant was that they have ways of tracking people down. Not legal maybe, but ways."

Lindy was wide-eyed. "Wow. The CIA!"

Bee Bee took her towel off and shook her wet copper curls. "Listen, this woman is very powerful. She said she married Leo when he was stationed in Virginia in the submarine corps. I never even knew he was in the service! She was thirteen years older than he was, and she had already been married and had a son. She was from a wealthy family and just lost her mind for him. He was in a navy band and they played at some charity ball she was cochairing. God, it was too familiar to bear!

"They eloped and he stayed with her for a few years, long enough to finish his tour and for her to finance some kind of ship-security business he'd started, sort of like that guy from Iran-Contra who put in security systems for Oliver North? Only for boats. Leo thought he could use all her connections with the yachting crowd in Bethesda and the Chesapeake Bay.

"He lost every dime and her family, who already disapproved, really put the squeeze on. Besides, she wanted to have another child, and he could hardly handle the one she had.

"One day she came home from picking her son up at school, and there was a note thanking her for all she had done for him, yackety-yack, and he was gone. She said it took her three years to settle his bad debts and get an annulment. But she still cares about the bum. I guess I don't have to explain that bit of insanity to you two."

They all smiled at one another, embarrassed by such a personal truth made so public.

Bee Bee rubbed her head with her fingers, shaking her hair dry. "She felt really bad about your daughter, Lindy. I know that's what made her say she'd help. She's a grandmother now and she really understands."

Willa looked at Bee Bee. "I keep trying to figure out his process. What it is that makes him run. It always seems to be about a child. Did you, I mean, you didn't have a baby, did you?"

Bee Bee's face tightened. "I had a miscarriage. I was really, really upset about it and I think he knew that it was starting to be an issue and that I'd want to try again. I knew he didn't want kids, but you know how that is—you never think they really mean it. Anyway, he left before it came up again. I've never thought about it like that, but that certainly could have been the reason."

Lindy felt the old anguish. "But it doesn't wash, Willa, because *you* left him."

Bee Bee looked at Willa enviously. "You did?"

Willa flushed. "Yes. But I truly believe—and I've given it a lot of thought lately—that he manipulated me into doing it. I mean, he was just behaving so badly, and he knew me well enough to know that I could take almost anything but a man behaving irresponsibly. He knew I was starting to lose faith in him, and I think he just couldn't stand it. He put the gun in my hand, so to speak. If I hadn't pulled the trigger, he would have been the one to leave."

They all sat quietly for a moment, each one lost in memory. A Leo moment held inside from a better time.

Trudy stormed in, breaking the quiet. "Look at you! Is this a wake for the bastard! Sitting around reminiscing about the biggest broad-basher ever to hit the dock! I know it's not my business, but this guy nearly killed this kid. Broke her heart right in half. Now she's gonna run off, when she's really starting to go places, to find the prick! He's still gonna ruin her life, even now! Took every cent she had, tryin' to produce records! That guy couldn't produce water from a faucet!

"He's the kind of schmuck that turns *gold* into *straw*! This is a terrible, terrible mistake, Bee Bee. Mark my words." Trudy's narrow face was twisted with fear. She was facing the loss of everything she and her husband had invested in; Bee Bee was now all they had left to see them through.

Lindy and Willa looked at Bee Bee. She was very still, but the flush in her cheeks belied her calm. "Trudy Dale, this is Lindy Lampi and Willa Snow. I know you don't mean to be rude, but we've already discussed this and you know my decision, so please just let us alone now."

Trudy crossed her arms protectively over her chest. She shook her head from side to side. "Sure. Sure. I'm going. I just have to say what's on my mind. This affects Mikey and me too, you know. We have commitments here. We can't afford to look like amateurs."

"Trudy, I've talked to Serena and it's fine with her. Actually, she's trying to milk it for PR value. I've taped all the new shows for the next series. It's really okay. And I'm *working* in Hong Kong! They pay me double what Serena does. Please just relax. It'll be fine. It's not about Leo. It's about a child's life."

Bee Bee spoke to her gently. She was so poised and patient for someone so young, that Willa thought she must have come from a family where she had grown up too soon, one rather like her own. She felt enormous affection for this big, handsome girl so unlike them but moving into their lives in a way that would hook them all together like a mountain-climbing team. Each of their destinies would depend on the one above and the one below.

"Yeah. Yeah. I know. I'm not unfeeling. But you're like *my* child. I saw this guy tear you apart. Walked out like the fucking Fuller brush man. Didn't even leave a note. Try to understand how it was for Mikey and me, watching it all and feeling so helpless!"

Bee Bee went over to Trudy and put her long, slender arms around her. "I know. But I'm not Leo. I'll be back."

The woman relaxed against her. The child with the tantrum over and the lollipop in hand. "Okay. You're right. I'm okay. You girls want some more coffee?"

Bee Bee kissed her. "That would be great." She crossed back to Lindy and Willa and leaned over the couch. "Have some more coffee. I'll be ready in a minute. I hope you brought your passports."

Lindy nodded. "We brought everything but machetes and poison gas."

"Here." Bee Bee handed Lindy her file. "Maybe there's something in this stuff that'll be helpful. There's even some medical information. He needed a physical for a commercial he produced." She left them alone to absorb the events of the last hour.

Willa had been right. The roller coaster was heading toward the top. She could feel her pulse throbbing, fueled by caffeine and excitement.

Lindy gasped. "Wills. He's the right blood type! I knew it!"

They waited for Bee Bee, drinking too much coffee and trying to find the next safe place to step, the peg hammered tight into the crevice above them, safe to receive the weight of their anxiety.

"Let's go," Bee Bee said, flinging an enormous duffel bag over her shoulder and slipping on her huge dark glasses. They were in motion now and there was no turning back.

Part II

Leo

CHAPTER 5

Come Back to Ancolla

N THE SEVENTEENTH AND EIGHTEENTH CENTURIES WHEN PI-rates roamed the world's seas, pillaging and plundering for pleasure and profit, two forms of pirate justice were used on enemy and errant crew. The plank walk was considered the most fearsome; humiliating and demeaning, a public topple into a savage, shark-infested nightmare. Marooning was the more humane and common means of justice. Convicted pirates were simply set ashore on some barren, sandy cay and left to rot, starve, dehydrate, or simply waste away from fear, loneliness, and despair. No one stayed to watch the process and there was always, for the hearty or lucky, the possibility of survival, denied to the strollers of the perilous plank.

On the islands of the Nineties, marooning is still practiced. The difference now is that it is self-inflicted and called expatriating. This practice, the relocating of an urban person from another culture to one of the self-styled paradise places (a lush tropical island somewhere in the world), is certainly not restricted to the Caribbean lands or to Americans, but they are the site and nationality of many a maroonee.

Certainly none of the marooned would see themselves this way. They mostly see themselves as fortunate, special escapees from the madness of modern existence; sensitive rugged souls who revere nature and want nothing so much as a simple life filled with sea sound and smell, frigate bird and brain coral, black rock crab and angelfish. A life of sun and jolly island folk, black star-swarmed nights, nutmeg floating on the rum punch, sweet marijuana incense tickling the nose, bare feet shuffling to the Rasta man's music.

They would never compare themselves to victims of pirate justice or to the pirates themselves, refugees from real life, dreamers and outsiders, wooed by the promise of whiskey and wenches, blood sport and bounty.

The open sea, and the "sweet trade" as piracy was mockingly called, seemed a much more exciting option than the whining wives and snively waifs, the crumbling row houses and brutal medieval bureaucracies that the original pirates left behind. The reality, however, like most realities, was far less glamorous than anticipated. Hundreds of scurvy-riddled, restless men stinking with sweat and excrement, feverish with typhus, yellow fever, and dysentery, crammed onto leaking, vermin-infested brigantines.

There were, of course, exceptions. A few pirateers and mutineers who saved their booty, returned home, or retired to one of the small, remote islands, living out their days in affluent quietude and escaping the scourge of disease, drink, and sex that lay waste to their comrades. But for most, the feral life led to feral death or to a peg-legged, syphilitic exile in some dagger-ready port.

It is not so much different for the marooned of today. They come to the islands with mind pictures clipped from travel brochures, not seeing the dry rot inside the sleek sailing hulls—the jet skis muffling the sound of apathy and desolation just below the clear blue water.

They arrive by sea or plane, dropping psychic anchor in a chosen harbor, with a past from which they have escaped and a future that they have let fantasy form. Some of these fantasies are more formed than others. They include living arrangements, attire, car, job, and other people. Others are merely floating thoughts, lazy half-formed yearnings. But they are all dreams, and like all dreamers they must wake up and face the daylight. The cockier and more calcified the dreamer, the worse can be his fate on these chimerical volcanic lands of alchemy and illusion. They do not like washed-up pseudo pirates from Philadelphia or Chicago, telling them who they are. They can be counted on to kick back, send storm and scorpion or other kinds of men, to punish the marooned dreamers of fragile dreams.

* * *

The rickety little Cessna touched down on Ancolla, and Rennie
Bowman took her first full breath since she had left Puerto Rico.
Home. Funny, she had been living on the little shit-kicker island, a
mere dot in the middle of the Sir Francis Drake Channel, for four
years and this was the first time she had ever used the word *home*
to describe it.

If anything, that was more a response to her visit with her father
and new stepmother than an endorsement of her life on Ancolla.
She unclenched her hands and opened her purse. She knew how
the Gibsons were about sharing a charter, and she was not about
to wait for them to ask her for the money. Randall the pilot, a
cheerful young man with corn rows and a sign pinned to the back
of his seat that said I'M THE GUY YOUR MOMMA WARNED YOU ABOUT
turned and smiled at her. "We gonna rock tonight. I hear Leo is
filling in for one of the Whalers. Gonna shake those brothers up!"

Thea Gibson, always eager to act like one of the locals, patted
his shoulder. "Everyone's so excited about the concert. Imagine
them bringing their whole show to Ancolla! How marvelous!"

Rennie handed her a check, which she passed to her husband
Arthur.

"How fortunate for all of us to run into one another like that!
This is so much the better way of coming down. Do you go up to
Puerto Rico often, Rennie? Maybe we can pool our round trip
next time. We have several artists we see there."

Rennie unfastened her seat belt, releasing her swollen belly.
"Actually, no. My father was appearing at the El San Juan. I just
went up to visit."

Thea smiled at her in that supercilious, social-climbing New
York art-world way that made Rennie want to bop her one. She
loathed the Gibsons—they were part of everything she was running away from. When she was around them and their WASP
friends, it was as if she were still in Rye with her grandmother's
group, her mother wandering in and out between nervous break-
downs and everyone creaking around with that ramrod in the
rectum, congealed upper lip–manner that had nearly destroyed her
and had destroyed her sister.

The Gibsons had been coming to Ancolla for years and thought
of themselves as its "discoverers." They had finally bitten the big

bullet, buying a large slice of beach-front property near the airport and building their dream house.

Now they were really unbearable. Full of patronizing anecdotes about the people and customs, ingratiating themselves with local restaurateurs and shopkeepers, showing off for their weekend guests; "Caesar will keep some lobsters for us even if we're late" —only to find that Caesar has no idea who they are and could not care less.

The islanders did their bidding, cleaned their dream house, serviced their cars and boats, their slow-moving, calloused feet flopping against the backs of their plastic sandals, scorning them silently; the Gibsons, grinning on, oblivious of the undercurrents all around them.

When Rennie had first arrived, they had taken her up with gusto. Not for herself but because they knew who her father was. At the time he'd been on a real roll, with his own television show. She knew what they were doing. If there was anything she'd learned growing up with a famous father, it was how people tried to use you because of that fact of birth. But she was lonely, vulnerable, and torn asunder by her parents' divorce and her sister's overdose, and she allowed it.

In fact, the party they had for her had changed her life. She'd met Brad Olson here and that led to her job and finding her house, and, of course, Brad led to Leo. Whether all that was good or not so good, she wasn't quite sure, but they had started her off, and for that, she tried to be nice to them and their obnoxious son, overlooking their chain-smoking, martini-guzzling élitism.

Since Leo had moved in with her they had pretty much left her alone. They did not approve of Leo. Too low-brow, too gigolo-ish for their crowd. Not that some of their female houseguests didn't request Rennie and Leo on their party lists.

Just thinking about some of those evenings at the Gibsons' made Rennie flush with anger. Good old Rennie. None of them saw her as any kind of a threat. It was almost as if she wasn't even considered as a woman. Just some bemused, blue-eyed trust-fund baby not to be taken seriously. Boozy, bosomy collectors' wives from Manhattan had practically grabbed Leo's crotch right in front of her, as if she didn't count.

The feeling was too familiar. Too painfully easy for her to slip into. Perfect victim. Brad called her "Monkey Eyes" because he said her eyes looked startled and bewildered, the way monkeys look. He had even brought her a picture of a blue-eyed monkey with the saddest face she had ever seen. The picture made her cry and Brad had held her, crying himself for having hurt her, which was the last thing he meant to do.

Rennie followed the Gibsons into the one-room prefabricated shed that served as Customs for the island. The Gibsons chatted on about the concert and the difficulties they were having with furniture deliveries from New York, but Rennie had stopped listening.

One thing that not having people think of you as imposing did, was make your performance of social niceties far less demanding. If she did not ohhh and ahhh, uhhuh and click her tongue in sympathy at Thea Gibson's travails, but chose instead to stand quietly, her black polarized lenses shielding her solemn monkey eyes, the Gibsons wouldn't think her rude or any duller than they already thought. Not being the center of anyone's attention did have its upside.

She had a lot on her mind today anyway. First, she had to get to the pharmacy before it closed and have her prescriptions filled. Then she had to go home and see if the Un Jill had everything ready for the party after the concert. Then she had to shower and change and drive into town and meet Leo by six. She looked at her Swiss diver's watch. It was already almost four. She felt like shouting. Being unmarried and pregnant was bad enough. Being unmarried, pregnant, and living with a man who had made it quite clear that that is the way you were going to stay, was worse. But being both and living a lie, as if you were neither, was really getting her down. She seemed to be rushing from one responsibility to another all the time. The business, Leo, the house, her family, and Brad.

Okay. If she was going to be honest about it, it was the scene in Puerto Rico that had tipped it. Her father, who was probably not that much older than Leo, and his blushing bride, who was younger than she was—and they were as happy as vampires at a blood bank. God, what a morbid metaphor! Rennie handed her passport to Lavaina, the Customs clerk. Well, the whole thing made her feel morbid. Her sister dead, her mother back in the loony bin, and her father blithely waltzing around the lobby of the El San Juan with his baby bride. He had taken one look at her, belly bulging and lip trembling, and she had seen not only surprise and disapproval, she had seen pity.

Poor little Rennie. Just like her name. She had been named Wren, like the bird, the little frail songbird, the Edith Piaf of birdlife. She hated it and kept her nickname when she grew up. She had always secretly thought that you took on the characteristics and maybe even the karma of your name. If she had a great big tough name like Madeline or Lorraine or something, maybe she would have made a stronger impression.

"Rennie dear, can we give you a ride? I left the car here." Arthur Gibson picked up her bag like a true gentleman and walked her into the main terminal. That was the *last* thing she wanted. She needed more time to think before she met up with Leo. She did not want to let her conversation with her father influence her. Leo would never put up with whining and badgering him about marriage.

"Oh, gee, thanks, but I've got to stop in town before the pharmacy closes. I'll just grab a cab."

She saw the Gibsons' son waving at them across the baggage claim, and she stopped. "I need some change, I'll see you tonight." She could not stand their son, more so because, until her belly gave away her secret, they were always trying to set her up with him. God forbid! Better Leo anyday than one of those spoiled, asexual prep-school jerks she'd been surrounded by all of her life.

"See you tonight, dear." Thea Gibson strutted away, looking as smug and self-deluding as Miss Piggy. In fact, that was exactly what Thea Gibson reminded her of. A tall, tan, twisted Miss Piggy. Piss-elegant on top but a hellion underneath. She was sure Thea and Arthur had violent drunken Who's-Afraid-of-Virginia-Woolf battles. Or maybe that was just wishful thinking.

When Rennie Bowman met Brad Olson, he had just come out of the hospital after months of postoperative agony following surgery on his spine. The doctors had told him that if he sailed again he could end up crippled for life, but he had little choice.

His father had given him a ten-percent interest in one of his catamaran charter boats, and that had propelled him into working so hard, he had wrecked his body. When he had to stop, his father took back the ten percent in return for paying his medical bills. When he came home from the hospital in Miami, all he had left was a job working on his own boat. His father had even repossessed his condo.

Brad Olson was a victim like herself, but his father was much worse than hers. Her father might be remote and egotistical, but at least he was generous and concerned about her welfare. Brad's father was a monster, using his son like a pack animal.

Rennie had some money to invest and needed something productive to do with her life, and Brad had gone to his father with a proposition. Lease them the cat on a payback with an option to buy. While they were waiting for the old bastard to make up his mind, they had met Leo at Mombo's place. Three years had passed since then, and they had all worked hard and done well as a team.

Mombo was a local legend, owning the best bar on the beach, which he had built himself like a deconstructionist sculpture from old car parts and driftwood. He came from a family that had been on Ancolla since slavery, and he knew people. He liked Brad and he liked Leo, who was tending bar for him. He liked to give guys like Leo a chance. Part of it was being the big cheese, offering aid to wandering white boys, having that control. But it was also that he really enjoyed people and wanted to be helpful. He was like an island godfather in that way. (He was also a notary and a certified captain and he even married people sometimes if they were drunk enough, having ingested one too many of his famous "painkillers.") Behind the bar was a hand-painted sign: "MOMBO'S: WHERE WHITE BOYS GO TO GET RED" and he liked it like that. Everyone who came to Ancolla ended up at Mombo's sooner or later and so Leo had found him and he had taken him in, given him a job, and found him a place to stay and a woman to stay with.

The woman was an island queen, the daughter of the governor and the ex-wife of the largest landholder. Her name was Athena Pidge and she was as hard as Bluebeard's heart and hated by everyone on the island. Leo did not know that at the time. He saw a tall, stately woman the color of pumpkin pie, with a flashing white smile, a new Mercedes, a large ocean-front home and a craving for tall, blond white men. Mombo cautioned him, "Watch yourself, she's got the head of a hog and the heart of a scorpion." But women did not frighten Leo Lampi.

She also had the libido of a mad dog in heat and that probably wore Leo down even before the other things he began to see.

Mrs. Pidge had quite a racket going for herself on Ancolla and several of the larger neighboring islands. She ran ads in the local press on the starving islands in the chain that ran from Haiti to Tortuga. She wooed poor young island girls with the promise of high wages and an easier life, offering to pay transportation and expenses, clothe and feed them, and find them work cleaning the houses of wealthy landowners and the hotel rooms of rich tourists. She offered to cover all legal services, expedite visas and work permits, and send them airline tickets. These too-good-to-be-true traps were set up and down the Caribbean and desperate young women fought over available spaces, leaving their worn-out mothers and dead-eyed babies, to earn salvation money provided by the goodly grace of Mrs. Athena Pidge.

The truth was somewhat closer to Fagin than Ministering Angel. Mrs. Pidge enslaved the terrified and helpless girls, forcing them to work as her personal servants from dawn until they went off to clean houses for ten dollars per day—no matter *how* many houses or hotel rooms they cleaned—from which she took daily deductions for the cost of their uniforms (at forty dollars per outfit) taxes, transportation, and housing.

In addition, the terms of their employment said that they were allowed to remain on the host island only if they were in the employ of Mrs. Pidge, and if for any reason they were dismissed, they would be deported at their own expense. The girls lived in sullen terror, taking out their rage on their employers, doing halfhearted work and returning tipless, to finish their endless days of drudgery by ironing Mrs. Pidge's underwear and cooking her dinner.

When Leo figured out what was happening, he left, taking with him a sweet, fish-faced Dominican girl called, mysteriously, "the Un Jill," who Mombo took in and saved from Mrs. Pidge. Mombo was the only person she feared and she let the Un Jill go, with her papers and her back wages.

When Leo came back to Mombo's, he had not been in the islands long enough and was still too naive in what Mombo called "the planetary legacy of racism" not to be outraged by Athena's behavior. "She's exploiting her own people! Those girls are terrified and trapped. Why don't you stop her? She's worse than a slave trader!"

Mombo had just smiled his wide, slow, big-toothed smile, capped with gold on either side of his upper and lower incisors, and stroked his salt-and-pepper beard. "You talk like a rabbit, mon. Everything in the islands is politics. Politics will ruin all of these islands. Nothing is what it seems. She is the governor's daughter, rabbit. Do you know what we call the governor? We call him Mr. Ten Percent. You want something done. A road. A beach developed. You give the governor ten percent. And *he's* the best governor we've ever had. At least greed is what motivates him.

"We have a hospital now and a concert hall and a community center. What about the new hotels? All because of Mr. Ten Percent. The last governor was honest, but he was also lazy and stupid and nothing, mon, *nothing* happened. It's the way it is. You rabbits all think like cartoon characters.

"Let me tell you about the Night of the Silent Drums. On the Island of St. John, more than a hundred years ago, many of the black slaves could not be tamed. They were African royalty, chiefs of their tribes, and they would not accept their fate. One by one they ran off and they formed an exile community at the end of the island, deciding among themselves which part of the island each of them would take.

"Every night the slaves played their drums. It had always been the custom. But on the Night of the Silent Drums there was no music. The chiefs came down from the hills, joined the slaves, and slaughtered every white man, woman, and child. Killed all of the Dutch plantation owners in their own beds. The only family spared was the owner of the Caneel Bay plantation, because a loyal servant had warned them and they escaped.

"Well, the white owners of Ancolla decided that they were probably next and they abandoned this island, leaving it to their slaves, who were not royalty. They divided up the land—my great granddaddy got quite a bit—and lived here without schools, electricity, or civilization until after the Second World War.

"This is part of our character. Part free man and part slave. Part capitalist and part lackey. But we are a bunch of slow motherfuckers, mon. Watch one of us work. We have a single agenda. We do one task at a time. That's why I like you rabbit bartenders—you can make three drinks at once, splash in three shots of vodka in three glasses, then pour orange juice in one, tomato in the second, tonic in the third. Not us, mon. 'I'll get to it, mon,' my guy says, and he does it slow. One order at a time.

"We hate the foreigners for coming, but without them we'd still be sitting in the dark, eating fish with our hands. I see everything here, mon. *Everyone* comes to Mombo's. The rich white boys showing off, wanting to impress me because I'm a motherfucker. I'm big and black and cool. White boys can't be cool like Mombo because they're scared and they feel guilty about us too.

"I know everyone on this island, and Athena is not the worst of them. White people don't like to look at human nature up close. Black people have no choice, so we are craftier. We see the things you hide from, and that's what makes you so scared of us. That is what we count on, rabbit. That is what we use."

On the night that Brad and Rennie met Leo, Rennie had been on Ancolla for a little over a year. She had leased a large modern house up in the hills for a very reasonable sum and had asked Brad to move in with her. The arrangement was not romantic, though if Brad had been able to find the courage to express himself to her, that would have been the way he wanted it. He had his rooms downstairs and she had hers upstairs. She refused to let him help with the rent. "Listen, I don't work for this money. I have a trust fund from my grandfather that just pumps it at me every month. I don't even think of it as mine, so it's one way I can help you out. I've got enough and we're trying to build something. Don't worry about it."

It was the nicest thing anyone had ever done for him in his life, and even though she didn't know it he loved her even more than he had all along and he would have gladly killed for her or died for her too, for that matter. He was a hurt man and she was a hurt woman, though she didn't talk about how or about her family much at all, really. But they'd come together to heal, and they were doing a fairly good job of it.

That night at Mombo's they had come across the island for two reasons. The first was that Mombo had told Rennie that he had a buyer for her car, which Mombo and Brad (or anyone who knew anything about Rennie's car) found absolutely hilarious. They called the car Big Red, because it was red and because it was anything but big.

The pathetic little vehicle had started life as one of those generic, disposable low-end Japanese exports and had been so misused and banged around by thoughtless sightseers, roaming goats, perilous potholes, and salty air, that it was barely breathing.

The proprietor of the Happy Beach Auto Rental had asked Mombo if he knew anyone willing to take the wreck off his hands. He couldn't rent it to anyone anymore, no matter how desperate to explore the scenic beauty of the tiny paradise, and Mombo had called Rennie.

Happy Beach was a one-room cement shack with a remnant of yellow-and-brown carpet that was too big for the floor and made closing the door impossible, and two slack-faced overweight island girls who made the simple acts of finding a car key, answering the phone, or (God forbid) typing a rental contract look as if they required the physical and mental strength of Arnold Schwarzenegger and Albert Einstein.

Sometimes it seemed to Rennie, even after four years on the island, as if everyone in Angeltown (which was as close to a city as Ancolla possessed) were underwater. Moving around with the clumsy, lead-footed effort of men in diving suits. Shop girls would lean over on the counter in the middle of a transaction and doze off. Cab drivers would put their heads against the side of their cars while figuring out a fare. People in line at the market would nod off against the bakery racks.

When she first arrived, it had completely mystified her. What was the matter with all these people? Waitresses closing their eyes in midorder and resting their heads on their hands. What could it be? No one could be *that* tired all of the time. Was it some island virus, a mass insomnia? Drugs? Rum? What she seemed to be dealing with were eight thousand permanently exhausted, bored, surly narcoleptics who couldn't make change.

One night, riding in a cab from Angeltown back to the boat, going over one of the treacherous mountain roads, she saw a man in the headlights, lying in the middle of the road and she had shouted at the cab driver. "Stop! Stop! There's a man in the road! He needs help!"

The cab driver just slowly maneuvered around the man, who was lying flat-out, with his head in the lap of a large-breasted woman who was stroking his face. "Stop! He's going to get killed. He must need a doctor!"

"Heh. Heh. Heh." The cab driver shrugged his shoulders, chuckling at Rennie as if her plea was the funniest, silliest thing he had ever heard.

"Heh. Heh. Heh. No. No. Lady, he not hurt. He jest resting. Taking a little rest."

"A *rest*? In the middle of the night? In the middle of the road!"

"Ya. Ya. He got a woman. He happy. Jest taking a little rest. Heh. Heh. Heh."

When Rennie recovered from the shock, she realized that she was like the newly blind learning Braille. All she could figure out were bits and pieces, and maybe that was all they wanted her to see and all that she ever really would, no matter how long she was here.

It had taken her four hours in the Happy Beach Auto Rental to transfer Big Red, but at the end she felt triumphant. It was hers. The fact that it could only work up a speed of three miles an hour uphill (and that was with only one passenger) and was often passed by dogs, goats, and motor bikes did not daunt her pride.

Mombo had laughed himself silly when Rennie took him for a ride. "You better eat a lot of beans and toot yourself up the hill—this machine needs all the power you got."

Brad put a new coat of paint on for her and patched the seats and got a new set of tires and he and Rennie bombed around Ancolla, dodging the emaciated chickens, goats, and pigs. They tore around the flat stretches and accelerated as fast as they could when approaching a hill, using the speed to push them up, then puttering and sputtering toward the top and sailing down in neutral. The car felt like them: bruised but still hopeful, with a survivor's gusto. It still made it to the top.

Finally, however, things were starting to come together. Brad's father had agreed to their proposal and they had hooked up with a rich misfit from Boston, who was in the process of buying an old hotel and scuba-diving complex on Blue Man's Bay, the best undeveloped spot on the island. He needed someone to run the dive shop and provide charter service. In exchange for supplying the catamaran and the diving equipment, which they already had, this kid, William (Billy) Bartlett III would give them a piece of the action and the potential for partnership in the whole operation.

So when Mombo called and said that he had a guy, an okay guy, who not only wanted to buy Big Red (Rennie had finally bought a real car and they didn't need her anymore) but was also looking for a boat investment, they jumped in their little symbol of hope over experience and barreled down the hill to Mombo's.

It was fish-fry night and the place was jumping. The Rasta band from Angeltown, led by a young Dominican woman with a beautiful husky voice, was wailing and tourists from across the island were dancing barefoot with each other or with Mombo's regulars, his island "trash men" mixing with bermuda-clad Yuppies from Connecticut, Mombo checking everything out, making sure the scene was cool and no one frightened off the spenders.

Leo was behind the bar when Brad and Rennie arrived and Mombo brought them over. If such a thing is possible, they both fell in love with him that night, feeding into him their mutual father-figure fantasies. Neither of them had ever met anyone like Leo before, and they empowered him with their need for someone who knew more about life than they did—more about boats and business and dealing with spoiled rich kids like Billy Bartlett (or "The Third," as Rennie called him), without getting screwed. They talked and Leo listened, refilling their rum punches and figuring out what it was they needed.

As it turned out, what they needed was a perfect fit with what he needed. A new life and a new career. He was the new guy in town and already attracting too much attention. He was not using his own name, driver's license, or passport. To all intents and purposes Leo Lampi had died in Miami.

He was Larry Yates now, though he still told people his nickname was Leo; otherwise he himself couldn't remember who he really was. He was Larry Yates with a passport and motor-vehicle seal of approval to back him up, and he had come to the islands because his marriage had broken up and he wanted to start a new life. He had sold his business and had a little money he wanted to invest. That is what he told Mombo and that is what he told Rennie and Brad. That is what he told Athena Pidge.

No one had any more reason to doubt him than they had to

doubt anyone else. They believed him enough to go forward. They believed him as much as all the people before them had believed him.

He was used to being believed, and of course, that in itself made him far more believable. Nothing Leo ever said was a lie. It was just carefully edited truth. They talked and Leo listened and by the end of the night—as the rum-soaked tourists staggered back to their air-conditioned hotel rooms, gleefully glowing from their "island experience": an exotic, worth-the-price-of-the-airfare evening mingling with the *real people,* dancing to the Caribbean beat —a new trio had formed.

If you wanted to know what was going on in the islands generally, and Ancolla particularly, you went to the airport. That is where all the taxi drivers hung out, waiting for flights to bring them fares. The taxi drivers were the strolling minstrels of modern Ancolla. The makeshift bar was always filled, and Ruby the barmaid was always busy pouring coffee and rum punches and popping open Coca-Colas and beers, shoving package pizza and frozen conch fritters into the microwave or reheating greasy frozen fries, until no one—not even Willie, who drank continuously and ate anything—would touch them.

The leader of the group was Louie, a native son with a wide gap-toothed smile and a beret. He kept them all in line, sobering them up if they were drunk enough to cast doubt on their ability to bomb over the impossible, barely paved roads with their usual élan. Louie was married to Eloise who ran the airport craft shop, a counter with her weavings, some island spices, and primitive tin paintings. Eloise was as quiet and silent as Louie was gregarious, but both of them possessed a wonderful natural nobility and kindness.

Rennie adored them. She wanted to be like them. She wanted to be friendly and open like Louie, and graceful and quiet like Eloise. At least if she could just be quiet the way Eloise was quiet. Silent but so present. Not someone to be taken lightly. Even the Gibsons didn't patronize Eloise.

Rennie waved to Louie, who was holding court in his indecipherable pidgin at the bar. In the distance she could hear Eloise's throaty, church-trained contralto as she always did in the afternoon when things slowed down and she sewed rather than sold. " 'Pack up your troubles in your old kit bag and smile, smile, smile.' "

Louie sprinted toward her and took her luggage. "Welcome home, blondie. I saw your father on the TV. Very funny man. Tells the same jokes I used to tell, only he whitens them up! Want to go home?"

"Thanks, Louie. But I need to stop in town first. Can you wait for me? I have to fill a prescription."

She followed him out, waving to Ruby and the guys and settled into the back of his van.

"Oh, boy. You know how that pharmacy is end of the day. Gonna take some time."

Rennie sighed. Suddenly she was so tired she could hardly talk. "I know, but it's doctor's orders. A baby thing."

Louie looked at her in the rearview mirror. "Oh-oh. Emergency service required. I will even carry you into Mr. O'Brien's at no extra charge. Shouldn't have gone off on no airplane in your condition. When Eloise was in the family way, I didn't let her walk around the chicken coop."

"Well, Louie, you know what they say—a good man is hard to find."

Louie nodded, chuckling at the compliment. "That's what I tell my wife. She is one lucky lady."

Rennie settled back against the seat and closed her eyes. She liked to listen to Louie talk; it cheered her up and calmed her down at the same time. "Tell me what I've missed, anything juicy?"

Louie laughed, flashing his wide-spaced teeth. "Yeah, yeah. Juicy as a bowl of bullfoot soup. We had some new blood come down, a big book writer from New York, wanting to do research on us for a novel.

"Well, he rented the Miller place up on the hill, and he gets in the cab with his pretty wife and his three young girls, showin' me the house pictures, like I couldn't find it in my sleep. They were so happy to be here, gonna stay *six* months, he say. Gonna put his girls in a local school. Heh! Heh! I am thinkin' this is one crazy rabbit!

"So I take them on the tour. Every time a little scrawny goat strolls across the road, they are squealing with delight. 'How cute! This is just what we came for!' they is sayin'. He wants to cut some deal, he says, for me to talk to him. He gonna pay me one hundred dollars a day to talk to him about the Island and the people. I am becoming very happy. I'm thinking of a new cab or a trip to Disney World. I am liking this book writer more and more.

"So we arrive at Mrs. Miller's and they are very cheerful about the beautiful view. Only trouble is, Mrs. Pidge sent some new girl to do the cleaning up. No one's been in that house for months, and this child does not know the ways of rich book people from New York. I'm thinking afterward, the poor girl probably just pushed the broom around and took herself a little snooze.

"Well, I'm helping them in with all their fancy luggages, and I hear a scream from the master bathroom. The pretty book wife comes running out of there like the devil hisself is after her. 'In the sink! In the sink,' she's screamin'. So her husband does the manly thing. He says, 'Don't worry, dear, I'm sure it's just one of the island lizards I've read about.' I'm not saying a sound, but I don't get a good feeling about this. Well, the man goes strutting off to save his family from the lizard in the sink, and a minute later he comes runnin' out, looking worse than she herself. 'In the sink! In the sink!' He's shakin' like a voodoo priest. So's I tell them all to stay in the hall and I'll see to it, but I'm feelin' a little peaked myself by now. In I go. *Ha!* The biggest, meanest, ugliest old millipede you have ever seen, just crawlin' along the sink, minding its business.

"Well, my cousin used to catch the devils, so I know what to do and I save the day, anticipating a very generous tip for facing the monster. They are all wide-eyed and grateful as you please and I leave them with plans to meet them in the morning and start my job telling about the 'Ancollan culture.' Ha! That is what he called it.

"So next morning I arrive bright and early and they are all sitting in the drive on top of their Frenchie luggage looking like they have seen the Beast.

" 'What hopponed, mon?' I says.

"Well, it turns out the millipede was just the beginning of their woes. This cleaning-up girl, she must have just snoozed and gone home. These folks had everything! Noseeums in the couch. Bird splatter on the floor. Rat turds on the sheets and those horrible-looking boxes of rat poison with the skull and bones that the girls are supposed to hide before the tourists come, all over the place!

"Now my book writer is trying to be the man of the family and he is calling Mrs. Pidge, who never takes calls at night because she don't want to hear no bad news before she makes her whoopie, so no one is answering.

"Finally they decide to take a walk down the hill to Nido's and have a couple of rum punches, some local food, and try to adjust. So first the pretty wife steps right on a sand bee, and he has to almost carry her into the restaurant.

"Now, it's reggae night there and all the yachties and locals are in, everyone is feeling good, and they start to cheer up. Pretty soon Nido's old flea-bag mutts wander in and the daughters start pettin' away. 'Oh, so cute,' they say.

"Well, then old Mr. Sticks comes up, seeing a new opportunity, and asks the oldest daughter, a lovely young thing, to dance. The blossom's too nervous about offending him to say no, so off she goes and they're dancing and he's twirling her around in that stiff-legged way of his, tipping his little porkpie hat at the family. So respectable! Pretty soon one of the boat girls, who knows about Sticks, she comes over to my book writer and she is a little inebriated, so she tells him, 'I wouldn't let your daughter dance with Mr. Sticks. He is a sick old pervert who does it with Nido's donkey almost every night.' Ha! Ha!

"Well, by now, the wife's foot is swelling up like a jellyfish and the flea bites from those old dogs are starting to itch those children and the book writer has the job of making his way across a roomful of crazy Rasta men dancing by themselves, you know how they do, looking pretty scary to city folks, and he grabs his little girl from the old donkey fucker and drags them all out.

"Now, they get home and the girl has not put up the mosquito screens or left the spray for them, and they are bitten to Jesus. Ha! Ha! I'm just happy he ain't no travel-magazine writer, or we poor fools would be catching parrot fish with a net from now on."

Rennie was laughing so hard her stomach hurt. "So what happened?"

Louie shrugged. "I took them over to Mrs. Pidge, who stormed around trying to do her jive. But this fellow is from New York

City and it's not so easy to pull a fast one about deposits. Then I took them to the airport and they went home. So much for Disney World. Ha! You should have seen those poor people. All red and scabby and hobbling and bleary-eyed. Welcome to Ancolla!"

Rennie sat forward. "What about the poor girl? Mrs. Pidge will kill her."

Louie shook his head. "Don't know. No one has heard anything. If she's smart, she went to Mombo's and he's hiding her till Mrs. Pidge finds herself a new man and quiets herself down." Louie stopped, checking Rennie's reaction in the mirror. Everyone knew that Leo had been with Mrs. Pidge first, and he was mad at himself for not thinking about it.

Rennie sighed. She was no match for Athena Pidge. In fact, if the truth was known, she was *scared to death of her.* Rennie had met Leo well after he had ended with her, but that was not how Athena saw it. No man had ever left her before, and Rennie believed they had not seen the last of the infamous Pidge Power.

Louie pulled up at the harbor parking lot, which was across the street from the center of Angeltown. Rennie reached to open the door, but Louie jumped out and ran around, pulling the heavy sliding door open.

"Don't you be reachin' for no doors now, blondie. Gotta keep that little lobster in there, nice and relaxed."

He helped Rennie out and she gave him a kiss on his almond-colored cheek. "Just like I said. A good man is hard to find. If I'm not back in twenty minutes, come in and chase everyone else out. Tell them you have ciguatera poisoning and you're having a fit."

Ciguatera was a bacterial disease caused by eating tainted fish and the islanders lived in daily dread of contracting it, since they all ate local fish, betting that the odds were in their favor.

Louie grinned and patted his beret. "I will look forward to it. Haven't had a good fit since old man Satchley dumped his septic tank into my garden."

Rennie made her way through the restless afternoon traffic to O'Brien's.

Angeltown was the center of Ancolla, and O'Brien's pharmacy was the center of Angeltown. It was housed in an old pink stucco building with large windows, shuttered at night, but providing during the day an eye-catching array of cough remedies, trusses, walkers, and Porta-Pottis, old Revlon posters covered with dust and featuring lovely if slightly out-of-style young women with brightly painted nails and lips—the closest any of the young island boys came to salacious viewing. Inside, the shelves were as sparse as *The New York Times* photos of Warsaw meat markets, with wide divisions between boil ointments and analgesics.

The most plentiful array was the local medicines, hand-lettered bottles and tubes, filled with exotic-sounding ingredients, promising to deliver far more relief than the overpriced foreign cures.

O'Brien's was a family business, handed down from father to son to the sons of sons. The new pharmacist was from the youngest generation of proprietors, freshly returned from college in Virginia and slightly more impatient, though probably as dedicated as his father, who worked beside him.

There were three medical doctors and many practitioners of island-style healing in Angeltown, but for many, especially the poor and frightened, the O'Briens were where they turned for diagnosis and advice. Because of this and the rather complicated payment procedures, more like some primitive barter system than any modern transaction, the wait could be interminable.

Rennie opened the glass door with the cardboard clock in the middle, and her heart sank. The line for prescriptions went halfway down the aisle. She picked up a local paper and a lonely Mars bar and got in line behind Lotty, the waitress at the breakfast café where she and Brad ate every morning.

They had a running joke about Lotty. For almost three years she had served them breakfast every day without ever acknowledging that she had seen them before. No "Good morning, nice day." Nothing. She would shuffle over, her head down, and even though they ordered exactly the same thing each morning, she would wait in silence until they told her what they wanted, writing it all down without a word. Every morning they made a bet that would be the day she greeted them with a wide grin of recognition. "Mornin', folks. The usual?"

Rennie smiled. Lotty looked right through her as if she were invisible. Something about the act flushed her with anger. Somehow it felt worse for her to be ignored here. At the café she was better prepared.

She munched on her candy bar, letting the hardness of the stale chocolate melt against her tongue. Old man Sticks was at the counter now, and she could see from the look on young O'Brien's face that he was having a hard time communicating with him. Rennie smiled, thinking of Louie's story. Maybe he was buying some Preparation H for Nido's donkey.

"The prescription costs twenty-four dollars, Mr. Sticks."

"Only got twenty dollars."

"Do you have a senior citizen's ID card? Then I can give you a discount."

Mr. Sticks reached deep down into the back pocket of his frayed brown polyester pants as if moving in slow motion. The lady behind him in line leaned her head against the pain-relief products and closed her eyes. He pulled out a wallet that looked as if it had been trampled by Clydesdales during the Civil War, and ever so slowly his gnarled arthritic fingers searched the cracked yellow plastic dividers as if it were someone else's wallet that he had recently retrieved from the street or the morgue.

Rennie watched, thinking that if he had been in a pharmacy in New York, he would have been beaten to death by the people in line behind him.

"Nope. Got my Legion card."

"That won't work." The young pharmacist opened the bottle and extracted several pills, rewriting the entire form. "I'll hold these for you, but you must go to the clinic and apply for your card and your medical benefits. Now, I know you don't have a phone, so I can't call and remind you, but you want to come get these pills before you run out. It's very important that you finish the entire course of this medicine."

"Yes, sir." Mr. Sticks handed him the twenty-dollar bill and took his pills, shuffling off, tipping his porkpie hat to everyone in line. Rennie couldn't help but feel better, seeing that Lotty was ignoring him too.

Rennie looked at her watch. She had been waiting over half an hour, and now she was going to be late for the concert. Her back hurt and she could feel her ankles swelling from the weight, the flying, the chocolate, and the humidity. She was carrying low and large for seven months, the doctor said; and she'd been having pain and spotting. He told her to take some hormone concoction and try to stay off her feet as much as possible. (That was a laugh.)

Even if Leo wouldn't marry her, even if he left, she wanted this baby desperately. Maybe because it was the first thing that was really her own. It was in her and she believed, in her deepest heart, that even if for the rest of her life she remained poor, blank little Wren bird to everyone else on earth, to this baby she would be the most important person in the world.

Oh, boy, she was really feeling sorry for herself! First of all, that wasn't true. Leo might not love her, but he cared about her. She was somebody to him. There were enough other girls on this island who had the hots for him, and she was the one he had chosen. And what about Brad? She knew Brad cared about her, maybe even loved her. She also knew he would have been a far better choice as a husband. Maybe they would have ultimately gotten to that if Leo hadn't come into their lives.

Finally the last diagnosis was made and Rennie was next. She was handing Mr. O'Brien her prescription when someone moved up next to her, reaching around her with one long, gold-bangled hand, making her nauseated with the heavy smell of jasmine and musk oil.

"Mr. O'Brien, I called about this." Athena Pidge towered over her. Rennie looked at the young pharmacist pleadingly, and he was just ready to tell Mrs. Pidge where the end of the line was, when his father ran forward, taking her arm. "I have it for you at the other counter, Athena." She turned, facing Rennie and glaring at her. Mrs. Pidge never greeted anyone first. She always waited to be addressed. Rennie felt faint.

"Hello, Mrs. Pidge," she heard herself saying, hating herself as the words fluttered out of her mouth.

Mrs. Pidge smiled, the most chilling smile Rennie had ever seen outside of a fright-night movie. "Well, well. It's the little mother. Welcome home, dear." She turned and allowed the nervous proprietor to lead her away, saving them all from a scene.

Rennie couldn't breathe. She held on to the counter waiting for the dizziness to pass. She *knows,* she thought, nodding to the young O'Brien who was concerned for her. "I'm okay," she whispered, catching her breath. *She knows everything we're doing. She must have her spies following us.*

He handed her the medicines and she stumbled toward the

door, wanting more than she ever had before in her life to go home, to be somewhere that was all her own.

Louie was sitting on his cab, playing gin rummy with Willie when she came rushing out. He jumped up and ran around to open the door for her, sensing in that radar-quick way that men who have grown up hustling for a living have, that something was wrong.

"What be hoppening in there? I saw Mr. Sticks come out and Mrs. Pidge go in. Quite a lot of coincidence for one day."

Rennie sank into the seat and put her head back. Louie closed the door and ran around to the driver's side. "Just keep that lobster calm, and I'll have the air-conditioning humming in a minute. Got it fixed like new this very morning. You be cool as a windy cay in no time."

Rennie smiled at him. "I'm okay. It's just hard to stand for that long. Let me close my eyes and rest a minute."

"You just shuffle off to dreamland, blondie. I'll drive so smooth, you'll be thinking you're in a hammock on Yellow Beach."

Tears slid down her hot, tired cheeks. Her defenses were lowered, hacked apart by the ominous presence of Athena Pidge, and so she could let more truth in. The truth was she was dreading the Whalers' concert. Not only because she was so tired and feeling so dumpy and fat and awkward, but because everyone on the damn island would be there. The Gibsons, Mrs. Pidge and her ex-husband, "The Third" and his band of bimbettes, and all the tourists and party-hardy crowd. She would be in the background and Leo would be in the foreground and women would hit on him and it would drive her wild.

Of course, Brad would be there, but Brad was bringing a date. Some schoolteacher from Maryland that he'd taken out on a charter. Great. She would probably end up losing them both.

Selfish, Rennie. Selfish and full of shit, she thought. But she couldn't seem to help the way she felt. She felt skinned.

Maybe it was all just hormones. Wouldn't that be nice? (Her sister used to call PMS "permanent menstrual syndrome.") She let the motion of the van comfort her. The AC was actually working and Louie was humming one of Bob Marley's old songs. It was the song, she remembered, that was on the car radio the night she knew that she was in love with Leo.

He was driving them to Billy Bartlett's in Big Red and she was in the front seat beside him. The car was so small that her leg was almost touching his and she could feel the physical power of his presence, the heat rising between them. They were all so keyed up about their big meeting with Billy that her nerves could hardly take any more stimulation, and she had moved her leg as far away from his as she could.

He turned his face toward her and winked at her and she thought, He knows what I'm feeling. All her life she had felt rather like a shadow. She had never in her entire life felt that anyone really saw her. Not in the way of Leo's wink. It was like he was telling her that he knew her. It was simply the most compelling response to her uncertain self that she had ever experienced, and she had felt a wave of passionate emotion crash down on her. *Splash.* She was in the deep blue lagoon of *amour.*

The funny thing about it was that she was now objective enough to understand that what she had injected into Leo's eye signal was probably just wishful thinking. If anything, it was Brad who really saw her. Most likely Leo's wink had been nothing more than a coconspirator's reassurance, but it was too late now for all of that kind of reasoning.

That night marked the end of weeks of work setting up their deal with Billy. They had all the first contracts worked out and they were driving over to Billy's house to present them. They were all spiffed up and they were all ready to go. Leo had already moved into her house, but nothing had happened between them. He was staying in the guest room. Rennie had hired the Un Jill to take care of the household, and she was living in the tiny maid's room. Brad had his own separate apartment down below, near the beach. It was as happy a time as Rennie had ever had in her life, and when she wasn't dumping on herself, she realized that it was probably as happy a time as any of them had ever had.

The Un Jill could now sit for hours in front of her own little TV, sucking her thumb and watching her favorite wrestler, Junk Yard Dog, an absolutely terrifying soul who wore a dog collar and leash, a big, overdeveloped black man on all fours, howling and barking like a cur. "Junk Yard Dog!" the Un Jill would shout out for no apparent reason, even when she was ironing or sweeping and not even watching TV.

Certainly it was good for Brad. His body was healing and he was without pain for the first time in years. He had a nice place to live and some hope for the future, and he was running the cat better than it had ever been run. He had made up his own ad, posing Rennie in a sexy little bikini, holding a platter of his specially-battered conch fritters and the marinated mushrooms that he diligently prepared every morning.

Make the most of our island paradise. Let Brad, Rennie, and Larry take you on the cruise of a lifetime. Gourmet cuisine and all the rum punch you can drink. Certified diving instruction and the latest in snorkeling and water-sports equipment. Have a day that will be remembered for a lifetime.

Their business had doubled, and most of their calls now were referrals from satisfied customers, and they were kind to each other with no old agendas clouding the present.

When she invited Leo to move in, he brought a little glamour and excitement to the group. They were still somewhat tentative together, like houseguests on their best behavior, but that also made each day a challenge, at least for her. She had put this small world together for all of them, and she was, in her own way, very proud, maybe even vain about that.

That was one of the things she had tried to explain to her father, showing him the ad and pictures of them all. But it was just too hard for him, his life was so different. She wouldn't even have *tried* to explain it to her mother or grandmother. She knew better. She was convinced when they thought of her at all, it was floating on a raft with a large, cool drink in her hand, getting a tan without a care in the world.

Anyway, she was just feeling sorry for herself, because she did have people who cared about her and a baby inside her that she could love and protect and raise the way she wished she had been raised. She even had a business. She had grown up sailing with her family, and Brad had taught her everything he knew about running boats. Now she was halfway toward completing the requirements for her captain's license. She *was* somebody.

"Buck up, Rennie," she muttered to herself, half out loud. If she didn't want to be treated like a victim, then she had to stop thinking like one. That's what Leo kept telling her, and he was right.

Leo never dumped on himself or showed self-pity. Neither of them knew anything about him, except that he had an ex-wife in Florida and he had been in the music business in California a long time before. She didn't even know how old he was! It was almost like that movie *The Man Who Fell to Earth.* He had just materialized in their lives. He never talked about his childhood or even mentioned a mother or father or brothers and sisters or where he had grown up. It drove them almost mad with curiosity, but they had quickly learned with Leo that if you pushed him or invaded the perimeter of his privacy, he would just flash those turquoise eyes at you and his jaw would go all tense and he'd close you out. They couldn't bear it when Leo closed them out, so they had learned not to pry.

It didn't really matter anyway. It was here and now that counted. That's what Leo said.

"All of this breast-beating Freudian bullshit that comes out of all those overeducated mouths. Life isn't like that. You just deal with it today. Everything else is a totally self-indulgent waste of time and energy, and it doesn't change shit. It is never going to fix one fucking thing that ever happened to you in the past or change any one of the sons of bitches who screwed you up. Grow up and let it go."

She tried. Boy, how she tried. What Leo didn't understand was what happened to that theory when you took it to San Juan and stuck it in a hotel room with your famous father and his child-bride.

She wiped tears from her eyes. When she and Leo had finally gotten together, one lazy dopey night when Brad was off the island on boat business, she was already so far gone, she could barely hear him when he told her that he could be with her and he could make love to her, but that he was worn out from relationships and he could never marry her or promise to stay with her and he *did not want* a family. He had been as clear as the water in Crystal Cove, but she was in love and did not think he really meant it. But he *did*.

Two of the most difficult moments of her young adult life had been telling Brad that Leo was moving into her room and telling Leo that, somehow, in spite of her diaphragm, she was pregnant. She had seen the look in his eyes and watched him shut down. It had not been the same since. She felt as if she were living with a spy or even a visitor from outer space (the Man Who Fell to Earth again) and that at any minute he would simply vanish, leaving her alone forever.

She was afraid to do or say anything that might upset him. She knew he had made her no promises and she could not blame him for not wanting the baby, but she did. That was the truth. She did blame him, more for failing to fulfill the fantasy she had created around him, than for anything else.

Louie stopped the car at the top of the road. It was too big to take down her narrow, steep driveway. She was so exhausted, she wished he could just sit her on her suitcase and slide her down the hill.

"Home again, blondie. Gave the little lobster the smoothingest ride he will ever experience." He hopped out and came around to open the door and pick up her bag.

"Thanks, Louie." They started down the drive to the white-and-blue house set into the hillside, hanging over the sea. Every time she walked down the driveway her heart skipped. It was so beautiful and so hard to believe that, at least for now, it was hers.

In the distance they could hear the sound of the Un Jill's TV. Louie chuckled. "Looks like wrestling day. That girl will come to no good. That man done put a spell on the poor child."

Rennie opened the door and Louie set her bag down on the tile floor. "Thanks. Will we see you and Eloise at the concert?"

"Maybe later. Got a big night, taking people back and forth. Eloise is working in the booth, selling crafts. We sneak in at the end. It's not the same since Bobby passed, just makes me feel bad."

Rennie paid him and he tipped his cap, whistling up the drive as if life were as easy and uncomplicated and hopeful and filled with joy as she wanted to believe it was.

"Junk Yard Dog!" the Un Jill shouted, and Rennie picked up her bag and went on with her day.

CHAPTER 6

Jesus Loves Me, This I Know

LEO LAMPI STOOD IN THE MIDDLE OF THE CEMENT-FLOORED bunker so optimistically called Sir Francis Drake Hall and shook his head. He lit a cigarette and walked forward toward the stage, which was jammed with enough synthesizers, amplifiers, electrical wires, lights, and instruments to rival a space station. What a bunch of bullshit. The contents of the stage represented everything Leo hated about modern life.

Here were a group of simple island men who had started out with nothing but beautiful God-given voices and some tin drums. Now look at them. It took a fucking barge just to transport their equipment. They lived at the mercy of every sort of technology, and at this very moment a power failure in the hall was threatening their ability to perform tonight. It no longer occurred to any of them to just turn all of the shit off and play for real.

Shades, the electrician who traveled with them but lived on Ancolla and led trail rides in the hills when he wasn't on tour, came up to him. Shades pointed at the booth and shook his head. He always wore dark glasses, had braided dreadlocks that hung in shiny black coils, like licorice twists, all the way down to his knees, and spoke only when there was literally no other way to communicate.

Leo stamped out his cigarette. "This is ridiculous, Shades. These guys started out with a piece of tin, probably part of someone's roof, some sticks, and a homemade guitar—and now if the fucking electricity shuts down, everyone spaces out like Milli Vanilli or some shit." Shades shrugged his shoulders and went back to work.

Okay, he had to be honest with himself. Part of his anger was that he was scared. This was the most important group he had ever played with in his life. It was a big deal that they had asked him, even if it was just for one local concert at the last minute, when their back-up drummer had gotten sick.

He had long ago given up the dream that he might one day really play serious music, but the loss continued to haunt him; being asked by the Whalers (who had heard him playing at Mombo's) was a real thrill. If they couldn't get the power back and the concert was canceled, he was at no risk of failing, especially in front of the entire fucking island.

Leo climbed up onto the stage and sat down at the drums. He hadn't played in a while and he wanted to double cover himself. Just keep the rhythm like they told him and let the flash come from the rest of them. Shades had hooked the drums up to some sort of computerized amplifier, and he couldn't figure out how to start it.

He felt old. Old and so fucking frustrated. Nineteen ninety-one. God. The future was here and he hated it. He had absolutely no interest in dealing with it. He did not want to "interface," as they called it, or "in your face," as he called it, with a computer, word processor, food processor, or any of the rest of the techno-trash cluttering our lives. He didn't even want to interact much with his fellow man.

He detested electronic music, compact discs, cellular phones, answering machines, and computerized or digital anything. He had absolutely no interest in a video phone that could show who was calling, a computer that could have a conversation, or any product that required an instruction manual.

Now that the next century was within periscope view, he resented more and more being pushed and bullied forward into a kind of life form that had no meaning for him. He was, he recognized, an endangered species. He was interested only in experiences and activities that he could perform with his hands, his reason, or his heart. He sailed mostly by the sky and one of his worst fights with Billy (Rich Brat from Hell) Bartlett had been about computerizing the cat. He still made coffee in a stovetop percolator, cooked everything possible on an open grill, hung his clothes outside to dry, had a wind-up watch, a manual typewriter, and of course, Big Red, a car that was the closest thing he could get to a toy run by ball bearings and rubber bands.

Now as fifty crawled closer he felt the fear of his future—this unwelcome new world that loomed over him in the dark of night —mocking everything he valued. He did not think it was going to be his kind of place. More and more it seemed as if he had finally been outrun by fate; the countdown to the end of the line was coming up.

He had been born too late, but he had been able to slide by, zigging and zagging around a future world that had always been far enough away not to overwhelm him.

Not anymore. Now it was everywhere. He couldn't even make a collect call without some terrifying voice simulation asking him questions. A machine asking him fucking questions and if he did not or would not respond, he was out of luck. Big Brother would certainly start with fucking AT&T.

Brad said he was unreasonable about technology and he didn't disagree. He was unreasonable about it. Why? Because it was so unreasonable itself! He had no gripe with progress; with men on Mars or under the sea; computer games, robot maids, microwave ovens, or the faxing of the universe. If that's what you needed. Cool. Have the party. It was losing the freedom of choice that drove him nuts.

You couldn't even buy a car anymore without all of that shit in it. It cost *extra* to have them take the junk out! A computer voice that told you when to stop, when to start, when to back up, take off the brake, put on the brake, fasten the seat belt. There were even some cars that had automatic belts that strapped you in against your fucking will!

There were "smart houses" run by computers being built by scientists and futurists. "Someday soon TVs may talk with washers, vacuums with doorbells," the article he read had reported. There he would be, stranded in the next century, the last hold-out, living in a "stupid house" without an "electronic brain" or window shades that raised themselves. Surrounded by neurotic appliances that couldn't communicate with one another and required weekly sessions with the stupid-house therapist who helped his

VCR deal with the loss and rage it felt from being so close to the TV but unable to have a relationship with it.

God! Rennie had already bought a camera that told her when to click! That in a nutshell was Rennie's problem. Just take the risk, woman. Click it and face the music. After a while even the camera stopped talking to her and he was sure, even though she never would admit it and just got mad at him for teasing her, that she felt rejected by it!

If it kept accelerating, by 2000 every appliance and convenience, gadget and means of transportation would be telling us what to do. Could anyone really want that? (In Japan, Shinto priests were being called in to bless new computers, and old parts were enshrined like the bodies of saints.)

It made him crazy just to think any further ahead than the next ten minutes. Which probably was in itself not so bad, because even ten minutes was more than anyone had any control over.

People thought it was really cool and New Age and a lot of other crap that he lived that way, but that is not why he did it. He really had no other choice. The past was far too painful and the future, far too frightening. Anytime he veered away from right this minute he was in thick shit. He stood up and lit another cigarette. Rennie would rag on him for starting to smoke again. The trouble with humans was that you couldn't just turn them off or pull the plug when they started telling you what to do. They were not voice simulated.

He jumped down from the stage and went out the side door. It was starting to get dark and the vendors were beginning to set up for the crowd. Spicy smells of street-food cooking filled his head. Caribbean barbecue and fried fish. He was hungry. No. He didn't want to feel logy. He would wait until after. Until the party.

The party reminded him of Rennie's return. He was not ready. Ever since he had come back from Aneconda he had been as edgy and tense as an overtightened guitar string. That's how he felt; like he was going to snap.

It had all started with that fucking crazy dream! He had turned Billy's ketch around and headed back and not stopped until he saw Angeltown harbor. The dream really blew his head open. He had never been very interested in psychoanalyzing himself or anyone else. He was superstitious about the entire process. He had always lived on his instinct and his gut and even though, God knows, he had messed up his life, he deeply believed that if he started analyzing things, he would mess it up a lot worse (and worse would probably mean dead or in prison). He chose to keep going in the only way he knew. But the dream had really unnerved him. What did it mean? Why would he dream about Willa, Bee Bee, and Lindy all together? Why were they after him?

One thing he had prided himself on was choosing women who were all decent and reasonable. He had used them and they had used him too, but he felt very little guilt because he had always been so clear about what he wanted. If they had chosen not to hear him, that was not his problem.

Probably the only real guilt he felt was about Maxie. He had wanted that baby with Willa (the only one he ever had wanted), and even though he had not left them he probably would have sooner or later. Regardless, he had abandoned his son, the same way he had been abandoned, and it was a dark and ugly truth that never left his heart.

He didn't feel that way about Tess, because Lindy had tricked him and in his code of ethics that absolved him. He had not wanted to get married again, let alone have another child—he had learned that much about himself after two marriages—and even though he did marry Lindy and gave it his best shot, he knew in his heart that he had never forgiven her and it had poisoned things.

But they were all women who could take care of themselves. They were all in better shape than he was financially and personally. He hadn't seen or read anything about any of them to trigger a memory, and because he held so fiercely to his motto of never, *never* telling any woman about his childhood or the women in his past, there had been no jealous scene with Rennie about his former loves. So what?

More likely it had to do with Athena. The male doll, with a large slash of chicken blood where his cock would have been, that she had placed in his boat locker. It was why he had taken off when Rennie left. He needed time to think and he always thought better at sea. Mrs. Pidge was the first real mistake in women that he had ever made, and it had unnerved him. It felt like his mistrust of technology. As if now even his instinct was threatened. He was losing the fine-tuning of his own inner radar.

How could he have been so mindless? He had always chosen
women who were strong and kind-hearted, if insecure. Mothering,
if you would, though that led to a lot of psychobabble bullshit and
he didn't like to look at it that way. But that is what he chose.
Women who adored him and would never do anything devious or
meanspirited, would never betray or abandon him.

Maybe above all else, in his heart he was still a four-year-old
boy whose mother had taken him off to what she said was a
playground, put him on the swing set, swung it real hard, and
when it finally stopped, she was gone. Gone.

The "playground" turned out to be a Catholic boarding school
and he had remained there (financed by the money she had left
with his birth certificate and instructions about his education), and
he had never seen her or anything resembling a relative again. A
father, he knew from nothing about. "Unknown" it said on his
birth certificate.

Women. Nuns, at first, were all he had known. But the first one,
la madre, was a real cupcake.

Maybe that's what Athena was about. A tiny bite on the old
poison goodie. Pidge was a bad momma. He had made a major
mistake in judgment. Why? Why now? Everything was coming
together for him for the first time in so long. Was that it? He had a
need to fuck up everything good?

Leo crossed to the parking lot where the road manager's trailer
was stocked with coffee and booze. Maybe it wouldn't be so bad.
Let Pidge cut the damn thing off. All it had ever done was get him
into trouble. Maybe it would be a relief. Naa. He'd probably just
start attracting some spiritual zealots, care-giver types who wanted
to make it up to him for his loss. Like the nuns. Of course, some
of them had had other things in mind. A perfect place for a Catholic orphan to learn about love—from some pimply-faced, man-
starved nun, with nothing on under her habit.

Tears filled his eyes. He saw himself back then. Barely twelve
years old. Jesus. He was freaking. He never thought about that.

Something was coming down. The dream was a warning. Maybe
it was about Pidge. Maybe it was about Rennie and the fucking
pregnancy. No one ever listened to him! He had come here in
utter despair and he had started over. He liked it here. He had
made real friends of Brad and Mombo, Louie, Eloise, and Rennie.

He liked these people. He enjoyed putting the deal together for them. He loved taking people out on dives and running the boats. He had a chance here. Brad and Rennie needed him. They looked up to him. He was like a hero to them. He knew how silly that sounded, but it was true. He always seemed sort of heroic to sheltered people and kids of privilege.

Even though they knew nothing about him they knew he was all alone. They never heard him complain about anything or any-one, and so to them he seemed beyond all that stuff. He seemed like a grown-up. He smiled to himself, taking the steps to the trailer in one stride and pouring himself a large container of coffee. Actually, compared to them he was.

No, that wasn't fair. They had helped one another. He gave them something they needed, a belief in themselves, and they had given him something he needed, a place to be. They were parents for him in that they had some security, and he was parents for them in that he had some wisdom. At least the kind they needed now.

He had always felt that someday Rennie would realize Brad was the guy she should marry and gravitate back to him. Leo had never thought that would end anything. They would just shift gears, change some toothbrushes around, and go on. He didn't mean to sound glib, he cared about her, but he also cared enough to know he was just a phase in her life, her "daddy" chapter, and treating her any other way would be deadly for both of them.

Well, guess what? Life was having, as fucking usual, the last laugh. She was going to have his baby and he was going to have to leave. God damn it! He didn't want to go. He was too old and too tired to start over again. He could never go back to the States, so where would he go? He could feel his heart accelerating from the caffeine and the fear. Maybe it wouldn't come to that. Maybe there was another way. Except for Pidge, he had always been able to deal with women.

In fact, he had never stopped being amazed by what he got away with. And not just with women either, though God knows, with women he had gotten away with murder. He could hardly even remember back to a time before he was aware of this thing, this power, if you will, over women.

They imbued him with all kinds of mysterious and special attributes he was quite sure he had never possessed. It was as if he were a blank canvas, a graffiti-clean subway car, an empty sheet of paper on which they could create their dream man, their figmentary relationship. All he had to do was keep his mouth shut. Talking too much was the quickest way to kill fantasy. Besides, they did enough talking for both of them. At least the ones who chose him.

That was probably why they chose him in the first place. He was quiet. They could do all of the talking, play both of the parts. It was fine with him. It made his relationships infinitely easier. They told him exactly who they were (or at least who they thought they were), and as a special limited offer, they told him who he was (or who they thought he was and who they wanted and needed him to be).

Sometimes he would just stand naked in front of the mirror and stare at himself dispassionately. He had never thought of himself as a vain man. He didn't even think he was particularly good-looking. Well, he was vain about his body. He had to admit that. Not that he thought he had a great body, but he cared about keeping in shape. He worked on it. Most of his life he had needed the fucking thing just to make a living. If he couldn't handle a boat, a scuba tank, a golf club, a fishing pole, or a tennis racquet he would have starved to death.

Well, maybe that was overly dramatic; there had always been someone along the road to help him (that power again), but no one ever helped him enough. And no one ever helped him without first connecting with him through sports or music. Music too—without good lung capacity you don't blow a very melodic horn. The drums and piano, even, took stamina and physical strength.

Still, he was not obsessed with being in shape. He rarely looked in the mirror except to shave or fasten a tie if he was playing. So what was it?

Corrine had told him he was the sexiest man she had ever seen and he had asked her, quite earnestly, what it was that made him sexy. "The look in your eyes." She told him. "You always look like you have seen something so sad, so bad, that it is all you can do to carry on. Wounded, Bambi-eyes. Terribly appealing, dear. Makes a woman want to save you."

He tried to find that in his eyes. But all he saw was a pair of pretty colored marbles. He could not see anything inside them.

Women had told him many things about himself, even women he hardly knew. They told him he was sensitive and vulnerable and brave and smart and funny and wise. They told him he was handsome and sexy and strong and mysterious and talented and deep.

They had also told him he was a liar, a bastard, a coward, a prick, a phony, a womanizer, a failure, a louse, and a queer; a lousy lay, a bully, and a lazy no-good son of a bitch.

Was all of it true? None of it? One from Column A and one from Column B? He didn't really care much anymore. Now he saw it all as their problem. He had never lied to any one of them. They had filled in all the blanks, creating him like some Frankenstein's monster out of their own longing, self-loathing, need, whatever. They invented him and then they recoiled in horror when the dummy walked and talked and turned out not to be Clint Eastwood, Ernest Hemingway, Vladimir Horowitz, Dizzy Gillespie, Marlon Brando, Spinoza, or whoever the hell else they had wanted him to be.

By now he could almost tell who would want what. He knew, for example, that all of the young rich girls, too young to even understand how old he was, who came with their families, eager to be free and away from their fat feathered nests, would always think he was Clint. Strong, silent, full of righteousness. A man who had walked away from the trappings of venal, materialistic urban life, because it was so corrupt. A man with a secret in his past. A man as unlike their pot-bellied, sun-burned, overworked daddies as possible.

The secretaries on package tours, more mature and less privileged, always went for Ernest. A creative man, sensitive and searching. They were willing to work and take care of him. They were used to bosses and remote men and had pretty much given up on Prince Charming, unless they could word-process his letters to Cinderella or something.

Then there were the older women. Divorced, maybe a little bitter and lonely. They always went for Marlon. They wanted to fuck. Get loaded and swim naked. Suck and be sucked. They also liked a lot of control, and Marlon—who could be tough, unfeeling and even brutal on command—could also be tortured, meek, and needy.

He had pretty well gotten it down to a science. Of course, it wasn't always that simple. It was never simple when he cared. Corrine was probably the simplest of his wives. She was rebelling and she wanted someone to rebel with but someone she could control. He would be a good boy, make her come, take her to fancy parties where everyone would see them, but she would call the shots, pay the bills, and thus keep him for her very own forever.

He accepted the rules of the game, though he knew that it never occurred to her that there were any, and he did what she expected him to do.

He wanted to please her and he wanted to help her break out of the suffocatingly snug minikingdom in which she had lived her entire life. He was very young and he still believed it was possible to change people. He saw himself as her deliverer both sexually and spiritually. He had even fantasized that one day, when he had made money from the boat-security business, they would sail off and he would write music and she would be his muse.

But it was not her dream, and even if it had been, she was too scared of change, too much a product of her background to dream it through. One night they had gone to see a Bergman film, *Smiles of a Summer Night*. He had been afraid, never having seen a foreign film before, that he wouldn't understand it and she would uncover a truth about him, something not written onto the page of Leo reality that she so scrupulously drafted, adding and subtracting paragraphs when they no longer fit her need.

He *had* understood it. He had, in fact, loved it. In one scene an old woman is listening to her daughter ranting on about her failed love affairs, and the world-weary mother says, "You cannot protect one single human being from suffering. That's what makes one so terribly tired." Tears had filled his eyes, and he had barely been able to control himself because he knew it was true. No one can hear anyone else's voice. No matter what you see or know is true, everyone has to find it himself and most people don't, at least not in time to do them any real good. It was the most truthful thing he had ever heard, because it applied to everyone he knew and especially to his wife, but it did not apply to him.

All of his vacuous, aberrant life he had been trying to find someone who saw him, who could point him in the right direction, who knew something true—a guide, a human north star who could help him set a course and lead him home.

All he ever found were people like Corrine who thought they knew everything and really knew nothing, and who were so busy playing all the parts that they never saw the curtain going down. Never realized until after he had left that the stage was empty.

The closest he had come to what he yearned for was Willa. Willa had had her paint brush, no mistaking it, but she did not just use him as canvas for her need. She listened to him. She believed in his talent and she made him believe that maybe he had something. Maybe he was not a fraud, a fabrication of fantasy, a cardboard dream man who got by on a facade and a certain glib facility for sport and sound.

She unsealed his deepest dream, and he allowed himself to believe that how she saw him might be the way he really was. Not just sparkle with ashes inside, but a core of good and gifts.

It made him vulnerable to her in a way he had never been able to afford. She did not need him to be rich or the best fuck in the Western world or the golden dragon slayer, father torturer, or whatever. She believed that he was talented and that they could live quietly together in a world of words she would write and music he would compose and raise Maxie and be in love and she made him believe it too.

When he saw the light in her eyes dim—because he saw that kind of thing—it had terrified him in a way nothing had before or since. It held the power of the old woman's voice; "That is what makes us so tired."

He felt overcome with exhaustion. As if every ounce of will and hope and energy had been sucked from him. What he had learned from Willa about himself was not what he had hoped to find. He was not that man. He was not that good. There was no great talent at the bottom of his Christmas stocking.

And yet he did not run, because this truth about himself was still more comforting than all the pretense, the years as a flashy backboard; a phony study of the player's ability, never tested in a real game. "We are all great stars at the backboard," he used to tell kids he taught to play tennis, when money was low.

He had let Willa lead him onto the center court at Wimbledon and he had been shut out. Her eyes changed and he changed, punishing her for what he saw in himself and what he did not have the courage to tell her he saw, putting her out of her agony.

He had never been much of a husband, and God knows, not much of a father, but he had come as close as he would ever come with Willa and Maxie. She had gotten the best of him, and when he knew it would soon no longer be enough, he had stepped on her love.

He always knew what his women couldn't take (since they always told him), and so he behaved in exactly that way, until he killed her love for him. When she asked him to leave, he knew he would never be the same again and that the women who came into his life afterward would suffer the consequences. Not that he would try to punish them for what he had learned with Willa, but because of the damage to his hope.

When he thought about Lindy and Bee Bee, it was always with great sadness. It was not their fault that they came afterward, when he had so little left to give.

Leo picked up a Coke and a bag of banana chips and headed back to the hall. The stage was now filled with crew. He looked at the expensive Swiss diving watch Rennie had bought him after he had admired hers. Five-thirty. He shook his head and swallowed the last of his coffee. This is when you really knew you were not in the States. Half an hour before showtime and everyone's doing the stuff they should have done hours ago.

It reminded him of an Italian television show Bee Bee had appeared on years ago when they were playing Milan. The host hadn't even seen her act, and then *ten minutes* before air time, they realized Bee Bee spoke only English! An interpreter ran over to say that she would sit beside her, on the air, and translate! Instead of a crew there was a bunch of crazy guys in tight jeans, running around pouring espressos and Pellegrinos for the guests.

They had a panel-style set where they sat Bee Bee down and some other musicians, all Italians, sat down too and Leo could see from the audience that all the name plates set up in front of them were wrong. Bee Bee's said SERGIO LUCA, ROME. A fat guy at the end, with a huge black mustache had BEE BEE DAY. He'd pantomimed to Bee Bee, who couldn't see him because there were so many people running around, and then all of a sudden—no guy with the clipboard or anything—they were taping!

Everyone talked at the same time, giving long-winded speeches to the camera. Bee Bee's translator kept whispering to her, "I can't quite understand them, but I think they're saying they don't like American music."

When it was Bee Bee's turn, she had about three minutes and then the translator started babbling on for another twenty or so, supposedly quoting Bee Bee, who hadn't said anything but that it was nice to be there and she was looking forward to attending the opera at La Scala. It went on forever and then it just stopped.

All the Italian television officials, the mayor of Milan, and a large audience of glitteringly chic Milanese had applauded one another and filed out to a lavish reception. They had laughed about it for weeks. The very thought of such a show on NBC was enough to send them off again. He had called her Sergio from then on.

Leo tore open the bag of chips and sat down on one of the hundreds of folding chairs provided by the concert promoters. The last thing he had ever said to Bee Bee was "Knock 'em dead, Sergio." Funny what you remember. He had kissed her and sent her onstage at Serena's, and by the time she finished he was gone.

That was not how he had wanted to go. He hadn't had much choice about it. The bad part was he had never been able to tell her that. God, what a prick she must think he was. He hoped she thought he was dead. With any luck, that's what everyone who knew him in Miami thought. Moses without the miracle. A trail leading to the sea and ending in the sea.

"Leo!" He turned and looked over his shoulder. Brad was moving toward him with an overripe brunette in some sort of green harem attire, hanging on his arm.

"Meet Marlene. She took the charter today."

Leo stood up and smiled at her. "Nice to meet you. Good day for snorkeling. I took two dive groups out this morning and it was clear as glass."

Marlene gave him one of those long, sliding, desperately available smiles. "It was great. Really great."

A schoolteacher from the Northeast, Leo thought, disliking her on sight. He should warn Brad about women like that. Women who said *great*. People who said *great* really annoyed him. It was the perfect pabulum word. It gave no information and served only to keep real conversation out. It was also almost always a lie. "How's it going?" "Great." It was what people said rather than communicate. It had its place, but to Leo it usually signaled someone shut down, out of touch, or just not very interesting to talk to. Besides, she was coming on to him. This was not what Brad needed, which meant that it was not what Leo needed either.

"Have you seen Rennie yet?"

Leo crumpled up the empty chip bag and tossed it into a trash container. "No. She's supposed to be here at six." Leo checked his watch. It was six. He laughed.

Brad put his arm around his date, pleased with himself. "What's funny?"

"Look at this place. It's six o'clock. All the ads say 'Whalers' Concert, Sir Francis Drake Hall, six o'clock.' All the tickets have printed on them 'six o'clock.' The doors aren't even *open* yet! The fucking ticket-takers aren't here. The *beer* isn't here. The *band* isn't here. They still haven't gotten the power to work! Can you imagine this in New York or L.A.?

"What really floors me is that somehow everyone knows they don't really mean six o'clock. But they all know what they *do* mean. Watch, all of a sudden everyone will appear, probably around seven fifteen. At least no one seems to mind. The locals expect it and the tourists are usually so mellow by the time they get here, they don't care."

"Rennie!" Brad waved. Rennie came in looking tired and confused. Leo moved up the aisle and kissed her. "What's wrong? You look like one of Willie's passengers."

Rennie smiled at him. "No way. I drove myself. I thought I was late. I thought you'd be mad."

Leo put his arm around her shoulder and walked her back down the aisle to Brad and the schoolteacher. "Why would I be mad—you're not in the *band*. I should have called you. They're obviously working on Ancollan time. Nothing's happening."

Brad came toward her, holding Marlene out like a badge of merit. "Hi, Momma! Marlene, this is Rennie."

The two women greeted one another warily, the itch of territorial imperatives twitching their senses. Leo and Brad made small talk, oblivious, in the way men can be, of the animal-pitched frequency of female jealousy.

"Leo! What is happening!" They all turned. Billy Bartlett the Third had barged in the side exit with his entourage. He seemed to be loaded. But then it was hard to tell, since he was always either getting, being, or recovering from having been loaded.

"The Third has arrived," Brad whispered to Rennie, and kissed her cheek. Evenings with Billy were increasingly falling under the category of hazardous duty. He was segueing rapidly from insecure and needy spoiled brat to petty warlord. None of them except Leo seemed to have any idea what to do with him.

He had been holding the new partnership agreement for months, dangling it before them but not signing. Only Leo seemed to intimidate him enough to keep their needs in play. He did not have to sign it. Mombo had told Leo the word was out that some outside guys from Lauderdale were interested in coming in, so they all knew that if Billy didn't sign soon, they could be hung out to dry, cut loose with nothing to show for all their time and effort. They had all agreed that tonight at the party Leo would try to talk to him and find out where they stood.

In the three years since they had hooked up with Billy, they had turned their venture, Blue Man's Beach Club, into the In place on Ancolla. They had the liveliest bar, the best food, the rooms were pleasant, and the dive shop and boat facilities were respected by "those in the know," as one of the diving magazines had put it.

Part of this cachet came from Billy's family's contacts and his party-boy image, but part of it came from Leo's strong, charismatic presence. Leo just had that. Where he was the action was. People gravitated to him. He made a party, a room, or a charter come alive. It had helped them immensely, and Billy was smart enough to value it.

All three of them—Brad, Rennie, and Billy—were cut basically from the same madras cloth. Billy was the least physically impressive of the three. He was one of those bland, sort of thin, sort of fair, sort of medium, sort of young, sort of receding, sort of guys who were indistinguishable by any feature, personality trait, or mannerism. He was almost impossible to remember or describe.

As if in reaction to his enormous physical plainness and general mediocrity of form and content, he made a loud noise. Every entrance was a cannon blast claiming the attention that was his due, no other way. He did not so much enter a room as attack it. Loud voice first, loud clothes next. He was never without a brightly colored Hawaiian shirt and some sort of cap or bandanna, and he was never, ever alone.

His days were spent recruiting the best-looking young women and the beefiest-looking young men in town for his evening prowls. The prowls started at Blue Beach and moved on, hitting every place where music, a party, or a visiting anyone was rumored to be, then moving to the water, taking off in one of Billy's boats to check out the Yachties, who were too hip to come ashore. When the season ended, he took his act back to Florida, where the season was starting. In July and August he was usually in the South of France; this summer, because of the deal, was an exception.

For Billy a night alone was a night of hell, a night that he was not in any way willing to risk. The real Billy Bartlett III was not on his dance card. The place where Billy hooked into Leo was there. Somehow Billy believed that Leo knew who he was (or wasn't) and if he made Leo mad, he might tell him. Rennie and Brad were comforting to him (as comforting as Billy allowed anyone to be) because they were marked, like him, by the same blandly pernicious, big blond tar brush of rich WASP familyhood that had left its sticky, permanent stamp on all of them.

His father was a bigger-than-life industrial monolith, one of those guys who advised Presidents and killed bears with a slingshot. He had mentally and physically overwhelmed his only son, snapping his slender spirit like a twig under a hunter's boot. He had crunched Billy and kept on moving. What was left, however, was a very unappealing person. So far none of them had ever found anyone who really liked Billy Bartlett. Rennie was convinced that, behind that lecherous, girl-collecting facade, he was gay, if he was anything. Men scorned and dismissed him, attending his soirées, drinking his French wines, accepting rides on his yacht, but making fun of him behind his back. Women did the same. The worst part of it all, at least as far as Brad could see, was that Billy was so obnoxious, such a drunken, spoiled, nasty little shit, that no one cared. He was not the Mouse that Roared but rather the Rat that Whined. It was sad, but it was mostly true.

They had all tried hard to be his friend. It was not in their nature to take advantage of someone and bad mouth him behind his back. Leo was really strict about that, and when Rennie and Brad would occasionally make fun of Billy, Leo would always stop them.

"If we talk, we walk." Not that they didn't talk about the deal and how to make Billy honor it—what Leo meant was the small-minded personal stuff or letting people gossip to them about Billy. That made Leo crazy. And what made Leo crazy neither of them was in any hurry to practice.

Lately, however (and maybe it was because of these guys from Florida), Billy had been so out of control that even Leo was letting a remark or two pass. They were all scared. He was so unstable now, he could do anything. If he blew them off, they would have to start over, move the boat, and worse, Billy would keep the reputation *they* had built. All their effort would have been for nothing. It was too depressing to think about.

Billy had his Walkman hooked on to a canary-yellow alligator belt and was dancing to his own music. He was surrounded by tall suntanned men and women in stylishly sparse outfits, all of whom seemed vacant and dazed. Everyone was loaded and everyone was dancing to Billy's beat. The tallest, blondest, and prettiest of the women was standing next to him, her eyes half closed, dancing by herself on the head of a hairpin, twirling strand after strand of her long, tangled blond mane and tossing them one by one back into the larger mass.

Leo looked at her. Marlene and Rennie looked at her. Rennie looked at Leo looking at her. Marlene looked at Rennie looking at Leo looking at her. Brad looked at Rennie and Marlene looking at Leo looking at her.

"So what is happening, Leo? This is like Deadsville! Who should I talk to?" Billy swayed back and forth, his flat pale feet sliding around on his rubber thongs.

Leo lit a cigarette. "It's cool. The band just came in and I can see Shades in the booth." Shades gave Leo the thumbs-up sign. "The power just went on. I'd better check the trailer. See you guys later." He turned to Rennie, sensing her distress. "Want to come with me?"

Rennie nodded and followed him out of the empty hall.

By seven o'clock all the tourists, mostly white people, had arrived. Many of them had been waiting outside since six, but with
the doors still locked and no one to let them in, Louie and Willie
and the guys had spent considerable time and energy reassuring
them that it was the right night, time, and place, and everything
would be fine. It had, however, been a boon for Eloise and the
food stalls and most certainly for the beer and punch booth.

Brad sat with Marlene and Billy's group in the front row,
watching people file in. Billy flopped up and down the aisles,
introducing himself to any attractive lone women and inviting
them, much to Brad's annoyance, back to their house for the party
afterward.

Brad watched the young American couples, many on honeymoon, settling in, striking up conversations with others like themselves. He was always amazed at this kind of social ease. The
Where-are-you-guys-from? kind of conversations he heard on the
boat every day. These people all seemed so relaxed in themselves
and with one another.

They were all similar in looks, interests, small talk, back-
grounds. These couples, freshly married, newly adult, all coming
from nuclear families of American middle-class expectation. Members of a church, a neighborhood, a professional organization.
They were so snug in their identities and their life choices. They
visited their relatives, went to church on Sunday, had (or would
soon have) two children, attended PTA meetings and church sup-
pers, became Brownie mothers and Cub Scout fathers, coached
Little League, went to see Aunt Margaret in the hospital, drove
Chevrolet station wagons. They were all Christians. They were all
Republicans. And they were all the keepers of the Dream.

By birthright he should have been like them, but he wasn't.
They only made him feel forlorn. It was as if he was lugging an
extra layer of something that they did not carry and whose absence allowed them to move on in that cheery, optimistic, talk-
alike, dress-alike, look-alike, think-alike, where-are-you-guys-
from? newlywed way that he would never share. He would always
be on the outside looking in. It would be his little secret. If it
walks like a duck and quacks like a duck . . . Well, he passed—he
seemed like them, but he was no duck. He was a fish out of water,

if he was anything. Flapping around on the dock, trying to get the hook out of his cheek.

Bringing Marlene had been a mistake. He didn't even like her. She was not a sincere person. She was obvious. He had done it to make Rennie jealous, to get her to take him seriously. Well, it had gotten her jealous all right—but not for him. Leo! Unbelievable. Marlene had practically stuck her tongue in his ear! What a joke. The whole thing was one big joke. His only friend and his only love. Maybe Marlene would go off with Billy's group at least, and he wouldn't be stuck with her for the entire evening. All he wanted now was to lose himself in the music and not think about what might happen later when Leo talked to Billy. "I'm going to get another beer. Want one?" He stood up. He needed some space and he did not want to have to make small talk with Marlene.

"Sure, why not," she said, and smiled at him, showing a smear of coral lipstick on her teeth. Suddenly he hated her. He hated women who acted like that. Cocky and teasing. He hated when they said things like, *Why not.*

"Okay. I'll be right back."

"Take your time." She winked at him. "I'll be fine."

He felt like smacking the stupid grin off her pudding face. He felt like crying. His back hurt from too many hours on the cat. Brad started up the aisle. The locals were coming in now, greeting one another, settling in. The room was changing, the energy swelling with the heat of the bodies. There was, as usual, no interaction between the tourists and the island people. It was as if some invisible dividing line were drawn down the middle of every situation. It still amazed Brad. If the locals talked to the outsiders and then turned to one another, it was as if they became different people. All the guarding and suspicion disappeared.

When he reached the door, he looked at his watch. Seven forty-five. The tech crew was onstage now, switching on the lights and equipment for the warm-up act. Good. It wouldn't be long now. Maybe he could hang around the lobby until they started. Then he wouldn't have to talk to Marlene. The thought made him feel worse. So much for the playboy life.

Rennie was all he wanted. Rennie and her baby. Even though Leo was the father, he thought of the baby as hers. Sometimes he

even thought of it as theirs, because he knew Leo would never stay
with her. He just knew it.

By the time Athena Pidge and her father arrived at Sir Francis
Drake Hall, they were too late to make an entrance. The concert
was almost over and the room was so jammed with sweaty, hyp-
notized, undulating bodies, who had long since abandoned the
pretense of "concert-goers" and were dancing, swaying, rocking,
and reeling. The carefully arranged folding chairs had been pushed
out of the way, and the entire room was filled with the hot, heavy
smells and sounds of people lost in the ecstasy of rhythmic abandon.

> *"You're running and you're running and you're running
> away—but you can't run away from yourself. . . ."*

None of this pleased Athena. Athena liked to make an entrance,
especially tonight when she had the gentlemen from Fort Lauderdale with her. She had counted on Billy Bartlett, Brad, and of
course Leo, seeing her with their pigeons. Well, she would just
have to move to Plan Number Two. She would take them to Leo's
party. Rather, they would take her, since they were invited and
she was not. Better. That would cause a stir. Athena was very fond
of causing a stir.

The police had cordoned off several seats at the back for them
and they took their places. She lowered herself, a queen before her
court, holding her head high and staying as still as steel. Moving to
music was so common.

> *"Running away, running away . . ."*

She checked the room, her eyes clicking like a camera lens set
too fast; without seeming to be paying attention, she saw everything.

Island men filled the floor dancing alone. The women—except
for a frenzied few—kept their seats, maintaining the stoic dignity
that was their only protection.

The rabbits danced wildly, slightly off the beat, the rhythms too subtle for their bodies. Stringy-haired, flat-bellied girls, with cigarettes propped in their chapped glossy lips, listlessly grinding their sturdy, solid torsos without emotion, pushing themselves against sun-brushed white boys, trying to dance black.

Billy Bartlett was hopping around as if his legs were encased in plaster casts. A puffy-faced woman in green harem pants was trying to get Leo's attention by shaking her sagging breasts and raising her arms over her head. How pathetic they all were!

Leo was onstage. He had taken off his shirt and his muscles were flexed, highlighted by the glistening sweat reflecting in the stage lights. Athena swallowed. He could still move her. She still wanted him. For this, above all else, he would have to pay. The spell must be broken. She had the blood of the greatest pirate of them all—the Danish cabin boy Ding Dong Wilmerding, captured when only a lad of twelve, who took to the pirate life with gusto. He was named for the ringing bells his musicians played in battle. The uncrowned Emperor of Soper's Hole, a rapacious and lusty leader whose blood ran in her veins, seed sown in one of his collection of island girls. Her father was weak, her mother long dead. She was his spiritual heir.

No one had ever loosened her control, except the white bastard. Mr. Yates. Mr. Larry (Leo) Yates, who had wandered in, shipwrecked and cast off, the sea slime from some other shore. For this he must pay.

"Stop that train—I'm leaving—and it won't be too long that I'm riding alone."

They all must pay. The three musketeers. Three white mice. What a joke! Without her father's consent the men from Fort Lauderdale could not invest in Blue Man's Beach. Without her father's consent Billy Bartlett could not expand his operation. Without her father's consent the three rabbits could not become partners, and without her people there would be no one to clean the rooms, cook the food, deliver the clean linens, or maintain the facilities.

What fools they were not to realize this! This was *her* island.

From the night that Leo had left her, taking the sick cow of a girl with him, costing her money and making a fool of her on her home terrain, revenge was all that filled her head. It was the only relief from the Leo lust that still drove her wild in the night. He must be punished for what he had done. They all must be punished.

Billy Bartlett held the land lease and his father was an associate of the men from Fort Lauderdale. Billy she must keep. But the others she must destroy. How this was all to come about, she was not yet sure. She needed something to use against them. Her father was more interested in his bribe than in her needs, but he was also afraid of her and liked to keep her happy. She was beginning to sway him toward her scheme to push Leo, Brad, and Rennie out and make her the partner on the project. Then Leo would return to her. He would have no choice.

Billy's father and the men from Fort Lauderdale were not stupid, however; and she did not yet have enough to offer them. This was what she needed to find. And she must get rid of the others. She must make them leave Blue Man's Bay and leave Ancolla. For this she already had a plan.

> *"I went downtown . . .*
> *I saw Miss Brown—she had Brown Sugar*
> *all over her buga buga . . ."*

What fools they all were. A bunch of greasy, grinning dominos. Black-and-white plastic pieces, she could send crashing with a clap of her hands.

> *"Kinky reggae . . . kinky reggae*
> *Right on . . . Right on . . . Right on . . ."*

At the party she would look for something extra to use.

CHAPTER 7

We're Gonna Have a Party

THE SUCCESS OF ANY PARTY DEPENDS LARGELY ON THE EX-pectations of the guests. If, for example, the art and museum–world folks that the Gibsons brought to Rennie's house after the concert had arrived at such a function in New York City, expecting sedate surroundings, polarized and career-focused conversations, a few discreet sips of white wine and a dainty canape or two, only to encounter a gyrating, reefer-reeking throng of half-naked frolickers of all sexual proclivity and racial identity, whose common goal was to get as crazy as possible as quickly as possible, they would have left aghast and offended.

By the same standard if the feverish group who found their way in the late night hours up the winding, potholed mountain road, had been greeted by a bunch of serene, sleekly tailored New Yorkers sipping Evian water and whispering over the Chopin about the patina in the primitive tin paintings on the whitewashed walls, they would have fled as fast as a lizard in a lightning strike, never again to attend such a deadhead disaster trying to pass as a party.

Expectation. A church raffle should not feature a naked blonde jumping out of the sponge cake and the afterhours-club crowd is not interested in ginger snaps and the Swedish Weavers Chorale performing old Norse folk songs.

Everyone came to Rennie's expecting to have fun. Fun, then, as the given, was easy to have. By midnight there was nowhere, inside or out, to sit, dance, move, or breathe. Everyone interesting on the island was there, from the mildly famous British movie actor known for his psychotically-tipped character roles and his drunken cockney wife, escorted by a group of Australian millionaires who had docked nearby, to the infamous Mr. Sticks (sans donkey). This was a party they would talk about for a long time.

Rennie already knew that. She had grown up going to parties and she knew a good one when she saw it. The fact that it was hers and her first made it even better. And this was the best part of any party, the middle. Rennie had always hated the beginnings and endings of parties. (Actually, she hated the beginnings and endings of everything—movies, books, meals, relationships.) With parties though she usually had more control. She could come late and leave early, thereby having to do only the middle. But not when it was her party and her house, which was probably why she had always been terrified of giving one.

Well, she had gotten through the beginning and Brad and Leo had promised her that she could leave and go up to bed anytime she wanted and they would do the end and the cleaning up, so she could relax now and enjoy her achievement. Rennie made her way slowly from the kitchen to the large open living room, looking for Leo. He was nowhere in sight. She saw Brad who, miraculously, had held a chair for her and she crossed to him, passing groups of people, many of whom she barely recognized.

A young man with purple smudges under his eyes, wearing a tuxedo shirt, jacket and bow tie and a black bathing suit, was hitting on a fashion model in a see-through polka-dot skirt and a tiny tank top that kept shifting to reveal her left breast. "When I'm lying on the beach, I'm happy. I don't know why I can't feel like that the rest of the time," she was telling him, while pushing her breast back into place.

"That's called a vacation, honey. Everyone's happy then."

A young baby-faced woman with close-set green-rimmed eyes was dancing with one of Mombo's cooks, who kept tickling her neck with his goatee. "Havin' kids really changes your life," she said to no one in particular.

Rennie reached Brad, who was talking to the Coopers, an amiable middle-aged couple who ran charters on their own yacht. There were many couples like the Coopers in the islands. Some had come to retire, gotten bored, and started small businesses.

Many had come because they had lost what they'd had on the mainland and needed a place to start over, out of range of the pitying looks in the veiled, patronizing eyes of their old comrades.

The Coopers were a couple like that. He had made a fortune in construction, only to see it fall apart from too much booze and too many bad investments. They had left their country-club life-style and come to Ancolla with just enough left to buy a boat. Milly Cooper told Rennie that their first year in the Caribbean they had earned what she used to spend on a *suit*. Eventually they built a nice business, taking wealthy families out for week-long cruises. Milly cooked and Bob captained and they let go of who they had been and became who they were now with good cheer and good grace.

It was only sometimes—late at night or at the end of a rough charter, when they would pull into the marina—that Rennie could see the loss in their eyes. They had the same habit of disguising this loss that all the expatriates did. They continually boasted about how much better their island life was and how glad they were to be here rather than where they had been. Rennie tended to doubt people when they said this. She knew it wasn't true for her, so it probably wasn't true for them (like the song said: "running away"). It wasn't a bad escape, but they all knew in their heart of hearts that that is what it was.

"Rennie! Sit down. You must be exhausted!" Milly Cooper moved over, making room for her.

Brad handed her a glass of water. "Want me to try and find some food for you?"

"Nope. Water is fine. Beer would be better, but I shouldn't."

Milly patted her hand. "Won't be long now. This is the hardest part. I remember feeling like a sea turtle someone had flipped over. Just this huge, solid shell imprisoning me, and little arms and legs jerking up and down, not getting anywhere."

Bob Cooper laughed. "Very sexy image, Mills."

"Sexy, my foot! We were just telling Brad about our last charter. I thought we'd seen just about everything after ten years down here, but these two took the cake.

"We left last Friday with what seemed to be a nice, normal young honeymoon couple. Well, we headed out toward Virgin Gorda and they went below to get settled and Bob is at the helm and I come out with one of my special trays with hors d'oeuvres and rum punch and I'm setting everything up—and suddenly there they were, naked as sea eels! I was so startled, I dropped the tray! Punch and guacamole all over the deck! 'I hope we didn't surprise you. I think we forgot to write on the application you sent that we're nudists. It's not a problem, is it?'

"Well, they were paying us top price, ten thousand for the week. For that money, in this economy, they could spend the week wearing their granny's garter belts, for all I cared.

"So, for three days we serve them dinner, stark naked. We serve them breakfast, stark naked. After lunch on the fourth day the man, who was six feet four inches tall—with appropriate size equipment, if you get my meaning—he goes up to sunbathe and he's spread-eagled on the deck. I am trying like all hell to act as if I am oblivious of this and his wife, who is staring at him with a very honeymoonie gaze, pokes my arm. 'Isn't that (pointing to his equipment) the most beautiful thing you've ever seen?' By the end of the week I never wanted to see anyone naked, ever again. So much for sexy!"

Brad and Rennie were enjoying themselves. They liked the-one-that-got-away kind of stories that all charter people had. Brad rubbed Rennie's neck. Rennie sighed, relaxing into his hands.

Brad sat forward. "Last month we took out this great big Nordic blond actress. I can't mention her name because you'd know her and her manager made us promise. Well, the manager takes Rennie and me aside when we're getting lunch ready and he says, 'Listen, I have to confide in you now because she's well known, and I'd hate to read about what I'm going to tell you in the papers.

" 'I give her massages and I am going to give her one after lunch, it helps her release tension. But she, uh, she, uh, suffers from an intestinal disorder and when she's touched, she, uh, releases *air*. Please ignore it. Whatever you do, *don't laugh*. I must have your word. I will make it worth your while.'

"Well, shit, we gave our word; looked like a big tip to us! So they eat and this girl does not speak one single word to us, it's like we're not there, and then the manager, or whatever he was, he goes through all this elaborate stuff, setting up the mats, the oil, pouring her champagne, giving her some kind of pills. Well, by then we are really curious, but we're playing it very low key.

"All of a sudden the guy touches her. *Bzzzzz!* I mean, we're talking air raid–siren farts! Every time the guy touches this woman it's like that old raspberry buzzer! Even *outside,* the whole deck is like toxic fumes! I swear to God, if we had lit a match, the entire boat would have blown up!

"Well, the guy said, 'Don't laugh,' but I thought we were going to explode! We stayed at opposite ends of the deck. If I so much as caught a glimpse of Rennie's face, I was gone. We eventually had to go below and lock ourselves in the engine room to get the hysterics out of our system. It went on for hours: *Bzzz! Bzzz!* Finally, when we could not stand another minute of it, he stopped. She slept for the rest of the charter. When we got back, she gets up and brushes right by us like Princess Di or someone, never said one word.

"I mean, how haughty can you be when you've just farted your brains out all across the BVIs in front of two total strangers! At least the guy didn't stiff us. We got a huge tip. We had to Lysol the entire deck! It smelled like someone's old ham sandwich up there for days!"

They were all laughing so hard that no one saw Athena and the men from Fort Lauderdale come in. They were doubled over, letting in the best part of any day, of any part of anytime on earth, the time when laughter loosens everything free and real and alive within us, making everything else, even ourselves, okay.

Leo leaned over them. "Look who's here," he said, and they knew that for them, the party was over.

"What does she want here?" Rennie's voice was as small as a child's. She looked up at Leo, her face white under the red of her sun-covered fairness, her round melancholy eyes searching his, looking for help.

A wave of rage hit him. He wanted to grab the Pidge bitch and toss her out. Rennie was the kindest, most decent person he had ever known, and she did not deserve whatever it was Athena had in mind. Leo knew she had something in mind. This was not a woman who made social calls. "Brad, take Rennie upstairs and meet me in the kitchen. It's time for a talk with Billy-boy."

Brad nodded. The Coopers were eavesdropping as discreetly as possible. They were not gossips, but on an island like Ancolla, gossip was the only real conversation. Newspaper delivery was irregular and the television reception was at best uneven. They lived by word-of-mouth reports on the doings of the others and whatever third-hand news from the mainland they could find, in between *USA Today* deliveries and the international edition of *Time* magazine.

Rennie let Brad help her up and they made their way as jovially as possible past the Coopers and the Gibsons and the others they knew, exchanging vacuous pleasantries. Good manners, always the last thing to go in civilized people. When the social niceties were breached, either a life was threatened, adultery interrupted, or a stroke, heart attack, or brain seizure in process.

Rennie made it up to her room, her smile in place, having thanked everyone, sober or interested, for coming and then collapsed on her bed. She sobbed into Brad's shoulder as much from the sheer tension release and the exhaustion of this very long, very complex day, as from the outrage of Mrs. Pidge invading her nest.

Brad settled her down and left, locking the door behind him. "I'll tell Leo to sleep down with me. You keep the door locked."

Rennie was unnerved enough not to object. It would be a relief not having to deal with Leo or any of it tonight. She wanted only to curl into a ball and lose herself in sleep, the baby turning and kicking, comforting her from the inside out. Tomorrow. Tomorrow she would deal with it.

Brad found Leo waiting for him at the foot of the stairs. He followed him outside and down around the deck. The sky was black as an ink pad stamped with yellow sticker stars. It was a made-up sky, a kid's cutout on Halloween.

Leo lit a cigarette. They were both looking up into the wizards' night world. The blackness, no matter how brilliant in its witchcraft, still a reminder of the murky dangers lurking behind the stillness. The mythical power of the voodoo curse; a virus that will hit one person and miss another, until next time.

"Those guys with Billy are the money men from Lauderdale. I think it's a good sign he brought them, Brad. If he was trying to cut us out, he sure as hell wouldn't parade them around here. I went up and introduced myself when you were with Rennie. They said they'd heard about all of us and were eager to talk about the project—so relax. We may be okay." Leo handed Brad his cigarette. Brad shook his head.

"What about Pidge? Rennie is just freaked out. She's up to something, Leo. I can feel it."

Leo, throwing his head all the way back, squinted into the moonlight, the way day sailors did in the sun. "Yeah. I know. First I'm going to get Billy. Then I'll try talking to her. Why don't you go down and play host to the Florida boys. Find out whatever you can." Leo stamped out his cigarette, sending the sparks flying off like tiny fireflies. "Boy, I'm tired. I wish everyone would just fucking go home."

They stood together for another minute. Men who loved the sea and being outside, taking the gift of a moment of peace in nature's blazing night world, preparing for the other, less appealing part of God's plan. The part that involved their fellow travelers.

Billy was dancing with Marlene when Leo found him. He was drunk but not any more than usual, not too drunk to listen. "Billy. I need a word. Please excuse us."

He took him by the arm and moved him away before the unpleasant woman could invite herself. Leo had been avoiding her all evening. The last thing he needed tonight, or *any* night, was another needy woman wanting to be serviced. Rage whipped against him.

All he had wanted to find on this fucking island was a place to be quiet and alone. How in the hell had everything gotten so complicated? Was it him? It must be. If he had just stayed away from the women, none of this would be happening. God fucking damn it! Where would he have to go? A leper colony? The gay section of Fire Island? He laughed to himself. Wrong, Leo. You've had your run-ins with those voyagers too.

The only answer was to make enough money to live on his boat (a boat he did not have anymore), a boat he would buy to sail the seas. Alone. Someday he would have that. Peace and quiet, a clarinet and a boat. Period. Maybe a few porno tapes for long, stormy nights or one of those inflatable female dolls with the sexually correct anatomy. One that didn't want to get married and have babies. One that didn't have a family, get jealous, angry, disappointed in his accomplishments (or lack thereof), or expect anything from him. One that he could just deflate and store in the supply locker. A perfect lifetime companion.

He maneuvered Billy across the terrace and down the steps to

Brad's apartment. Billy wobbled along beside him, feeling to Leo almost as if he had no bones in his body. There was something feathery and wispy about him, as if he were not made of flesh, blood, and muscle.

Billy grinned at him. "So, big guy. What's the emergency? I was just starting to unwind."

"Billy, cut the shit. I'm just tired enough to say something I'll regret. Tell me what the fuck is going on. In you trot with Pidge and the Suits from Lauderdale, never mentioned a word to us that they were already involved or that they were negotiating with you. You've been squirreling us around with the contract for months. It's not right. We've worked too hard for you, man. We trusted you and I want to know what this means."

Leo's jaw was rigid and his eyes flashed. Billy looked up at him as if he were a sea god, or worse, a father. A fierce, overpowering father like his own, who could tread on him and never slow down. The difference was that Billy wanted to be Leo's friend, wanted his approval and respect. He no longer had any such aspirations toward his own father.

He giggled, fear and substances shaking his nerves. "Hey, my main man. I'd never pull any shit like that! I've got the contract all ready to go. I swear, buddy.

"When these guys called me, I held back, I admit it, because I didn't quite know how to work it out. I mean legally. I mean, what part of what do you guys get, you know? So I had to talk to my old man's lawyers and stuff, and it's cool. These guys really dig what you've done. They like the image, that we're the quality dive club and all. They want you guys. It's cool! Tomorrow. I'll bring it over tomorrow. Really. I could use the back-up. I mean, these dudes are tough. You're good at this stuff. Just chill out, man. We're happening."

Leo could feel the tension in his head ease a bit. "What about Pidge?"

Billy shrugged his shoulders. He pulled a joint out of his washed-silk shorts and started to light it. Leo took it out of his hand and put it on Brad's dresser. "I said, what about Pidge?"

"Hey, man. I don't know! She was with the guys. I think she wants a piece of our action. She wants more than the concessions. She's buttering up the boys, but I've got the lease. Her old man's going to get his fat ass greased as usual. So I don't think she can do much but stick pins in dead cats and that jazz." Billy giggled, pleased with himself.

Leo did not respond. "She's trouble, Billy. Be careful and keep your fucking mouth shut. You are way over your head with her. Don't try to be a big shot. She'll have at you, Billy. And we'll all suffer. Do you hear me?"

Billy nodded and held his hand out for the joint. "I hear. I dig it. I'll be cool."

Leo nodded, releasing Billy from his command. "Okay. I want you to lead the animals back to the ark. Start getting everyone out of here. Rennie's not feeling well. I'll see to Pidge. You'll be back here tomorrow at noon with the contract. Right?"

"Right. Gentleman's honor, man. We're out of here."

Leo waited until Billy left, preparing for the last task. Always save the worst for last, Corrine had taught him. What a ridiculous way to live! The opposite was the way. Get the worst part over first. That's what he would do from now on. That would be his new-way-of-living resolution number one. The first post-Pidge resolution. He would flip his operating style.

When he got back upstairs, however, Athena was gone, having slipped out without any drama, as if she'd known he was coming to confront her, as if she could sense him wherever he was or whatever he was doing. Since he had not seen her go, he could not know that she had taken his photo, the only one he had let anyone take of him since he had been on the island. A shot on the cat that Rennie had begged him to let her have. He'd been squinting into the moonlight, like tonight, all alone on the deck. It was in an antique silver frame that had belonged to Rennie's grandmother, and Athena had slipped it into her pocket as she glided, sleek and quick as one of her felines, out into the night.

Ten A.M. the morning after the party everyone at Rennie's house is well into their day. Rennie and the Un Jill are busy putting everything back in order. Leo has gone for a run on the beach. Brad has just returned from his morning therapy swim and is talking to Billy on the telephone.

"Leo said you were coming at noon with the contract."

"I know. I know. But the guys from Lauderdale want to go out on the cat. It's important, Brad. I think we should all go. I'll bring the contract with me."

"Okay. But Rennie's not up to it, she's got to rest. You'll have to help out."

"No problem. I'll even wear a bikini."

"That'll put them off their lunch."

"So I'll see you guys there at twelve."

"Yeah. I mean, I haven't asked Leo yet. We've had the boat docked for repairs. We haven't booked any charters this week because he's been working on it. So if he says it's not cool, you'll have to stall them."

"Tell him, to make it cool. It's *muy importante,* dude."

Brad put down the phone and shook his head. He did not have a good feeling about any of this.

Rennie came up behind him and handed him a fresh cup of coffee. "What's up?"

"Billy wants us to take the boat out. Show-and-tell for the guys from Lauderdale."

"I thought it was in the shop?"

"It's back in the water, but it may not be ready. Anyway, he's not bringing the contract over. He says he'll bring it with him on the charter. I hope he's leveling with us. I don't know, I feel really spooked today."

Rennie kissed his cheek. "Me too. Someone took something last night."

Brad faced her. "What?"

"It sounds silly, I guess. I noticed it first thing when I came down, because I keep it on the table by the window so I can see it from everywhere in the room. The picture of Leo in that silver frame my grandmother gave me. It's gone."

"Maybe it just got misplaced. Someone could have picked it up to look at it or moved it to make room for glasses and stuff."

Rennie shook her head. "I've looked everywhere."

"Who would want that? I mean, the frame is nice, but none of these turkeys would appreciate that kind of antique, and what would anyone want a bad Polaroid of Leo for?"

"I don't know. I just know that it's gone."

Leo came in, his T-shirt wet with sweat. "What's gone?" He was still out of breath.

"My picture of you."

Leo inhaled, wiping his face with his shirt. "You sure?"

Rennie nodded.

Leo looked at her. One of the things she loved about him was that he always respected what she said. If she said it was gone and she was sure, that was enough for him. He never did any of that awful, male macho stuff, not trusting, or believing that women ever knew what they were talking about. The kind of stuff that her father had done to all the women in her family. It made her feel great about herself when he took what she said seriously.

It reminded her of all of those thrillers she'd watched where the woman sees a monster or a madman or people from outer space or her dead child, and no one believes her. She turns to her husband or boyfriend and they always act like they kind of believe her, but it always turns out that they don't. In the end they are always revealed to be the patronizing scumbags we knew they were all along, and she is saved from a life of lies with a chauvinistic bozo, usually by the detective assigned to her case, who does believe her and also falls in love with her.

Rennie smiled at Leo. That was her problem. She had watched too many movies like that and had somehow lost track of the limitations of reality. Probably if she came in saying that little purple men had taken the photo, Leo wouldn't believe her either.

What about Brad? Would he— What was she doing! Was that to be her *test* of who cared about her? Brother! She hoped these thought patterns would wash out of her with the afterbirth. They made dealing with people extremely stressful. Come on, Rennie. She turned away from them both, thinking they might be reading her weird thoughts, and went to get Leo's health drink.

Leo followed her. She handed him the drink. "Pidge," he said, and she nodded. She knew he was right, and she was so grateful to him for saying it, not pretending or hiding it, that tears popped out of her eyes and rolled in two fat wet lines down her shiny cheeks.

Brad came up to them. "Leo. Billy called. There's been a change of plans. The Lauderdale boys want to go out on the cat. Billy wants us all to go. He says it's important and he'll bring the contract with him. Is the boat ready?"

"No, it's not ready! But I guess it will have to be. Meet me there in an hour. We can make do. But we can't use the sails. They'll have to settle for a motor cruise."

"Fine. Why don't we just go over together?"

Leo gulped down the drink and headed for the shower. "I've got something to do first." He winked at Rennie, that same wink that had gotten her into all of this in the first place and she winked back, wiping the tears from her compliant face.

Athena Pidge lived in a house at the top of the tallest hill on Ancolla, hanging over a beautiful green-water cay. The cay was called Long Nose Cay because—even though the water was so clear you could see the schools of silver fish swimming right through it and the sand was so fine, it melted under wandering toes like chocolate fudge—it reeked from some fetid smell. Most likely rotted sugar cane, one of the by-products of the manufacturing of local rum. But there were all kinds of stories, island lore, as to the real cause—all of them grisly and scary enough to keep many folks from buying property in the lush and lovely hills that lined the beach. This was fine with Athena. Athena's house was called the House of Blood because it was painted bright red inside and out. Everything in it was red except the floors, which were pink. The effect was somewhere between a huge beachfront box of Valentine candy and hell, depending on the state of mind of the visitor. To Leo, it had been the latter.

Down below, set back from the cay, was a hotel, the only one on Long Nose, owned and run by Athena's uncle and his family. From the air or sea Pidge Point Inn was the kind of place that graced travel brochures designed to show a fantasy view of Ancolla. The peeling paint, the rusted-out dryers in the laundry room and the broken-down video-game machines and three-legged pool table in the "Game Room"—all of its flaws and peculiarities were hidden.

The shabby condition of the rooms—long dead ACs, phones that never worked, toilets that flushed into an illegal and probably contaminated drainage ditch (emptying the mess into the idyllic, clear waters of the beach, another reason, so the taxi drivers said, for the smell)—were not in evidence. Neither were the surly barkeeps and unfriendly waitresses or the hustlers who roamed

the patios, looking for tourists with "inclinations" and large pockets.

By far the most interesting thing about Pidge Point Inn was the
graveyard, which was set smack in the middle of the "Garden
Court," between the "Swedish Sauna" and the "Game Room."
Here were buried the bodies of all the Pidges from the uncle's
side. The graves were the only well-tended area of the hotel and
were the subject of much gallows humor among the package-tour
guests, young army and marine recruits on leave, and foreign visitors, whose unknowing travel agents had seen only the brochure.

In its favor, Pidge Point Inn was lively, with the best reggae
bands on the island, cheap but strong local rum drinks, and tasty
(though suspicious) barbecue. Uncle Pidge made a living, protected by the laxity of his brother's rules on hygiene, taxes, and
permits.

Athena hated her uncle and wanted nothing more than for the
vile, tacky place to disappear. In fact, one of her plans for the
future included just such a scenario. When she had found Leo, he
seemed to be her way to achieve this.

Leo could run the inn. She would get rid of her uncle and re-
create Pidge Point. For such a task, she needed a man. Leo was the
closest thing to a real man she had ever found. Now he was gone
and helping the rich rabbit build her competition. So. Pidge Point
Inn would wait for a while. Like all good pirates, Athena was not
impatient. She could roam, finding the right prey, the ship with
the crew too sick from scurvy and battle to resist. Her uncle was
old and had only lazy, worthless children who posed no threat to
her desires. She would wait. Something would turn up.

She had taken the first step. Bright and early she had gone into
Angeltown to the post office and mailed off the photo of Larry
Yates with a note to her friends in Miami. "Please find out everything you can about this man. It is of urgent importance." These
friends were in the drug business, and they knew everything about
everyone in Florida.

If there was anything she could use to get Leo back, they would
be able to find it. So that was an important step requiring patience
and inner calm. These tests of nerve appealed to Athena. She liked
to conquer herself as often as possible, it kept her in form.

Of course, there was only so much patience that a woman of her restless nature could endure, so she had moved forward on her other scheme, just in case. She had, of course, heard about the fabled partnership agreement, and it was not good news. That was why, while the party was keeping all the rabbits and island big-eyes like Mombo occupied, she had sent her flunky to set the bomb on Brad, Rennie, and Leo's precious cat.

Without the boat what would their partners want them for? What would the gentlemen from Lauderdale think? Businessmen were as superstitious as voodoo cultists. They would run right into her waiting, perfumed arms. The boat was in for repairs. No one would be on it. A terrible accident. A terrible shame. Leo would be broken. So even if the photograph led only to the water's edge, she was not waiting idly by.

She was not surprised to find Leo at her door that morning. She could see the hate in his eyes, and that she did not like. She could not believe he could prefer any other woman to her. She could not believe he no longer desired her. She had always had any man she wanted. She was majestically beautiful. She was a former Miss BVI in the Miss Universe contest, and she was fantastic in bed. How could he not succumb? Well, when he was weaker, he would not be able to resist. She would just have to be patient.

She met his eyes when he accused her. She said nothing. She neither confirmed nor denied his accusations. "I'm sorry to hear the little mother is so upset," she said. "I will ask around and see if anyone has heard about the heinous crime." She was mocking him.

"Why?" he asked over and over, but she just smiled.

"Why, *what*, rabbit man? Why is the sky blue? Why is the sea salty?"

"You can't hurt me, you know," he said, his fluorescent eyes stabbing her heart.

"I see, Mr. Jesus Christ," she replied.

"No. Not at all. Jesus suffered for us. I suffer only for myself, so you can't hurt me."

"We will see," she said, but she was no longer quite so confident.

Then he turned and over his shoulder she heard him say, "We're taking the boat out for the Florida guys. I'll be back here at four o'clock, and I want the picture and the frame."

If Leo had looked back, he would have seen that Mrs. Pidge was no longer smiling. If he had seen her face and waited, she might have told him about the bomb and everything that happened would have been changed.

But he did not stop. He was too angry and too late to stop, and by the time she had recovered enough to go after him, he was sailing downhill in his silly red car and she had locked herself inside her House of Blood, afraid to turn back. It seemed that voodoo worked two ways. This had never before occurred to her.

Part III

Everybody

CHAPTER 8

Ginsenging in the Rain

"LISTEN TO THIS." WILLA ROLLED OVER ON HER STOMach. "Researchers are puzzled about what anomaly in the cultures of Eastern Asia promotes the psychiatric disorder called koro, in which men or women become panicked by the fear that their penis or nipples will retract into their body and kill them."

Lindy came out of the bathroom, swathed in thick white towels. "Oh, yeah, that. They call it penophobia or nipplrexia."

Bee Bee finished her pushups and fell forward. "Really?"

Lindy threw her a towel. "Of course not, *really*! That's the weirdest thing I've ever heard. Actually, I can see the penis thing. What would happen to a guy whose schlong got sucked back up inside him? He'd be a girl, right? I can see these Asian studs not liking that idea one tiny bit. But the nipple thing is a little tipped, excuse the pun. I mean, where would they go? What would it threaten?"

Willa yawned. They had been back in Hong Kong for three days, and it had been raining steadily the entire time. The first two days they had all been too tired to care. They had spent the past two weeks chasing wild geese across Indonesia. Now they were getting restless.

"I don't know. Maybe it's a fertility symbol. I mean, the nipple means motherhood, feeding a child, and it's also an erogenous zone; it's part of femininity and sexuality. What's interesting is that they don't have problems with anorexia or agoraphobia, like in our culture."

Lindy threw herself down on the bed next to Willa. "Listen. If I had to eat this shit every meal forever, weight would no longer be a concern. A little dim sum goes a long way, *and* they live ten people in tiny little apartments coated with peanut oil! No wonder they don't want to stay in the house.

"Do I need a degree in sociology to figure that one out? The Oriental women are small-breasted, right? So maybe the nipple being sucked backward means more."

Lindy reached for her phone book. "I like the penis part. Picture a room full of Chinese guys in a mass panic attack clutching their boing-boings. What would they do to stop it? Tie the boing-boing to the bedpost? Sit on it? Maybe surgical tape or safety pins? If they're not circumcised, clothespins might work. I bet they have clotheslines in their bureaus just in case of an attack.

"I guess married guys could train their wives to grab hold and not let go for anything, unless of course, the wife was having a simultaneous nipplrexia attack and had to hold on to her tips at the same time. That would be a problem.

"Well, if they had kids, the kids could be called in. They could be trained, like for earthquake drills, or they could get the old folks to help. Everyone here lives with some old folks. However, if they live alone and all else fails, there's always Krazy Glue. I'll take my Nobel prize now."

Bee Bee and Willa watched her. When Lindy did monologues, Lindy was deep in her own panic attack.

Willa looked at the clock. They were all hungry and edgy and they had a lead to follow at some nightclub called the Volvo, but they were waiting until it was morning in New York. Lindy hadn't talked to Tess in almost a week, and they were all feeling the tension.

"Funny. The girl is funny." Bee Bee got up and gave Lindy a kiss and went off to the shower. They had been together twenty-four hours a day for six weeks and had become closer to each other than any of them would have believed possible of three ex-wives or three anyones.

They had moved into a tiny, private sleep-away camp that was as much a part of their lost girlhoods as their present woman-hoods. None of them had sisters, and none of them had ever been to anything remotely like camp. The intensity of their mission had certainly accelerated the intimacy, but that in itself did not explain the level of bonding that had developed. After all, it could just as easily have turned them into snarling, irritable enemies.

Lindy told Willa after the first week, "If we were here for any other reason, we would be having the best time of our entire lives."

They had left Bee Bee's house, filled with nerves and hope, and headed straight through the needle's eye.

Corrine Brandmore looked like someone's genteel and proper maiden aunt. Perfectly groomed. Perfectly coiffed. She lived in a perfectly decorated mansionette in Spring Valley, D.C., with perfectly trained springer spaniels, a perfectly dry, gracious elegance, and the stiff, overbred manner of Washington society. She seemed as unlikely a choice for Leo and as far away from themselves as possible. She was nearing sixty but seemed older because of all the "perfectlies." It made them uncomfortable, and they tried valiantly not to be intimidated by the ambience.

But once they got beneath the surface of Mrs. Brandmore, wife of the famous cabinet officer and patroness of the arts, she was really quite down-to-earth and fascinated by their plight.

Bee Bee thought they had given her a long-needed shot of Adrenalin, something to keep the circulation going in a life as overstructured and controlled as an astronaut's space walk. Also it brought Leo back to her, and they could all see the effect of that. When she talked about him (even after almost twenty-five years), her eyes glittered and red splotches appeared on her powdery white neck.

"Well, I've done my homework, girls. I've been busy as a bumblebee since you phoned me. I must say, it took a little getting used to. But once I put my mind to something, I'm like a tomcat. Is that the right image? Well, you know what I mean."

A maid appeared with a tray of tea things. "Your call, Mrs. Brandmore," she said, gracefully lowering the tray.

Corrine nodded and stood up. "Excuse me one moment, I have to take this call. We won't be disturbed again." They watched her walk, with her light, finishing school–style across the pale, antiques-filled room to the phone.

"Barbara. So good to hear from you! I am so grateful for your support. I know what your schedule is like. You are a *saint*!" She listened, murmuring appreciatively. "Thank you so much, this will help us no end." She finished, setting the phone back in place as if it were Meissen, and coasted back toward them. "Barbara Bush. I *had* to take it."

Willa kept her eyes away from Lindy, knowing contact might be deadly to their cause, hoping Lindy would keep her mouth shut and not say what she was probably thinking. (No shit. Barbara, Mrs. President, fucking Bush. I am *sooo* impressed!)

"Now. Where was I? Oh, yes. After the shock—and a flood of memories, I might add—I made some calls." Corrine pushed her little tortoiseshell magnifying glasses up high on her well-shaped nose and picked up her Pierre Deux notebook. "This is interesting. The last credit-card charge Leo Lampi made was an American Express cash advance for fifteen hundred dollars, which was never repaid. That was in February of 1986. Nothing with his name on it has been transacted through an American bank or a national or international charge company since that time. It's almost as if he had ceased to exist."

Lindy's stomach tightened, and for a moment she thought she would scream. "But he sent you a card from Hong Kong last year! He does still exist. He was obviously tapped out and running from bad debts, so it figures that he wouldn't be using credit cards."

Corrine rubbed her chin. "Yes. I suppose. But I made a mistake about Hong Kong. It wasn't last year, it was three years ago. I misfiled it. I'm sorry." Lindy crossed her arms over her belly. Corrine watched them. "There is also another possibility." She took off her glasses and leaned forward conspiratorially. They all leaned with her.

"He could be using another name or identity. This must all be in the greatest confidence—my husband would murder me if he knew I was telling you any of this—but it is not at all uncommon. The same process as the witness-protection program works for many other people, with and without the benefit of official approval. He could be living a new life as another person."

Lindy's stomach unclenched. "Yes! That would make sense! I mean, the way he left Miami, just vanishing like that. Bee Bee told us that guys came around for weeks asking about Leo! Where he was, when he'd be back, and not classy guys either. *Miami Vice* types. Maybe he got into trouble and they were after him for money and he just split. Maybe he wanted them to think he was dead! Great! That makes sense! What do you think, Bee Bee?"

Bee Bee sighed. Lindy was so desperate to believe anything positive about where Leo was. "Well, don't think I haven't thought about it. But he left his boat! He adored that boat. Why wouldn't he have gone off on his boat? They finally came and repossessed it. That's what made me think something had happened to him. What doesn't figure is that there was no other reason. We were getting along really well. I don't know, but it's worth exploring."

Corrine nodded. "Right. I agree. I've already started the ball rolling. If he's gotten false identification papers in any major city, I think my friends can find out. I've called in a lot of markers on this, but it's a very worthy cause and I'm delighted to be able to help."

After a while the maid reappeared with more tea and Corrine excused herself to "have a little chat with the gardener." They were quiet, letting the strangeness of the event settle in.

Bee Bee put her cup down next to a stack of personalized note cards, embossed with Corrine's initials and rimmed with lines of gold and sapphire-blue. "The Brandmores request the pleasure of your company for cocktails on July 1."

The notes were all printed in gold. Bee Bee picked one up, letting her finger wander over the satin-shiny letters. She tried to imagine a life like Corrine's that included specially printed invitations inviting people for drinks. It hurt her inside just to think about it. Somehow it seemed so safe. So normal and refined. She handed the card to Lindy. "Leo made a mistake. He should have stayed with Corrine."

Lindy passed the card to Willa. No one said anything. They were thinking about what Bee Bee had said.

Willa reached across and put the card back on the pile. She felt like a freshman at the housemother's first tea party. "Do you think she knows anything about Leo's childhood? I mean, he was still really a kid when she married him."

Lindy popped a cucumber sandwich into her mouth. "Can't hurt to ask."

Bee Bee spooned three teaspoons of sugar into her cup and stirred briskly. "Do you know what his name means?"

Willa and Lindy shook their heads.

"*Lightning,* in Italian. Well, almost. Lightning is actually *lampo.* Someone told us when we were in Italy together."

Lindy licked her fingers. "I never really thought of him as lightning. Thunder would be closer."

Corrine entered holding a leather scrapbook. "I found something." She smiled at them proudly. "It's our first-year book." She settled down on the sofa, and the three of them nestled close to her as if they were about to see friendly family snapshots rather than the pictorial history of the first love affair of their common husband.

They studied each one as if memorizing the likeness. He was so young and so handsome and happy-looking. Corrine stood tight at his side in every shot, smiling up at him with her fresh debutante beauty, looking like an adoring older sister. They were everywhere together. Leo in a tuxedo at the Chevy Chase Country Club. Leo in a naval uniform. Leo in a swimsuit. Leo on their boat.

This was not the Leo any of them had known. This was Corrine's Leo. Willa couldn't help thinking, sitting on the three-hundred-dollar-a-yard Fortuny silk sofa, sipping English tea from French porcelain cups, only a phone call away from Mrs. Bush and the Heart of *Democracy,* that Leo was becoming more and more like a hologram. An image that re-created itself in time and space, taking many forms, living many lives, but no more tangible than his name. Mr. Lightning. A flashing of light produced by a discharge of atmospheric electricity from one cloud to another.

They turned the pages until it was time to leave for the airport. Only when they were in the cab, Corrine waving them off with promises to keep in touch, did they realize they had never asked her about his childhood. Somehow by then there didn't seem to be any point.

Hong Kong had been good for them. It was a city crackling with the energy of uncertainty. A mysterious and beautiful woman with a possibly fatal disease. It conducted its business of commerce and avarice, poised on the edge of time running out; the lease ticking away and China watching across the water, biding its time. This gave the city a prewar vitality, a sense of danger and excitement even more intense than before.

For Willa and Lindy, who had never been much of anywhere, especially not since the realities and responsibilities of adulthood and motherhood had claimed them, there was open-mouthed awe. Bee Bee was their leader in this town. She breezed into the airport, taking charge of customs, luggage, and her two suddenly shy and uncertain companions, with the ease and assurance of a package-tour guide.

A young moon-faced man in a chauffeur's outfit was waiting for them at the baggage claim.

"Hello, Chen." Bee Bee held out her hand, impressing Lindy and Willa, who hung behind her like little girls. "These are my friends, Ms. Lampi and Ms. Snow. This is Chen."

The small man bowed and motioned for them to follow. "It is good to see you, Miss Day. We have missed your presence."

"It's nice to be back, Chen. How's the Emerald City holding up?"

Chen stopped in front of the most beautiful car Lindy and Willa had ever seen. A gigantic hunter-green Bentley that looked as if it had been lacquered with liquid mirror.

"Please." Chen opened the back door and Lindy and Willa stumbled in. Bee Bee sat up front so that she could talk to him.

"You ask how Hong Kong is. She is scared, Miss Day. No one knows what will happen. Things are not good. More and more people are leaving. But we still hope that nothing will change. We will have good joss and Hong Kong will prosper."

"Chen, if things are slow at the hotel, do you think we can book some time with you? I have a reason for being here besides singing. You know this town better than anyone, and I could use your help. I'm trying to find Leo."

Chen looked at Bee Bee ever so discreetly. "Mr. Lampi has come back here?"

"We think so, but we're not sure. I'd like you to help us find him."

Chen nodded, a small smile pulling at his face. "Sure thing. That will be adventurous. My mother says I need to have adventures in my life. She read it in the tea leaves."

Bee Bee laughed. "Good. Maybe your mother can find Leo in the leaves too."

When they pulled up in front of the Regent Hotel, Lindy scrambled out of the car and grabbed Bee Bee's arm. "Bee Bee, what is this? This does not look like a Holiday Inn to me. The *car,* the *Regent*! This is *not* in the budget!"

Bee Bee patted her back. "Part of the perks. I get a suite and Chen when he's not busy. If he works extra, we'll have to pay him but it doesn't cost that much. Everything else is comped. Food. Room service. Everything."

Lindy's mouth dropped. "No shit. Boy, that Lampi sure could pick 'em."

"Pick whom?" Willa came up behind them.

"Wills. This is all free! It's on the house. The room, the food— everything! The less money we spend, the more left for Tess's transplant. This is great news."

Once they knew that they were not paying for the splendor, they allowed the magic of Hong Kong to buoy them up. No city in the world, not even New York, creates the crackling fizz, the internal effervescence of Hong Kong.

The lobby of the Regent Hotel beckoned them in, a polished, purring playground of steel, chrome, leather, and glass, pulsing with the tinkling sounds of voices and bodies in perpetual movement. Japanese, Korean, French, Italian, Swedish, British, American, Spanish—businessmen from the ends of the earth, huddled in hives of commerce, phones ringing, laptops humming; bar girls with China-doll faces and fishnet stockings circling continuously, faces blank and painted red lips sealed, while men made money.

Hong Kong was a city of money. Money was what moved it forward. It smelled like money—gold, silver, silk, suede, steel, oil —sniffs of potent, intoxicating possibility. A city of joss, of lucre and pleasure. A city where one could conquer or disappear, taste forbidden fruit, indulge in perversion, gluttony, lechery, greed, and endlessly spend money.

People who hated to shop woke at four A.M. and wandered darkened, garbage-stinking streets to find the best place to buy things it had never occurred to them to want. Tourists quested. Missions of acquisition were plotted and planned with rigor and seriousness. Every day in Hong Kong was the bargain of a lifetime. Cartier pens and Vuitton purses, South Sea pearls and hand-beaded sweaters—all so cheap, so once-in-a-lifetime never-before-or-since affordable, that no one could resist the temptations. No one.

The malls bewitched, mazes of malls, soaring up into the smoky sky hanging over the harbor, lining the lobbies of every hotel, every inch of street space in every quarter of this tense, voracious, vigorous little village of vices, lured with its silent signal. Come in. Enter here. English spoken. Visa, American Express, tourist discount. Come.

Hong Kong was a whore in a Chanel suit with a million dollars' worth of Eurodollars and a ticket to Switzerland in her oversized alligator shoulder bag.

They put her on immediately and she fit perfectly.

By the end of their third week in Hong Kong, however, she was beginning to feel a bit too tight. Bee Bee was working two shows a night, so Willa and Lindy, fighting the allure of the Bargain every step of the way, would take off on their own with Chen in the early morning while she slept. They followed every conceivable lead given by anyone.

The doorman at the Peninsula Hotel said Leo was living on a junk in Aberdeen Harbor (it turned out to be a surly Brit with a very bad temper and a loaded pistol, which scared Chen almost out of his beige silk custom-tailored chauffeur's suit).

An ancient toothless woman who ran one of the herbal-medicine shops said Leo came in to buy buffalo-testicle powder for potency ("just what the man needs," Lindy had muttered). The bow-legged old crone led them for miles to the apartment complex where she had last seen him. "Yes, he lived here," the landlady, a slinky, slack-faced wench from Australia, told them, smiling in a way that made them all extremely uncomfortable. "He moved out years ago. Think he must be long gone by now. A roamer, he was."

Their frustration and fear were offset only by calls to Alice and Tess. Tess was nearing the end of the chemo course, and the doctors were very pleased. "I see a remission comin'," Alice told Lindy, helping her get up for still another endless day of no joss and angst-filled lurkings in the land of Leo.

Sometimes Lindy felt that this was some perverse penance she

was paying for having run off with him in the first place. Now he
was back in her life and in her head as if he had never left. She
knew it wasn't easy for Bee Bee either, being back in the place
where they had gone, freshly in love and newly married, full of
energy and ardor. Sometimes she could see it in Bee Bee's eyes, a
wince or a wistful, cloudy glance and Lindy knew she was remembering something.

Willa handled her feelings by organizing everything, charting all
courses of action, keeping financial records, making lists of leads,
circulating photographs, and keeping her mind so full of the business at hand that there was no room in it for Leo, the man.

By the time Bee Bee's contract was ending they were no closer
than the day they'd left Washington. Corrine sent cheery little
faxes saying, "Still working on it, hang in there," and not much
else. They needed outside help, though they hated to break down
and hire a detective. And who the hell would they find here anyway? The police had been useless. Charlie Chan was long gone
and the whole prospect seemed an admission of defeat.

They were all in the lobby café having breakfast, trying to figure
out what to do next, when it looked like their luck was turning. A
hive of Asians, all dressed in formal wear even though it was
morning, began forming in the lobby. Lindy pointed. "Take a
look at the sign: THE AMWAY GOLDEN CIRCLE AWARDS."

Willa laughed. "Asian Amway. I love it."

Hundreds of people were pouring into the lobby on their way
to the ceremonies, all looking self-satisfied and delighted to be
part of such a grand occasion.

"First prize is a solid-gold box of biodegradable detergent."
Lindy played with her omelette, enjoying the spectacle.

Out of the crowd an overdone young Chinese woman in a
shocking-pink ruffled party dress, waved at them. Lindy looked at
Willa. "Wills, don't tell me you're a closet Amway girl."

Willa put on her glasses. "I've never seen her before."

"I have," Bee Bee said, lifting her hand in a brisk but unenthu-
siastic wave.

The girl padded across the lobby, moving through the throngs
of happy award-winners toward Bee Bee.

"Miss Day! Miss Day! What a fond surprise!"

Bee Bee did not smile. "Hello, Jasmine. How are you?"

"I'm quite great. I've risen high since last you saw me. I am in charge of the entire Indonesian Amway distributionship! I am living in Singapore now. I am only present for the awards. I will be on the stage with celebrities from all over the planet. Including the Crown Prince of Malay and Mr. Bob Hope of Hollywood."

"How nice," Bee Bee said quietly.

Willa and Lindy were watching her. They knew she was not introducing them for a reason. "A go-for-it girl in a go-for-it world," Lindy whispered to Willa.

Jasmine moved closer. "Scandalistically speaking, I was very dismayed to hear about the ending of you and Leo Lampi."

Bee Bee smiled. "How did you know about me and Leo?"

The girl stuck her pink chin up, just slightly taunting.

"He was back here for quite a while after your disconnection, and I put three and three together."

Lindy put down her fork. "He was?"

Bee Bee jumped, as if coming out of a daydream. "Jasmine, these are my friends, Willa and Lindy. We are here trying to find Leo for a very important reason. If you could tell us where he is, I would be most grateful."

The girl grinned at them, showing small, pointy white teeth. "Gee. I would enjoy to help. Scandalistically speaking, he was working a lot of afterhours clubs, playing music and sometimes tending bar. But I haven't been in Hong Kong for over three years. So I don't know about the current. Last I saw him, he was hanging out at Chung Fang's club in the Bird Market, getting into serious t'ai chi and stuff. He was there every morning for breakfast. A real weird place, scandalistically speaking."

She turned to see where her herd of happy co-workers was heading. "I must depart. I have a multitude of things to prepare. Why don't you and your friends come to the ceremony as my guests. Maybe by then something will recur to me. Leo stays inside the brain like bad ginseng. Right, Miss Day?"

For a minute Lindy thought Bee Bee was going to stand up and pummel the tiny pink thing with her large-knuckled American fists. "Right." She replied so softly, she was talking to herself.

"I will leave passes for you at the entrance. Now I must meet the international winners outside on the miranda." Jasmine skipped off like Judy Garland on the road to Oz, to join the merry merchants of house-to-house soapwares.

Willa shook her head, "Outside on the *miranda?*"

Lindy did not laugh. "Can Chen find this place?"

"Chen can find any place."

"Let's boogie," Lindy said, and she and Willa took Bee Bee by the arms, offering their support, understanding without prying that this girl had caused trouble in Bee Bee's love life, a trouble that, knowing Leo, they all understood only too well.

They heard the Bird Market before they saw it. They also smelled it. Chen could not get the car down any of the tiny streets that crisscrossed the market, so they had left him and set off, following his hand-drawn map and two of their senses.

"Here! Turn here!" Willa pointed left and they all turned into a sight that stopped them in their Reeboks (the shoe of choice for hunting down former husbands).

"Holy shit!" Bee Bee whispered.

"It's bird and there's nothing holy about it." Lindy pointed her camera and clicked. "Tess would love this."

Spreading before them was a sweeping, chirping birdland of caged and captured feathered friends hanging in a vast collection of cages from simple to sublime, an aviary mall. A parakeet slave market. A lovebird brothel with something for every taste.

Birdmen, old and young, some carrying cages already occupied by previously purchased pets, wandered through the squawking, foul-smelling streets, checking out the flapping merchandise.

Wizened old women, with gold teeth and black, hooked toenails hanging over their dirty sandals, screeched like their captives, pushing their wares at the customers. Grown men swaggered by, holding their daintily delicate cages in brawny fists, cooing at the tiny dove or mini-parrot inside, browsing through rickety straw-covered shelves filled with pretty porcelain water dishes, tiny silver seed bowls, the finest straw for the precious droppings, the finest carving for the handle, the softest silk for the cover.

"Imagine this on Rodeo Drive," Lindy whispered, causing Willa to dissolve in giggles as they wandered transfixed by the sights surrounding them.

"We're here." Bee Bee pointed to a building at the corner of the longest street in the market that looked as if it had been bombed out and only recently returned to use. Not restored, simply reoc-cupied. It leaned sideways, its filthy, rutted facade cracked and covered with grime.

They both turned to Bee Bee as if expecting her to offer some explanation.

"Don't look at me. Leo never took *me* here. I'm as clueless as you are."

Lindy inhaled, as if sensing she would not be breathing deeply for some time. "Okay, girls. Let's go. Stick together and I'll do the talking."

Chen knew the club well and he had told them what to do. They were to walk up the stairs and keep going all the way to the top. Then they were to ask for the owner, Chung Fang, using Chen's father's name. This had seemed simple enough in back of the luscious Bentley cruising the streets in serene comfort. It be-came less simple on entering the Birdmen's Café.

On the first floor dozens of half-naked young Chinese men, each with a bird in a cage, were smoking pipes, drinking tea, throwing dice and seeming to converse in a competitive way about their birds. They all turned and stared at the intruders. The only other woman present was one of the ancient, stooped tea ladies, who ran from group to group pouring and passing huge metal steamer baskets filled with mysterious foodstuffs.

"Move, keep moving," Lindy whispered. They were intimi-dated by the titters and cold stares of the men around them.

"Maybe women aren't allowed in here?" Willa followed Lindy.

"Don't be silly. Chen or 'the Miranda Decision' would have told us. Women have more sense than to show up at this hellhole —that's why they're not here."

Bee Bee, who was quite a sight in her huge dark glasses and baseball cap, glared at two men who were mimicking them. She was so imposing, they stopped and turned away. "Lindy, let me go first. This is where being large pays off. These little guys just hate it."

"Good idea." They were on the second floor, which looked exactly like the first, but even dirtier. Bee Bee moved to the front and they forged on. The stairs creaked and crunched beneath them. Tiny old women almost bent in half with age, lost calcium, and the weight of their trays and metal baskets scurried around them effortlessly while they huffed onward.

"I wanna smoke what these grannies smoke." Lindy, now bringing up the rear, was panting. "They look like they couldn't pick up a chopstick, and they're passing us with all that junk on their backs, like the bionic woman. No more Jane Fonda for me. I want the secrets of the Orient. I want Suzie Wong's Workout."

"Lindy, shush." Willa pulled her up the last step.

They were standing in a tremendous room surrounded by enormous, dust-covered windows that soared to the tallest ceiling, outside of a Gothic church, that any of them had ever seen.

Swirling on wires, encircling the entire perimeter of the space, were hundreds of cages of birds, mostly covered with elaborate fabrics.

On the floor were scores of old men, half dressed, sweat-stained from their morning of t'ai chi, drinking green tea, and reading piles of Chinese newspapers on tables encrusted with bird turds. The floor matched the tables, but had the added enticement of large globs of brown tobacco mulch, the result of badly aimed shots at one of the carelessly placed spittoons.

In the center a group of younger men were comparing parakeets as if they were status symbols, placing bets and chain-smoking small, unfiltered cigarettes. The trio were struck dumb by the sight, as if they had been transported through space, beamed down by the Starfleet into a grotesque and bizarre alien social.

An old man, who looked like an emaciated Ninja Turtle, motioned for them to take a table.

"Bee Bee, he wants us to sit down there!" Lindy grabbed Willa's hand.

Bee Bee stepped forward. "Give me something we can sit on. Willa, do you have a newspaper in your bag?"

Lindy nodded. "Willa *always* has a newspaper in her bag."

Willa reached in. *"The Herald."*

"Great. We'll spread it out, but do it as subtly as possible—we don't want to offend them."

They followed the turtle man, looking straight ahead. As they reached the table a customer with a black bandanna tied around his shiny bald head spat a wad of tobacco, missing the spittoon and covering Lindy's bare leg with vile brown slime.

"*AGGHHAH!*" Lindy screamed, recoiling in horror.

Silence filled the room. Even the birds shut up. "Lindy, I've got Handi Wipes and Neosporin in my purse. Calm down." Willa moved her forward. All eyes were riveted to them.

"I don't care if they hang us up like the goddamn beakies, put that paper down," Lindy said, moaning.

Willa extracted the paper and as discreetly as possible, with three hundred sets of prying brown eyes nailed to her, she spread it over the bird-soiled bench.

"Okay." She slid in.

"Don't touch anything," Lindy gasped, shuddering with revulsion. They were small now and less conspicuous. Laughter began to return, birds resumed their chirping. They were the object of mirth, but an adjustment to their presence had been made.

Willa pulled out her Handi Wipes and ointment and handed them to Lindy, who went to work with the same zeal she reserved for serious feminine hygiene.

"*Yick!* If I get something from that old creep, I am sending Chuck Norris up here to stomp his spleen." She wadded the soiled papers up and threw them into a spittoon. "Look at these lunatics. I mean, comparing *birds*. They might as well just unzip or unwrap or whatever the hell they do and set the real McCoys on the table. I mean, talk about cock of the walk—this is so phallic, I may up my won-tons."

They huddled together like first-time sinners in a filthy confessional.

"Okay. We've got to find Chung Fang. How do we go about that? I am not wandering through the crowd, inquiring as to his whereabouts. Besides, I don't think anyone here speaks English."

Before they could ponder their situation any further, a portly little man wearing a brown loincloth and carrying a large gilded cage stormed over to their table, yelling at them and pointing to Bee Bee.

"What is he saying?" Willa and Lindy turned to Bee Bee.

Because she had been in Hong Kong before, they always assumed she understood what people were saying.

"I keep telling you, I'm just a little Las Vegas lass. I have absolutely no idea."

The man was so upset, he was jumping up and down, causing

his stomach to jiggle and bounce. Lindy leaned toward him, vamping slightly. "I know a wonderful exercise for that, sir."

Willa elbowed her. "Shh. He might understand you."

"Give me a break. Do you not think that if this guy could speak English, he would have figured out by now that we don't know what he's saying?"

Bee Bee stood up, hoping height would help. This just inflamed him and he began pointing at her head and screaming over his shoulder. Several of the old women came running and one of them grabbed Bee Bee's skirt, pulling and pointing.

"This is turning into *Gulliver's Travels.* We've got to do something!" Bee Bee held on to her skirt.

Willa and Lindy slid out of the booth, moving up against Bee Bee forming a barrier between her and the women.

The man was shrieking and pushing his cage at them. His bird was shrieking. The ladies were shrieking. Now men from all over the room were moving toward them, pointing and yelling at Bee Bee.

Willa turned to look at her. "I think this is the part of the picture where we run for our lives."

Lindy grabbed Willa's arm. "But we haven't found Chung Fang!"

"Willa's right," Bee Bee whispered. "If we're *dead,* he can't help us. Let's get out of here."

"Ladies. May I be of service?" A tall, thin gentleman, wearing a madras summer suit and Brooks Brothers loafers and leaning on an ivory-headed cane, was making his way toward them.

"Yes, please. We can't understand them. What have we done?" Bee Bee's voice was louder than she had intended.

The man raised his cane and moved the crowd away from them, shouting in Chinese at the chubby man with the screaming bird. "I apologize for my friend. It is your dark glasses, miss, and your cap. They upset the birds. Please remove them and all will be well."

Bee Bee took off her cap and the glasses. The angry man bowed and returned to his own table. The old women tottered back to their work.

"Let me guess," Lindy said, moving toward their savior. "You're Chung Fang."

"At your service," he replied, and led them out of the fetid feathered nest and into the cool Mandarin splendor of his private office. He served them tea and almond cookies on sparkling clean plates.

"Leo Lampi? Oh, yes. He went off with an old friend of mine. A very rich man who needed someone to captain his yacht. They were going to spend several months in the Indonesian archipelago. I can give you the last address I have for him. I believe it was in Jakarta."

Mr. Fang, the perfect host, led them down and back to Chen. "I myself hate birds, but business is business," he said, and left them to recover from their ordeal.

"Scandalistically speaking"—Lindy sighed, slumping down in the cool, lush comfort of the car—"the Bird Market sucks."

Two days later they left for Jakarta.

The only thing they learned in Indonesia was that America was no longer the center of the universe. At times, they felt like recently freed refugees from some Third World dot on the map. Indonesia, like Hong Kong, was throbbing with progress, techno-futurism, wealth, energy, and the edgy, intangible aura of the new kid in town. New York seemed like some nursing-home shut-in, out-of-step, left behind—a tired, slovenly, delusively arrogant derelict, whose rummy, jaundiced eye was on the wrong ball.

They scoured the archipelago, Lindy pushing them onward more relentless as each frustrating, futile day passed. "Remember why we're here. This is about Tess—we're not on a singles tour," she repeated over and over, a frenzied mother's mantra to stave off her own fear. They talked to yacht-club managers, hoteliers, gamblers, millionaires surrounded by stunning women from all over the Orient, bejeweled and superior with their waist-length marble-sized pearls and couturier clothes, oblivious of the three exhausted wanderers.

Asian dandies in exquisitely tailored Italian suits and Turnbull & Asser suits and ties listened to their tale with amused impatience. By the end of the first week they had given up all efforts to compete with the glittering raven-haired beauties and their crisply dressed, unctuous male counterparts; forgoing makeup and hair care as their frustration mounted.

Leo Lampi had left Hong Kong sometime in the last four years and fallen off the edge of the earth. No one in Indonesia had ever heard of him.

They returned to Hong Kong, desperate and demoralized. The hotel gave them a special rate on their old suite, but it was certainly not the same as when Bee Bee had been working. They all knew time was running out. They had one more lead, courtesy of Chen, who heard that Leo had been tight with Timmy Tang, a singer who was working at the Volvo nightclub. After that, they had no plan and there was no new lead in sight.

Lindy picked up the telephone. "I'm calling New York."

They all gathered around her on the bed.

"Yeah?" Alice picked up the phone on the first ring.

"Alice? It's Lindy. Tell me everything."

"Gee whiz. This long distance is unbelievable. You always sound like you're in the next room! Ain't that somethin'!"

"Alice, I'm not in the next room and while you ponder, I pay. Talk!"

"Right. Right. Okay, there is good news and there is bad news."

Lindy could feel her pulse throbbing through her fingers against the receiver.

"The good news is she's in remission! The docs are real happy. This kid is a trouper. We just got the new tests back yesterday, and they want to put her back into the hospital right away, keep her clear of all bacteria until we find a donor. So that's the good news. She's been through the wringer, but she made it. She and Maxie celebrated last night. He took her out to dinner. The cutest thing I ever saw, those two kids, going out . . .

"Okay, enough blubbering. The bad news is—you know this anyway—she's gotta get the bone marrow while she's in remission. The sooner the better. They've been testin' all kinds of nice folks comin' in, tryin' to help—but no match. Found the father yet?"

"No." Lindy's throat felt like it was filled with shards of glass. "We're doing everything we can. We've circulated his picture all over the Orient. We're going to try hiring a private detective."

"Wow. Just like the movies! Well, don't get one of those old wienies like the Equalizer. Get some young beef. Maybe Magnum or—who's that fella on *Miami Vice* reruns?"

Lindy laughed. "Don Johnson?"

"That's the one. I'd take him down a dark alley anyday."

"Don Johnson would certainly cheer up the trio, but aside from the fact that he is an actor and not in Hong Kong, I don't think he's likely to take the case. Alice, can I talk to her now? We've got a lead to follow tonight, and it's getting late here."

"Yeah, sure. I'll wake her. Don't make no sense to me, that you're all upside down over there. Hold on."

Lindy wiped the tears from her face. "She's in remission, which is great; but it means we have very little time left to find him."

Willa and Bee Bee each took hold of one of Lindy's hands.

Bee Bee smiled. "Don Johnson?"

Lindy rolled her eyes. "Alice's detective of choice."

"Don't even think about it," Bee Bee said, connecting them all to the wretched displacement of their woman need—the yearning for male protection to comfort and help them through the blackness—the Prince they had been denied.

"Momma!"

Tess's sleepy, sweet voice tickled against her ear, opening her heart and flooding her with joy. "Oh, baby. My baby girl! How I miss you. I miss those sweet cheeks! I'm going to come home and give you one thousand cheek kisses. You will never need blusher ever, in your life. Your cheeks will be permanently pink from smooches!"

Tess giggled. "Mommy, you are so weird! Did Gramma Alice tell you the good news?"

"Oh, yes, she did, honey. But am I surprised? No way. It's like Willa told you—God has his hand under you, baby. Everything is going to be fine."

"I'm so happy, Momma! Maxie took me out for Italian last night. I went out to a restaurant! It was great. I mean, I'm bald as a bean, but I wore one of your slouchy hats and no one could tell. Did you, I mean, have you . . ."

The glass was back in her throat. "No, baby. But we're getting closer. I can feel it. I promise I'll let you know the second we find something. I know you're going back to the hospital today. I'll try to call you tomorrow. The time thing makes it hard sometimes. Do you know that I think about you every single second?"

"I sure hope not! That would be totally boring. Don't turn into one of those Granola-bar mothers who spends her entire life on her kid. It's too Fifties, Mom!"

Lindy laughed. "Well, I can tell you're better, you're talking to me in that sardonic, adolescent manner I've missed so much."

"No, Momma! I'm never going to be like that again. I'm a much nicer person now—ask Grandmother Segal. She thinks I'm practically a saint."

"I think I'd rather have a wise-ass. Speaking of which, those are the other cheeks I miss, but I guess you'll never agree to letting me cover them with kisses."

Tess squealed. "Mother! You are totally crazy!"

"Crazy about you! I don't know when I'll be home, baby. But it won't be long now, I promise."

"I know. Just take care of yourself, Momma. Don't get all worn out. I'm fine. Really. Momma?"

"Yes, baby?"

"I love you more than anything in the whole world."

"More than Baskin-Robbins double chocolate chip?"

"A zillion times more."

"Me too, Tessie. Hang on, baby. Momma's coming."

Even though no one had said it out loud, when Chen pulled up in front of the Volvo nightclub and released Bee Bee, Lindy, and Willa, or rather unleashed them, into the misty midnight, they were all approaching the evening as a farewell to Hong Kong. As such, the Volvo was a consummate choice.

They had taken considerable time dressing for this last assault on the netherworld of the city, restoring their ruptured egos after Indonesia and armoring themselves for their last chance, the end of the climb without the summit in sight. They arrived in full battle gear, steeling themselves with mascara, and lip gloss, masking their quivering assailability as best they could.

At the entrance to the Volvo two of the largest men any of them had ever seen stood guard. They were dressed, for some unknown reason, like Indian Sikhs, replete with flowing gold-and-crimson gowns, jeweled sabers, and mammoth vermilion-and-silver turbans. Flanking them were a dozen tiny Japanese girls wearing American high-school uniforms and hopping around to football pep-rally music, their grins as frozen as the rictus of horror-film skeletons.

Behind the welcoming committee was a pair of massive glass doors, which were opened by another set of giant Indian men to reveal an antique Volvo automobile circling on top of a shimmering chrome turntable. In the center of the entry hall was an escalator lined on either side by a tuxedoed chorus line of stone-faced women from all parts of Asia, heavily made up, wearing top hats and carrying walkie-talkies, with the single-agenda deadpan characteristic of airport security guards and highway patrol officers.

The leader of the greeting committee stepped forward, blocking their path. "Name, please," she demanded with all the warmth of a cryogenics technician.

Bee Bee stepped forward. "Day. The Regent Hotel made the reservation."

The woman screeched something into her walkie-talkie. Someone at the other end screeched something back.

The woman snapped the fingers of her free hand, and a rookie from the end of the line stepped forward.

"Follow," she said, and led them to the escalator.

"I think we may be heading into Bird Market II." Lindy turned back to Willa. "What's with the Vulva?"

"*Volvo.* Vulva is the private part, Volvo is a Swedish car as seen above. They are decidedly different symbols."

"Maybe it's just a bad translation. The joint seems more vaginal than mechanical to me."

They had reached the midpoint on the escalator ride, and the nightclub could now be seen through the blinding pink fluorescent lights.

"Holy Moses!" Bee Bee turned to see their faces.

A wonderland of decadent delight spread out before them. A mammoth, city-sized space, curving in pink velvet swirls of banquettes and bubbling Plexiglas waterfalls. Overhead, pink satin hearts and bows bobbed on silver tinsel dotting the entire gargantuan interior like candy stars in a pink plastic sky.

Down the center, transporting frolicking groups of men, all well dressed and well oiled and representing every semicivilized country on earth, were a fleet of mini antique Rolls-Royces driven by beautiful young girls, each in a white chauffeur's suit.

On the dance floor a troupe of young American blondes were singing slightly off-key. " 'When those cotton bales get rotten, you can't pick very much cotton. In them old cotton fields back home.' "

Dancing to this improbable tune were a large cluster of unescorted Japanese matrons, still wearing their print housedresses and sensible shoes, as if they had been kidnapped in the middle of their chores and herded off to enforced temporal pleasures. Some of the women were having what appeared to be a very good time, leaping and shaking and looking as if control might soon be a concern.

The Top Hat led them to a plush shocking-pink booth near the dance floor. "You want hostess?" she asked, her face impassive, her eyes cold.

"No. Just drinks." Bee Bee handed her several Hong Kong dollars and she turned, still unsmiling, and stalked off, confiding her displeasure to her walkie-talkie.

Lindy leaned over to Bee Bee. "What did she mean about a hostess?"

"They have girls to drink with you and entertain you and it costs a fortune. They hate women coming alone because usually, unless they're gay, they don't use the hostesses."

Lindy nudged Willa. "See, I was right! Vulva it is!"

They sat back trying to absorb the spectacle before them. Aside from what appeared to be busloads of tourists from Japan and Korea, the vast powder-puff space was filled with men.

At each table, depending on the size of the group, beautiful young women of every nationality sat provocatively, wearing lavish revealing dresses, almost robotic in their practiced seductiveness. None of them spoke, but rather nodded, murmured, smiled without showing teeth, poured drinks, and generally created a sexual charge and an incentive, a sort of fleshy bonus program, energizing and fueling the conversation and wit of the men surrounding them.

As each new group drove up and extricated themselves from a Rolls, a top-hatted dominatrix would appear, leading a group of nymphettes from which they could choose any or all. The girls followed these harsh-faced women like marionettes or wind-up dolls, self-conscious in their overrehearsed runway walks and too-high heels. Creamy baby breasts bobbing like ivory apples above their spangly evening barrels.

Lindy scanned the room. "The only way you could be overdressed in this joint is if you were wearing the chandelier from the lobby of the Waldorf-Astoria."

Willa picked up a pamphlet from the table. It was an ad for an exclusive jewelry boutique. "Listen to this. A jewel for today, born to be so. That completes, but that, in the same way, would be different from everything else. That shines on its precosity, for the peculiarity, for the variety of chromatisms. Precious stones, from the foolishest Island. *Mings,* because your unicity prove itself on little, precious details."

"Save that." Lindy reached for the glossy brochure. "I think we've discovered a new language. Chinglish."

"What you having?" A young, flat-faced girl kneeled before them, looking as if she would be more at home in a soda shop than a nightclub.

Lindy smiled. "Okay, gang. Tonight we are celebrating. My baby's in remission and we are going to triumph! Dom Pérignon and bring us an ice bucket filled with unicity to keep it very, very cold!" The girl jumped up, more pleased with the order than she had expected to be.

"Wait a moment." Bee Bee stopped her. "We are trying to find Timmy Tang. Do you know him?"

The girl pulled away. "He on next. I be back."

"See!" Lindy hugged Bee Bee. "We're in luck. Good joss is coming. I can feel it."

Willa was writing something down in her ledger. "Normally I would kill you for the Dom Pérignon, but we are running well under budget, thanks to Bee Bee."

Bee Bee blushed. She was still shy at their praise.

The little waitress was back, followed by a busboy who looked even younger. They went to work on the business of champagne, serving with vapid efficiency.

"To Tess!" Lindy raised her glass and they all clicked. "May the Vulva be with us!"

Willa took a long, slow sip. She had never drunk Dom Pérignon before, and she knew it was entirely possible she would never drink it again. She closed her eyes, letting the tingly cool bubbles slide down her throat. "Ummm. What precosity."

The lights, if it were possible, grew dimmer.

From somewhere above them an overamplified and nondenominational voice said, "Ladies and gentlemen, the star of our show, Mr. Timmy Tang."

"It's our man!" Lindy reached over into the bucket and refilled their glasses.

A beaded pink wall of curtains slowly parted.

"The sequin alert just went off." Bee Bee moved closer, trying to see over a very tall blonde at a table of loud and animated Australians.

A full orchestra slid forward on a moving stage of solid Plexiglas. From offstage a deep, mellow voice could be heard:

> "You're just too good to be true.
> Can't take my eyes off of you . . ."

Suddenly bounding onto center stage and into the spotlight came the owner of the improbable voice. A human Mickey Mouse with a Fu Manchu mustache.

"This is not happening. This entire thing is a dream." Bee Bee lowered her head onto Willa's shoulder to muffle her mirth.

> "You'd be like heaven to touch.
> That's why I love you so much . . .
> Oh, pretty baby, trust in me when I say . . ."

The Magic Kingdom character was clad in a pink satin tuxedo, with a V-necked T-shirt beneath, revealing a few black chest hairs and a huge diamond-and-gold chain. He pranced around the stage, thrusting his tiny pelvis forward, causing the Japanese housewives to convulse with erotic overstimulation.

"I want him. I want him now!" Lindy took off her shoes and curled her legs up under her. "I may be in love here."

When the waitress returned they ordered another bottle of champagne and gave her a note for Timmy. "Please tell him it's a matter of urgency," Bee Bee whispered, making her point with a wad of bills. "Okeydokey," said the girl, who had decided they were not deadbeats after all.

The show ended with Timmy and the American blondes doing a lively cross-cultural rendition of "The Yellow Rose of Texas." The lights went up and hostesses and their clients took to the dance floor, the men with lecherous enthusiasm, the young ladies with jaded stoicism.

"Here he comes!" Lindy poked Bee Bee and pointed to Timmy Tang, now dressed in a black leather suit and white silk shirt, making his Mickey look complete. He strutted up to their table and clicked his little patent-leather heels together, bowing to Bee Bee.

"Bee Bee Day. What a trip! I am one of your biggest fans. I caught you in Singapore and Geneva. They don't make 'em like you anymore. Let me buy you ladies a drink."

Bee Bee blushed. "Thanks, but we're fine. Will you sit down for a minute?"

"Sure thing. I'm cool for an hour now."

He pulled up a small stool and plopped down beside Bee Bee, with whom he was clearly enamored. "I love your style."

"We've never met before, have we?"

"Nope. But I've always wanted to. What brings you to Hong Kong?"

Lindy leaned forward. "Mr. Tang. My name is Lindy Lampi and this is Willa Snow. We're all here to find Leo Lampi, and we were told you knew him."

Timmy's mustache wiggled up and down. "Lampi? Your name is Lampi? You his sister?"

Lindy swallowed. "Not exactly. We are all his ex-wives."

Timmy found this idea intensely amusing, and they waited while he squealed and rocked back and forth on his little pink chair. "No way! No fucking way! No wonder Lampi was so eager to split this scene. Three ex-wives! What a putz! Hee-hee!"

Lindy motioned to the waitress for another glass.

"Have some champagne, Mr. Tang."

"Timmy. Hee-hee-hee!"

The girl banged down the glass and Lindy filled it. "I don't mean to be personal, but you're not from China, are you? Sounds more like Brooklyn to me."

"Newark, but I speak Chinese. My parents came over in the Forties. I'm US of A all the way. But I can't make a living there. Here, I'm a star."

"I see." Lindy handed him a glass. "So what can you tell us about Leo?"

Timmy drained the glass and refilled it. Willa inhaled. At that rate, they would be heading for a third bottle in no time.

Timmy turned to Bee Bee. "Listen, is this cool? I mean, I haven't seen Lampi in years, but he was my friend. If this is some alimony trap, I'm not playing. You're a pro, Bee Bee—entertainer's honor, right? What's the score?"

Bee Bee looked at Lindy. Lindy nodded.

"Okay, in strictest confidence. We were all married to Leo at different times, but we didn't know of one another—rather I didn't know about Willa and Lindy. Leo disappeared and left me in Florida almost five years ago. No one seems to have heard from him since, except we traced him here and it appears that he was here about four years ago. Lindy's daughter is very ill, and we need Leo for a bone-marrow transplant. The situation is urgent. We are desperate for some information that can help us find him, and we have very little time left. If you know anything, please help us!"

Her eyes were filled with tears and little Timmy's cartoon face was quivering. "Jeez. What a story! Never knew Leo had any kids. Wow! Sure. Sure. I have two kid sisters. Boy! Okay. Let me think." Lindy refilled his glass and he drained it again, motioning for the waitress and pointing to the bottle. Willa nudged Lindy.

Timmy was concentrating, his wide brow furrowed under his shiny slick black hair.

The girl appeared with a third bottle of champagne. "No check for this table." Timmy patted her behind and the girl grinned at him, revealing the existence of a personality.

Willa exhaled.

"Okay, here's the deal—but I am betraying a confidence here. The last thing I need is a guy like Lampi as an enemy. But a sick kid . . . that's gotta come first.

"So Leo shows up here, about the time you said he left Florida. He's real quiet, even for him. Down too, very bummed out. He tells me he needs a job and a place to stay, but he's undercover, sort of, and he can't use his papers. I figured it was a divorce thing. I knew you guys were married, Bee Bee.

"Anyway, I got him a job backstage. They use part-time guys all the time. They paid him cash. I let him stay with me for a while, till he found a place. He never said what happened, didn't want to talk about it. No broads either. I mean, look at this scene; Godzilla could score here, and we know how broads were about Leo, but he was definitely not interested.

"Anyway, one night after the show we go out for a beer, and he asks me if I know anyone who can get him a new ID. He says he's met a rich guy who wants to hire him to run his boat, but he can't use his papers. Bad debts, he says.

"Well, shit. This is Hong Kong, there's a rice-head on every block making IDs, so I set him up with someone. Two weeks later he split. Thanked me and asked me to forget he was ever here. If anyone came looking for him, I hadn't seen him. Then he was gone. Never heard one word from him again."

Lindy moved closer. "Did he tell you what name he was using?"

"No way. I mean, the whole scene was real Ludlum stuff. He wanted me innocent. Maybe he was being a buddy. Didn't want me to know anything that could cause some Guido to shoot my kneecaps off."

Willa refilled his glass generously. "What about the guy who made the papers? He would know."

"No good. He's in jail in Macaw. Wait a minute!" Timmy perked up. "There's a special hostess here, a Swedish broad. She had the major hots for Leo. One night just before he left she got wasted and followed him home. I remember she told me he was trying to calm her down and he went to get her some coffee and she went through his stuff, trying to find airline tickets, something, so she could follow him. We're talking major Fatal Attraction. Let me see if I can find her."

Lindy stood up. "What's a special hostess?"

Timmy giggled. "You ladies are from Kansas, right?" He raised a tiny arm, exposing large gold cuff links and pearly manicured fingers and pointed toward the distant back end of the club. "See those mirrored doors? That's where the big-time business guys entertain. The special hostesses work there, and they do a lot more than dance with the suckers or pour drinks. *Comprende?*"

"I'm going with you," Lindy said, reaching down for her shoes.

"No way. I'm telling you, this is one tipped tootsie. If she heard you were looking for Leo, she'd freak. She's still nursing a major rejection complex. Besides, no outsiders are allowed back there— one of the managers would stop you. Just chill out, I'll be back."

Lindy watched him disappear into the pretty backlit fantasyland. "Please, God," she whispered. They all held hands, watching the twistings and twirlings of the dance-floor zombies, aware of the absurdity of their presence in such a place for such a reason. For the first time in weeks there seemed to be nothing to say.

Finally Timmy leapt back into his little chair, grinning broadly. "Okay, here's the deal. I'll tell you what you want on one condition." He turned to Bee Bee. "You sing one song with me."

Bee Bee laughed. "You've got it." She stood up and he jumped to his feet. He hardly reached Bee Bee's abdomen. "Larry Yates," he said, leading Bee Bee off.

Lindy fell into Willa's arms and they held each other, shaking with relief. "It's working, Wills. It is."

"Ladies and gentlemen, the Volvo is very proud to have in its audience tonight the wonderful and talented American singer, Miss Bee Bee Day." The audience whistled and cheered. Bee Bee waved and walked to the mike to join Timmy.

"She has graciously agreed to join me for a song. Maestro."

Willa and Lindy let go of each other and turned to the stage, in awe of Bee Bee's ability to stand up there in front of hundreds of strangers and sing.

"She's incredible," Willa whispered, still holding Lindy's hand. "We never would have gotten this far without her."

Lindy and Willa picked up their glasses. "To Bee Bee."

It was after three when they got back to their room, and they were all giddy and overtired, woozy with wine and renewed hope. There was a message under the door. Lindy picked it up and carried it over to the window, letting the moonglow strike the page.

Willa followed her. "Why don't we turn on a light?"

"Not yet. I've adjusted to the dim." She opened the envelope.

"It's from Corrine. Important news, she'll call us at four A.M., Hong Kong time."

Bee Bee unzipped her dress and kicked off her shoes. "How about sandwiches and coffee?"

"Great. Club sandwiches with lots of mayonnaise and double French fries. No coffee—why waste all that lovely champagne?"

"Good thinking." Bee Bee picked up the phone.

Lindy pulled her dress off over her head and tossed it on the bed. "It's more good news. I can feel it."

They all marched to the bathroom together and took off their makeup, each following her own prescribed beauty-and-retiring ritual with rote efficiency.

Willa, who never bothered much with cosmetics, always finished first. Lindy watched her neatly lining her brush with toothpaste.

"Do you ever think about what we have to do every day just to go to work? I mean, it is really pathetic. On a highly hygiene day —I mean, when the whole wad has to be done—you start with washing and setting and conditioning the hair; filing and polishing the nails; creaming the hands; shaving the legs and underarms; bleaching the hair on the upper lip; tweezing the brows; exfoliation masque for the face; sloughing cream for the bod; baking-soda scrubbing for the yellow teeth; placement of contact lenses. Then let's see—mascara, eyeliner, blush, powder, foundation, lip-lining and sticking, drying hair, selecting clothes, brushing lint off clothes, ironing blouse, struggling into pantyhose, which is always one size too small. Combing out and spraying hair, jamming earrings in lobes, filling purse with all necessary paraphernalia. No wonder we're already so tired when we leave the house!"

Willa laughed and stepped into the bathtub. "Well, that's one way to look at it, but what I see happening is that women, at least women with any money at all, have turned most of that stuff over to other people. Someone does the hair, waxes the legs, plucks the brows, does the nails—all the feminine stuff that we couldn't wait to do when we were kids, I mean, remember, Lindy? That's how we spent every weekend—doing our nails, fixing our hair, shaving and plucking away in ecstasy. Then we grow up and we can't wait to have someone else do all of it for us.

"If we could find someone to wipe our butts, we'd do it. It's the ultimate status that we don't do any of those things for ourselves anymore. We don't cook either. Modern Woman does not do anything she doesn't have to do, and she only has to if she can't afford to hire somebody to do it for her."

Bee Bee wiped cold cream off her face. "It's true. I haven't done any of those things for myself since I was eighteen."

The door buzzer rang. "Food!" Lindy grabbed her robe and raced out. They were all suddenly famished.

The room-service waiter, a fey, bland little man who had served them for weeks but never seemed to get more comfortable being among them, meekly arranged their dishes and tiptoed backward out of the room.

Lindy wasted no time pulling off the silver domes to reveal their treats. The door closed behind him.

"If he had a dick, he'd be dangerous." Lindy stuffed French fries into her mouth. She was nervous about Corrine.

Willa bit into her sandwich, mayonnaise oozing down her freshly scrubbed chin. "Uh-oh. I feel a monologue coming on."

Lindy smacked her fries with a huge thick wad of ketchup. "You're right. Champagne always makes me gabby."

Willa licked her fingers. "So does fear."

Lindy ignored her. "I like this concept: Dick Dangerous. I see it as an adventure comic in the Dick Tracy mold. *The Daring Days of Dick Dangerous.* Okay. Is he physically attractive? How would we draw a physically attractive Dick? Well, that's a problem. Maybe a long, slender pink one. Very patrician. With a little neat mushroom top. Circumcised, of course. What about hair?"

"How 'bout a little yachting cap? That's more elegant." Bee Bee slid a piece of bacon into her mouth.

"Perfect. So. What's the story line? Dick Dangerous has come to Hong Kong, stowing away in the Fruit of the Loom boxer shorts of a TWA pilot, to find his lady love who has been sold into white slavery."

"Gina Genitalia!" Willa grinned.

"Willa Katharine Snow, my word! Okay. Good. So he cleans up in the bidet in the men's room of the Peninsula Hotel (very sentimental and colonial is our Dick), throws on his waterproof foreskin trenchcoat, pumps a little air into his jet-lagged testicles, and bounces off into the rainy Hong Kong night to find Gina. He arrives at—"

"The Vulva Club!" Bee Bee reached for a fry. Lindy moved the plate closer to her own.

"She's hoarding, don't let her get away with it. She's been a fry hoarder since infancy." Willa pushed the fries back to the center.

"Who can eat at a time like this! Dick is being thwarted by the dyke in the Fred Astaire costume, a former SS officer who, through the miracles of plastic surgery and sheep's-urine injections, is working as a nightclub door blocker."

"Dick flashes his badge, pinned discreetly beneath his left ball. 'I have police business.'" Willa swallowed.

"No reservee, no luckee." Bee Bee licked her lip.

"Dick's masculine pride is hurt. In a fit of pique he explodes, sending a stream of powerful love juice straight into the Chinese Nazi's steely eyes. *Arghhhh!*" Lindy falls back against her chair.

"She is blinded by the spew and Dick makes his move, bouncing high over her head and down into the smoky darkness where he settles in, disguised as a table ornament, glad for once that he is pink. He bravely lets himself become flaccid and inconspicuous so as better to observe the evil scene, unnoticed.

"We can sell this. I see a series. Right after *The Simpsons*." The phone rang. Lindy jumped up and ran for it. "Oh God, oh God. I am over the top, my eyeballs are shaking!

"Hello?"

"Who am I speaking to?" Corrine's carefully modulated voice.

"It's Lindy. Tell me quick. I am barely coping."

"You're going to be very proud of me, dear. He *is* using phony papers. The name is Larry Yates."

Lindy wilted. "We know. We found out tonight. But it's still a great big world out there."

"That's true, dear. But I've narrowed it down a bit. It seems there's a woman who's sent a photo to some very unsavory men in Miami of a man matching Leo's description who's been using the name Larry Yates. She is inquiring as to who he is and anything else they know about him. Well, one of the gentlemen who works for these thugs is an undercover agent for the Justice Department, so I was informed. It seems Leo borrowed money from these men and left without repaying it, so they are very eager to find him."

"Not before we do! That would be horrible!"

"Well, I would suggest you head back on the first plane available. The woman's name is Athena Pidge, and she lives on some godforsaken island in the British Virgins. It's called Ancolla."

CHAPTER 9

Fantasy Island: The Reality

AUGUST IN THE CARIBBEAN IS ONE OF THE MONTHS that travel agents refer to as "the low season." This has more to do with the fact that people who live where winters are cold prefer to flee then to climates where winters are warm than to any negative aspect of summer in the Caribbean. If the truth be known, many places like Ancolla are nicer and considerably cheaper in the summer.

August is quiet. The warm water and sweet, balmy nights are saved for the enlightened, for those on a budget, and for the residents. It is a lazier time, even by island standards, and also a pause at the cap of hurricane season, which begins its twitchy, teasing approach as September nears.

Although two years had passed since the horror of Hugo, this August was still close enough to cover the already naked backs of the survivors with the gleam of heightened anxiety. Everyone still remembered and no one wanted to go through *that* again. It made people edgy, the way they are for years after an earthquake. Tempers were short and the consumption of local smoke and demon rum was definitely up.

There were so few tourists on the island that the presence of any new arrival was noted by all. And so the landing of the flight from San Juan carrying three bedraggled white women in urgent need of the address of Mrs. Athena Pidge caused quite a stir in the otherwise dead midday heat of the Ancollan airport. Even Ruby put down her potato-fryer to check out the activity.

Louie, moving with an accelerated version of his usual gregarious grace, scooped them up the instant they passed Customs, raising the ire of Willie and the others who, though lazing their day away in August apathy, saw an opportunity for big tips and intrigue, an enticing enough option to bring their heads to a fully upright position.

Louie tipped his beret and grabbed their bags, struggling under the weight but refusing their offers of assistance, piling them into the van while touting its excellence, fine tires, new brakes, compact-disc player, and superpower air-conditioning.

He was pushing the air-conditioning because he had hardly ever seen passengers who looked more in need of resuscitation.

"Where are you ladies entering from?" he inquired, smiling his adorable gap-toothed smile to full effect.

"Hong Kong." Lindy sighed, falling back against the seat.

Louie shook his head, his shoulders shaking with mirth. "Some travel agent must have a very unusual sense of humor."

"It's a long story." Willa yawned, taking out her travel-sized Evian spray, which was an extravagance that had more than paid for itself in hourly revitalizing shots. She sprayed all their eagerly offered faces, parched into puckering from heat and forty hours of airplane air.

"I feel like a singing raisin." Bee Bee moaned, patting the water into her skin.

Louie eyed them in the mirror. "That is my very favorite American television commercial. I am quite fond of the singing raisins."

Willa leaned forward. "So you really do know this Mrs. Pidge?"

Louie nodded. "On Ancolla everyone knows Mrs. Pidge. Even the goats and chickens in the road could take you to the House of Blood."

Lindy, Willa, and Bee Bee made eye contact. They were now revived. Lindy moved closer to Louie. "The House of *Blood*?"

Louie grinned, knowing he had another captive audience. "Yes, ma'am. That is what we call the house of Pidge, because it is red and because the rumors fly about what happens in the privacy of Mrs. Pidge's evening hours."

Lindy laughed. "You're kidding. Are we talking house of ill repute?"

"I am not saying that there is nothing ill-reputing occurring in the House of Blood, but the rumors in question are concerning black magic."

Lindy rubbed her head. "Swell. We were hoping for more of a kindly old church-going granny."

Louie found this notion intensely amusing. The more he laughed, the more nervous they became.

Willa tapped his shoulder. "Excuse me, sir."

"Call me Louie, *sir* is for the old men."

"Louie, do you think you could pull over for a moment somewhere so we can talk. I think maybe we need a bit more briefing before we, uh, march up and ring this woman's doorbell."

"Athena don't have no doorbell. She have a very fat voodoo doll with a shark-tooth necklace that rattles when you shake it."

Lindy lit a cigarette. "Sounds real neighborly. How's she fixed for vicious attack animals?"

Louie pulled off the road onto a tourist photo-opportunity spot. The view was breathtaking.

Bee Bee opened the door. "Let's stretch, it's lovely here." The three exhausted nomads climbed out and stood near the edge, looking out over the sea.

Louie stood behind them, feeling pride in his home. "If you like, I will be happy to take a photo for memory of my beautiful island."

"Oh, thank you!" Willa pulled her camera out of her purse and the three of them moved together, the mountains and sea behind them.

Louie went at the task with the grave seriousness of purpose of Avedon shooting a *Vogue* cover. "A bit closer together. No, please, miss, because you are taller, it is hard to balance, kindly move to the center. Very good. Now a very wide American toothpaste smile. When I count three say ciguatera."

They obeyed, though the smiles were less than dazzling. "Ciguatera." They relaxed while Louie spread a blanket for their talk. Lindy watched him. "So, Louie, what's ciguatera?"

Louie took off his beret and scratched his shiny head. "Not something cheerful like it sounds. Very bad illness we get from eating infected local fish. It makes you paralyzed and all the senses become mixed up—seeing smells, hearing colors—but it produces a very nice photo-quality smile."

Willa laughed. "So far we have a dragon lady who lives in a House of Blood and seafood is a no-no. What else can you tell us about Ancolla? We will pay you for your time."

"That is most American of you. What do you desire to know? I can speak on the subject of Ancolla for quite a while. I was once hired by a famous book writer from New York to speak to him on a daily basis about the Ancollan culture. I would have earned enough money to take my dear wife and children to Florida, Disney World, but unfortunately he ran into some difficulties caused by the lazy cleaning-up girl sent by Mrs. Pidge and returned to New York rather suddenly."

Lindy looked at Willa. "So our Mrs. Pidge—when she's not ill-reputing for her personal pleasure, drinking chicken blood, or pulling the teeth out of sea creatures—runs a maid service?"

Louie patted his beret back into place. "Mrs. Pidge provides many services. She is a former Miss BVIs in the Miss Universe contest of beauty and the daughter of the governor of our island. She is a woman of much power and can be helpful in many ways. But there have been some rather upsetting incidents surrounding Mrs. Pidge in the last week, and I must warn you that she is not in a very happy mood at the moment. It is uncommon for Mrs. Pidge to be cheerful, but this mood makes dogs howl and rabbits scurry from her path."

Bee Bee's eyes were as wide as a child's upon hearing her first ghost story. "What kind of events?"

"A boat, a fine charter boat owned by some very nice friends of mine, was blown up. Mrs. Pidge has powerful connections on the island, but the scum who planted the bomb has confessed. He was told no one would be there—that it was just to scare away a spell.

"This boy is a bad penny, but he is no killer and he was not about to spend his ragged life in jail for Mrs. Pidge. He named her to the police and now she is trying to get her father to intercede. But we are all hoping that sometime soon the policemen will arrest her and take her evil from our land."

"Gee." Lindy hugged her bare knees. "Maybe it's not such a good idea for us to show up now. We're just trying to find someone. We were led to *her,* but maybe you can help."

"I would be honored to try. This is a very slow time for business, and I am free as a sea bird."

Willa frowned. "You said that the boy was no killer. Does that mean the people on the boat were killed?"

"Two men killed, three men injured. It is the worst thing to happen here since Mr. Hugo almost blew us away."

Lindy swallowed. Her heart was racing and beads of sweat popped out on her upper lip. Primal, animal intuition flooded her. "We believe that the man we're looking for was being investigated by this Mrs. Pidge. It is urgent that we find him. His name is Lampi. Leo Lampi. Have you heard of him?"

Louie shook his head. "I am very eager to help. But I do not know this name, and I know the name of every rooster on Ancolla.

"The only fellow here called Leo is not named Leo. It is just his, what do you call it in America, his not name?"

Lindy swallowed hard, "Nickname?"

"Yes. His nickname. But he is named Larry Yates."

Lindy grabbed Willa's hand. "That's him! My God! We've done it! We've found him! Louie, you angel! You adorable dear man. I could kiss you! Where is he?" Lindy saw his face and stopped.

Willa and Bee Bee, who had been watching Lindy with joy, now turned toward Louie, who looked as if he had just seen the evil specter of Athena Pidge hovering over them. *"Sweet Jesus,"* he whispered.

Lindy crawled across the blanket and took hold of his shoulders.

"What? *What?*"

"That is my friend Leo. He was on the boat."

Rennie was screaming. The pain was unbearable. "Keep pushing," the doctors were yelling at her. "Push! Now! Harder!"

"I can't! I'm afraid!"

"Yes you can! Now! It's coming. It's out!"

Rennie gasped, afraid to look, "Just tell me, is it healthy?"

"Yes. Beautiful and healthy."

Rennie exhaled. "Is it a boy or a girl?"

A doctor took off his mask and grinned down at her. "It's a chicken!"

Rennie sat up, her heart pounding. She had had the same horrible dream every day for a week. The Un Jill was stirring beside her. "Junk Yard Dog," she muttered. Rennie pulled the sheet up over her.

She looked at the clock beside her bed. Five P.M. The sun was riding the rim of the cloud bank, getting ready to settle down a bit. She was still so tired she felt like crying. Even the doctor-prescribed naps didn't help.

She slipped into her thongs and tiptoed out of the room. She made her way carefully down the stairs, unable to see over her belly now and terrified of falling. Actually, since the bombing, she was terrified of everything. Maybe it was silly to have the Un Jill sleep in her room, but neither of them thought so. Mrs. Pidge was still free and now they had neither Brad nor Leo to protect them.

She poured herself a glass of lemonade and walked out onto the deck. The sun shone over the water, casting lines of green and powder-blue across the sea. *Leo's sea,* she thought, tears falling on her sleep-damp cheeks. God. What a nightmare!

Rage flooded her. Rage at Pidge and rage at herself. There she was, still the little Wren bird hiding under the covers! This monster had destroyed everything she cared about, the entire life she had built—and what was she doing about it? Nothing! The pregnancy made her so vulnerable, she was so afraid of hurting her baby that she had let herself be bullied and humiliated by Athena.

At the Emergency Room, right after the accident when Pidge had arrived, full of phony concern, she had been hysterical enough to lash out. "You did this! I know you did it and you'll pay. You'll rot in hell for this!" she screamed, the police holding her back.

Athena had ignored her as if she were a recalcitrant child having a tantrum and turned her shoulder. Something about that gesture, the turn of the shoulder, the discounting, dismissive motion, had struck her an unabsorbable psychic blow. Some things cannot be ignored. Some wounds must be avenged. She had to do something to reclaim herself. But she did not know what. She was all alone now and there was no one to help her.

She sat down on a folding chair and sipped her lemonade. She remembered a conversation she had had with her father long ago, when he was first famous and she was confused by what it meant to their lives. Her family had always seemed rather unspectacular and not particularly noble or nice. She had always associated success and stardom with reward for greatness. She tried to explain this to her father.

When she was through, he had taken her hands in his—a gesture which he had never made before. "Rennie, let me tell you something that will save you a lot of grief. Life is never fair. Never. You either get more than you deserve, like me, or less than you deserve. That's just how it is."

She had never forgotten it. She closed her eyes and let the sun warm her tired face. "Okay, God. If it's all the same to you, I'll take the more-than-I-deserve part now."

She also understood that, before she could get anything positive back from this tragedy, she would have to stand up and fight. "How?" she whispered, waiting for an answer inside her own head or outside in the universe.

The doorbell rang. Rennie extracted herself with some difficulty from the canvas sling and shuffled across the cool tile floor to the door. She kept it locked now. She looked out the glass windows on the side and saw Louie's happy face. She undid the lock. She was glad to see him.

The door opened to reveal Louie and three nervous women hovering on the steps behind him. "Hi, Louie. What's going on?"

"These ladies have traveled all the way from Hong Kong, China. Please, Rennie. I do not want to disturb the lobster, but I highly recommend that you invite them in and let them tell you a most amazing story."

One hour later, after a conversation so layered with emotion and information that they were all exhausted, even Louie and the Un Jill who were only spectators, they all had a wealth of new facts. Rennie had known nothing about any of them, except the shadowy existence of Bee Bee as the ex-wife he had left in Florida. Now she had all the parts of the puzzle that made Leo Lampi the ultimate heartbreak, and the trio had their hope back.

Leo was not dead. Leo had been at the bow of the boat with Brad when the bomb went off, and both were thrown clear. He did have a concussion and had been in and out of consciousness for a week. Brad had second-degree burns on his back and three fractured ribs. One of the Fort Lauderdale guys had been making a phone call ashore and had suffered nothing but a severe shock.

Billy Bartlett and the other gentleman from Florida had not

been so fortunate. Both of them were sitting almost literally on top of the bomb, in a macabre, seafaring version of the warhead-riding scene from *Doctor Strangelove,* and they went up with it.

Rennie had gotten a call from the hospital, but she did not know whether Brad and Leo were survivors or victims until an hour after she arrived. The trauma had sent her into false labor, and she had held on to the baby by sheer force of will. She was not going to let Athena win.

Billy's father had flown in, demanding an investigation, and Rennie and Brad both told him they thought Athena was behind it. Leo was still too out of it to talk much to anyone, but the island police seemed to be even more afraid of Mr. Bartlett and his British lawyers than they were of Athena and her father. So there was a chance that justice might be served. But even the lawyers said they needed one piece of concrete evidence. "All we have is the word of a Rasta reedhead against the governor's daughter. We need something solid."

When the women were all through talking, they were silent for a while, trying to sift through their feelings. The Un Jill went off to bring lemonade and Louie went to call Eloise.

A whirring sound broke into their reverie. "What's that noise?" Willa asked, turning toward Lindy.

"My pocket recorder. I thought taping all of this might come in handy." Lindy opened her purse and pulled out the tiny machine and switched it off.

A cool breeze crossed over Rennie. Her prayer had been answered. She had asked God and the doorbell had rung and into her life these women had walked, bringing their torment and need and history, bringing her an answer. Rennie leaned forward as far as her stomach allowed. "May I see that?"

"Sure." Lindy handed it across to her. They all watched Rennie looking over the tiny bit of magical technology. She put it down on her knees and beamed at them. "I've got it. I know how to get Pidge, but I need your help. Here's the deal. You can all move in here and stay with me until Leo is well enough to leave the hospital . . ."

Rennie saw Lindy's face. "I'll take you all down there tomorrow, and we can talk to the doctors. Yesterday they told me they thought he could come home in a few days. Then he'll need a couple more here to rest up. Don't worry, Lindy. We'll get him on a plane with you in time. If we all band together, he'll have to help."

She hesitated. They all watched her. "He wasn't going to marry me. He didn't want this baby. I know he won't come back, but it was only a matter of time anyway."

She sat up straight. Admitting it all made her feel better. "Okay. Now, this is what I need from you." Louie tiptoed back into the room. "Louie, I need your help too. I have an idea how we can get Athena to confess."

She was no longer tired, and she was no longer afraid.

Athena Pidge lay back in her red tile tub, counting her money. Her money, of course, was not in the tub. The tub was filled with the requisite hot water and medicinal oils. The money was in her several numbered accounts in the Bahamas. She was merely adding it up. Everything was in order: her passport, the pilot who would fly her out at a moment's notice, her false identity papers, her fake second passport.

It was unlikely to come to that, but Athena liked to be prepared. She knew, and they knew she knew, that they did not have one piece of real evidence. She had been practicing her magic every night, sending curses to all of her enemies. She would triumph—and soon, broken and defeated, Leo would return.

She stepped out of the tub admiring her long, strong, tea-colored body in the three-way mirror. She stroked herself—her breasts, her pubis—fire filling her. That was all it took, a hand brushing herself and she was consumed with desire, but only for Leo. Damn him! No one else could satisfy her anymore. She spent her nights trying one poor bastard after another, only to be left howling at the moon like some rabid bitch in heat.

But finally, after the horror of thinking he had been killed, she had something useful. Her friends from Miami had sent her a letter concerning the subject of her inquiry. If she told them where he was, he was a dead man. She would use it to get him back, if necessary. She would use anything. So now she knew who he really was and why he had come here.

"There's a contract out on this guy, so please let us know if you hear from him," her friend had written.

Her friends trusted her because they had enough on her to send her to jail for a very long time. She was supposed to burn all communications with them immediately, but this time she did not do it.

She put the letter away in her red heart box, along with the picture of Leo, which she returned to its frame, having held it above her, to release her lust. How disgusting, for a woman like her! Masturbating to a Polaroid picture of a man who had scorned her!

She slipped a flame-red caftan over her head and wrapped her hair in a towel. She moved into the kitchen to see if the girls had left her ironing and dinner in proper shape. She had a new boy coming tonight, very young and handsome. Maybe tonight she would break the spell. She poured a large glass of French burgundy and carried her hors d'oeuvres plate across the pink tile floor to the gold-mirrored dining table.

She stopped, anticipating something. The voodoo doll rattled.

Athena took her glass and glided barefoot to the door. She opened the peephole and looked out.

Rennie Bowman was on her doorstep. Three rabbit women were standing behind her. Athena smiled. This might be interesting.

"Sorry to disturb you, Athena. But this is a matter of some importance to both of us. May we come in?"

Athena opened the door. "But of course. My door is always open to visitors. Please sit down." Athena made a wide, sweeping gesture with one long, satin-covered arm.

"I think we'll stand, if it's all the same to you," Rennie said firmly, though her back was killing her.

Athena strode to her red velvet throne chair. "Well, suit yourselves. I am going to sit and drink my wine. How may I help you?"

Rennie moved closer to her. "Athena. I am afraid you and I have both been used by our friend Leo."

She turned and motioned to Lindy who was dressed in a black suit, not in fashion for a tourist on summer holiday. Lindy opened her purse and flashed a wallet displaying a large, shiny badge, which she flipped quickly into Athena's face. "Lorraine Smithers,

FBI. I'm here on government business, ma'am. I understand that you are acquainted with Leo Lampi, alias Larry Yates.

"These ladies are the victims of Mr. Lampi. He is wanted in three states on charges of bigamy and embezzlement. Apparently you sent out an inquiry to Miami about a man resembling our suspect, and one of our informers tipped us off. I am authorized to arrest him and take him back to the States. I am just following up on why it was that you sent his picture out."

Athena's face was blank, but her knuckles tightened around the glass.

"I see. Well, I also had my doubts and before I became involved in such foolishness myself, I wanted to make sure he was on the up-and-up."

Bee Bee stepped forward. She was wearing a skintight Lycra minidress and five-inch heels. She blew a bubble and snapped it back into her mouth, causing her enormous gold earrings to shake. "Aw, come on, honey. Cut the crap . . . I know all about you from my pals in Miami. You had the hots so bad, it was sickenin'. Leo told them, when he first met you, that he was gonna pick you off like a clay pigeon at the rifle range. He's been settin' you up by playin' you off this poor young girl. You talk tough, but you're a bigger fool than we were."

Bingo. They all knew a direct hit when they saw one. Hubris was Athena's Achilles' heel, maybe even her *Achille Lauro.* She stayed statue-still, but Rennie saw the shock in her eyes.

Rennie turned to Willa, who was made up like a Hollywood disco dancer. "Listen, would you all wait outside for a minute? I'd like to talk to Mrs. Pidge alone."

Willa shrugged. "Sure. I just want to get down to that hospital and arrest the jerk and get out of this third-rate rat hole."

Athena had reached her limit. If she was a silly romantic fool and her island the subject of scorn to such trash as this, then who, after all, was she? "I think that is a very good idea. Leave at once!" Athena turned away from them, not seeing Willa duck down behind a chair.

Lindy and Bee Bee strutted to the door. "Okay, but hurry it up."

Rennie walked across to Athena. "Well, I guess it was all for nothing, Athena. I mean, if the reason you blew the boat up was to get revenge and get Leo back, what a waste. All it did was kill the two men who might have made you rich, or at least richer."

Athena whirled around, her face contorted. "How dare you talk to me like that! You nothing, you bloated little rabbit turd! Do you think that I am such a fool? It was a perfect plan. No one was supposed to be on board. It would have destroyed the boat and Leo's pride and taught you a lesson! How could I have known that that moron Bartlett would want to take it out! It was days away from being seaworthy! An evil spirit came with the full moon! I will still have my vengeance on all of you. They have no proof!"

Rennie smiled at her and turned away. She walked as quickly as she could to the door, out of attack range. She opened the door and rattled the shark teeth.

Willa popped out from behind the chair. "Did you get it?"

Rennie nodded, patting her purse and pulling the hidden microphone out of her sweater. "Got it."

Athena stared at them. *What is this?*

Willa moved Rennie through the door. "I think in the movies they call it a sting, Mrs. Pidge. We've got you on tape, and I am an eyewitness to your confession. Very nice to meet you. Oh, and hey, nice floor."

They motioned to Louie who was waiting down below with Mr. Bartlett and the chief of police. "We got her. Come on up."

When Mrs. Pidge was safely in the police car, Rennie went back into the house to find her picture. It was hidden in the red heart box next to Athena's bed on top of the letter about Leo. Rennie took everything, leaving a hollow valentine.

Two A.M. Lindy.

She lay in the dark, looking up into the whirling ceiling fan above her head. She was alone but so stuporously tired that she could hardly enjoy it. She had to stay awake a little bit longer. She had to be ready for tomorrow.

The Family Reunion from Hell. Rennie had been so kind, taking them in, giving her the guest room and Bee Bee and Willa the two bedrooms in Brad's apartment. How lucky they were to have found her first!

She thought of a second scenario, without the hand under them

—the one protecting Tess—leading them to safety. All it would have taken was some other cab driver, who didn't give a shit. They would have been dumped on the Blood Queen's doorstep, and God only knows what horrors would have befallen them.

She yawned and stretched her arms up, the way she always had as a child. What a wild night! There they were, having traveled so far on what might well have turned into another trail to the precipice, all dressed up like Halloween tricksters, entrapping Leo's former mistress in a hasty, but extremely clever sting! Rennie showed great potential.

They had come home from police headquarters and put their hostess to bed. It was clear to all of them that what Rennie had done tonight had healed something in her, and her gratitude for their help had touched them all to the point of tears. What a darling kid! She had to hand it to him—he still knew how to pick 'em.

Except for Pidge. She had no idea what *that* was about. Well, maybe it was the beginning of the Leo luck running out. Sooner or later life does catch up with us. Only a fool really believes he can outrun himself. So, what did she really feel about all of this? Better be clear, kid, before tomorrow. Was she jealous? She rolled over onto her side and curled up. No. How could she be jealous of Rennie? She felt so sorry for her. She knew that this was not someone Leo would stay with. She felt protective. Motherly, if you will. Oh, brother, was that pitiful! So, what else?

When Rennie showed her the picture of Leo in the silver frame she had recovered from Mrs. Pidge, it hurt. He still had it. She hadn't seen him in almost ten years, but he looked about the same, only better. She did love him. It was the wound that had never healed. If it had, she probably would have found some other sucker to marry her and give Tess a home. Maybe she would have even found Wheezie.

So, okay, the truth was the truth. She hadn't told Willa about it. It was much too embarrassing to admit. But what if it got in the way of taking him back to New York? Well, all she could do was deal with it honestly within herself, and save her bravado for Leo.

Now that she was so close, another feeling was coming back. Desperation. It was almost impossible to keep the reality of Tess, waiting in a sealed room in a New York hospital, on the back burner of her overheated mind.

For a moment, when she'd first heard about the boat accident, before she found out that Leo was not seriously wounded or dead, her entire being had seemed to slip away from her as if pieces of herself had suddenly broken apart, as if the stabilizing core—the anima of her soul—which had held her together and given her the strength to handle the last eight months of her life, had exploded. It was the most terrifying feeling that she had ever had, because in that instant she lost herself, splinters of her spirit whizzing by in a hail of psyche shrapnel.

She curled tighter into a ball. Willa had seen it in her eyes and removed her fists from Louie's trembling shoulders and held her, rocking her, whispering to her, until the rest of the information had gotten through and the fragments inside her head had rejoined one another. He was okay. But he was not okay enough to go *tomorrow*. And the big *if* still remained. What *if* he refused?

Before Rennie went to bed, she had given Lindy the letter she had taken from Mrs. Pidge's heart box. There *was* a contract out on Leo's life! If he knew about it, would he still go with her, when a phalanx of newspersons might be waiting eagerly for his arrival?

Okay, if he didn't know, they didn't have to tell him about the letter. But if it was true, it was also true that the bad guys could still find him (courtesy of Mrs. Pidge) before they got him safely to the hospital. Corrine was their best bet. Corrine had told her that she had gotten Leo a new passport with a different name and would help get him into the country quietly. She would call her first thing in the morning and just get it done. No, *first* she would call home and tell Tess that they'd found her father.

Tears filled her eyes. Come on, God, you've been great so far—I mean, considering you're the fucker that got us into this mess to begin with. Sorry, I didn't mean to call you a fucker, but you can understand that I still have a little bit of ambivalence about the Lewd Comedian. I mean, you could have given it to me instead, if you had to prove some kind of big metaphysical point, or punish me for my wicked ways. But I'd say we're almost even now. Just let Leo's concussion heal up real fast and let him agree to come home with me, and of course, he's got to be the match. *And* it's got to take. Then we're even, we'll call it a day. Okay?

Lindy wrapped her arms around her legs, the way she had always done on North Beverly Drive after a fight with her mother, and rocked herself to sleep.

Two A.M. Willa.

She sat up and turned her reading light back on. It was the third time in two hours. Damn. She got up and went into the bathroom, scrounging in her makeup kit for the sleeping pill donated by Bee Bee, veteran traveler and expert on time zone–induced sleeplessness. She took one and washed it down with the remainder of her lemonade. She had forgotten to ask Rennie if the tap water was drinkable, and she was taking no chances. She crawled back into bed and waited for the release. The deep, muscle-releasing chemical peace that she saved for emotional overload.

Why was it that everything that helped you feel better had a downside? Addictive, cancer-causing, fattening—or all three. Now even sex wasn't a safe release. What a predicament. She turned the light out, waiting for sleep. She could hear the sea down below. Rennie's house was on a bay, so there were no crashing waves, only the sliding rhythm of the water moving against the moon's tug. It was so amazing how it did that! She had never been able to grasp why all the water just didn't fly off the planet. She took a final lemony sip and settled back against the pillows.

She remembered sailing in San Francisco Bay with Leo and asking why the sea didn't fly off the planet and how he hadn't made fun of her but had tried in his calm, careful way to explain it to her.

It all made perfect sense, but she still found it inexplicable. Maybe no more so than the fact that they were here, and just down the way, Leo Lampi was lying in a hospital bed, completely oblivious of their presence or the turmoil of events leading up to it. She shuddered, seeing Lindy's face when Louie said that Leo was on the boat . . .

She was worried about Lindy. Something was going on that she had not told Willa the truth about. She knew her too well. She could feel it. It was only right for Lindy to do the talking when they confronted Leo in the morning, but she was very anxious about it. What a way to start a summer day!

She'd try to talk to Lindy in the morning and see if she could get her to tell her what was wrong. Lindy was getting more frantic and it would be harder, being this close, for her to keep cool. God, she understood! It was all she could do herself to keep from charging down there and dragging him onto the plane!

Poor Lindy. Poor little Rennie. What a sweet kid. What an un-Leo-like choice. She was probably very good for him, but he was not very good for her and it seemed that she was beginning to accept that.

They really should have the doctors castrate the bastard before they release him. It would save all the future Rennies a lot of grief. Was she really so angry at Leo? She yawned. The pill was working. She had not felt this relaxed in months, maybe even years. No. But then she had never been able to stay mad at Leo. Somehow she just never blamed him for anything. She had always seen Leo as their victim as much as their oppressor. He had always told her and Lindy the truth about who he was and what he wanted. They just didn't listen.

Leo was a man who needed a woman. Maybe a mother figure, but a loving, adoring woman. He did not need or want a family. He was not interested in sharing his woman. They wanted to turn him into Ozzie Nelson, even though it was his un-Ozziness that had entranced them. Well, that's what nice girls did when they lost their panties for a not-nice boy; they tried to turn him into someone safe. That wasn't Leo's fault.

Even Maxie. She had loved having Maxie all to herself, not having to compromise her parenting with anyone else's input. Did she feel guilty about leaving Leo and depriving Maxie of a father? Sure. But what she knew that Maxie didn't was that if they had stayed, the damage done by having a father who could never have made a deep emotional commitment to him would have been worse.

It was only that last night before they left, when Maxie had come to her room and she had seen his anguish about the possibility of Leo returning, accepting that it was too late for his fantasy to ever come true, that she had been swamped with doubt about her choice.

At least Maxie was coming to terms with Leo early in his manhood. A man who would leave his son without saying good-bye would probably have hurt him more by staying around.

Okay. Ambivalence would be what she had to look for tomorrow. Feeling sorry for Leo and not hanging tough enough for Lindy. She was floating off, sinking down into sleep. With all the pain, there had been so many gifts given to her this summer. The gift of Lindy's return to her, in a deeper and more loving way. The gift of Bee Bee and of Tess and Maxie finding one another, and even of Vilma Segal taking them all back down the rugged trails of their childhood. She was not the same woman that she'd been two months earlier, not the same at all.

She was braver and her heart was more full of love. She knew what this meant too. It meant that she was almost ready for the risk of a relationship.

She was closer, after all these years, to loving someone her own size.

Two A.M. Bee Bee.

She locked the door to her bathroom and sat down on the toilet seat, pushing the pillow she had taken from her bed against her face so that Willa wouldn't hear her crying. She had no real idea why she was crying, but she had been at it for almost an hour and she was nowhere near through.

Maybe it was just exhaustion. No. If it had been exhaustion—and God knows she had certainly freaked out before from too many hours in too many airports—she would have just let it out and fallen into deep, dark sleep. This was different.

What did it feel like? It felt like the night her mother had died. It did. That dark terror, a loss so unacceptable that there is nowhere to hide from it, no way to cushion the blow. Was that it?

Bee Bee stopped crying and raised her anguished face. Yes. That was it. Tomorrow she would see Leo. Now that she knew he was alive, she knew that he was really lost. But it was more than Leo. It was Lindy and Willa. It was almost over. A few more days and they would take Leo and go home. It would all be over. They would go back to New York together, bonded by their history and their children, and she would go home to Miami, alone. Companionless and Leo-less. Or at least stripped of the fantasy that he had either been taken from her against his will or had died.

She no longer had any idea how she had lived before or how she could possibly just go back and pick her old life up where she had left it. She knew it was selfish to think like this. These women had come to her because they were trying to save a child, but they had given her the most emotionally satisfying, loving, and intimate two months of her entire life and she loved them. Now she would lose them too. Two more mothers leaving her in the middle of a transformation, in the center of becoming without a guide through the terrifying tunnel into the light.

She stood up, placed the pillow on the seat, and walked to the sink. It was dark in the room and the shadows lined her face, making her look old and gaunt. She turned on the faucet and let the cool water cover her hands, holding them against her face until the water ran out between her fingers. "It'll be okay, Beeb," she whispered, refilling her hands. This was new, this talking gently to herself. She had heard Lindy doing it and she had tried it and it worked. Maybe she was becoming a mother to herself. Maybe that would be enough.

"Tessie?"

"Momma!"

"We've got him."

"Oh, my God. Where are you?"

"Somewhere in the middle of water. You know how my geography is. Except for one disastrous trip to Hawaii with your grandparents and Willa a thousand years ago, I have never been on an island that wasn't serviced by the Midtown Tunnel. It's called something like Coca-Cola—but it starts with an A."

"Lika Aoca Aola?"

"Very funny. Ancolla—that's it! Anyway, he's here and I'm going to see him this morning, I just wanted you to be the first to know. I'm quite proud of us. We never even hired a detective. Maybe this is my true calling, Lindy Lampi, Private Eye."

"Momma, you are so great! I knew this was going to be a good day. I just knew it!"

"Will you tell Grammas Alice and Segal for me? It's very hard to make calls from here."

"Sure." Tess paused. "When are you coming home?"

"Well, it's a little complicated but don't you worry, honey. As soon as we can make all the arrangements. Within a week, tops."

"Oh."

Her voice was small, too small for Lindy's taste. "Are you okay, baby?"

"A-okay. Like your island."

She had paused just a second, but in that pause Lindy knew that Tess was not okay at all. Her stomach flipped and a wave of nausea passed through her.

"Hey, kid—this is me. What's wrong?"

"Nothing, Momma. Just the bad dreams again. I'm doing fine, Dr. Davis is pleased. I mean, they're all hovering around waiting for a match, and that's all a little creepy, I mean, they try to be subtle, like, 'Have you heard from your mother?' But I mean, I'm not dumb. It's just that I miss you, Momma."

God. Please. "I know, baby. Just a little bit longer and then I am never going to leave you again, ever for the rest of your entire lengthy life. I'm going to stick to you like a sweaty thigh on a vinyl couch."

Giggles filled her dizziness. "Oh, Momma. You are really so totally twisted. Wait till I tell Maxie that one!"

"Just make sure I receive proper credit. You know how I feel about stolen one-liners."

"Okay. Go get him, Detective Lampi. I'll be waiting."

"Tie a yellow ribbon 'round the old IV. I'm a comin'."

"Corrine? Lindy. We've found him."

"Fabulous! What can I do now?"

"Well, it's a little tricky. He's been in a boat accident and he's in the hospital with a concussion, which should hold things up for a few more days. I've already talked to his doctor, and he thinks he'll be able to come home in a day or two; then he'll need a few days to rest up. Of course, we haven't seen him yet. He may die from the shock before we can get him out of here."

Corrine laughed. "How I would love to be a fly on that wall! He's not seriously hurt?"

"Naw. You know, the luck of the Leo. But we really need your help. His girlfriend—"

"His *what*?"

"His twenty-something-year-old *pregnant* girlfriend—you were thinking maybe he'd found Jesus?"

"No, but even finding the condom counter would do."

"No kidding. In all fairness to Mr. Love 'em and leave 'em, I don't think he's to blame for this one. She's a very sweet kid and she's taken us all in—we've become sort of an American harem.

"The bottom line is that she intercepted a letter proving that there is a contract out on Leo in Florida and if they find out we're bringing him back . . . well, you can fill in the rest. Also, if Leo finds out, I doubt that he's going to be overly eager to jump on the jet with us. Not that he's going to be eager anyway. But if we can promise him a new ID and a silent entry and exit with some kind of security, it may make all the difference."

"Say no more. I'll Fed Ex the passport, the rest is just a phone call away. All I need is your flight number and arrival time."

"Corrine, you're a very classy dame. I owe you a big one."

"You owe me a visit with your beautiful daughter when all this is over. Now, go get the bastard!"

"Thanks." Lindy hung up. That was certainly the message of the morning. She felt like a star quarterback just before taking the Super Bowl field. Go. Go. Go.

She picked up her coffee and walked out onto the terrace. It was still early. No one else was up. She stood against the railing, looking down onto the empty white beach. A large black dog was chasing a dragonfly round and round in circles, trying to catch it. His boundless energy and hopefulness toward the impossible task touched her. Round and round he went, panting and jumping.

Lindy smiled. All anyone ever needed to know about the continual triumph of hope over experience could be learned watching a big, sloppy black dog, filled with longing and frustration, trying to catch a dragonfly on the morning beach.

"Hi." Rennie came up behind her carrying a glass of milk.

"Hi. What a beautiful day. Maybe we should just tan today and do Leo tomorrow."

Rennie laughed. "Sounds good to me."

"There was a woman on the plane, wearing a T-shirt that said SHE WHO DIES WITH THE BEST TAN WINS. I wanted to ask her what she wins. Or how about adding on the back SHE WHO EXPIRES WITH THE MOST WRINKLES LOSES or SHE WHO DEPARTS WITH THE LARGEST MELANOMA GETS A YEAR'S SUPPLY OF COPPERTONE, but by the time I had figured out all those hilarious retorts, we were here." Lindy sighed. "I guess I'm nervous. I always do schtick when I'm nervous. You probably have no idea what schtick is."

Rennie sat down in one of the difficult deck chairs. "I certainly do. My dad's a comedian. I was weaned on the Borscht Belt."

Lindy sat down beside her. "Oh, *that* Bowman. Did you live in Beverly Hills?"

"Off and on, but my parents got a divorce and my mother's family was all in Rye and Manhattan, so I came back East and then they shipped me off to boarding school."

"Better choice."

"Oh, I don't know. At least B.H. was real phoniness. Not all of that WASP tightass hypocrisy."

"Well, the Beverly Hills you saw was really different than the one we grew up in, in the Fifties. It was normal for Willa and me to hit Jimmy Durante's cook for homemade cookies, then pop over Harpo Marx's fence on the way to see Zeppo's kids; wave Dinah Shore off to her tennis game at Dino's place; bump into Rita Hayworth taking her daughter by Aly Khan, to Saks for school clothes. I mean, this was just an afterschool walk around the block.

"All these legendary people had kids or grandkids that we knew. Everyone seemed just like an ordinary family. You'd hear singing coming out of Gene Kelly's house or piano tinkling from Oscar Levant's or the Minnellis'. Every once in a while someone we were really nuts about, like Bobby Darin, would be in a meeting at some famous producer's house and his kid would sneak us in, but mostly we just took it all in stride.

"Jack Benny would give us a wink strolling down Rodeo on his way to his agent at the Morris office, and Uncle Milty always had a joke for everyone. Just like any kindly old neighborhood uncle in Middle America."

Rennie put down her milk and rubbed her stomach. The baby was doing double gainers this morning. "Well, in the Seventies, I must tell you, it was a lot more jaded and pretentious than that! All anyone cared about was power and status. The thought of Warren Beatty's or Jack Nicholson's maid popping up with a plate of goodies for the kids on the block is really riotous.

"Do you remember that line in *Sleeper* when Diane Keaton asks Woody Allen what it feels like to wake up after being asleep for two hundred years and he says, 'It feels like spending a weekend in Beverly Hills'?"

Lindy threw her head back. "I love that! I'm stealing that!"

The Un Jill moved in behind them.

"Phone, Rennie. The hospital."

Rennie and Lindy turned toward her. Her eyes were so wide and her pink round lips so pursed that she really did look like one of the drawings of a golden cod that Brad kept on his desk.

Lindy stood up and helped Rennie out of the impossible chair and followed her to the phone.

"I see," Rennie said, while the Un Jill and Lindy huddled behind her. "Good. Very good. We'll be right over."

Rennie put down the phone and turned toward them. She was not going to cry. "He's fully conscious. He's fine."

Lindy let out a war whoop and hugged the Un Jill. "Let's boogie, ladies. I'll get the girls and we are out of here."

They decided to take both Rennie's car and Big Red, because the hospital was on the far side of the island, and most likely they would not all be staying around. Rennie gave Bee Bee and Willa a crash course in the peculiarities of the spunky little wreck. Lindy, who could barely manage the automatic transmission on a brand-new Buick, chose to ride with Rennie.

To balance their weight going up and down the steep hills between Rennie's house and the hospital, she suggested that Willa drive and Bee Bee sit in the backseat. These suggestions made more and more sense to the two of them once they were under way.

"First hill coming up," Willa yelled, picking up as much speed as she could. Bee Bee was spread out across the backseat, distributing her weight.

Willa hit the upgrade, keeping her foot to the floor, but about halfway up the speedometer started to fall. Twenty. Fifteen. Twelve.

Willa shrieked. "She wasn't kidding! We're dropping by the second. We still have a third of the hill to climb and we're down to eight miles an hour!

"Would you believe five? We are going *five* miles an hour!"

"In a minute we'll be going backward!"

"Oh, God! Bee Bee. Get out! Quick! Out!"

Bee Bee flung open the tiny back door and jumped out of the car. Willa moved forward, creeping toward the top. "Can you make it on foot?"

Bee Bee waved her on. "I'm fine. I'll meet you!"

The hill, however, was far steeper than it looked. Bee Bee arrived huffing and puffing, only to find a long downward slide, with another hill looming ahead.

Bee Bee crawled into the backseat, her chest heaving. "I'm out of shape for this. How many of these did she say there were?"

"Three in a row, then two more, not as bad on the other side of the island."

"And this is the easy way?"

"So it seems. I guess we should have had them follow us instead of taking the other road."

"No. It's more important for Lindy to arrive in one piece. Okay, hit it."

Willa threw the rusty gear into first.

They sputtered over the ridge. "Okay, get ready. I'm going to swing her into second to build momentum. Hang on!"

"To what?" Bee Bee braced herself with her long, bare legs.

They flew down the hill, hitting the second rise so hard, Willa's head jerked back as they were propelled forward into their second climb. "Here we go again!" Willa pushed the pedal as hard as she could. "Rats! Fifteen. Ten. Four."

"I'm going, I'm going!"

Bee Bee jumped out and trudged along beside the car. She leaned in the window and grinned at Willa. "Do you understand that I am walking as fast as you are driving?"

Willa could feel the hysteria building. "Don't make me laugh, Bee Bee. If I start now, I won't stop. You don't know that about me, but once I start I'm gone. Peeing in the pants, the whole thing. I am not going to confront Leo with urine on my shorts."

"Oh, great. So I get to arrive a sweaty, dehydrated wreck, but you don't want a little dribble to keep things equal. How about I drive the next one and you walk?"

"Fair enough. If there is a next one. I am now going one mile an hour, according to the speedometer."

"Should I push?"

"Can't hurt."

They were about twenty yards from the crest. Bee Bee leaned against the back window and pushed. "Please let me know as soon as possible if you start going backward. I have limbs at stake."

"We're holding steady at one m.p.h. Call Le Mans."

"Naaaaaaaaa!"

Bee Bee jumped away from the car. A lone mangy goat had come up behind her, brushing against her thigh.

"What's happening?" Willa turned her aching head.

"A goat just passed us, Willa." This was too much for them. Willa steered the car to the crest and Bee Bee fell into the back, screams of mirth filling the stifling interior as Willa slammed them back into first and started down into the final assault. "A goat passed us! Haaaa!"

"Not for long!" Willa slid Big Red into second and sailed past the insouciant nanny, flipping the bird as she flew. "So long, sucker!" she screamed out the window, sailing into the third ascent like an island pro. "Maxie will never believe this," she said, laughing, proud of herself in the way only a timid, fearful person can be proud when she's done something risky, reckless, bold, or out of character, and survived. The rest of the trip was a breeze.

They bombed into the Angeltown clinic parking lot, where Rennie and Lindy were waiting for them.

"How'd you do?" Rennie said, telling by their sweaty, wind-blown faces that it had not been easy.

Bee Bee was still recovering her composure. "One mile an hour at the summit, and a goat passed us."

Lindy looked at Willa. "*You* drove this? Miss 'I've never had a ticket, not even for parking' Snow? I am very impressed."

Bee Bee took out her compact and lipstick. "She was fantastic! Completely fearless and determined. I'd fight beside her in the gulf."

Willa blushed. She was loving this. "It was nothing."

They all stopped the patter. The diversion had anchored them.

Lindy took a long, deep breath. "Rennie's already been in. He's asleep, but the doctor said we can wake him anytime."

"Does he know about us yet?"

Rennie shook her head. "No. No. I think that's for you all to do. If you don't mind, I think I'll go up and see Brad. I'll meet you in the lounge."

They all smiled at her. Lindy hugged her. "Absolutely. We'll come get you when it's over. If the place is still standing."

They all walked arm in arm to the front door. Lindy opened it and held it for everyone. Rennie pointed down the hallway on her left. "Three A." Her voice was so thin and sad that none of them knew what to do or how to comfort this decent girl who was waddling down an empty linoleum-covered hall to wait for the end of her love affair.

Lindy turned and took one of each of their hands. "Okay, Exes, let's find our Y."

CHAPTER 10

Come Fly With Me

THE DREAMS CAME AND WENT, FLOATING LEO UP AND DOWN, in and out of consciousness. It was a twilight reverie, the most peaceful time he had ever had. Only once, when the fat, torpid old nurse had put him on the bedpan with her cold puffy fingers and never returned, did he feel anything close to discomfort.

As long as he kept his head still and they kept pumping whatever it was they were giving him for pain, he was content. He had never been in a hospital before, and so he did not even know enough to be nervous. All he knew was that the doctor and Rennie had told him he was going to be fine, all he needed was complete rest until his memory fully returned and his concussion healed.

Not once in his entire life had he ever stopped moving, physically or mentally. He had never been afforded that luxury. Except for that first year with Corrine, he had never had a mental or physical vacation; there had never been any way around the daily tension of knowing that he had to keep slugging away, trying to keep his life from falling apart. That had been as far down the list of goals as he had ever gotten—trying to keep everything from collapsing around or on top of him.

It was a lousy way to get a time out, but at the moment it almost seemed worth it. He dozed. His head was still so thick. There were enormous holes in his recall, and he could not remember anything about the day of the accident. Rennie had sat with him all through the first night while he asked her over and over to tell him what had happened; but even while she was telling him, he would forget what she was saying.

He still couldn't remember anything after his run on the beach the day it happened, but he was holding bigger chunks of what Rennie told him. The doctors said that this was common with concussion. He thought of what he had read about Alzheimer's disease. What a terrible thing that would be—for the holes to never close up, to lose your life while you were living it.

He clicked the thought out. He wasn't letting any bad thoughts in, only musical thoughts that he was singing in his head. Sinatra: "As long as you kiss me and the world around us shatters, how little it matters, how little we know." Cuts from that album Lennie Tristano recorded just before he died. Tunes, words, and melodies humming in his head, filling him with joy.

"When Sunny gets blue, she breathes a sigh of sadness, like the wind that stirs the trees—"

"Leo."

"People used to love, to hear her laugh, see her smile, that's how she got her name—"

"Leo."

"Since that sad affair, she's lost her smile, changed her style, somehow she's not the same—"

"Leo, wake up."

"But memories will fade and pretty dreams will rise up where her other dreams fell through—"

"Leo!"

"Hurry new love, hurry here to kiss away each lonely tear—"

Someone was calling him. Maybe whoever it was would go away. He wasn't ready to be conscious yet. Consciousness meant reality and facing his predicament. Instinctively he knew that the voices calling his name would demand that he face what he could avoid after the crack on his head; everything he had gotten time off from having to deal with. He didn't want to come back. Not just yet.

"Leo! Leo!"

"And hold her near when Sunny gets blue . . ."

He opened his eyes slowly, trying to control the headache that came with vision. He was surrounded. Women were surrounding

him. One on either side leaning over the metal safety bars and
another at the foot, leaning toward him. Nurses? No. They were
wearing colors, not uniforms. What did they want? Faces swam
into focus. Leo shut his eyes. Jesus! It was the dream! The Wilis!
He was having it again. They were back.

"Leo! Enough already. What is this? Sleeping fucking Beauty?
Wake up!"

That was no dream. That was . . . that could only be one
woman.

Leo opened his eyes and this time there was no blur, no misty,
dozy reverie to couch reality. Lindy stood at the end of his bed,
hands on hips, glaring at him. Flanking her, like overzealous
mothers guarding an infant's crib, were the other players in his
troubled past. Willa. Bee Bee.

His head was pounding. His heart was pounding, but his voice,
when he tried it, was composed.

"Three guesses. I won the lottery: the Messiah has come: or I'm
dead."

Lindy swallowed, trying to control the shaking in her hands
and jelly in her knees. "You forgot *Candid Camera, This Is Your
Life,* and *America's Funniest Home Videos.* You've lost your edge,
Lampi."

Leo laughed. Pain shot through his head and he winced. Bee Bee
automatically reached toward him. "Are you okay?"

He looked at her and smiled, that same old crooked, quizzical
smile that had done her in the first day she met him. "Hi, Sergio.
You cut your hair. I like it."

Bee Bee felt the blush start somewhere in the middle of her back
and move like an oil fire up her body across her shoulders, hitting
like twin firecrackers in the freckled ovals of her cheeks.

"Thanks," she whispered.

He turned toward Willa. "Wills. It's been a long time. You look
great."

Lindy could feel the jealousy and hurt. Everyone would get
their pat but her. She had to put that aside. Use the hurt as righteous indignation, make the bastard pay. She could feel Willa's
eyes on her. Willa had tried to talk to her before they went in, but
Lindy knew what Willa would ask her and she could not talk
about it. Willa was trying to warn her, and Willa was right. Cool

it, Lindy. Clamp the big mouth. If you make him mad, you give
him an excuse for not helping. Stuff it.

Leo met her eyes. He winked at her. "Lovely Lindy, the leader
of the pack. Better just spit it out. I can feel the pressure of a
monologue needing release."

Lindy laughed. He had given her one too. A doggie treat for
each of them, but it helped. She took a deep breath.

"Tess is sick, Leo. Really sick. She has leukemia and she needs a
bone-marrow transplant and you seem to be her last hope. Believe
me, I've been everywhere else. That's how I found Bee Bee and
Corrine helped us too."

Leo sat up straighter. "Corrine?"

Bee Bee nodded. "That got us to Hong Kong and one thing led
to another and here we are."

Willa moved closer to Lindy. Bee Bee followed her lead. "We're
staying with Rennie. She's been a jewel."

"You're staying with *Rennie?*" Leo could feel the net closing
over him. A dolphin trapped with the albacore.

Tears streamed down Lindy's face. "Look, I know this is all a
little bit much for you to handle all at once, but my baby is handling a helluva lot worse. She's going to die, Leo. You've got to
come with us. I've arranged everything. Corrine's husband has
promised security to get you in and out without any attention. We
know you can't go back to Florida . . ."

"You do?" Leo looked at Bee Bee.

Willa put her arm around Lindy. "Leo we know just about
everything about you now—we've all put our pieces of the puzzle
together. You don't have to be afraid. We don't want to hurt you.
We don't want anything from you. We just need your help for a
couple of days. We've got a new passport for you and if you need
money . . ."

"Gee, this is great. You've just worked it all out."

Lindy wiped her face. "Yes. We're trying to make it as easy for
you as possible. Though why we . . ." Lindy felt Willa's elbow in
her side and changed her mind. "Anyway, we even helped Rennie
sting Mrs. Pidge last night."

"*Sting, Mrs. Pidge?*"

"It was great, you would have loved it! We went over there and
told her that I was an FBI agent . . ."

Bee Bee joined Willa and Lindy at the end of the bed. "Lorraine Smithers!"

"I used Brad's captain's medallion. I even had his gun in my belt. Rennie gave it to me."

"Good old Lorraine." Leo gripped the metal railing.

"Lindy said that we, Willa and I, were your wives and you were wanted for bigamy and embezzlement and she, Mrs. Pidge, was supposed to be your next victim . . ."

"Bigamy and embezzlement?"

Willa laughed. "We left, I mean, we pretended to leave. I ducked behind a chair and Rennie—"

"Rennie was great!" Bee Bee took Lindy's hand.

"Good old Rennie!"

"She had my pocket recorder and Rennie got her to confess. Willa was a witness and Mr. Bartlett and the police arrested her. So you don't even have to worry about any of that. She can't hurt any of you anymore."

Leo's lips were a white-hot line of rage. "Well, this is just all terrific news. I bet old Rip Van Winkle has nothing on me. I get a bump on the head, and lo and behold, I wake up a week later and my entire life has been lived for me. All I have to do is take a quick trip to Manhattan and squeeze out some bone marrow and all my worries are over."

They were quiet. They could feel his anger. Leo never yelled. He just got that white line around his mouth and talked so slowly and steadily and sardonically. It had always scared the shit out of them.

"Too much, too soon," Willa whispered to Lindy.

Lindy was ready for him now. Tess had centered her. Her voice softened. "Hey, Lampi. Be a mensch. She's your kid. She's a beautiful, lovely girl with her whole life ahead of her. I know you're pissed, but you know us all well enough to know that we would never have walked back into all of this pain, not to mention the blows to our pride, if it wasn't really important. You loved us once; hell, you married us! You gotta do it!"

Leo let go of the railing. His head hurt so bad he felt sick to his stomach. He had never felt so utterly helpless in his life. They were all standing there, so sure of themselves. So righteous. Three beautiful, brave, wonderful fucking women who held his future in their noble demand.

He closed his eyes. His anger was gone. "I'm really sorry about Tess, but I can't go back there."

Lindy looked at Willa. He must know. She would have to risk it.

"Because of the contract?"

Leo stiffened, then he laughed. Why not! They knew everything else. "Yeah. I go back and I die, maybe even before you can get me to the hospital. I have a feeling Pidge tipped these guys off about me."

Lindy felt hope returning. "No! We picked up the letter they sent her last night after the sting. She was smarter than that, probably because she still has the hots for you. They told her to tell them if she heard from you. But you should probably leave here anyway, and with Corrine's new papers and the security, we can cover you. No one will know you're there and afterward you can start a new life somewhere else."

The headache was blinding now. He had to sleep. He could not absorb anymore of this maelstrom in the middle of his melody line. "You must think I'm fucking Felix the Cat. Just what I need, another new life! Let me just rest now. My head hurts. Come back later. It'll give me something to look forward to. Great seeing you all, but I have to sleep now."

They watched him. No one moved or spoke. Each was lost in her private Leo memories; feeling long-buried emotions too personal to share. They stood together like eavesdroppers.

Leo slept until he could no longer keep his eyes closed. When he opened them, his headache was gone and Brad and Rennie were sitting beside his bed.

"Hi." Rennie's voice was barely audible.

"Hi."

"How do you feel?"

"How do I feel? Disappointed. I was expecting the Rockettes."

Brad laughed. "It's been quite a day."

Rennie kept her eyes on Leo. "Are you mad?"

Leo smiled at her. "At you? No. At myself? You betcha." He remembered something. "Billy's dead, right?"

Brad winced. "Right."

"This is my fault. If you hadn't gotten messed up with me, none of this would have happened."

Tears filled Rennie's eyes. "Don't say that. None of the good things would have happened without your help. You mustn't feel like that. Right, Brad?"

"Right. Listen, the Pidge thing was just bad luck. Who would have thought the broad was that wacko! Maybe it won't be so bad. My dad will collect plenty of insurance—maybe we can work something out with him on a new boat.

"The lease on Blue Man has been turned over to Billy's father and he likes me, and of course, he hates Pidge; so when we get out of here, we can talk to him. It'll be okay, Leo. We'll start over. It may even be better now without Pidge and, I know it's wrong to speak ill of the dead, but without The Third jerking us around all the time."

Leo smiled at them. Two eager, kind souls who still needed him. God, what was it he had that made people continuously want to justify and forgive him? "Are you okay, Brad? I keep asking Rennie to tell me what happened, but pieces still slip away."

"I'm fine. Some burns, a few cracked ribs—nothing serious." His face was impassive, but Leo saw his lip tremble. "So what happens now, buddy?"

"I don't know, Brad."

Rennie leaned toward him. "The doctor says if you feel up to it, you can go home tomorrow. Brad too."

"Great," he said, feeling despair cover him. The place of peace was casting him out, and Leo knew that he would not have another respite like this, not as long as he lived.

"Leo? You're going to help Lindy, aren't you? You've got to go with her. I saw a picture of Tess. She looks just like you."

Brad reached over and took Rennie's hand. "Give him a little more time to get his head together, Ren. I mean, how often do your three former wives show up and drop a little nuclear warhead on your lap?"

"Thanks, Brad, you're a better friend than I deserve, but I might as well start dealing with the truth right now. I've always thought that there were three kinds of people. The ones who want to see the truth, the ones who want the lie, and the ones who don't see anything. We're all truth types, so let's get on with it."

He pulled himself up higher, feeling the heaviness in his still fuzzy head. He looked at them. "You guys are the best friends I've ever had. I want you to know that. The last three years have been the happiest of my life. But it's over now. I have to leave here. Pidge isn't through with me, and even if she is, it's only a matter of time now before the guys I'm in trouble with find me.

"I did something really stupid in Florida. I wanted to produce an album for Bee Bee. I wanted to show her . . . well, it doesn't matter now, but I trusted the wrong guy. I borrowed money from bad people and I couldn't pay it back. I couldn't give them my boat because it was mortgaged to the teeth. I didn't want to put Bee Bee in danger and I was ashamed, so the night I heard about the contract I just split. I thought if we made enough money on this deal, I could pay them off and cancel the hit, but it wasn't to be. So I have to go and I won't be back."

Rennie and Brad were crying. Leo pulled no punches.

"Hey, believe me, I am doing you both the biggest fucking favor of your young lives. If I hadn't come along, you two would be married by now, which is what I hope to hell you do after I leave. You'd start out as best friends, which believe me, I never did with any of my wives and it doomed every relationship. Get married and give my kid a home. I have never been the guy for that job, and Rennie, you know that I never misled you about that."

Rennie nodded, feeling the baby churning, as if sensing his potential abandonment right through her womb. "What are you going to do?"

Leo sighed. "First, I have to finish off this hammer in my head. So if it's okay, I'll go home with you tomorrow and try to get my strength back. Then I'll have to see."

Rennie knew that she should back off, but she had changed. She had stood up to Pidge and she had faced the loss of Leo and now she had nothing left to be afraid of. "What do you mean, 'you'll see'? You mean you might not go with them?"

"You wouldn't understand, Rennie. Life isn't always black or white, right or wrong. I am not going to talk about it."

Leo was mad. Rennie had pushed a button, but now that she had started she needed to finish. "Try me!"

"I don't want to hurt you, Rennie. Please go now."

Brad put his arm around her, trying to calm her.

"No! What wouldn't I understand?"

Leo's mouth grew tighter and whiter. He could feel the fury that he had fought all of his life, filling him. "You women, you fucking self-righteous martyrs from fucking Mars! It's always about how selfless and wonderful you are and how heartless and terrible I am!

"It was fine for Lindy to trick me, get herself knocked up and manipulate me into another marriage that I never wanted, because otherwise I was the world's biggest heel: but if I choose not to walk back into the life of a kid I hardly knew and who wouldn't know me if I parachuted into her bedroom, if I should choose not to be made responsible for her *survival,* I am a fiend, a prick beyond pricks, an animal, and of course, a monster!

"You too! I told you and you did it anyway! Moping around like I was the fucking Hillside Strangler or something! *You* wanted a baby. I was just your sperm bank, kid. I am not making myself into a heroic figure, but all the trouble in my life has come from trying to meet the insatiable needs of a bunch of self-absorbed little girls who just don't listen to a word I say!

"Now I wake up with my life in shreds and a contract dangling over my bare ass and I find an entire fucking drill team of women pulling me back into their agendas. Well, no one is going to do that to me again. Ever!

"I made a couple of gigantic mistakes in my life, for which I may pay the Big Price. But no one is going to make me do anything because I'm supposed to feel guilty for being such a swine! Tess is *not* my responsibility, and I am not so sure I am willing to die for her.

"Okay? I said it. Now you can run home to 'the girls' and make popcorn and curl up to talk about what the husband from hell just said. But it's still *my* decision, and I will be the one and the only one to make it."

Rennie stood up. She had never felt stronger in her life. She turned to help Brad up. Then she faced Leo. "You're right, Leo. Everything you said is true. I don't blame you for feeling just what you're feeling. But I also think part of it is just a childish temper tantrum. I think you'll see that sooner or later and do the right thing, because whatever you are, you are not a coward.

"You'll do it because it's the right thing to do. If you can live with this, then I suppose you're either the most fortunate man on earth or the most tragic. I won't say anything to 'the girls.' It's not my place. There's plenty of time for that when you get home. I love you, Leo, but I'm on their side."

Leo never slept that night, so the image that kept floating before his dry, itchy eyes could not be called a dream; but it was a vision, a view through a corroded periscope. A little boy on a great big swing, crying for his mother; swinging higher and higher and all alone.

Two days later Leo came home. The Un Jill returned to her room off the kitchen; Willa moved in with Lindy; Bee Bee stayed where she was, Brad replacing Willa as her roommate. It all worked so easily that an outsider stopping by would have had no sense of the tension underneath or the uniqueness of the circumstances.

There was nothing to do now but wait for Leo to recover. Lindy had already booked a flight at the end of the week, allowing him four full days after the hospital. Of course, Leo did not know this yet, no one but Corrine did, not even Dr. Davis. That was Corrine's department. The truth was, they could all use the rest before facing what was waiting back home.

Leo was quiet, venturing forth from Rennie's room only to walk on the beach or lie in the sun, not speaking much to anyone. They hovered over him, bringing food and freshly squeezed juices, vitamin compounds, and cold packs. It was in their best interest to see him heal as quickly as possible.

Leo was not a guy who liked subservient, hovering women under any circumstances, but a quartet of them only served to irritate him more. Only Lindy, who was especially lousy in this role, had broken through his surliness and made him laugh.

"So, how would the Sultan of Brunei like his eggs this morning?" she asked, bouncing across the deck to where he was lying in his French bikini swimsuit, letting the sun work its magic.

They had not spoken a personal word since the hospital, but when he laughed, she felt her insides flutter. She was alone with him on the deck in the sun, and she was having an enormously hard time keeping her eyes off his groin.

He looked up at her. "You always could make me laugh."

Lindy clutched her book against her chest. "Yeah. That's me, always leave 'em laughing."

He watched her. "Sit for a minute. I don't want any eggs unless they're golden."

She curled up beside him, still holding her book.

"What's the book? I thought you were a magazine fiend."

"I am. But now they have all these self-help books that are just like twenty magazines mushed together, so I'm raising my brow, so to speak. You know the kind: *Stupid Women, Brilliant Choices; Women Who Love Too Little, Too Late, Too High, Too Low, or Too Close to the Equator; Cher on How to Spend Five Hours a Day on the Magic Stairs and Still Have the Energy Left for an Eighteen-year-old Bagel Maker; Jane Fonda Tells You How to Adjust Your Politics to Your Love Life and Firm Your Inner Thighs at the Same Time; Goldie Hawn Reveals Her Secrets of Giggling and Screaming and Being Girlishly Adorable Throughout Menopause; Linda Evans's Guide to New Age-Middle Age with Perfect Hair Color and a Two-thousand-year-old Channeler Growing out of Her Neck*—stuff like that."

Leo reached out and took the book from her. "*Love, Medicine, and Miracles.* You're a fraud, Lucinda. Spunky, but bullshit."

"Don't call me that. You are not on the list of people who can call me that. Not even Wheezie can call me Lucinda."

Leo laughed. "How is old Wheezie?"

"He's running Hollywood from the front seat of the biggest German automobile I've ever seen. He's sort of a glitzy Desert Rat."

"Is he still in love with you?"

Lindy laughed. "How did you know that? I never knew—until this summer."

"Because he did everything but fling himself into your arms every time he saw you."

"He did? I never noticed. Anyway, he's fine. He's been a real prince through all of this. Even Gerrold has helped."

Leo raised his feathery blond brows. "Gerrold? The dashing dentist! Remember that Christmas card he sent us with a picture of him in a Santa suit with a giant plastic molar on his lap and engraved on the bottom 'A white X-Mas begins here'?"

"These cards are coming back to haunt me! I had blocked them all out."

She looked at him, wondering how much to tell. "Actually, Gerrold made our trip possible. He gave me back all the jewelry he bought for me. Remember when I left, I didn't feel right about taking it? Well, he still had it all. I'll have enough left to offset most of the costs of the transplant."

Their eyes locked. She waited, but he said nothing. This provoked her.

"Want to set your head a-pounding? Guess who he's married to now."

"The Tooth Fairy."

"Very funny. No. He's married to that little piece of work with the enormous incisors that you used to see. Honey."

Leo roared. "No shit! Poor Gerrold."

Something about this mirth annoyed her. "They're very happy. They live in a great big French château monstrosity in Bel Air, with their chunky but very special ten-year-old *twin* daughters."

Leo stopped laughing. Their eyes met again and he watched her. Lindy hated it when he looked at her like that. It always made her feel that he could see right through her. "Lindy, I'm sorry I hurt you. Maybe we can talk about it."

"No. I don't want to talk about it. It's all over and done with. I . . . it's just about Tess now. That's all." She was too near him and she could not risk letting him move any closer to her wound. She stood up and leaned over, sliding her book out of his hands. Her fingers grazed his warm muscular arm. It was all she could do to keep from hurling herself on top of him. *Oh, God, please.*

"No golden eggs. I'll bring coffee." She did not look back.

The evening of Brad and Leo's return they had eaten on trays in their rooms, but by the afternoon of the second day, Rennie and the trio realized that something like a dinner party would have to occur.

The thought of all of them sitting down to supper made them so uneasy that they had pushed it aside by concentrating on the menu.

Bee Bee had not cooked a meal since she was opening cans of

SpaghettiOs for her kid brothers in Las Vegas and Rennie was hardly able to get in and out of a chair, so Willa and Lindy leapt into the fray, checking provisions and preparing to set off on foot for the store down the beach.

The Un Jill was riveted to *Donahue,* which had managed to circumvent the terrible static and was beaming in an interview with some pop psychologist. The woman, who admitted to having been married and divorced four times herself, was now an expert on married sex. "Fifty minutes of sex is perfect," she was saying as Willa and Lindy entered the kitchen, list in hand. The Un Jill shot up as if she had been caught with a porno tape. Willa laughed. "Fifty minutes a *day?*"

Lindy rechecked the list. "No way. She must mean a week."

Willa retied her sneaker. "Maybe a month."

Lindy grinned at her. "Why Miz Snow. You have grown up. I was sure you'd say 'a year.'"

Willa stood up. "Well, if I were comparing it to my life, I would have. I was trying to generalize."

The Un Jill put her hand over her mouth. "Ho-ho-ho."

Lindy smiled at her. "Now, don't you be laughing at a couple of horny old broads. It may happen to you too someday."

The Un Jill covered her face, she was not used to attention.

"It already hoppened. Ho-ho-ho."

Lindy counted the money in her pocket. "Oh, really? That's not what I heard about you. You're just waiting for some hunky wrestler to carry you off."

The Un Jill lowered her face into her lap, muffling her voice. "Junk Yard Dog."

Willa and Lindy both laughed. Lindy tickled her. "That's it. He sounds like every girl's dream lover, but, probably not a best bet for a husband. How would you introduce yourself? 'Hello, I'm Mrs. Dog'? Or 'Hi! I'm Mrs. Junk Yard'? And what about your babies? The Dog children? Better have Louie introduce you to some nice fellow with a decent last name."

"Ho-ho-ho!"

Bee Bee and Rennie came in. "What's so funny?" Rennie had never heard the Un Jill laugh before.

Willa smiled. "We were teasing her about her wrestler."

Bee Bee moved over to the television set. "At least she has

someone to be teased about. Hey, I know that woman. She was on
my show in Miami. I wouldn't let her advise me on how to change
a Band-Aid. She's a lunatic. The only coherent thing she said in
twenty minutes on the air was that, at thirty-five, American
women either look twenty-eight or forty."

Willa checked the refrigerator to see if Rennie had enough butter. "That's coherent?"

"Well, at least it was a complete sentence."

Lindy put on her sunglasses. "It's also true, come to think
about it. Now, that's even more depressing than the dinner we are
facing. Let's go, Wills."

Rennie followed them out. "Did the Un Jill tell you about the
store?"

Lindy turned around. "It's down the beach and everything is
rotten."

"Not everything. But be really careful about bread, cheese, and
milk—and under no circumstances let them talk you into the fresh
fish. They're notorious."

Willa waved. "Right. We've been warned. Paralysis and seeing
sounds or smelling colors or something. We're thinking more of
spaghetti and meatballs."

"Check the pasta. Some of it's been there a long time."

They set off down the beach, the sun on their backs, enjoying
the walk and the time alone together. They were quiet, letting the
sea sounds soothe them.

"Listen." Willa moved away from the water, following the echo
of a woman's voice.

At the edge of the path down to the beach was a small, perfectly
tended graveyard, and behind it, a miniature white church. The
door was open and from the cemetery in the sand, they could see
right inside.

Willa motioned for Lindy, who followed her. They stood in the
shade of the graveyard, listening to a sturdy coal-black woman in
a grass-green dress, who stood shyly before the small room full of
Ancollans.

"When I come here, I have no money and no place to stay. The
Reverend and his people took me in and found me work. I'm
going home to my children tomorrow, so I want to offer my
thanks to the Reverend and all of you."

The woman moved forward, holding her hands under her heavy breasts. She started to sing a low, crackling harmony, the voice so powerful and so racked with emotion, that Willa reached out and held on to Lindy's arm.

> I love you, Jesus. You is my everything,
> I can't complain.
> I love you, Jesus. You gave me work to do,
> You gave me work to do, I can't complain.
>
> I love you, Jesus. You wake me up each day,
> You wake me up each day, I can't complain.
> I love you, Jesus. You gave me everything,
> You gave me everything, I can't complain.

The woman's face was wet with tears, and circles of sweat had formed under her firm ebony arms. Willa and Lindy had lowered their heads, joining her prayer.

They stood there after the woman had finished, overcome by the humility and gratitude in her song.

A woman with so little to call up from the temporal world that they had lived their lives in; counting such simple blessings, with so much joy and strength, moved them in a way that they had never been moved by any sermon in any upscale church or synagogue. They felt the force of the woman's faith buoying them up.

Later it would be a memory that Willa would write about and a song that would never leave.

By the time they reached the market the sun was slipping down behind the clouds, and the old man with one remaining tooth who ran it was anxious to close.

Not that the selection would have been much better earlier in the day, but there was nothing on the shelves that did not have either dust, an expired USE BY . . . date on the package, or both. They settled for two mangy heads of lettuce, several cans of sweet corn, a double pack of frozen chicken parts (too frozen to be exactly sure which parts), two cans of black beans, and a dog-eared box of Uncle Ben's minute rice.

They trudged home along the darkening beach, still too moved by the woman and the brutal beauty of her song to speak.

"So, are we cooking the Last Supper or what?" Lindy said finally, when the silence became too heavy.

"When's the flight?" Willa sighed, realizing how much more stood between them and Tess.

"Three days from right now, but he hasn't said a word."

"Want me to talk to him?"

They were back. Lindy looked up and saw Rennie and Leo standing on the deck above them. "Sure. You always knew how to handle him. But not before dinner. Dinner will be weird enoug..."

Willa moaned. "Good thinking. You know Leo. Leo's like Switzerland!"

Lindy sighed. "Yep. You got it. Talk to him after dinner. Can he drink?"

"The doctor said wine, nothing hard."

"Fine. *I'll* pour. We'll loosen him up first."

The Un Jill and Bee Bee were waiting for them, and they all began the strange but familiar female process of preparing food that they never would have chosen, for a meal they never would have planned.

But Leo was tired and had no appetite and Brad's burns were hurting and so it was the women who ate and the women who made conversation with a mixture of relief and disappointment at having lost one of their last chances to look at Leo again, to figure it all out.

It was later, at Lindy's insistence, that Willa climbed the stairs, carrying a couple of beers (also Lindy's idea) to Leo's room. Rennie was in the kitchen, watching an old *Fugitive* rerun with Bee Bee and the Un Jill. Lindy, who could no longer sit still long enough to eat, let alone watch TV, was pacing back and forth down below on the beach.

Willa knocked. Everything in her was yelling *Don't do it!* She knew that pushing Leo was always a mistake, but there was no arguing with Lindy about it and she could certainly empathize.

"Come in."

Willa balanced the beer cans in one hand and opened the door. Leo was lying on the bed, his bare chest and head propped up against the pillows. He was not reading or doing anything, as far as Willa could tell. He seemed surprised to see her.

"I brought you a beer. Are you hungry?"

He shook his shaggy blond head. "No, thanks. The beer will do just fine."

She walked across to him and set it down on the night stand as if she were afraid to touch him.

"How was dinner?"

Willa popped the tab and took a sip. It was cold and the bubbles tickled her nose, making her shudder.

"That bad?" Leo smiled.

Willa rubbed her nose. "No. It was fine. The beer's too cold . . ."

"You never were much of a beer drinker. I think I gave you your first one."

"You did. Beck's, at that funny bar on Van Ness near the old Jack Tar Hotel. It's probably gone now. They had terrific French-dip beef sandwiches and every kind of beer on earth."

"It was the day I met you, remember?"

Willa felt like crying though she didn't know why. "It was all because I decided to walk down the right side of Van Ness instead of the side I usually took. I was wearing a T-shirt that said MAKE LOVE, NOT WAR. Oh, God, how embarrassing! I was so virtuous! You came up beside me and said, 'Okay.' But I had no idea what you were talking about, because of course, I had just thrown the shirt on and didn't even know anything was written on the back. I said something brilliant like, 'Okay, what?' "

"You said, 'What's okay,' to be exact."

"And you said, 'I'll agree to make love, not war—but only for today. Tomorrow I may want some combat.' "

Their eyes met. "You were so funny, but then again every person under thirty in San Francisco in the Seventies had one of those T-shirts, so you had probably gotten a lot of mileage out of that line."

"I admit, I'd worked on it. But I'd never actually used it before."

"Really?"

"Really."

Willa took a long sip. This was not the conversation she had intended to have. "Well, your instincts were certainly correct—two Beck's and I was out of the shirt."

"You were out of a lot more than the shirt."

Willa could feel the blood surging up into her neck. "I really was a virgin, Leo. I never thought that you believed me. I mean, why should you have? I certainly jumped into it without much of a fight. I still don't know why—I had held out like the Warsaw Ghetto for twenty-two years! Something just . . . I don't know. Maybe I thought I would never see you again, a stranger in the night and all, so I wasn't risking doing it and having you reject me. But I *really* was."

Leo laughed. "I see the spider neck blush—some things never change." He was quiet for a moment, remembering. "I certainly did believe you. I would have known, even if you hadn't invested a fair amount of our first six months trying to convince me that you had never done anything like that before and would most certainly never do it again, even while we were doing it again and again."

Willa covered her neck with her hand. "Oh, God! Stop it. I can't take it. It's too humiliating. You must have thought I was the world's silliest female."

"I thought you were magnificent. I was also very flattered."

"Oh, come on, Leo! Women have probably been flinging themselves at you since you were first walking upright, maybe even before. What happened with me must have happened to you all the time."

He was hurt. She could see it in the slight tightening around his eyes. "I'm not like that. I choose very carefully. I always did. You were special. No one like you had ever responded to me before."

Something was happening to her that she would not have thought possible. She was letting him back in. She wanted to touch him and curl up next to him with her head against his hard lemon scented shoulder, so that she could fall asleep the way she had all those years ago, feeling safe in his arms in a way that she had not felt safe since.

"What was so special about me?" she said as softly as if she were praying.

"You know, I've been lying here all night, just thinking about you and Lindy and Bee Bee and Rennie and Corrine too. Quite a list! I was trying to figure out what you all have in common, since you're all so different on the surface of it. Well, you just answered it for me.

"None of you knows how special you are. You're all marked in the same way. When you were kids, no one ever told you who the fuck you were! You're strong as hell, but there's not enough self-esteem in all of you put together to fill a cereal bowl.

"That must be what I gave you. I validated something in each of you that no one ever had, especially no *man* ever had. With you, well, it's pretty obvious. You never had a father or a brother—and that mother of yours, wandering around like Blanche DuBois.

"If any of you had found what you needed in your families or relationships, you wouldn't have touched a bum like me with a laser gun."

"You're not a bum, Leo."

"Yes, I am. I'm a bum and I'm a failure. You were the first person who knew that, and you were the only one I couldn't stand to have see it. Do you know that?"

"I didn't. Thank you for telling me now. It really helps make some things clearer. I don't blame you for what happened to us."

"Not even about Maxie?"

"No. I'm not proud of it, but I liked having him all to myself."

"How is he?" Leo knew that he should not have asked; he no longer had control of the road ahead in this conversation.

"He's great. He just graduated high school with honors. He's going to BU in the fall on a tennis scholarship. The sports definitely came from your gene pool. He's a wonderful athlete, he's . . ." She stopped, knowing that if she said the next thing, it would take the conversation off this perilous, seductive road and back where it belonged. Part of her did not want to do it. "He's in New York with Tess. It's quite wonderful to see them together."

Leo put his head back and closed his eyes. His breathing was shallow. Willa turned her head. She had never seen him cry and even though she was not sure he was, she did not want to watch. She stood up and walked into the bathroom. "Gotta pee. The beer always does that."

When she came out, he was waiting for her, his reserve back in place. "I know why you came up, Willa. It's okay. You did your duty. Let it go now. Believe me, I am aware of the deadline."

She started to deny it, but she stopped herself. It would have come out like a lie. She had come in for that; what she had not planned on was all the feelings she had brought in with her.

He had been her one true love, and in a way, she had been his
and even though they had both traveled far and many others had
taken her place, standing there in the dim light of another
woman's bedroom, without saying another word, they were back
in the Haight-Ashbury in 1970; they were in love and nothing
mattered but each other. What they brought back to the table now
was the knowledge that no matter who else had or would enter
their lives, they would never quite feel, and could never again risk,
what they had risked together. Some loves are just like that.

"Try to get some sleep," she said, opening the door and leaving
them both all alone.

They were all waiting for Willa when she came down. Lindy,
who had just come up from the beach to join them, was agitated
from the exercise and the anticipation. "Well?"

Willa shook her head. "I'm telling you, Lindy, we can't handle
him like that. Believe me, he's aware of the pressure. Let's just take
the next two days and try to relax. Get some sun, stay out of his
way as much as possible, and let him find his own road to it. It
won't work otherwise. I know how hard this is, honey, but please
try to let go. It's going to work. If we've gotten this close, we're
not going to fail now."

Lindy slumped down on the wicker couch beside Bee Bee and
put her head against her shoulder. "You're right, as usual. I'll try. I
may need drugs. Hold on to the sleeping pills, Beebs, I haven't
slept more than three hours since we landed in this bathtub."

Bee Bee kissed her cheek. "Let's all try to get some rest." They
helped Rennie out of her chair and followed her up, slightly envious that it was she going into the room that held the purveyor of
so much of their anxiety and all their attention.

Bee Bee was playing Billie Holiday. Everyone was on the beach
or taking a nap and she had the house to herself. She had been
playing on Rennie's out-of-tune spinet for quite a while. Playing
always anchored her and she was badly in need of its stabilizing
force. "If I take a notion, to jump right in the ocean, ain't nobody's business if I do."

Her eyes were closed and she was so focused on the bliss the
music brought that she didn't see or hear Leo come up beside her.

When she opened her eyes, he was there and she paused, feeling shy.

"Please don't stop." He sat down beside her on the bench. She had not been this close to him in five years. She did the only thing she had ever been able to do to protect herself. She sang.

After a while he joined her and they played together, working their way through all their favorites.

"Do 'Earthquake.' " He lit a cigarette and she began singing the song that she had sung in public for the first time the night she met him, with a throaty, bitter edge that made it more effective. "After waiting around for years, hiding from myself in a cozy vale of tears . . ."

She stopped. It was all just too much for her. She lowered her head. "I can't," she said, and he put his arms around her and held her.

"Rennie told me what you said." She kept her face turned away from him.

He nodded, holding her tighter. "I made a mess of it, Bee Bee. I didn't want you involved, but it's really better this way."

She raised her head and pushed away from him. "Maybe for you. I was never given the opportunity to decide that for myself."

He stroked her face, wiping the tears away so tenderly that she started crying all over again. "Bee Bee, I was holding you back. I tried to keep up with you and all I did was almost get us both killed. I still think you're going to be a star and I'm not going to play out some fucking a-star-is-born scenario. We'd just end up hating each other."

She put her head back against his shoulder. There was nothing more to say. The worst part was that she knew it was true.

Way back at their beginning she had already started turning down opportunities that threatened her marriage, that would have propelled her too far ahead of him, too fast. She had known it, but her feelings for him were too strong to listen to common sense. Or to Trudy or even to Leo, who had told her then the very same thing he was telling her now. As much as it hurt and as much as she still wanted him right where he was, holding her, playing beside her, she began to feel better.

She had come to terms with something. She still loved him, but not enough to stop herself. She felt free of the burden she had been carrying since he had simply vanished from her life all those years ago. She sighed and sat up, turning toward him.

"Want to hear a new one I've been working on? It's about you."

"Sure," he said, and kissed her forehead. She turned back to the keyboard, the place that never failed her and always gave her back a better part of herself.

And so the second day passed and the night and they all slipped down into their own recovery plans, sleeping and sunning and reading and leaving one another as alone as possible. No one had the energy left for conversation, speculation, confrontation, or obliteration of the hope that two days hence Leo would be well and docilely set off to do his moral duty. Even Lindy let go. The last news on Tess had been good, so a few days more or less would not threaten anything.

They all relaxed, having made their peace one on one with Leo; and having gotten this far, they treated themselves to the luxury of time off, to the magical healing of the water and the sun, lazing like pampered kittens licking their sore places and regaining their energy.

It was now the men who were shouldering the anxiety and stress. Brad was faced with losing Leo and starting over with nothing, unsure of his future and of what Rennie would do. He had been assigned the responsibility for "doing the right thing" about the baby and seeing her through, though he was still in so much physical pain he could hardly stand up. He had no one to turn to for comfort. Rennie had retreated into herself and Leo . . . well, Leo had enough on his plate to feed the entire marine corps.

Leo did feel, in fact, as if he were standing on a land mine, one of those evil little circa-Vietnam jokers that you could hear ticking under your toes, just waiting until you moved. He could hear the ticking. There was no way back and no way forward.

He realized now that the dream had been his warning, and he had totally misread it. He should have just set a different course and kept on going. Now he was ambushed—as much by his love for all these frustrating fucking women as he was by the circumstances.

There were just too many feelings strafing him for any one man to handle, especially one who had lived his entire life by moving faster than the feelings and staying one step ahead of the booby traps. They had stalked him and they had found him and they had freed themselves of him and he had done his best to help them do it. Now they were whizzing around in his car and floating in the bay and grilling hot dogs while he was frozen in place trying not to move, listening to the ticking under his feet, alone with the mortal danger beneath him. Tick. Tick. Tick.

He held on as long as he could. He stood it until the end of the last day. Until the peril overcame him and he moved. *Click.*

An afternoon nap is a wicked sleep. Sensual as the cat for which one of its forms was named; a cat in the late-day sun, licking itself, luxuriating in an indolent narcissism, yawning in lazy delight.

Naps feel different from other sleep. They are time out from daily life; quiet in the middle of bustle, an indulgence as lush and guilt-producing as a fat, thick slice of double-chocolate cake; the butterscotch sundae of slumber.

An afternoon nap, with freshly bathed bodies and cool, clean sheets, birds chirping, waves tossing, boat motors humming, soothing sounds magnified by the quiet of sleep, is as far from the Weight Watchers' sleep program (seven hours and no nonsense, then back to business) as sleeptime gets. And so naps are lascivious, mischievous devils, waiting to release lust and longing, impossible desires and all the temptations of the night into the daylight.

Leo woke up. His cock was hard, it pushed against his Speedos, making him wince. Rennie was asleep beside him, her stomach swollen and red from the sun, rising and falling like a birthday balloon on a windy day.

He stood up and walked to the window, his erection throbbing and pushing him, propelling him forward. He saw Willa down below, floating on a bright yellow raft, dark glasses covering her eyes. He did not think about it, he moved into his need, his rage and frustration as locked in to his libido as a fat worm on a gleaming baited hook. He went out the screen door and down to the cove.

There was a bottle of sunblock on the towel beside Willa's unread book, and he picked it up and waded out to her. He braced the raft against his chest, so gently, so smoothly, that she did not even open her eyes, lost as she was in her own verdant napscape.

He unscrewed the cap and covered his broad, calloused hands with the creamy sun-warmed oil. He paused, knowing that when he touched her everything would change; he would be taking this fantasy that had haunted him for years out of his head and into reality.

There was the possibility of losing even more control, feeling even more cornered and helpless than he already did. Leo had always used sex for power, to bind the feelings of worthlessness that stalked him; and here he was before the supreme risk, but he had gone too far now—the pressure inside him was too great. He could fuck them or he could kill them, was the way it felt.

He lowered his hands onto her thighs and spread oil up toward her pubis. She raised her glasses and tried to sit up, but he reached out with one hand, yanking down her bikini top and oiling her cool white breasts. "Shhhhh," he said, and it was enough. Willa moaned and reached out with her hand to touch him. He took her hand and held it against her belly, caressing her breasts with his free fingers.

"My God," she whispered, surrendering in a way that she had never surrendered herself before, the sea and sun and longing all melted into this pleasure. It was not the same as it had been with Leo all those years before—even Leo was different. Aggressive rather than languorous and passively sexual; he was telling her, taking charge of the act, taking the decision and the responsibility away from her. This was as close as she had ever come to her most primitive erotic fantasy, and her desire overwhelmed her defenses.

She moaned and he released her arm, filling his hands with more oil and pulling her bikini bottom down her legs, leaving her slippery and naked in the afternoon light, floating on an inflated tube and not caring how it looked.

He slid his fingers inside her and she gasped, coming before he could even reach her clitoris. Nothing had ever felt this good. She reached out for him and he pulled himself up onto the raft, and entered her, driving himself as far inside this woman whom he had known so well, whose body had been his and was now new again, like the first time, only without the uncertainty, without the shyness of new love.

He thrust into her, making the raft rock and the water ripple around them, and she came again and again. Spasms shaking her, she clawed at his back in an abandon that he had always sought with her and had never before found. Somehow she trusted him more now that she had nothing to lose.

This enraged him and the rage hardened him and he finished without coming, sliding out of her and back into the water, leaving her like a merman or sea monster, leaving her to believe, if she should choose, that it had all been part of her nap, part of the lulling island murmurs that filled her wandering mind.

He felt stronger and surer of himself than he ever had before in his life. He stalked the beach, his erection pushing tight against his wet trunks; he saw Bee Bee pulling into the driveway, returning from her shopping trip to town. Big Red was sputtering and Bee Bee was struggling to find reverse. She backed into place behind the fan palms and he crossed to her. She looked over at him and he walked right up to the window and opened the car door, turning off the key and pulling the brake. She allowed it, as compliant as one of the Un Jill's rag dolls. He took her arm and pulled her up to her full height and they stood face-to-face, his cock pushing against her shorts. He kissed her, holding her so tight that she could feel him almost inside her.

"Get in the back," he said, and she did, as dazed by his power as Willa had been. She had not been with anyone since he left, and in his claiming her, he opened all of that need at once. He pushed her back against the far side of the broken-down little car, a ridiculous car for two big people to tryst in, but more exciting because of it.

He pulled the elastic waist and her shorts and panties slid down her sun-brown legs and he spread them wide, holding one in each hand and mounted her. She pushed her fist against her mouth, muffling her moans that continued until she was drenched with sweat and collapsed on her side, curled up like a child on the sagging, creaky leather seat of his toy car.

He was panting now, the effort to keep control growing more difficult, but the fury propelling him forward. He was living his deepest, darkest fantasy and he thought, as he climbed the steps and made his way down the hall to Lindy's room, maybe he was living every man's deepest fantasy. He would do it for all of them;

he would be the fucking sacrificial lamb of Eros, the snake in the Garden with a hard-on; he would do it for Adam and Everyman.

Lindy was lying in the bathtub, her eyes closed and the warm, bubbly water sheltering her. He opened the door and without pausing he climbed into the tub. She opened her eyes. "No," she said.

"Yes," he said, and she sat up, her eyes clouding and he slipped off his suit, standing over her, and she laughed. "Holy shit," she said. "It's on fire."

He pulled her up and turned her around so that she could lean against the towel rack and he entered her from behind, pressing her forward, holding her large, soapy breasts in his hands, kneading her nipples the way he remembered she liked it. She had never let him do it this way, but she was wiser now and she tightened against him. "Oh, Jesus. Fuck me, Leo. Just fuck me," and he did.

When he came back to Rennie she was awake, lying on her back, her face soft from sleep.

He moved across to her and she watched him tentatively. He tore off his trunks and lifted her gown and she sighed, not really wanting to, but he took her face in his hands and he looked at her in a way that he had never looked at her before—as if she was important to him. He was almost over the edge of his control and she could see his need. "I love you," he said, pressing himself against her warm thighs. He shouted something, but she could not understand the words and he reached for her hand and she held him while he came, coming in a way that he never had with her before, his body shuddering, holding nothing back; and then he fell down beside her, dripping with salt and sweat, sound asleep.

"Safe" is what he had shouted and for just this moment, he was.

What Leo had forgotten was that there was no safety for long, behind enemy lines. There was always another danger, maybe just one step away, and no one, nothing, on that side of the frontier could be trusted.

If there is any truth to the superstition that bad things always come in threes, it gained credibility as a theory during the next twenty-four hours in the lives of Lindy and Leo.

It began with a knock on the door as Lindy dozed on her bed, recovering from her bathtub encounter, and she heard the Un Jill whisper, "Miz Lindy. Telephone from New York."

She grabbed her robe and ran. Alice never called her unless it was urgent. "Alice? What's going on?"

"Sorry to bother you."

Lindy had never heard her sound so solemn. Her throat closed. "What is it? Tell me!"

"I don't wanna scare you. I know you're doin' your best to get the guy back here, but we just got the results of the new blood tests and it don't look quite right. The white cells are movin' up a little. Now, they could settle back down—she's still holding—but you know how it goes. Gotta do the transplant while she's in remission. So, what I'm sayin' is, the sooner, the better."

"The day after tomorrow, if I have to carry him. But not a word to anyone. Just call Corrine in Washington, the way I told you."

"Good. They'll be all ready for you. Want me to tell Tess any mushy mother stuff?"

"No. I'll tell her myself in person on Friday."

The trio had planned to drive down the hill for dinner, needing privacy to conduct the conversation about how to push Leo forward, but the dinner plans had been made before Leo's troop movement, and they were all feeling the intimacy barriers created by what each of them felt to be a betrayal of the others.

Lindy had received the phone call just before getting dressed for the evening and had still not told any of them about it. This did not help the mood at the table.

Willa watched her fiddle with her fork, unable to eat even her French fries. "I see French-fry depression. Something's wrong. Tell me, or I'm taking the potatoes."

Lindy bit her lip to keep from crying. "Alice called. The last blood test doesn't look so terrific. We've got to go. While we're sitting around waiting for His Highness to make up his mind, Tess is free-falling."

This was more than Bee Bee could stand. She had done something wicked and wanton and lost sight of her friend's suffering.

"I have to tell you both something that happened today. I'm so ashamed. It was weak and selfish of me and I don't want it to come between us. I—I had sex with Leo. He came at me when I was coming back from shopping. He got into the car with me. I just couldn't help myself!"

Lindy stared at Bee Bee. Willa stared at Bee Bee. Lindy looked at Willa. Willa looked at Lindy. Willa looked at both of them. "I was on the yellow raft," Willa said, the spider rash crawling back up her neck.

Lindy picked up a handful of fries and stuffed them into her mouth. "I was in the bathtub."

They were silent, absorbing the information.

Lindy broke it. "What is this? 'The Three Bears'? Who's been sleeping in my bed! Well, if he's fucking Goldilocks, I'm the fucking Terminator. I've had it! Enough. Let's go get him!"

Willa grabbed her arm, holding her down in the chair. "Whoa! Think a minute. He didn't *rape* us. We all wanted it. Be honest. We owe Bee Bee one for telling the truth and saving our friendship, but it doesn't change anything. It won't make him go, though I would say it indicates that his concussion is pretty well mended. We can't go flying into his room like three deflowered damsels. It will make him defensive, and we could hurt Rennie in the process."

Lindy finished off the fries. "I bet Rennie got the best of it. I bet two plates of French fries that he saved her for the curtain call."

"Oh, God." Bee Bee put her face in her hands, her shoulders heaving with laughter. "What a motley crew we are."

"You really did it in that Tinkertoy?" Lindy wiped her mouth.

Bee Bee nodded from inside her hands and they all joined her, laughing as much at the absurdity of their situation as at what they, ever fools for love, had done.

They arrived back at Rennie's, having decided to call an emergency meeting with Leo to tell him about the phone call and demand that he go. They did not think beyond that. If he refused, they were helpless.

No one would ever know what might have happened if everything that followed had occurred logically and collectedly, as Willa's strategy intended; but what was waiting for them when they returned was Brad, who was holding a computer printout.

"Lindy, I've just picked up the National Weather Service storm warnings. Did you feel the wind on your way home?"

Lindy nodded, afraid to ask the next question.

"I hate to bring bad news, but there's a hurricane watch up. They're expecting at least major turbulence to hit us in the next twenty-four hours. I've got a bad feeling about this. I mean, hurricanes are often much ado about nothing—they change course at the last minute or break up over the ocean. But the way it looks now, this one is headed straight for the Virgins. Even if we only get the storm, they'll close the airports and stop all boat service. You won't be able to make calls or get out of here until it's over. I don't want to alarm you, but I think you should go as soon as possible."

"How soon?" Willa said, putting her arm around Lindy, who was standing as stiff as a stick and drained of color.

"Now."

Rennie stood on the stairs, listening. The rain had started. She felt something loosen inside her. *No way.* She gripped the railing. She would hold it in. She had done it before. She was not due for another three weeks. "Brad, will *you* talk to him?"

Brad looked at her. "I'll try." He crossed over to her, moving slowly, every step still painful.

Bee Bee reached out and Willa and Lindy moved toward her. They held on to one another. The end of the adventure was in front of them. "Friends forever," Lindy said, clutching them to her in a gesture more vulnerable and open than Willa had ever seen her make. "Forever," they all said, not wanting to release one another.

By the time they were packed and ready the wind was howling so fiercely and the rain was pounding so mercilessly, they all knew that there was no way they could leave.

They huddled in the living room, surrounded by suitcases, waiting for Brad to come back. Lindy held her knees tight against her chest, rocking back and forth, her eyes shut tight, trying to keep herself from screaming. Please, please, please, she prayed inside her head. There's got to be something I can do!

Rennie sat on the sofa afraid to move. The contractions were coming about twenty minutes apart. There was no way they could get across the island to the hospital in this tempest. The roads were so bad, they washed out during a drizzle. Louie could probably get there in his van, but the phone lines were down and there was no way to reach him. She did her birth-breathing, trying not to panic.

Willa tiptoed across to her. "Are you okay?"

Rennie nodded.

Willa kneeled beside her. "No you're not. You're in labor! We've got to get you to the hospital."

Rennie leaned closer, not wanting to upset Lindy. "Can't. The roads will be flooded."

"Can we call the doctor or an ambulance?"

"The phones are out."

Rennie gasped as a contraction hit. "Brad knows how. You have to . . . to get your captain's license. So does Leo. We can manage."

"Let's get you into bed." Willa helped her up.

"Take me to Un Jill's room. The bed's higher and it's closer to the kitchen. They always seem to need hot water in the movies."

Bee Bee and Lindy encircled her. "Is it the baby?"

Willa helped Rennie up. "We need Brad. Go get him, Lindy. Bee Bee, get Jill and put fresh sheets on her bed."

Lindy sprinted up the stairs and down the hall. She could hear Leo's voice through the door. "Are you fucking crazy? Not even a pelican could get out of here now! You told them that? Are you trying to get us killed? The airport closed hours ago."

"Yeah, but *you* can fly. Billy's plane is just sitting there."

"Fly where? I'm not Lindbergh. I haven't flown in months."

"If the tank's full, you can get to San Juan."

"I couldn't even get to the airport! In the morning maybe, when it clears. I haven't even decided to go. I don't trust Corrine. The only things she's ever arranged in her entire life are dinner parties and opera benefits. Now I'm supposed to put my life in her hands? Lindy is frantic, she'd tell me anything to get me back there. You're asking me to walk into a bullet—that is, if we don't die in a plane crash!"

Lindy knocked. She had heard enough. She knew what she had to do.

"Yes?"

She opened the door, standing in the shadows. She did not want Leo to see her face. "Brad, Rennie's in labor. They need your help."

"Great. Fucking great!" Leo stood up and reached for his jeans.

Brad turned from him and moved awkwardly to the door. "I knew it. I should have driven her over the minute I heard the reports."

Lindy watched him go. She had to do something. She had to stop Leo from going downstairs. "Leo. Wait a minute. We need you to carry something down to Rennie. It's too heavy for me."

"Okay." He sat back down and slipped a sweatshirt on over his head. She was running now, down the hall to her room.

What could she do? What? She slipped out of her skirt and pulled on a pair of jeans and grabbed a sweater from her carry-on bag. Wait. The gun. Brad's gun from the sting. She grabbed her purse and turned it upside down, shaking every last lipstick and used toothpick, fuzzy Q-Tip and rusty paper clip out onto the floor. There it was.

Her hands were shaking. She had never handled a gun before. She slung her purse over her shoulder, stuffing her wallet and passport back inside, jammed her feet into her sandals, and raced back down the hall to Leo, not bothering to see if the gun was loaded.

He was sitting in the dark, his shoulders stooped, a POW waiting to surrender. He heard her enter and he turned.

She was pointing the pistol at him. She gulped air, knowing that if he saw her fear, he would overpower her, taking the weapon as if it were made of paper. *For Tess.* She had to be strong for Tess. She had to get out of there, before they were trapped and all was lost.

Her hand steadied. "Okay, Lampi. You're coming with me right now. You are going to get us out of here tonight or, I swear to God, I will blow your fucking head off."

He stood up and she cocked the gun. He raised his hands. "You know what the odds are?"

"About even. Better than sitting here. I remember the hurricane that hit the Caribbean. People were trapped without any communication for weeks. No way, Leo. We're going down and out that door without a word. Take Rennie's car—the keys are still in it. Go!"

She backed up and let him pass, staying out of his reach; he did not resist her and they moved quickly through the hall, down the stairs, and pausing for just a second, as if sending their farewell to the others, they crossed the threshold of protection and stepped out into the tempest of the night.

Halfway to the airport they hit a washout and the car stalled. The rain was relentless, making it impossible to see, and the roads were too muddy to provide any leverage for pushing. Leo was behind the car and Lindy was in the driver's seat, trying to follow his instructions when Louie pulled up in his van. Lindy jumped out of the car, determined to reach him before Leo.

"Louie, please, take us to the airport. We've got to get out of here before the hurricane!" Lindy covered the gun with her sweater.

Leo yelled to Louie over the wind. "Can you get us into Billy's plane?"

Louie grinned, excited by the adventure of it all. "No problem. I know where he kept the keys. It's just been sitting there like a wingless bird."

"Get in!" Lindy motioned with the hidden gun and Leo got in next to Louie. She climbed into the seat right behind them.

"Let's just push Rennie's car over to the side," Louie said. This meant that Leo would have to get out and help him. Lindy clutched his shoulder with her free hand. "No. No time! It'll be okay. They closed the road behind us. Go. Just go, Louie!"

Even with all his experience and four-wheel drive, it was still almost four o'clock in the morning by the time they reached the airport and made their way across the deserted rain-slick field to Billy's small plane.

Lindy had put the revolver in the pocket of her sweatshirt and Louie was still unaware of Leo's plight. Leo, however, seemed resigned to his fate. He waited quietly for Louie to bring the key from Billy's hook in the flight office.

When they were seated inside, Louie's enthusiasm began to ebb. "This is not such a very good idea. No flight plan, no runway lights. What can I do for you?"

"Go inside and turn the fuckers on, Louie. You could probably run this airport single-handed. If the radio's still transmitting, call San Juan and tell them we're coming."

"You got it, mon! At your service!"

"Be sure and give San Juan our approximate route, so they can send a rescue plane if we don't make it."

Louie saluted, and started to climb down, the wind threatening his beret. Lindy yelled across to him. "Louie, tell them all I'm sorry. Tell Willa to try and get Corrine and tell her that I love her and . . ."

Leo started the engine. The tank was almost full and everything seemed to be working. He let his breath out. "You want to chat or you want to fly?"

He waved Louie clear and let the engines rev while they waited for the runway lights. He looked over at Lindy. He could almost read her mind. "I see you're beginning to understand that the girl who freaked out on anything smaller than a seven forty-seven is about to set off on the aviation equivalent of balsa wood and rubber cement. Still fiercely determined?"

Lindy was too frightened to speak. She pulled the gun out of her pocket and pointed it at him, nodding her head up and down.

"Lindy," he said, so gently the words felt like love play. "Put that away. I mean it, I'm not going to run off. They're never going to let me into the country without a passport anyway, kid."

Lindy was soaking wet and her teeth chattered. She reached into her purse and pulled out the new passport that Corrine had Federal Expressed to her that morning. "No problem, *Elliot Jackson* of the Albuquerque, New Mex, Jacksons."

Leo laughed. "*Elliot?* Do I look like an Elliot?"

"Better than a swell name on a toe tag in the morgue." Lindy handed it to him with a folder. "Here's a driver's license, open airplane tickets to New York, and two thousand dollars. I'll give you another eight thousand after the surgery. That should help you get back on your feet."

The lights went on. Leo moved slowly forward. "Look in the back. There should be a waterproof nylon bag on the floor." Lindy picked it up and heaved it into her lap.

"Open it."

Lindy unzipped it. Inside were wads of hundred dollar bills. "My God, there must be twenty thousand dollars in there."

"Probably closer to fifty. Billy's drug fund. Keep your money, Lindy. I'll be fine. He owed me almost that much for my share of the shop. Dump the other stuff in there and put on your seat belt. Let's do it."

Leo picked up speed, but the wind held him back. He turned the plane around, so that the wind was behind him, and lifted off into the squall. Lightning shot through the sky in the distance. Lindy swallowed a scream. *Tess,* she said over and over to herself, a mantra against her terror.

They fought the wind, altering the course as they flew. Leo shouted instructions to Lindy, who held the navigation chart on her lap, shining a flashlight on it as the plane bobbed and weaved. Time seemed frozen. It felt as if they had been flying for hours. It was getting lighter. Finally he passed over St. Thomas and Leo could see a small cluster of islets that, if the chart was right, marked the way to Puerto Rico. Once he reached land, there were plenty of places that he could set down if he had to.

The rain lessened, slowing to a drizzle, and they both let their breath out. The wind was eating the fuel, but with the rain easing, visibility was better and the plane was lighter. "We may be okay now," Leo said, and Lindy exhaled for the first time since takeoff. "The next land, past these sandbars, is Puerto Rico. See if you can find any small air field near the south coast. Just in case. I'm going to radio San Juan. Let them know we're coming in."

They surged forward. They were almost there.

Something flashed, a crackling, blinding shudder; a sizzling zap of light, like the finger of God. "What is it, Leo?" Lindy grabbed his arm.

It was the worst thing that it could be. "Lightning, baby." Smoke was filling the cabin. Leo tried the throttle. "It hit the wiring. We're going down. Brace yourself. The wind should help us."

The sky was moving toward dawn and he could see land in the distance. They had been thrown off course by the wind and he was not quite sure where they were, but he knew there were reefs lining the length of the channel. "How well do you swim?"

"Why?" Lindy's eyes were dilated.

"Because the farther out I can set her down, the less chance we have of breaking up on a reef. Asshole Bartlett never packed life preservers, so I won't go for it if you're not a strong swimmer."

"Captain of the Beverly Hills High team. I've got a killer breaststroke. Do it!"

Lindy closed her eyes, feeling them falling out of the sky. Her stomach was somewhere around her throat. It was like one of those horrible nightmares where you just keep falling, but never land.

They hit the water hard and the plane spun around, flipping over.

"Out! Out!" Leo unbuckled her harness and grabbed the bag, pushing open the door and pulling Lindy out after him.

The ocean was churning and the plane, which was low enough on fuel not to explode, was rocking hard. Lindy stepped out onto the wing, clutching her purse. She climbed on top of the plane and sat there.

Leo looked up at her. He could see her fear. "I never knew you were a swimmer," he said, trying to center her in the moment.

"Well, you didn't stick around long enough for water sports."

He smiled. "Okay, Captain. I'll go first. You stay real close to me. It's still pretty dark and it's very hard to see in the water. If you get tired, roll over onto your back and just let the water carry you. I'll call your name every few minutes. Please answer me, so I know you're there. Remember, if anything happens, roll over and float it out. The water's choppy, but it's warm and there aren't any big waves. The wind is behind us, which is good—it should push us to shore. Okay?"

Lindy nodded. Leo turned and hoisted the bag over his shoulder.

"Leo?"

"Yeah?"

He answered her without turning around, so he could not see that she was crying. "Thanks, Leo."

"Thank me on shore," he said, and lowered himself into the sea.

He swam for a minute, getting used to the current, finding his rhythm. He could not hear Lindy and he turned, calling her name.

"Keep swimming!" she yelled to him, and he realized she was still sitting on top of the plane.

"What the fuck are you doing! Come on!"

"I can't swim, Lampi! My mother wasn't into it."

"You said you were captain of . . ."

"I *lied.* I'm gonna just sit here and wait for the rescue plane. I'll be okay. You go on. Swim, Leo. You better swim and keep on going until you get there. Swim, you bastard, because I am not going to get my hair wet for nothing!

"You're more important than I am now. You can save Tess and I can't. Go! If you come back here, I'll shoot you, I swear to God I will! I'm fine. I like it here! Go!"

He knew it was useless, but he started back and she fired at him. She would do it too—he knew that and he knew what she was saying; he knew that was what she wanted of him and so he turned around, his head pounding and his muscles already knotting from the effort, and he swam. He swam. He swam.

CHAPTER 11

The Long, Lonely Road

WHEEZIE SPRINGER WAS IN HIS CAR ON THE WAY TO A SIX A.M. power-breakfast meeting in Westwood, when he heard the first news of the hurricane watch on the Virgin Islands. He turned his car around and headed back toward Beverly Hills. He had not slept all night, waves of dread and premonition slipping over him one after another.

The night before Lindy had left him and gone back to New York, they had worked out a briefcase full of possible scenarios. She had made him promise that if anything should happen that made Wheezie believe she was not going to bring Leo back, or if Tess's condition suddenly changed and she couldn't be reached, he was to go to Gerrold and convince him to let them test the twins.

No one had heard from Lindy in two days, and now he knew why. Maybe he would turn out to be a hysterical fool, but something in him that he could no longer ignore was telling him to move.

He called Gerrold's house while he made his way in the already congested early-morning traffic to Bel Air. "Gerrold?"

"Yes."

"It's Mark Springer. I'm sorry to call you so early, but it's urgent that I speak to you. Can I come over?"

"Meet me at my office in fifteen minutes," Gerrold said furtively.

When Wheezie pulled into the parking lot, Gerrold was sitting in his car. The twins were beside him on the front seat, looking cheerful and slightly agitated.

Gerrold got out and walked quickly over to Wheezie and slid into the front seat beside him. "I know," he said, more somber than Wheezie had ever seen him. "I've always known. I assume the Leo plan hasn't worked out. I called the airport. We're booked on the eight-thirty to Kennedy. The twins are about to have the longest ballet class in history."

Wheezie smiled at him. Gerrold was not such a nebbish after all. "Are you going to pay big for this?"

"Me? She's the one who's told the great lie all these years. She'll freak, but she'll be too scared that I'm going to leave her to do anything about it.

"I have one requirement. The girls know about Tess being sick and what they may have to do. They were crazy about Lindy and they're very excited about helping, but they *don't* know and must *never* know that I'm not their father. That, I can't handle. Any problem?"

"Not that I can see."

"Good. Let's go."

Leo Lampi staggered into Dr. Davis's office at Beth Sinai Hospital. He was suffering from exposure and dehydration and he had not slept in two days. He leaned against a chair, trying to keep from passing out on the doctor's desk. "I'm the father," he said. "Has the Coast Guard called? Is Lindy here yet?"

He had not stopped moving since he crawled ashore. Lindy had given him instructions, but he had only followed the part about the hospital. He had not called Corrine.

"Come with me," the doctor said, and Leo followed him. The next thing he remembered he was in another hospital bed, clean and conscious, and the doctor and a hawk-faced little woman with a bad black wig were standing over him.

"Is it okay?"

He saw tears in the woman's tiny black eyes. "You're gonna be fine."

The doctor put his arm around her. "You were delirious when you came in—you kept saying something about a plane crash. We took the liberty of testing you without consent, Mr. Lampi. I hope you will forgive us, but time is running out. We assumed, since you were here, that it was all right."

Leo stared at them. "Is Tess okay?"

Alice nodded. "Yep. That Lindy—she's psychic. She said it hadda be you. They're gonna do the procedure in about an hour. You a *paisan*? Pray to the Virgin, pal."

"Have you heard anything about Lindy? I called the Coast Guard and Air Rescue. She should be here by now."

Alice's face tensed. "Haven't heard nothin'. You were supposed to call Corrine. She's on her way. She'll have the news. Her guys have kept the press from talkin' about the plane goin' down. That's to save *your* heinie, buster, so keep quiet. That Lindy ain't gonna let a little water stop her."

Leo looked at her. "What's your name?"

"Alice." She pulled the covers up over him and checked his IV. "Maxie waited as long as he could. He left yesterday, hadda start college."

Leo winced. She saw him. "Does Tess know I'm here?"

"No one knows. We were told to keep a lid on about you. Besides, she'd wanna know where her mother is and it doesn't seem like a good idea to say we don't know. Frankly, I'm not sure it'd be good for her to see you anyway. She's real nervous about the whole thing, and she's not so strong right now."

"I understand." He thought that he would feel relieved, knowing that he did not have to face Maxie or Tess, but he didn't. He felt broken. No place to hide, Leo, he said to himself, his eyes still on the small, spicy broad who seemed to know all about them. At least he matched. It had not all been for nothing.

She pulled out a pocket light and leaned over him. "You had a concussion, Lindy told me. Look at me." He obeyed and she shone the light into his face, making his eyes water and hiding his tears. "What the hell were you doin' out there like that? You coulda had a brain hemorrhage."

Leo laughed. "What did you just say about Lindy? She sure as hell wouldn't let a little thing like that stop her."

"Quite a dame, that one," Alice said, and slammed the bars of his bed into place. "You sleep. Nothin' more to do now, 'cept that prayer I told you about."

Leo closed his eyes. His head ached and his entire body felt as if it were encased in lead. He prayed. Hail Mary, full of grace. He had not prayed since he'd left the nuns, but it came right back to him. It held so much memory and so much sorrow and he had buried it far down where it would not hurt him; but he prayed for his daughter, and he prayed for her mother.

When he woke up again, Corrine, Wheezie, and Gerrold were waiting.

When Willa and Bee Bee got off the plane from San Juan eight days later, they had been totally out of phone and media contact with the mainland since the night they'd delivered Rennie's baby.

The hurricane called Daphne had nipped them, saving the worst damage for Ancolla's larger neighbors, but it had completely shut down all services and knocked out the radio tower and all the telephone lines. They had left on the first plane possible, without stopping to buy a newspaper or make a phone call. They had sent Lindy a fax with their flight information and fled.

Maybe Wheezie was not the last person Willa expected to see waiting for them at baggage claim, but he most certainly was a surprise.

Willa ran to him, sobbing in relief against his shoulder and leaving Bee Bee standing timidly behind her. "Oh, Mark, it's so good to see you."

Wheezie held her, feeling her fine, fragrant hair against his chin.

She remembered Bee Bee and pulled herself together. "Bee Bee Day, my dear old playmate, Mark Springer."

Wheezie extended his hand. "We've met before. In Vegas about six years ago."

"Of course. Nice to see you again."

"I've got a driver out front. Let me help with your bags."

They busied themselves with the task of arrival and followed him out to an enormous stretch limo, which made Willa smile.

"Hooray for Hollywood," she said.

He winked at her. "Gotta give my girls the full treatment."

They fell into the plush comfort of the seats, the smell of cheap room deodorizer being the only reminder that this was a New York rental and not Wheezie's personal transport system. Wheezie gave the driver directions and closed the sliding panel between them. He had asked for the biggest car they had, for reasons other than wanting to impress them.

Willa smiled at him. "You look great, Mark."

"Thanks, you too."

Willa and Bee Bee exchanged looks. "Stop it. We know how we look. We look as if we hadn't had a decent meal, night's sleep, or peaceful moment in weeks. Not to mention hot water."

"Well, all of that is about to change."

Willa swallowed. His eyes looked funny. "You have to tell us everything. What happened to Leo? Did he get here? We were . . . well, it's a long story, but Leo's friend Rennie—she went into labor and we were helping her, and the next thing we knew, the baby arrived and Leo and Lindy were gone! We've been berserk ever since. Our friend Louie on the island said that they took off into the storm, and that was the last we heard! Did Leo ever show up?"

Wheezie nodded. There was nowhere to go now but straight ahead.

"He matched."

"Thank God." Bee Bee put her head in her hands.

Willa could feel the pressure behind her eyes. Her stomach turned over. "Tess?"

Wheezie leaned forward, touching her knee. "Tess is fine. I called Gerrold. He kidnapped the twins—well, not really, but we had them here as backup. The procedure was really tough though —it's a relief we didn't have to put them through it. Leo was great. I think he needed this—to do something for someone. I think it helped him forgive himself. It was like that, like an apology to Tess and Maxie."

Bee Bee and Willa collapsed into each other's arms.

"Oh, God, it worked! It worked!"

Wheezie waited for them. They had a long ride still ahead and there was no rush toward the next question.

They let go of each other, tears streaming down their tired, haggard faces. Willa reached out for his hands.

"I can't wait to see Lindy! She must be wild with joy! The twins! I should have known she'd have held an ace. Poor Leo, what we put him through!"

"Leo was fine."

Wheezie looked out the window.

"Is he still here?"

"No."

"Oh," Bee Bee said softly, and they were both quiet. They had never even said good-bye and now they would never see him again.

Willa sighed, trying to make light of it. "So, where's our girls? Are they home yet?"

"Tess will be home in two weeks or so."

"Life goes on," Willa said, starting to let go of Wheezie's hands. "Is Lindy at the apartment?"

Wheezie held on to her. She looked at his face. His eyes really were funny. "Willa. Lindy didn't make it back. Lindy's dead."

Everything that happened after that was a blur to Willa. She vaguely remembered hearing someone scream and realizing that it was her and the car stopping so Bee Bee could be sick and a kind of howling—not crying or yelling, but a wailing, coming from all of them—overcoming them.

Somehow she was back at Lindy's apartment, Bee Bee was asleep in Lindy's room, and she was bathed, her hair was washed and hanging in moist, tangled strands down her back. Wheezie had gone to pick up some food, she thought, and she was alone in the dark on the couch she had slept on that first night, when they'd stayed up plotting and reviving their friendship, when the summer hung before them filled with passion and purpose.

No one else knew about Lindy yet. Wheezie had waited for her before telling Vilma. Willa sat in the dark, trying to figure out what to do next. That is what she had always done when what was happening to her was too engulfing, submerging her logic like a dummy in a diving bell. That was how she felt—dumb, muddle-headed, opaque, and unable to see out of this deep and terrible swamp that she had sunk into.

Her entire emotional life had been flipped upside down and there she was trapped on the bottom, unable to find the surface of her loss. Willa heard Vilma Segal's heels clicking across the parquet floor. She opened her eyes. It was almost dark and the old woman loomed over her like an apparition in the twilight. Her bright red mouth was turned so far down at the sides that Willa thought if she squeezed her cheeks ever so slightly, the corners would meet, forming a circle above her trembling chin.

Willa could see that her hands were clenched into fists, but she stood tall.

"My daughter is dead, isn't she?"

Willa nodded, not trusting what sort of sound might emerge from her throat.

Vilma straightened up, the opposite, Willa observed, of the literary clichés that described old people as shriveling or shrinking after a loss. But Vilma seemed to expand, to grow larger from the truth. She stood tall, looking down at Willa, the sounds of the street echoing through the silence.

"May I sit beside you?" she said, and Willa nodded again and the old woman crossed the room, her high heels clicking, but less firmly now, as if she had become suddenly drunk. She lowered herself down beside her daughter's oldest friend and even though Willa could barely see her face, she knew that she was crying. "May I hold your hand, Katharine?" she said, and Willa reached out to her.

Lucinda Lindy Evelyn Segal Barnes Lampi had not been the easiest person to love, and they both knew, sitting voiceless in the shadows, that she would not be the easiest person to mourn.

Corrine had brought the news with her to New York. First to Wheezie and Gerrold. Later they had all gone together to tell Leo. Wheezie and Gerrold were almost unable to speak, so Corrine did most of the talking. The Coast Guard and Air Rescue had circled the area as carefully as possible, but the storm had really kicked in soon after Leo had reached the nearest town at the edge of the island.

The plane must have been swept into a reef by the wind, and the force had caused a gash that pulled it under before they could get to her. That was their best guess. All they knew for sure was that she was gone. Several days later a fisherman found an Italian leather sandal on the beach. It was all that they ever found of Lindy.

When Corrine told Leo, he listened, his face taut and sealed. When she was through, he got up out of bed, walked to the closet, put on his pants, his dirty sweatshirt and boat shoes, still soiled and stiff from the sea.

He threw his bag over his shoulder and walked past them without a word and out of the room.

Corrine ran down the hall after him, alerting her security people, who tried to follow, but he had vanished into a cab before they reached the street.

That was the last anyone saw of him.

On the dresser beside his bed he had left several envelopes. They were all marked PRIVATE on the front next to the recipient's name.

There were letters for Willa and Bee Bee. There was one for Lindy and one for Rennie and the others were for Maxie and Tess. Wheezie gave them all to Willa. It was more than Tess or Maxie had had before, in a way more than any of them had had.

It was almost two months before the doctors felt that Tess was strong enough to hear about Lindy, and by that time Willa had run out of all conceivable excuses. The day they told her, Wheezie came in from L.A., and Bee Bee came in from Miami. Alice was there and Maxie came down from Boston and Vilma, who was still in residence, came from across the hall. They all took turns holding her; no one said much, no one could have.

The child was inconsolable.

Two days later Willa brought Tess a mailing envelope that Wheezie had held for her. FOR TESS: JUST IN CASE was scrawled in Lindy's large, artless handwriting on the front.

"Do you want me to sit with you?" Willa asked, waiting while Tess opened it, taking out one of Lindy's pocket recorders and a small envelope with photos inside.

"No, thanks," Tess said, trying not to cry. Willa nodded.

"I'll be right outside."

Tess put the recorder on her bed and pushed the Play button. She curled against the pillows, hugging her knees to her chest, the way her mother always had.

The sound of her mother's voice hit her so hard that for a moment she did not think she would be able to stand it.

"Tessie, if you are listening to this, it either means that you have been going through my drawers without permission, in which case you are grounded, or that something horrible has happened to me, meaning that you are free to go through my drawers forever and can have anything—make that *everything*—you want. (This even includes my Karl Lagerfeld black cashmere turtleneck-and-cardigan set; but you had better make damn sure that I'm not coming back before you take it.)

"Oh, God, Tess, I don't mean to make jokes! If you're listening to this, it must mean that I've come to an untimely end and you are most likely not in a joking mood—you better not be!—but since I'm recording it while very much alive and my gray growing in is the worst thing I believe is really going to occur on this journey, it's kind of hard to find the proper mood. Also, you know how I am; I always make jokes when I'm scared and I am a little bit scared, so please forgive me.

"I don't think I ever told you how your grandfather died. He was on the dance floor at the Cocoanut Grove nightclub in L.A. doing the fox trot with my mother. I guess that was a perfect way for him to go—doing one of the things he loved best with the person he most adored, but it kind of left me out of the whole process. So I made a promise to myself when you were a baby that I would never leave you like that, that I would have something prepared from me to you. Well, thank God for the tape recorder because if I'd had to write this, it would have been more like 'See Jane Run.'

"There should be an envelope with this, Tessie, and in it are some pictures of me from when I was about your age. I was going to show them to you on your thirteenth birthday: it's taken me a while to deal with you seeing them, and I'm not proud of that. When you do, you will know something about me that may make your adolescence easier. Maybe it will help you forgive me for being so vain and self-conscious.

"I kind of hate to break your illusions about me, but as you can see, I sure didn't start out cute and it screwed up my values pretty well for a long time and I don't want that to happen to you. Of course, you were born beautiful, and that makes some things easier, but not many, kiddo.

"If I had to do it all over again, I would have loved good old Lucinda Evelyn Segal more and left her the hell alone.

"You can laugh when you look at the pictures, as long as it's a genteel laugh—no screaming with hysterics, please. That would hurt my feelings and don't for a minute think wherever I am, I'm not watching over you. Death has no meaning to a Jewish mother —all I'll be getting is a better view.

"Also, in my underwear drawer is a copy of a novel that Willa was writing about our childhood—mostly my childhood. You can read everything but the last three pages. I want your word of honor!

"I feel kind of bad about not having much else of importance to leave you, baby. No heirlooms, family treasures, artwork. I mean, aside from a few Karans, some Armani, and a drawerful of hot rollers, there's not a lot.

"For most of my life I was not much of a person, Tess. It's the truth. I was not a wonderful girl. Even you, having you, I did to get Leo to marry me—not particularly noble. It didn't work either, not that it should have; but what it gave me was a miracle, far more than I deserved. It gave me you, baby. You are by far the best thing that ever happened to me in my entire life and the best thing about me and I'd like to think that I rose to the occasion, that I became a better person because of you.

"I've been watching you for almost thirteen years now and I want to tell you what I see and I want you to promise me that you will never discount what I'm saying just because I'm your mother, and that you will wear it inside yourself, like a big warm fuzzy robe to keep you snuggly and safe.

"You are a wonderful, funny, smart, beautiful, kind, generous, loving, very special young woman, and you are brave and courageous in a way that few people ever are. Don't ever doubt what I'm saying, and don't ever let anyone mess with your head about yourself. You are the best, and it has been my honor to know you.

"Now comes the really hard part. If something should happen to me while I'm trying to find your father and you blame yourself for it, I couldn't bear that, baby. It's the one thing that would make me really pissed off at having to die now.

"I need to hear you promise out loud; 'I promise Mom I will not mope around and feel guilty. I promise that I will grow up healthy and strong and have a really wonderful, happy, productive life. I promise I will learn from my mother's mistakes and wait for a fabulous guy who will love me forever and I will never doubt that my mother is still with me and is proud of me. I will live for her and make her happy that she was in some small way able to help me!'

"Promise me, Tess—otherwise I won't rest in peace, and we've both seen far too many of those soul-in-torment movies for you to let *that* happen to me.

"(Oh, before I forget, I am charging all the airplane tickets on Am Ex, so if I've died in a plane crash, make sure Wheezie gets them to pay up!)

"Speaking of money, you will be fine, honey. I've made Wheezie and Willa my executors and Willa your guardian. What little I have goes to you, and Grandmother Segal put everything she has in trust for you a long time ago, though she will probably live to be two thousand years old. For now at least, she'll provide your school and living expenses. Don't worry, kid, you'll be rolling in it. I also have an insurance policy on my life, and I doubled it when you got sick. Wheezie will take care of all of that, don't you worry. You just get well and back to the business of growing up.

"Wherever I am, darling, I know I will always be with you and you will always be with me.

"Oh, Tessie, I am so hoping that this will be saved for one of our future Mother/Daughter most-embarrassing-moment evenings. You're the only thing in my life worth living for, so you'd better live it well enough for both of us, my angel. I love you so, princess. Just remember all the good stuff—forget how I looked in the morning and that I never got up to make you pancakes and all that June Cleaver jazz. Have the best life, Tessie."

"I promise, Momma," the sobbing child whispered over and over, rocking back and forth, holding herself close.

There was a picture that Willa had given her that Tess kept by her bed. In it, her mother and Willa and Bee Bee were standing arm in arm on a hill with the ocean behind them, smiling at the camera.

Willa said it had been taken the day they arrived in Ancolla, by the cab driver named Louie. It made Tess feel good to look at it, because her mother looked so happy. She was smiling in a way that Tess had never seen her smile in any other picture—even some of the modeling ones where she looked so beautiful but not like a real person. Not like a happy person either.

Tess thought that her mother had looked happy in this picture. She had never really had any friends while Tess had known her. But there she was with her two best friends on her way to get Leo, and she looked hopeful and playful. Tess liked to hold this image in her mind. She liked to think that that was the way her mother was now, in heaven, feeling hopeful and loved.

Some days, when Tess was not able to keep her promise to Lindy, the worst part of the pain was that she understood now the way her mother had felt when she got sick. She knew what that had been like for her mother and why her mother had been willing to do anything to keep Tess with her. She would have done anything too.

She would do anything to bring her mother back, to wipe away the horror in her heart, the horror of the truth—she would never, ever see Lindy again.

Sometimes she had to shake her head, just shake the thought out. It was just not possible to believe that her wonderful, crazy mother was not, at any moment, going to bounce into her room, in that duck-walking way of hers, fling herself down beside her on the bed, and hug her tight. "Hi, baby," she would say, her full lips nuzzled against Tess's cheek. "Tell me every single thing that happened to you today. Spare no detail, however minute."

She would roll her eyes. "Oh, Momma, you are so weird," she'd say, and they would flip on *Oprah* or a *Murder, She Wrote* rerun, cracking jokes and arguing over whether to send out for a pizza or Chinese. Just them together against the world.

"How do I do this?" Tess kept asking Willa, who would just hold her and they would hang on to each other. She had promised her mother and so she did the best that she could.

But all the way inside her, even deeper down than where her heart was, something was torn; it was ripped to shreds and it hurt so bad that she knew it would never, ever—no matter how old she got or how great her life became—it would never be right again. All she could hope for was that it would get smaller, small enough so she could live with it.

Epilogue

Two Years Later

Mark (Wheezie) Springer and Willa Katharine Snow were married in New York City on Tess Lampi's fifteenth birthday. They all had a great deal to celebrate.

Rennie and Brad came from Florida, where they now lived with their two-year-old daughter who, they all noted, looked exactly like Rennie and nothing like Leo.

Bee Bee was there too. She was living in New York in Lindy's old apartment, preparing for a one-woman show at Carnegie Hall. The Dales had retired, moving to a condo Bee Bee bought them in Fort Lauderdale and freeing Bee Bee to let Wheezie take over her career. Since then, everything she had done had turned to gold: Her "Earthquake" single, her album, her show.

Wheezie had brought the same magic into Willa's life. In a way, it was almost inevitable that they would end up together. They were bonded by more than Lindy now and by all of those years of their childhood. Now they shared Tess.

In the beginning, when they first sensed that their friendship was turning into something more, Willa was struck by the irony that this was the second man she and Lindy had shared. Wheezie had loved Lindy and would probably never feel quite the same passion for her, and Leo had loved her and had never felt quite the same passion for Lindy.

After they became lovers, she told Mark this, and he held her and told her about his time with Lindy in L.A. Willa started to